**He'd known this was a bad idea, but he'd been out of options, now all he wanted to do was stay alive...**

Sid fired the weapon, its report reverberating across the walls of enormous room, and its round impacting the edge of the table, sending a squadron of wood splinters into the air. Leveraging upward, Tommy forced the table even higher, knocking Aslan out of his chair and onto the floor. Scurrying to one side to avoid the table, Jainukul reached out and grabbed the envelope from Aslan's hand before retreating to the edge of the platform. Sid backed up and fired another round. Tommy could feel the wake of the bullet pass across his left temple and heard it hit a metal object someplace in the lobby behind him. Letting go of the table shield, he rolled to the right and scooped up the abandoned Colt Woodsman.

Stepping back again, Sid stumbled on a chair. Swiftly raising the Woodsman barrel, Tommy pulled the trigger. With a short loud pop the small gun shuddered in his hand, spewing hot chamber gases into his face and stinging his eyes.

Grabbing his throat, Sid fell backward over a table. More shots echoed from the walls in the massive lobby, and Tommy rolled behind the overturned table.

Tommy jumped from the platform and sprinted for the hotel's entrance. One of Jainukul's men shot at Tommy. The round was so close that it buffeted his shirt as it passed by. Glancing back, Tommy saw Jainukul hunkered down next to a large planter, filled with flowering flora bursting from its top. Continuing his run to the front exit, Tommy could see that Aslan had crawled across the platform toward Sid's motionless body.

The soft classical piano music amidst the gunplay provided an amusing audio equilibrium as Tommy raced to escape the pandemonium.

Once a sought-after engineer and manager of complex construction sites across the country, Tommy Luck is now nothing more than an unemployed drunk. His life is simple—drink himself into a stupor each night and run each morning to minimize the effects of the daily hangovers. The only problem is that he's short on cash and would do just about anything for money. Approached by a mysterious man and offered a sizable fee to deliver a flash-drive to Bangkok, Tommy is suspicious. But, without a lot of options, he reluctantly accepts the seemingly simple task. What he doesn't realize is that he's been selected for the job *because* of his destructive lifestyle—and the fact that no one will miss him if he "disappears."

KUDOS for *Tommy's Luck*

In *Tommy's Luck* by Patrick Ashtre, Tommy Luck is offered a job delivering a flash drive to Bangkok. Since Tommy is an unemployed drunkard at the time, and the offer is very lucrative, he has little choice but to accept, even though he's suspicious. Turns out that his suspicions were correct. Tommy was selected, not only for his familiarity with Thailand, its people, and culture, but also because he *is* an unemployed drunk with few ties to the community and no one would miss him if simply "disappears" after the job is done. But Tommy has a few surprises of his own, and, as his bosses soon discover, he isn't as easy to "disappear" as they might have thought. Tense, exciting, and fast paced, the story will grab your attention from the very beginning and keep you riveted all the way through. ~ *Taylor Jones, The Review Team of Taylor Jones & Regan Murphy*

*Tommy's Luck* by Patrick Ashtre is the story of a man whom most people would underestimate and misjudge. Our hero, Thomas Bacon Luck, was once a successful engineer who worked on projects all across the country. But when someone under him dies in an accident, Tommy turns to alcohol to ease the guilt he feels. When the story opens, Tommy is unemployed, an alcoholic, and desperate for cash. He is offered a job delivering a flash drive to a buyer in Bangkok, Thailand, based on Tommy's experience from time spent in that country. Tommy doesn't buy the story, but the pay is too good for him to turn down. Reluctantly, he accepts the job and heads for Bangkok, but as soon as he arrives in Thailand, he begins to cause trouble for his new employer. Unpredictable, clever, and no one's fool, Tommy is determined to make the delivery on his terms, ensuring that he will be able to collect his money and survive. But his enemies are numerous, resourceful, and have access to large amounts of money. All Tommy has are his wits, his instincts, and his friends in the country. But will that be enough to ensure his survival? Having read Ashtre's first two non-fiction books about Thailand, I was delighted to revisit the familiar places detailed in those books. Ashtre cleverly weaves his mystery/thriller into his knowledge of the Thai country and its people, creating an intriguing and well written tale that will have you turning pages from the first one to the last. ~ *Regan Murphy, The Review Team of Taylor Jones & Regan Murphy*

# TOMMY'S LUCK

## PATRICK ASHTRE

*A Black Opal Books Publication*

GENRE: MYSTERY/THRILLER/INTERNATIONAL CRIME THRILLER

TOMMY'S LUCK
Copyright © 2017 by Patrick Ashtre
Cover Design by Jackson Cover Designs
All cover art copyright © 2017
All Rights Reserved
Print ISBN: 978-1-626946-21-7

First Publication: FEBRUARY 2017

Published by Black Opal Books **http://www.blackopalbooks.com**

# DEDICATION

*To Alison, Amelia, and Benjamin*

Thailand Road Map

——————  International boundary
★  National Capital
+–+–+  Train
– – –  Expressway
———  Road

0   50   100 km

www.Thailand-Ticket.de

# CHAPTER 1

*Mexico City, Mexico, 7 May 2015:*

Jimmy Santos strode down the street, maneuvering along a crowded sidewalk, brushing shoulders with people outfitted in a montage of working class clothes. An occasional woman dressed in a white blouse and colorful skirt or man in a suit could be spotted in the rambling crowd. The smell of fried chilies, corn, and chicken mixed with exhaust fumes from a procession of passing late model cars and trucks. It was a hot day, making the usual heavy smog hanging over the city seem all that more ominous. Colorful red, green, and white tattered ribbons and ripped banners still hung precariously from the lampposts and walls, evidence of the recent Cinco de Mayo Celebration. Local food hawkers standing next to their stainless steel rolling kitchens and vendors in front of their shops called out, tempting potential customers. Mixed between the shops were small cantinas and restaurants, filled with an earlier evening crowd.

Recognizing the cantina described to him by his employer, Jimmy stepped under a small wooden sign hanging above the sidewalk heralding the La Laguna Azul Cantina, or the Blue Lagoon Bar. A big man, Jimmy had strong legs supporting a barrel chest, with thick arms and neck. While he had grown up in Los Angeles, California, his short bushy black hair, light brown skin, and soft flat facial features marked him as having a Central American Indian lineage. With dark polyester trousers and a tight fitting yellow cotton imitation Lacoste polo shirt, Jimmy looked like a local.

Walking through the arched doorway was like stepping back in time. A thin layer of dirt grated under the soles of his shoes as he stepped onto its terracotta-tiled floor. The brick walls were painted brownish-tan with no decorative embellishments, except for a black plastic clock and a faded picture of Pancho Villa in a worn frame, both in need of dusting. An old wooden bar, running along one side of the room, with no mirror or bottles of liquor adorning the wall behind, was manned by a thin and wrinkled bartender dressed in a red plaid shirt and white apron. A veil of smoke hanging in the air, fed by the bar patrons' glowing cigarettes, twisted into misty contrails by three slow-moving ceiling fans.

The cantina was filled with men sitting around heavy round wooden tables on a variety of wobbly chairs. Some dressed like Jimmy, as if they had just stepped from behind a low-paying desk job. Others, clothed in dirty jeans and T-shirts, looked as if they had just departed a nearby construction site. Most of the tables were topped with a bottle of cheap tequila, accompanied by small clear glasses partially filled with the yellowish liquid. A spattering of brown beer bottles shared the same space as the tequila and glasses. Saying little to each other, the men were undoubtedly drinking away the memories of overzealous and demanding supervisors or the recollections of a day of hard labor. Two young female waitresses—both with long black hair, dressed in short green dresses, red sashes, and white ruffled blouses—worked to keep the bottles and glasses full.

Jimmy saw the two men at a table in the corner of the smoky room, both appearing to be Mexican. One, short and skinny with a lazy eye that looked wide, was dressed in neatly ironed black jeans and a white western-style shirt. The other, wearing Wrangler blue jeans, was the same height as Jimmy but lacked his bulk.

This man had narrow-set eyes and deep pockmarks on his

face with half of his left eyebrow missing. He wore a black silk shirt and matching vest with a heavy gold chain looped around his neck, a seemingly unlikely wardrobe choice, to Jimmy, on such a hot day.

Jimmy knew the two men were there to meet him because of the out-of-place laptop sitting at the center of the table. The two men looked quizzically at Jimmy as he entered the cantina, likely wondering if the big man could be the one for whom they were waiting. Jimmy smiled and nodded at the men and began working his way toward them, weaving through the tables of bar patrons. Both men nodded back with unsmiling faces.

As Jimmy moved his large body through the crowded bar, he inadvertently knocked up against a chair of one patron and then, a few steps later, bumped a shoulder of another. The victims of the accidental collisions both turned with scowling faces then, once observing the offender's size, both quickly looked away, returning to their drinks and muted conversations.

"*Buenos tarde, caballeros,*" Jimmy said, greeting the two men as he approached the table. "The smog is not nearly as bad as usual today." These words had been given to him to confirm these were indeed the men he had been directed to meet with by his employer.

"The smog is always bad, except when the sun is down," the skinny man replied in heavily accented English. It was an unusual statement that made no sense but was the response for which Jimmy had been expecting and hoping.

Pulling out a chair from the table, its wooden legs scraping across the dirty terracotta-tiled floor, Jimmy lowered his massive body onto the seat. The joints of the chair groaned under the weight. Glancing down at the tabletop, he examined its rough surface. With deep gouges and burns from unattended cigarettes, the heavy wooden table showed years of wear. One of the waitresses stepped up and tapped him on the shoulder, asking him what he was drinking. He ordered a beer.

"Have you the flash-drive?" the skinny man asked.

"I do," Jimmy replied as he pulled a thin silver flash-drive from around his neck and put it on the table next to the laptop.

Opening the laptop, the skinny man turned it on and then picked up the flash-drive. Once the Windows desktop appeared on the screen, he plugged the device into the computer's USB port, moving and clicking the cursor onto the appropriate icons. The flash-drive's contents appeared on the computer's screen. As the skinny man inspected the files, the waitress brought Jimmy's beer, setting it on the table in front of him. Taking a long drink of its ice-cold contents, Jimmy casually watched the skinny man moving the curser from file to file.

"It is confirmed—this is what we expected," the skinny man said, pulling the flash-drive from the USB port and closing the laptop.

"Then we're finished," Jimmy announced. "It was nice doing business with you gentlemen." Smiling, he took another long drink of beer.

Acknowledging him with a grunt, the two men pushed back from the table, leaving Jimmy alone without saying a word. Jimmy remained at the table, drinking and flirting with the waitresses, both of whom ignored his efforts. Between his flirtatious advances, Jimmy glanced at the time on his wrist-watch, waiting for the second meeting of the day.

He didn't have to wait too long. A tall fit man dressed in a dark blue suit and an open-collared white shirt walked into the cantina ten minutes later. With short dark wavy hair, bushy eyebrows, and light brown skin, the man could have been Mexican or any other nationality lying near or south of the equator. Jimmy waved, and the man began making his way over to the table as the other patrons nudged one another, gesturing toward the well-dressed person crossing the cantina. He was an anomaly for that cantina. His attire marked him as outsider, and that made him an oddity.

"Good afternoon, Jimmy. I hear everything went well," the well-dressed man said with a crisp Midwestern-American accent as he sat down across from Jimmy.

"It was pretty easy. I got the right reply to my comment about smog and then handed them the flash-drive. They plugged it into the laptop and checked its contents, and then they were off. Easiest money I've ever made."

The waitress approached the table and asked the well-dressed man in Spanish if he wanted something to drink. The man looked puzzled at her question.

Jimmy repeated the question in English. "Do you want something to drink?"

"No thank you," the man responded and, as Jimmy began to translate his response back into Spanish, the waitress turned and walked away.

"I guess she understood what you said." Jimmy chuckled, while looking over his shoulder at the waitress's green-skirted bottom swaying back and forth as she weaved through the cantina clientele.

"As I was about to say, it is always pleasant when the de-livery goes smoothly," the well-dressed man said as he pulled a thick envelope from his jacket pocket and handed it to Jim-my.

His eyes widening, Jimmy took the envelope and lifted the folded top, peeking inside. "Ten thousand?"

"It's all there. You can count it if you like."

"Not in this place. I wouldn't make it to the door." Jimmy laughed. "I'll have to trust you."

"Jimmy, I have another delivery and was wondering if you might have a recommendation."

"I'll do it," Jimmy blurted out, hoping for the possibility of earning more easy money.

"This one is in Thailand. I need someone familiar with Thailand. Preferably, someone who knows the language."

Sighing, Jimmy paused for a moment, thinking about the man's question. Then a smile crossed his face, as if some pleasurable memory had come to mind.

"As a matter of fact, I do. He's a bit like me, though. A big drinker but always gets the job done."

"What's his name? Where does he live? I'd like to contact him and see if he meets our requirements."

"Last I heard, he had just moved back to the States from Thailand."

Taking another long drink of beer, Jimmy drained the bottle. The waitress saw him emptying the bottle from across the room and ordered another from the bartender.

"That was about six months ago. His name is Tommy. Tommy Luck. I think he lives in the Washington DC area. Maybe Arlington or Alexandria. I haven't talked to him directly but heard the news of his return to the States through a mutual friend."

The well-dressed man took out a pen and pocket-sized notebook and began writing the information down. "You don't happen to have an address?"

"Naw, no address. Just a name and general area."

"His name is Tommy Luck?"

"Thomas Bacon Luck is his full name," Jimmy added.

"That is an unusual name." A raspy cluck erupted from the well-dressed man's mouth, making Jimmy wondered if it was his version of a laugh. Looking up at Jimmy, the man then asked, "Is he the only one you can think of?"

"Yeah, if speaking the language is a requirement. Not too many Americans speak Thai. It's a tough language to learn. A tonal language. A lot of the words sound the same to us Westerners but have big differences with just the way you pronounce them. A lot of those Southeast Asian languages are the same."

"Thank you, Jimmy," the well-dressed man said as he pushed the chair back and stood up. "If we have another delivery in Mexico, I'll give you a call."

"Please do," Jimmy replied, encouraged by the well-dressed man's parting words.

Continuing to drink for several more hours after the well-dressed man had left, Jimmy stood up to leave and could feel the effects of all the beers he had consumed. Slightly dizzy, he made his way to the arched door, again bumping into several of the seated bar patrons. Their reaction mimicked the earlier victims. Even in a drunken stupor no person was foolish enough to challenge a man of Jimmy's size.

Lampposts illuminated the now dark and nearly empty sidewalks with a yellowish glow and few cars moved along the once-busy avenue. Walking back to his hotel, Jimmy passed a small group of men taking turns drinking tequila from a bottle on the steps of an old tenement. A little farther up the street, a tired-looking prostitute in a short black dress with fishnet stockings and scratched patent leather high heels, clearly past her prime, asked him if he wanted a date. Jimmy ignored her. Stopping by a small convenience shop, he bought a bottle of tequila. Four blocks later, he approached his hotel, carrying the tequila bottle in a brown paper bag.

It was a cheap hotel, used by the local prostitutes on an hourly basis. The hotel entrance was marked by a small flickering blue neon light that simply stated *Hotelero*. The lobby was small and need of a good cleaning, and the night clerk, a thin and somber man dressed in a dirty white T-shirt, sat behind a dark wooden counter with peeling veneer. A wide chicken-wire screen separated him from the hotel's clientele.

"Not much protection there, pal," Jimmy commented to the clerk while tapping on the chicken wire. "I could be through that in ten seconds."

The clerk passed the room key under the screen without uttering a word. Picking up his key from the counter, Jimmy walked past an aged elevator with gated doors and a *no funciona* sign hand written in thick black ink on yellowing paper fixed to its call button. Climbing a set of narrow steps leading to the upper floors, he drunkenly bounced off the walls of the stairwell several times while struggling to the third floor.

After unlocking and opening the door, Jimmy paused at the threshold, teetering against the frame. The walls, covered with a faded floral wallpaper, were faintly illuminated from a single bulb hanging from the hallway ceiling behind him. A metal-framed bed and thin mattress, along with a small wooden bed stand in need of paint, made up the only furniture. A small window provided a view of the neighboring building's brick wall. With no maid service, Jimmy's bed was unmade and the sheets looked as if they hadn't been washed in weeks. The room smelled of a mixture of urine and mildew.

A nearly indistinguishable shadow crossed the room's wall and Jimmy felt a narrow blade slip between the ribs in his back. The pain was excruciating as it pierced through the nerves surrounding the ribs and grated across the bones as he turned to confront his attacker, dropping the brown paper bag with the bottle of tequila. Its contents shattered and spilled onto the floor at his feet. The sheer power of Jimmy's spin forced his assailant into the doorframe and, with the impact, the man lost his grip on the blade handle. It was too dark to make out his attacker's facial features, so Jimmy grabbed the man's hair and slammed his head against the doorframe, splintering the wood. As the man's head bounced off the wooden frame, he fell to the floor.

A wave of fatigue overwhelmed Jimmy, and he began coughing up blood. As he reached down to grab his assailant, the man pushed Jimmy away with his feet. He stumbled backward, falling onto the small bed. The bed's metal frame shrieked a high-pitched squeal under his weight.

The collision with the thin mattress buried the blade farther into his back. Sitting up, Jimmy attempted to reach around and extract the weapon but the thickness of his arms became an obstacle. He could not reach the blade handle. His attacker stood up in the doorway, rubbing the side of his head and watched in silence.

Unable to find the strength to stand, Jimmy knew he was dying. He realized that the blade must have punctured his heart or aorta, disrupting the flow of blood to his body. He breathed heavily but to no avail. Life-supporting oxygenated blood never arrived.

"*Por qué?*" Jimmy weakly asked, falling back onto the mattress, the bed frame squealing again. When the man did not respond, Jimmy asked again in English, "Why?"

"The world won't miss you, James Santos. You're a

drunken idiot," his attacker replied in American-accented English, the voice sounding unusually soothing.

Jimmy knew the man was right. He would not be missed. Before taking his final breath on a dirty unmade bed in a budget hotel room in Mexico City, Jimmy thought of his old friend Tommy Luck. He wondered if Tommy would have a better outcome during his delivery.

# CHAPTER 2

*Denver, Colorado, 28 November 2010:*

It was a cold day with gusting winds, the chill seemingly cutting through his jacket and burning his face. The weather was such that Tommy was considering closing down all construction above the tenth floor on the building in downtown Denver. Holding onto one of the steel beams on the eleventh floor, Tommy looked out onto the city below as the winds nudged him from side to side. Standing next to Tommy, his assistant Jim, a short stout man with a large red nose, wore a heavy tan jacket, dirty yellow hardhat, and jeans. Jim's cheeks matched his red nose from the cold.

Looking at Tommy, Jim said, "Gavin is concerned about the crane."

"The winds aren't that bad. I'm more concerned about the combination of wind and cold. This wind chill can dull a man's responses. One good gust and a slow reaction could send a worker over the edge."

"That's why we use safety lines." Jim reached up and straightened his hardhat. "Gavin says there's a rattle in the crane."

Tommy shrugged. "It's an old crane."

"And it was recently certified, but Gavin says there's something wrong. He's been complaining about it for a couple of days."

Looking at Jim with a stern expression, Tommy asked, "Why am I just now hearing about the problem?"

"You've been busy with getting this project back on schedule after that freak snowstorm."

"What seems to be the issue?" Tommy shifted his gaze to the tower crane. "Could it be a problem with the slewing unit engine or gears?"

"Gavin doesn't know. He just says there a shimmy in the movement that shouldn't be there."

"A shimmy?"

"He said it has a shimmy."

Tommy watched the crane's jib slowly spin and its hook lower. "What do we have left to do with the crane today?"

"Two more beams need to be delivered to the twelfth floor." Jim looked at Tommy with concern. "It'll take a week to replace that old crane."

"Let's bring a team in to inspect and recertify the unit. Tell Gavin to deliver the beams and then stop for the day. I want someone inspecting the crane no later than tomorrow morning."

"The company is going to fight us." Jim shook his head. "It was certified last month."

"Tell them—" Tommy suddenly saw a tremor in the crane and turned to Jim. "Tell Gavin to stop everything and get off that crane. Get the riggers clear. Now!"

The crane shuddered again and a loud screeching sound echoed through the steel girders of the building. Tommy looked on in horror as the crane buckled below the cabin, the jib jerking into a forty-degree cant from the mast. Tommy sprinted for the construction elevator attached to the side of the building while listening to Jim scream instructions into his radio. His hands shook as he jabbed the button for the ground floor. As the cage began lowering, Tommy looked out and watched as the cabin and jib broke free from the mast and fell, punctuated by an ear-piercing loud clatter of metal that seemed to shake the elevator cage.

When the elevator came to a stop at the bottom, Tommy ran to the crumpled crane cabin where three other men were pulling twisted pieces of metal aside. Dropping to his knees, Tommy peered inside the mangled cabin. Gavin looked at Tommy and reached out with one hand. Tommy stretched his arm inside and took Gavin's bloody hand. Tommy watched the life fade from Gavin's broken body.

# CHAPTER 3

*Arlington, Virginia, 10 July 2015*:

It was another hot day in Northern Virginia. Unemployed, Tommy Luck was two hours into his daily jog along one of the many trails that crisscrossed Arlington, Falls Church, and Fairfax. Sweating out the libations from the evening prior, Tommy's feet kept pace with music filling his ears by means of a small set of earphones plugged into his cell phone, his thick brown wavy hair bouncing with each stride. The narrow paved path passing below alternated between sunlight and shade produced by the large overhead oak, maple, and elm tree limbs.

Trotting down a pathway leading into Ballston, Tommy pondered the memory of Gavin's death in downtown Denver nearly five years before. Even though he had not known there might be problem with the crane until several minutes before it came tumbling down, Tommy had felt a colossal amount of guilt and drank himself to sleep for a week straight after the incident. With vivid clarity, Tommy could still see Gavin's lacerated face looking up as his life ebbed. Tommy could still remember the feel of Gavin's hand, sticky with blood. He could still recall the smell of grease and dirt. But what truly troubled Tommy had been Gavin's eyes.

Those eyes had expressed a mixture of sorrow and pain, seemingly asking Tommy some unknown question. It was that unknown question that would haunt Tommy for years to come.

Tommy's daily jog would last up to four hours, a far better way of filling a day in his current jobless state than any other option he could think of. The incessant jogging also provided a physically wholesome counterbalance to an otherwise unhealthy lifestyle. Not to mention the daily jog kept Tommy worry free of gaining weight due to his excessive use of alcohol. Both the jogging and drinking had been a part of his daily rituals for a number of years and in his view were representative of his Freudian ID and EGO. As long as those two habits were in balance, he was in equilibrium.

Forty three years old and standing just under six foot tall, Tommy was not a big man and while he currently considered himself 'slender' it had not always been that way. At the end of career in construction management he had developed plumpness he had come to despise. Only after resurrecting the daily run had he reduced his girth. With deep blue eyes surrounded by a spider web of fine wrinkles coming from a life of working outdoors, and high cheekbones given to him by Swedish heritage, Tommy had a boyish handsomeness.

Tommy had always been capable of attracting a woman with only a wink and a smile. This talent was partially responsible for his current financial woes. Having amassed a large sum of money managing high profile construction sites across the United States, Tommy had enjoyed bouncing from city to city, state to state, seeking out new surroundings. A personal life exhibiting the same unusual desire for change, Tommy had a wandering eye which, understandably, neither of his former wives had tolerated. After his last divorce, he had packed up his belongs and moved halfway across the globe, once again in search for new surroundings. Twice divorced with three children, he was now living on what was remaining of his once bulging saving account that had not been taken by an unsympathetic divorce court judge.

The music faded and his cell rang, and slowing his pace, Tommy removed the ear buds. Having just turned down a trail with thick layers of large oak branches hovering above, he felt immediate relief from the hot sun.

"Tommy here."

An unfamiliar man's voice with a midwestern-American accent asked, "Mr. Thomas Luck? Mr. Thomas Bacon Luck?"

Tommy focused on keeping his slowed pace at a steady cadence. "That's right. What can I do for you?"

"Mr. Luck, my name is John Smith and I represent a small technology firm here in DC. I was given your name by a Mr. James Santos, who I believe to be a friend of yours."

"Wow, I haven't heard from him in years."

Tommy and Jimmy Santos had attended the same university in Southern California in their youth. With a shared interest in drinking, Jimmy and Tommy always managed to get into trouble when together. The two friends lost touch when Tommy moved to Maryland to attend graduate school. Occasionally, Tommy would hear what his former collegiate companion was up to through mutual friends. He imagined Jimmy kept track of him in the same haphazard fashion. Last Tommy had heard, Jimmy was working personal security someplace in Central America.

"So what's Jimmy up to these days?"

"Mr. Santos has completed some recent business for me in Mexico. Last time we spoke, I told him I was looking for a unique talent, and Mr. Santos recommended I contact you."

Tommy slowed to a walk. "I would imagine that most of my friends consider my unique talent is the ability to get into trouble where there is none to be found. I'm not sure what other distinctive skill I might possess."

"You've spent time in Thailand? You know the culture and the language?"

"I have indeed and I know a little of the language. I certainly don't consider myself fluent."

In fact, Tommy was more than proficient in both Thai and *Isaan*, the two primary languages spoken in Thailand. Having spent several years on a small island in the Gulf of Thailand owning and operating a pub on the beach at a popular European tourist destination, he began feeling guilty about his parental absence and closed it up six months ago to spend time with his children. Out of work since then and bored, he had recently considered returning and re-opening the beachfront bar.

"I might have an opportunity for you to earn a sizable payment for a small delivery to Bangkok," John Smith offered.

"Sounds interesting but wouldn't FedEx be easier?"

"I was wondering if we could meet and discuss the proposition," John Smith asked.

"Sure. I have an open calendar." Tommy softly chuckled. "You name the date and time."

"This evening at five o'clock on the National Mall would be best for me. Let's meet at the entrance to the Smithsonian Castle. You do know where the Smithsonian is, right?"

"Of course I know where the Smithsonian is. This meeting, not to mention your delivery job, sounds a bit mysterious. How do I recognize you at the Smithsonian?"

"I have a need for discretion. I'll find you."

"All right, it's a date. I'll see you there...well, at least you'll see me," Tommy replied, disconnecting the call.

Reattaching his headphones, he began running again. For the remainder of his jog, Tommy thought about how he could use the cash, however much it might be, offered by John Smith.

Tommy finished up his run, showered, and called his most recent ex-wife to tell her he wouldn't be able to see the kids today. At three o'clock he drove his ancient white Chevy pickup to the nearby East Falls Church Metro Station parking lot, catching the Orange Line to the Smithsonian Metro Station. Wearing faded jeans, a short sleeved dark blue T-shirt advertising some San Diego beach bar, and flip-flops, Tommy arrived at the National Mall forty minutes early.

# CHAPTER 4

*Washington DC, 10 July 2015:*

Tommy leaned up against a tree near one of the coarse gravel paths that bisected the interior of the National Mall, allowing him a view of the red stone Smithsonian Castle's entrance. The National Mall was hot and humid, even at that late time of the day, and he could feel sweat beginning to form under his dark blue shirt. Listening to the busy traffic from the distant Constitution and Independence Avenues, his shaded vantage point allowed him to clearly see the tall Washington Monument above the tree tops to one side and the majestic white Capitol Building in the distance to the other.

Tourists, dressed in a variety of international brightly colored casual clothes with cameras dangling from their necks, milled around the sidewalks, gravel pathways, and the building entrances. Several security officers, in black pants and white shirts with oversized red patches identifying the company currently holding the Smithsonian security contract sewn on their shoulders, lazily took a break smoking cigarettes on the sidewalk in front of the building.

The red Seneca sandstone walls of the Smithsonian stood out against the other architecture on the National Mall. Its tall spirals of Gothic Revival design hovered above the emerald green trees and contrasted against the Ionic style pillars adorning the other buildings. Elm trees stood beside the Castle and lined the sidewalks, wrapping around the entire Mall and its foot-trodden and browning grassy interior, providing some repose from the heat in the form of shade.

Examining the Mall, with his shoulder pressed against the rough white bark of a poplar tree, Tommy remembered his first trip to this grassy park some fifteen years before. He and a woman had visited the National Mall for a day, wandering through the various tourist sites and museums. Tommy hadn't really paid attention to the historical significant of this section of Washington DC.

At the time, he didn't care about L'Enfant's vision of a grand avenue or spectacular vistas of the Washington Monument or the National Capital. His focus had been his companion, a shapely blonde-haired and green-eyed woman with a quick wit. A smile spread across his face as he recalled the memory.

Eventually, he married the woman and they would conceive two children together. His smile faded as quickly, remembering the painful demise of the marriage, and how cheating and lies crippled a perfect partnership, making him forever cynical about love and commitment. Once told by a friend, attempting to reassure him of the wonders of love, that affairs were to be expected over the course of any relationship, he simply nodded his head at the notion.

Tommy knew he would never allow himself to be placed in a position of emotional commitment again. He didn't trust himself to ever create another long-term obligation in matters of the heart. He had failed at every attempt.

Pushing the memory away, Tommy focused on the upcoming meeting with John Smith. Having never been employed in any type of clandestine work and given the circumstances of the possible offer for what seemed an odd job, Tommy thought a little extra time taking in the surroundings prior to the meeting might be a good idea.

Peering out over the roaming crowds, he was largely ignored by the passing tourists who were inundated by the sights. Some looked his way, but they could have been chance glances or had sensed Tommy had been watching them.

Several of the people near the Castle's entrance caught his eye. One was a middle-aged man with thick dark hair, sitting on a short retaining wall under a brass life-size statue of Professor Joseph Henry across Jefferson Drive from the Smithsonian. Dressed in khaki pants and a white short-sleeved shirt, it was hard to tell the man's height but to Tommy he looked short, maybe five feet four inches tall. With pale skinny limbs and small hands, the man's face was unremarkable except for dark beady eyes. The beady-eyed man was reading a newspaper but had yet to turn the page in the fifteen or twenty minutes that Tommy had been watching. There was also a couple standing under several large trees not far from the brass statue. The man, blond, mid-twenties, dressed in blue jeans and a green polo shirt, was playing with his cell phone. With large sad brown eyes, his hair looked as if it had been bleached from too much sun.

Tommy figured him to be a swimmer, the chlorine water used in swimming pools being the bleaching culprit. His girlfriend or wife, a pretty brunette, appeared to be twenty-five or six years old with sparkling blue eyes. Dressed in a red and green floral summer dress, she was kicking dirt around with open toed flats. She had light brown skin and small round breasts. Obviously together, they had yet to say one word to one another.

At five o'clock, Tommy left the shade of the tree he had been leaning against and walked across the Mall to the narrow arched entrance of the Smithsonian Castle. Standing just outside the entrance he tried not to look out of place but the meeting's setup began to concern him. Tommy didn't like being in the position of not knowing what was going to happen next, preferring situations where he understood all the options, allowing some level of control. Tommy's eyes darted from the beady-eyed man to the bleached-hair man and pretty brunette, looking for some sign the meeting was getting ready to take place. He wasn't disappointed with his improvised warning system.

Shortly after five the bleached hair man and pretty brunette's attention turned to a tall fit man, about five or ten years younger than Tommy, wearing a stylish two piece dark suit, white shirt, and red tie. Tommy's first thought was the man must be hot with his wardrobe choice in this weather. The well-dressed man approached Tommy.

"Mr. Luck, I am John Smith," the man introduced himself, smiling and holding out a hand.

While his accent was clearly Midwestern, John Smith seemed to have Middle Eastern ancestry, his skin having a light coffee tint and his hair, while cut short, was dark and naturally wavy. Dark eyes and thick bushy eyebrows clinched his lineage.

"How'd you know it was me? By the way, your name suits all this mystery and you can call me Tommy," Tommy greeted John Smith, shaking his hand.

It was a firm and short shake, easing Tommy's nervousness, as he believed you could tell a lot about a man when you shook their hand. John Smith's was an easy confident shake.

"I have my ways," John Smith replied, his dark eyes not leaving Tommy's blue eyes.

"So what's the deal?"

"Not here. Let's move over to the center of the Mall. Less people and more privacy," John Smith said, gesturing toward the grassy interior of the Mall.

"More mystery, Mr. John Smith, I'm not sure I like the way this is going."

"Mr. Luck—Tommy, this is a completely lawful opportunity, and as I said on the phone, I have a need for discretion. Let's move over to the Mall where we can discuss the proposition without the threat of eavesdropping. You'll understand better after I've described my offer."

They walked toward the center of the National Mall, crossing the narrow Jefferson Road in front of the Smithsonian Castle, over the sidewalk surrounding its interior, down a set of the concrete steps encircling the brass statue of Joseph Henry, and onto a coarse gravel pathway leading across the heavily trodden grass. The beady-eyed man paid no attention to them as they passed by, convincing Tommy he had been wrong about the man's presence. Midway across the Mall, stepping onto the dry grass, John Smith began explaining the opportunity.

"As I said on the phone, I run a small technology firm here in DC. We specialize in highly confidential corporate security technology."

"You said you represented this firm on the phone, not run it. We're not talking corporate espionage are we?" Although at this point Tommy thought he would probably consider anything to make money. If nothing else, he figured he might be able to get a free round trip ticket to Thailand out of the deal.

"Run. Represent. Not much difference is there? Actually you're close, as it pertains to espionage. It has to do with technology that protects a firm or organization from corporate espionage. In this case it is security software that is embedded into a firm's database that monitors and controls access to sensitive information by identifying and tracking access with pinpoint accuracy. As with most database security programs, if the identity or access point is suspect and does not meet certain parameters, the files cannot be accessed. One of the differences with this software is that if someone were to attempt to access certain information, and they did not have the proper authorization to do so, the program pinpoints their identity, both as an electronic fingerprint and a global location. Their identity is revealed, and they don't get the information, making it a bad day for the failed intruder.

"Another difference from other security programs is that if the sensitive information is downloaded by an authorized individual on an authorized terminal, the program inserts a beacon into the data so wherever the information is viewed on a machine with a network connection, the same information in sent. If it is viewed on a machine without a network connection, the program registers the viewing and sends the beacon out if the file ever finds itself on a network. The program overcomes all current technological advances designed to screen the locations and identities of illicit database access abusers—or hackers."

"Why not just encrypt the program and send it electronically?" Tommy shrugged his shoulders.

"It is a highly specialized program that we do not allow to be transmitted via the internet for fear of exposure to outside sources." John Smith continued to explain, "Once it is established on the source server it provides its own self-defense security. But during transport, whether via wire or manual delivery, it is susceptible to exposure."

"I say again, why not just encrypt the program and send it electronically? It worked for Wikileaks with all those Department of Defense documents."

It seemed to Tommy that manual delivery of this program was overkill for protection—if not more risky.

John Smith smiled. "Although Wikileaks posted the DoD documents as an encrypted file prior to releasing the information to the public, do you think that the American Intelligence community had not already broken the encryption, viewed the documents prior to their release, and known what the files contained? Do you think this agency did not erase the most damaging details contained in the files? And if we did encrypt and transmit the program, then should we encrypt the encryption key and send it electronically? And then send the encryption key to encrypted encryption key...or should we encrypt that, as well? We are under constant high-tech surveillance. The protocol we use has proven to be secure."

"What about that Phil Zimmermann guy, didn't he solve all that with something called PGP?" Tommy asked, scratching his wavy brown hair.

John Smith playfully asked, "Are you a computer scientist?"

"No."

Looking at Tommy with a wiry grin, John Smith said, "Then you need to trust me. This is our protocol. This is how we do deliver our merchandize."

Looking into John Smith's eyes, as if trying to determine

his genuineness, Tommy then asked, "So you're looking for a delivery boy for this security software? Why me, and why all the secrecy?"

"The code is sought after by many of our competitors, as well as those that would want to learn how to breach the security of those databases protected by the software. My office, my employees, my home, my movements are under constant surveillance by people and organizations seeking to obtain this program."

"Does that mean we are being watched right now?" Tommy raised his eyebrows to highlight the question. He could see a thin sheen of sweat building on John Smith's brow and cheeks, produced from a combination of the hot weather and his dark suit, no doubt.

"I have taken the necessary steps to ensure we are not being watched. In fact, I am currently on a private jet at thirty six thousand feet, destined for Denver at this moment." A small dry cluck erupted from John Smith's mouth and Tommy wondered if it were his version of a chuckle. "As the delivery is to be in Thailand, we sought out someone with your qualifications because of your knowledge of the country, the Thai people, and the Thai culture—the language. We have found in the past this small talent can pay dividends if there are problems at the delivery site. And the fact you have been recommended by a trusted source is as important."

"Thank you, Jimmy. As I said, I am not fluent in the language. Assuming I accept, when, where, and how much?"

"The delivery date is set for ten days from today in Bangkok with detailed delivery site location and instructions forthcoming. There is a ten thousand dollar fee to you—after all expenses paid, of course."

"You're running a tight timeline. What if I say no?"

"It is important, for security reasons, that we run a tight timeline. Information on the deliveries tend to have a way of, let us say, leaking out. And of course we have an alternate delivery person but you are our lead candidate." Arriving at the center of the Mall, John Smith stopped walking and turned to face Tommy. The faint sound of gravel and dry grass being crunched whispered under the soles of his shoes.

Tommy glanced over his shoulder and saw the bleached hair man and pretty brunette had moved to a tree at the edge of the Mall adjacent to the spot John Smith had chosen to stop.

"Sounds interesting and pretty easy for that much money," Tommy commented, looking back to John Smith.

"We have had issues in the past that have required the delivery person to earn that much money. Not often, but on occasion, there have been problems to what might appear to be an easy job."

Tommy raised his eyebrows and asked, "Like what?"

"The individuals and organizations desiring this program will stop at nothing to obtain a copy. We have found the current protocol for delivery provides sufficient security."

"You didn't answer my question. What kind of problems have occurred in the past requiring the delivery boy to earn his money?"

"Let's just say, that in the past several of our deliverymen, well versed in the culture, the people, and the language of the delivery country, have been able to spot problems before they occurred, and have been imaginative and flexible enough to modify the delivery or delivery sites," John Smith calmly explained.

"You still haven't answered my question. What kind of problems? Have any of your delivery boys been hurt, maimed, or killed?"

"Never," John Smith answered while smiling confidently as a trickle of sweat broke from his left temple and rolled down his cheek.

"Did Jimmy Santos' delivery go smoothly?"

"His delivery went very smoothly. One of the smoothest we've had."

"Good for Jimmy," Tommy replied, holding out his hand. "I'll think about it. You got a number I can call and let you know the answer?"

Tommy wondered to himself who he was kidding, he was

ready to take the money and run, but like all job offers, he didn't want to seem too desperate.

John Smith extracted a card from his jacket pocket. "Don't take too long to decide, Tommy. As you pointed out, I am on a tight timeline."

The card he handed Tommy had a simple *JS* printed in the center, with a number in smaller print just below. As John Smith turned and began walking away, the bleached-hair man and the pretty brunette took up a parallel course. Tommy watched the pretty brunette's floral dress as it floated back and forth across her slender tan legs when she strode away.

"One more thing," Tommy called.

As John Smith stopped and turned, the bleached hair man and the pretty brunette awkwardly duplicated his maneuver.

"What is it, Tommy?"

"What's the name of your tech firm? That's probably important information for a potential employee."

"Dual Tech of DC," John Smith said, before turning and continuing his departure across the brown grass.

The bleached-hair man and pretty brunette stood still for a few moments, as if trying to halfheartedly persuade Tommy that they were not connected with the mysterious John Smith, before resuming their parallel tracks.

"I'm not sure I like all this mystery, Mr. John Smith," Tommy quietly said to himself as he examined the unrevealing business card.

Walking back to the metro station, Tommy checked over his shoulder several times to see if he was being followed. He saw no one. Boarding the Orange Line Metro bound for East Falls Church, he left the train at the next station as a precaution, delaying his exit until the last possible moment. He then picked up the Yellow Line to Crystal City. From Crystal City he hopped on to the Blue Line to Rosslyn, once again delaying his departure from the train until the last possible moment. Finally, he boarded an Orange Line train back to East Falls Church.

Departing the metro station at East Falls Church, he shook

his head. "That was a wasted effort. They undoubtedly know where I live."

As Tommy walked toward the metro parking lot, in the reflection from a glass-covered advertisement board, he saw the beady-eyed man from the National Mall exit the station behind him. Ignoring the man, Tommy walked to his aged white pickup and drove home. Stepping through the front door of his small house, he turned on the television, retrieved a bottle of Jamison whiskey from the cupboard, and drank himself into a stupor. He was asleep by nine.

# CHAPTER 5

*Chaloklum, Koh PhaNgan, Thailand, 20 November 2012*:

The wide white beach extended along the shores of the enormous bay, each end punctuated with grey rocky outcroppings covered in lavish green tropical flora. Crystal clear water, tinted light blue, reflected the sun. Tall palm trees drooped over the sand as water lapped at its edges. Tommy could feel the hot Southeast Asia sun on his shoulders and fine grains of cool sand between his toes as he and Lawan walked along the beach. Her hand, in his, felt soft and smooth. The briny smell of the sea was carried on a soft breeze, as Tommy contemplated what he needed to do.

"It's time," Tommy whispered just loud enough for Lawan to hear.

Looking at Tommy walking at her side, Lawan asked, "Time for what?"

"It's time I returned to the States."

Tommy could feel a slight quake in her grip before she released his hand. He could feel a sudden tension in the air. He glanced over and saw a confused expression on her face, a knitted brow over bewildered eyes.

"We are going to the United States?" Lawan asked in a confused tone.

"No. I am going to the United States," Tommy replied, trying to keep his voice from revealing his welling emotions.

"We have made a good life here. I don't understand…" Lawan's voice trailed off.

Not knowing how to explain everything he was feeling, Tommy said again, "Its time."

"But I love you."

"I love you too."

"But why?"

Stopping, Tommy turned and took her shoulders into his hands. "You deserve better, Lawan. I will eventually hurt you and you deserve better."

"But I don't want better. I am very happy with you."

Releasing her shoulders, Tommy walked away without looking back. His emotions vacillated between love, sadness, and regret, nearly bringing him to tears. He walked from the beach to their small apartment over their business and packed his bag. He left the island on the ferry that evening and Thailand the next morning.

# CHAPTER 6

*Arlington, Virginia, 11 July 2015*:

Blinking from the light pouring through the window, Tommy awoke from a dream and placed his hands over his face. It had been a memory really, a recollection from his past, and one he had often. Walking on a beach of fine white sand with crystal clear water lapping its edges to one side and tall lazy palm trees to the other, he had looked down into the eyes of a beautiful Asian woman. The dream had recounted a departing farewell, nearly word for word. It had been a painful conversation with a woman he had fallen in love with. It had been a decision he would always regret. But Tommy knew himself too well.

Love and commitment were fleeting concepts in his world. Tommy had learned that the pain of separating could come in one of two forms: a well thought out and orderly departure or a separation amidst the chaos of lies and deceit. Even filled with a seemingly endless love for the woman, he had chosen the previous, and got out before it all went to hell.

An all too common hangover took hold, and Tommy's memory shriveled to an overwhelming ache in his head and nauseous rolling stomach. After his morning routine of eating a small breakfast and watching the news for several hours, he dressed for a run.

Stepping out of his bungalow, he scanned the cars along

the street. Having run by the same cars for over six months, he had come to recognize each and, on this morning, he noticed an out-of-place white nondescript sedan, a late model Ford Taurus, a block and a half from his house. He could see someone sitting in the driver's seat of the car. Stepping back into his bungalow, Tommy grabbed the card given to him by John Smith.

The phone rang three times before John Smith answered.

"Good morning, Tommy."

"John Smith, are you having me watched?" It was more of an accusation than a question, as the dull headache from his alcohol binge the night before made his words sound testy.

"It is both for your protection and to ensure that our meeting occurred undetected. And I must say, I am happy to see you have taken the precaution to notice," John Smith commented. "That is a desirable trait for the upcoming delivery."

"What trait would that be, paranoia? You might recall I haven't agreed to deliver your software and being watched was not a part of our deal."

"As I said, we have monitored your movements in order to protect both you and the delivery."

"I hate to tell you but your team is about as discreet as a Christmas parade along the streets of Mecca," Tommy replied before disconnecting the call without waiting for an answer. Walking out the door, he began his run.

Alongside the white sedan he stopped abruptly and knocked on the side window with an open hand. Sitting in the driver's seat was the bleached hair man who had been with the pretty brunette on the National Mall the day before.

The young man's sad brown eyes looked up at Tommy as he rolled the window down and smiled. "Can I help you, sir?"

With his hands on the roof of the sedan, Tommy leaned close to the open window. "Your boss just called and said you can go home. Take the day off and go for a swim. Your services won't be needed at this location anymore."

"I'm not sure what you mean, sir."

A cell phone on the passenger seat began chirping, announcing an incoming call, and Tommy said, "That's your boss now. Have a nice day," before trotting off.

Tommy liked to run. It cleared his head and gave him an opportunity to ponder the day before him. It also aided in minimizing his daily hangover from the previous night's drinking, sweating out the residual effects of the alcohol. This run he mulled over the mysterious job offer by John Smith. He justified taking the job because he needed the money. He considered the possible risks and countered them with his knowledge of Bangkok and Thailand, not to mention all the people he knew in the country. Just as he was ready to admit that he would take the job, Tommy became suspicious about the high pay and ease of the task. He was also worried about his lack of knowledge concerning John Smith and his mysterious high-tech firm.

"This just seems like it's too easy and good to be true," Tommy muttered to himself while jogging down a path leading to Falls Church.

The white sedan was gone by the time Tommy returned three and a half hours later. Walking into his bungalow drenched in sweat, Tommy pulled out his laptop, opened it up, and punched the power button. After a short wait the Windows desktop background and icons appeared, and Tommy double clicked the internet explorer. The Google search engine quickly materialized on the screen. He typed in *Dual Tech of DC*. Google immediately came back with several sites containing the key words. Scanning the results, Tommy picked the most obvious and double clicked his choice. A webpage appeared with the Dual Tech company logo on one side, a silicon chip laid over two cogs, and the familiar face of John Smith on the other.

Tommy laughed. "Wow, his name actually is John Smith."

He scanned the website propaganda before picking up John Smith's card and calling him for the second time that day.

Three rings later, John Smith's voice echoed from the phone's tiny speaker, "Tommy, nice to hear from you again so soon."

"You and three rings, is that a habit or is the phone always three rings away?"

"Just another protocol, Tommy," John Smith explained. "Three rings allow the security system on the phone to engage."

"I should have guessed as much. Against my better judgment, I'll deliver the software."

"Excellent," John Smith answered, clearly happy about Tommy's decision.

"What next?"

"We will coordinate an airline ticket and lodging. I'll get back to you concerning the departure date and time. We will meet prior to your flight out, and I will provide you with the package, some pocket money, and further details. Any other questions?"

"I'll have to think about that, but for now no questions."

"With your approval, I would like to resume the surveillance on you—benefiting us both, of course," John Smith requested, his voice remaining confident.

"I'll bring your watchman coffee in the morning. Or better yet, station the pretty brunette in my bungalow. I await your call, John Smith."

Tommy's schedule of running and drinking continued, with the exception of an occasional visit with his children, sometimes at his bungalow and sometimes at a park or a community pool. He cherished those moments, making his daily routine bearable.

Two days later, John Smith contacted Tommy.

# CHAPTER 7

*Kansas City, Missouri, 9 August 2009:*

Tommy was hunched over his desk, examining the architectural drawings of the building under construction outside. Through the small window in the portable office that looked as if it had been built from shipping container, skeletal steel girders thrust from a lot filled with cranes and trucks. Men dressed in flannel shirts, jeans, and hardhats moved about the site with natural efficiency.

The door to the office swung open, and a man wearing a dark suit stepped inside, silently eyeing Tommy at his desk. Tommy recognized the man as an assistant to one of the three investors of the building. Assistant might have been what he called himself, but to Tommy he seemed more a muscle-bound thug with dim eyes.

"What can I do for you?" Tommy asked, straightening up and placing his hands on his hips.

A strange tenseness seemed to wash over the small office as the man stepped up to the desk. "The boss has changed your supply order," the man responded flatly, as he laid several documents on the desk.

Taking the documents, Tommy inspected their contents. "Sorry, but this won't do. These materials are substandard and not specified on the architectural design."

"Boss said—"

"I don't care what your boss said, the answer is no. Tell your boss that if he has a problem with that then he needs to come down here himself and talk to me."

The big man stepped forward and slapped his hand down hard onto the desk, the sound echoing off the walls. "The boss says you'll use what's on that list."

Tommy calmly looked into the man's eyes. As the man began to speak again, Tommy swiftly grabbed a stapler from the corner of the desk. The man's eyes widened as Tommy swung the stapler down and slammed its edge onto the thug's outstretched fingers. Before the man could let out a high-pitched bellow, Tommy took the stapler and smashed it into the side of this head. The man teetered for a moment before falling to the floor, unconscious.

Opening the top drawer of his desk, Tommy retrieved a small pen like device and slipped it into his shirt pocket. He then took his truck keys from the desktop and causally walked from the office. Climbing into his white Chevy pickup, parked just outside the door, he drove off the construction site. Tommy drove several blocks to an office building on a back street of the city and double parked the truck out front. Before stepping from his pickup, he grabbed a hammer that had been sitting on the seat next to him.

Stepping into the office building, Tommy nodded to a young receptionist as he walked by. The young receptionist, seeing the hammer in Tommy's hand, grabbed a phone and began making a call. Tommy assumed she was calling the office manager or possibly the man he was intent on meeting.

Walking down a wide corridor to a stairwell, Tommy climbed the stairs to the third floor and found the office he was looking for. Another receptionist with a panicked expression silently watched as Tommy strode past and opened the door.

A silver-haired man in his seventies with wire rim glasses sat behind a large oak desk wearing a white open collared shirt and gray slacks. Two men wearing tailored suits and jackets stood on either side of the desk with blank expressions, as if a man walking into their boss's office with a hammer was not an unusual occurrence. The office had expansive windows looking out onto the downtown Kansas City skyline.

The older man smiled. "Mr. Luck, I see you've received my instructions."

"Yes, Mr. Wigglow, I have."

"I do hope my assistant is all right." Mr. Wigglow gestured to a heavily cushioned chair in front of the desk. "Please take a seat."

"He'll be fine," Tommy replied, sitting down. "He's enjoying a nap on my office floor at the moment."

"Isn't there a metaphor about not shooting the messenger?"

"A quote from Shakespeare in the play *Henry the Fourth*."

"Ah, you are well read, I see." Mr. Wigglow calmly shifted in his chair. "I've never had a man come to my office and threaten me with a hammer."

"The hammer's not for you. I made the assumption you wouldn't be alone. The hammer was designed to equal the odds against your henchmen."

"I'm not sure a hammer would equal the odds against what they have under their coats."

"You're right." Tommy chuckled morbidly. "I only brought one hammer. I didn't expect two thugs."

Mr. Wigglow leaned back in his chair, scrutinizing Tommy for a moment. "I never leave anything to chance, Mr. Luck. You will use the updated materials list."

"No, Mr. Wigglow, I will not."

"You will regret this act of defiance."

"Is that a threat?"

"Call it what you will, but you will use the updated list."

"Mr. Wigglow, I hesitated to take this job when I learned you were one of the investors. The only reason I accepted, in the end, was because of a plea from one of the other investors who happens to be a good friend. He was concerned that you would attempt to use vendors clearly linked to your little criminal empire. Based on this updated materials list, I can see his concerns were well founded. Maybe I should have convinced my friend to back out of a project partially funded by you."

"Your friend was coerced into his investment role, just as I will compel you to continue managing the project with the updated materials list." Mr. Wigglow laughed. "We all have families, don't we? We all want to ensure to their wellbeing, don't we? You have received a sizable down payment for your services and will continue with our contracted agreement."

"Thank you, Mr. Wigglow."

Mr. Wigglow looked mystified. "What?"

Tommy cocked the hammer back and threw it, striking the man on the left side of the desk in the forehead. As the second thug began reaching under his jacket, Tommy pulled a tang knife from his boot and threw it. The knife struck the man's right shoulder as he pulled a nine-millimeter Beretta from under his jacket.

The man squealed and grabbed his shoulder with his left hand, dropping the weapon to the floor. Tommy vaulted over the corner of the desk and struck the man in the face with a closed fist. The man fell to the floor on top of his weapon. Plucking his knife from the man, Tommy calmly walked back around the desk to the overstuffed chair.

"It's amazing what you learn working on construction sites with a tough crowd of men," Tommy explained, once again sitting across from Mr. Wigglow. "One of the reasons I have become successful at the trade is that I react to threats efficiently and swiftly. But what really gets me riled up is when someone threatens my family. I imagine that, even though you're a devious bastard, someone out there loves you and you likely love them back. If one hair on any of my family is hurt, I will come for you and your loved ones with a vengeance and level of violence that will surprise even you."

"You will regret this day."

"Think twice before you act, Mr. Wigglow. I am going to walk out of this office and drive back to the construction site. I will manage the project till it is complete, using my materials list. I will honor our contract only because of my friend."

# CHAPTER 8

*Arlington, Virginia, 13 July 2015*:

Having just eaten a small breakfast, Tommy was reflecting on an event that occurred six years ago. It was the memory of managing the construction of a skyscraper in Kansas City and the man who sent an emissary requesting changes to the engineering plans in the form of materials. It had been a transparent attempt to reduce the cost of the building and, knowing that the changes would have affected the buildings integrity, Tommy had dismissed the proposal. When the financier had threatened his family, Tommy had acted swiftly and viciously, toppling his two henchmen. Before leaving the man's office, Tommy had delivered a threat of his own. Tommy had learned over the course of his career that people never change and the silver-haired Mr. Wigglow would always be a despicable character.

While Tommy could control what took place on the construction site, he didn't want to be associated with the caliber of individual he had found himself working with. A reputation meant everything in the construction business, and Tommy didn't want his sullied by a bad business relationship. The only reason Tommy had offered to remain at the project was because of a friend.

The next day Tommy was arrested for assault by the Kansas City Police Department. The charges were quick dismissed when Tommy presented a pen like recording device with his conversation in Mr. Wigglow's office. Tommy left the project and, several years later during a severe storm, the building had a catastrophic structural failure that killed several office workers.

A ringing cell phone broke him from his thoughts about the leaving the construction site all those years ago.

"Good morning, Tommy," John Smith's voice greeted him.

"You always seem to call at the right time, John Smith."

"I have spent some time learning your daily schedule," John Smith said. "Up by seven, you turn the television on by seven-thirty. Depending on whether whatever you're watching holds your attention, you begin daily run around ten o'clock, for up to four hours. You pick up your children around three o'clock, followed by a trip to the grocery store at four o'clock in the afternoon. You shop for each day's meals, a very interesting and unusual habit for an American. You cook dinner for your children and begin drinking no earlier than four-thirty in the afternoon. With Jameson Irish whiskey as your drink of choice, you're normally intoxicated by five-thirty or six. You take your kids home by seven, much of the time driving under the influence—you should really consider changing that particular habit. I'm just trying to keep this convenient for you, Tommy."

"Wow, you really know how to sum up a pretty dismal existence," Tommy replied. "Knowing my lifestyle, why in the world would you trust me with the package?"

"My investigation of you and your past was far more extensive than just identifying your current personal crises. The excessive drinking has been a decade-long problem but does not seem to affect your overall performance. For instance, the other day when you suspected that you were followed, you managed to shake one of my best agents. It was only because he knew your destination that allowed him to catch up at the final metro station. You have a history of an insightful decision making process."

"More like a two-decade-long drinking problem and one

that probably is not best defined as a 'current personal crises.' Maybe 'enduring' would make a better descriptive adjective. How did you know that I was headed home from the National Mall and not to meet with one of your competitors or go out and feed my nightly addiction?"

"It was after five o'clock and you were headed home for a drink," John Smith answered. "You very rarely drink in public while in the United States. On the other hand, drinking in public overseas seems to be a part of your personal policy."

Tommy could feel John Smith's confident smile on the other end of the line. "Thais tend not to indict people for their imperfections. I imagine it all has to do with their Buddhist roots. I like drinking with them. John Smith, I am a self-proclaimed drunk who is normally intoxicated by six o'clock each night. I make great decisions when the sun is up—after that it's hit or miss. I ask again, does that not worry you?"

"I will admit you were a difficult decision for me, Tommy," John Smith explained. "With you, I had to read between the lines. After an intensive investigation into your past, I learned that you have never failed to rise to the occasion. Two days ago, at the National Mall, I met you after five in the evening. You broke from your habit and had not started drinking because you were interested in what I was going to offer you. You are like the genius child failing out of grammar school. As the genius child fails to do his homework because it's too boring and easy, you choose to drink because life is too easy and you are bored. When you are not bored, you perform."

"Thanks for the vote of confidence John Smith." Tommy chuckled. "So when do I leave?"

"You're booked on a United Airlines flight tomorrow out of Washington Dulles with a layover at Tokyo Narita, arriving in Bangkok at eleven thirty in the evening, day after tomorrow. I have arranged lodging for you at the Imperial Queen's Park Hotel on So Twenty Two. There will be a driver waiting for you at the airport in Bangkok."

"I doubt you arranged anything. One of your minions, I

imagine, did all the legwork. I know the flight and Queens Park well. By the way, it's Soi Twenty-Two, not So Twenty-Two—Soi, like in soy sauce—it roughly translates to street," Tommy corrected. "What about the delivery?"

"Takes place on the twentieth. Instructions will be provided on the morning of the delivery. After the package is delivered, you'll be catching another United Airlines flight the following morning at six-thirty. Isn't there a song about 'One night in Bangkok makes a hard man humble'?" John Smith clucked a short raspy snort, confirming Tommy's earlier suspicion that he had an unusual laugh.

"That song's about a chess game. Probably doesn't apply to this situation."

"I wouldn't be too sure, Tommy. Chess is exactly what we are playing. However, for this one, we are on the same team."

"Are we the white or black game pieces?"

"The white of course, Tommy. I will pick you up at ten tomorrow morning and drive you to the airport. Don't forget your passport."

"One last thing, John Smith."

"What is it Tommy?"

"Will your people be following me in Bangkok?"

"I think that is prudent, do you not, Tommy?"

"How will I know between your guys and someone else interested in the delivery? You know, between the white pieces and the black?"

"What are you asking me?"

"Let me do this delivery without the white noise. With your guys following me, I won't be able to discern if someone else is in the game."

"I can't do that, Tommy. Protocol. However, you will recognize at least two, as they are the same agents who took part in our meeting at the National Mall and your subsequent surveillance," John Smith offered. "We are a small team."

"The pretty brunette and the bleached-haired guy with you at the National Mall, or the beady-eyed man who followed me home?"

"You're good, Tommy. You even identified my man who followed you into the metro. I didn't think he stood out," John Smith replied, clearly surprised Tommy had identified all his agents at the National Mall.

"He needs re-training," Tommy replied flatly. "Reading a newspaper for thirty minutes without turning the page was a dead giveaway that he wasn't there to see the sights or keep up with current events—actually they all need retraining."

"That's the entire team. If you see someone else, they're a black piece."

"Somehow, I think you have more up your sleeve than three poorly trained employees. See you tomorrow, John Smith."

Later that evening—after spending the afternoon with his two youngest children, his daughter Ann, son Will—Tommy walked down to the old Chevy pickup parked along the sidewalk in front of his house. They had spent their time together playing chess, a game both the kids seemed to enjoy and one Tommy had learned as a young boy himself. Slightly tipsy from five glasses of Jameson on the rocks during their back-to-back games, Tommy nearly fell over as he pulled the heavy driver's side door open. It squealed in displeasure as it rotated on its hinges.

More inanimate disapproval sounded as he climbed in and slammed the door shut. The age of the truck evident in its old drooping doors, Tommy had to reopen and slam the door shut again to get the handle to latch. His son, tall and lanky for his age with wavy brown hair and high cheekbones that had obviously been given to him by his father's side of the family, pulled the passenger's side door open and slid into the center seat.

Tommy's daughter, a petite brunette with similar facial features and brown eyes, climbed in next to Will and pulled the old door closed, it responding with a similar racket as the driver's side. The passenger side door didn't droop as much and closed on the first try.

As Will slid across the worn and cracked blue vinyl bench

seat, he looked up at Tommy. "Dad, why don't you and Mom like each other?"

"It's not that we don't like each other. We just have a hard time agreeing on things."

"Will, don't be a jerk," Ann sounded off.

"Ann, it's okay. He can ask those questions," Tommy replied, trying to stifle an argument between his two children.

"She's a good mom," Will argued. "Do you think you could ever love her again?"

Tommy paused before inserting the keys into the ignition, thinking about the question. "Will, your mom and I had some good years, and I will always love her for giving me you and your sister. But everyone's needs and desires change throughout their life. You will never stop changing—both mentally and physically. The trick is to make sure you change with the person you're with. Your mom and I didn't. A lot of job-related separation made sure of that."

"I love her."

"I know, buddy. I know," Tommy said as he started the pickup.

"Dad and Mom don't get along. It's a fact of life," Ann added.

Tommy chuckled under his breath. "That is a fact."

The smell of coolant leaking from some valve or fixture under the hood immediately filled the truck's cab. He had thought about taking it to a shop to fix the problem but had decided that spending time with his children outweighed losing his only means of transportation for several days—not to mention spending money he didn't have on a problem that had not become critical.

Pulling away from the curb, Tommy could feel the effects of the Irish whiskey and hoped that his ex-wife would not realize how much he had drunk. A five minute drive later, they pulled up to a small tan bungalow with an enormous oak tree out front. The house was surrounded with freshly planted flowers and a thick rope was draped over one of the oaks high limbs. Tommy could remember how difficult it was to get the rope over that limb in order to make a swing for his children when they had first moved into the house. He had had to tie a heavy weight to the end of a thin nylon cord and then tie that to the rope, before throwing the lead over the limb and hoisting the heavier line up.

He chuckled to himself, remembering nearly knocking himself out as he threw the weight over the limb, and it swinging back down onto his head.

Noticing the house had long grass in the front yard and small saplings growing from the gutters as he climbed out of the pickup, Tommy thought for a moment that he should come over after returning from Bangkok to mow the lawn and clean the gutters. He quickly dismissed the idea for fear of having a confrontation with Sarah, his ex-wife. Sarah made him nervous, and he avoided her at all costs.

Walking up to the front door, Tommy could feel himself become tense. His ex-wife's simple presence had an effect on him that had never been duplicated. As a result, Tommy had come to despise these short child exchanges. He wasn't sure whether his nervousness was a result of his guilt over past infidelities or brought about by her relentless criticism of his lifestyle, or, more likely, both. Whatever it was, he dreaded the next few minutes.

Dressed in a bright red robe, Sarah opened the door and placed her hands on her hips, scrutinizing Tommy's every move with displeasing eyes before asking her traditional first question of, "How much have you had to drink?"

"Not enough to put up with the inevitable inquisition I'm about to experience."

Sarah was a tall woman with bright green eyes, and thick blonde hair. She had been knockout beautiful in her youth, thin and agile, but age was beginning to take its toll, adding deep crow's feet wrinkles around her eyes, thick loose arms, and wide hips. Tommy could still see her youthful beauty but doubted whether if anyone else could.

"You're drunk—again," Sarah hissed at Tommy.

Will called over his shoulder, "Love you, Dad," as he

slipped past his mother and disappeared into the house.

Similarly, Ann said, "See yah, Dad," before gliding between her mother's imposing body and the door frame.

"I'm not drunk," Tommy retorted as he reached out for a black iron hand rail leading up the front door to steady himself.

"I'm going to call the police next time you drive our children home drunk."

"Call them if you like. It'll make a pleasant childhood memory for the kids—the local sheriff hauling their father off," Tommy growled back. The two silently stared at one and other for a few moments before Tommy said in a softer voice, "Looks like I'm off to Bangkok for a few days."

"Back to your Jimmy Buffet lifestyle?"

"No, I got a short term job. Some guy needs something delivered to Thailand, and I fit the job description," Tommy responded, successfully keeping the simmering anger out of his voice.

"Wouldn't be nice if you really did get a job. Something you could actually make some money to help pay the bills around here."

"It's just for a couple of days. I should be back in about a week, or so."

"I hate you. I hope you never come back," Sarah spat before slamming the door.

Rather than get angry, Tommy felt a wave of relief as the door slammed in his face. The scent from the flowers planted around the house and the neighbor's freshly cut grass suddenly filled the air.

Tommy quietly laughed as he turned and walked back down to his pickup. "Another semi-successful transfer of the children."

Tommy drove home and finished off the bottle of Jameson before passing out on the couch.

# CHAPTER 9

*Arlington, Virginia, 14 July 2015:*

Sitting in his living room waiting for John Smith, Tommy contemplated the twenty-three hour trip to Bangkok and the initial unpleasantness finding oneself twelve hours off schedule. Standing up, he shook those thoughts from his head and prepared himself for the long trip.

At ten, a black limousine pulled up in front Tommy's bungalow.

As he walked out the front door, carrying a small suitcase, John Smith stepped out to greet him. "Good morning, Tommy," he called out from next to the limousine's open door.

"Good morning, John Smith. With the presence of a limousine, it seems like we've dropped all the discretionary protocol."

"It would appear so, wouldn't it, Tommy? At this point, you should consider the fact that the delivery taking place has been compromised."

"Protocol?"

"Protocol."

"Are your employees on the same flight or will they be meeting me in Bangkok," Tommy joked in an effort to inject some levity into what seemed to be a very somber meeting.

John Smith did not reply.

The driver placed Tommy's suitcase into the trunk and

they departed for the airport. Seated in the back of the limousine, without saying a word, John Smith handed Tommy a large manila envelope. Reaching inside, Tommy pulled a cell phone out.

"To ensure we stay in contact, Tommy. I wouldn't want you to worry about running up your own minutes," John Smith said, attempting to add some levity of his own.

Next Tommy pulled out a smaller envelope containing money.

"Petty cash for expenses."

"How much?"

"Five thousand. That should be sufficient for the five days you're in Bangkok—it is not an expensive city, from what I understand."

Tommy looked at John Smith with a wiry smile. "That's not necessarily true. Will you require receipts?"

"That is nice of you to ask, but no. No need for receipts," John Smith replied, smiling back.

He then pulled an airline ticket from the envelope with the name *Thomas Bacon Luck* printed as the passenger.

"First class, thank you, John Smith."

"Nothing but the best for you, Tommy."

Lastly, Tommy pulled a silver flash-drive, with a navy blue neck strap from the large envelope.

"The package?" Tommy asked, turning the flash drive over in his hand, examining the small device.

"The package. Please don't let it leave your person until the delivery."

Tommy put the flash-drive's cord around his neck. "There are two security checks along the way. One at Dulles and one at Narita. The flash-drive will have to be run through the X-ray machine at each."

"Keep an eye on the package, Tommy."

"What if I lose it?" A question Tommy realized he should have asked before.

"That has not happened yet. Please don't be the first to do so."

For the remainder of the ride to Dulles, Tommy and John Smith sat in silence, both pondering the task before them. When the limousine pulled up to the airport, Tommy stepped out onto the sidewalk and the driver retrieved his suitcase. John Smith remained seated inside while offering his hand to Tommy.

"Good Luck, Tommy."

"Don't worry. Luck and I are well acquainted."

As he turned and walked into the airport, Tommy could not help but think something had changed in the demeanor of John Smith. The limousine and his silence seemed to indicate a game changer. It was almost as if John Smith had lost his confidence. Approaching the check-in counter, Tommy spotted the pretty brunette and the beady-eyed man in the economy check-in line.

"John Smith's surveillance team," Tommy quietly muttered to himself. "They really do need to be re-trained at this surveillance stuff. Well at least I got first class. Obviously not standard company treatment... Let's hope it's not they're equivalent to a last supper."

A tall pale man with freckles and red curly hair, dressed in dark slacks and a light blue shirt, standing against the wall of windows across from the ticketing counters, caught Tommy's eye. The tall man appeared to be reading a newspaper but Tommy felt is if he was watching him. He quickly dismissed the idea to paranoia.

As Tommy stepped away from the counter, after checking his bag, he looked back. The tall redheaded man approached the counter where Tommy had checked in, showed his identification, and began talking with the attendant.

# CHAPTER 10

*Suvarnabhumi International Airport, Thailand, 15 July 2015*:

A s a first class ticket holder, Tommy was one of the earliest to depart the aircraft at Suvarnabhumi International Airport just outside of Bangkok and the first in line at the immigration counter. Marked as a priority passenger's belongings, his bag appeared quickly on the luggage carousel. John Smith's employees, in the economy section, wouldn't be as lucky.

The officials at the customs counter eyed Tommy but didn't stop him as he walked through the 'Nothing to Declare' exit from the baggage claim area into the airport's busy terminal. The sights and smells of Thailand always brought Tommy's spirits up. He found it to be a fascinating country and culture that always surprised him when he least expected. As he stepped into the crowded airport lobby, he felt at home.

Tommy walked past a skinny man dressed in black pants and white shirt holding up a sign with the name 'Thomas Bacon Luck' printed in thick black ink and proceeded to the taxi stands on the lower level of the airport. He had considered John Smith's parting demeanor during the long flight and decided it would be best to operate in a low profile for the time being.

As a part of maintaining that low profile, he had removed the battery from the cell phone provided by John Smith in the event it had some type of tracking device embedded within. After all, John Smith did run a high tech firm and Tommy assumed that his expertise extended beyond software. Descending on the escalator, he could see rows of yellow and green, and hot pink taxis on the street outside through the large floor to ceiling windows on the lower level of the terminal. Lines of people waited, attendants filled out destination forms, and tasked taxis. The scene resembled a chaotic beehive of activity.

Stepping outside through large turn-style glass doors, the night air was heavy with humidity and the unique smell of Thai spices prickled his nose. Tommy knew Thailand came alive as the sun went down and the heat from the preceding day dissipated into the night. He joined one of the long lines waiting for a taxi, and was spirited and shifted by the struggling crowd.

The line moved quickly and as Tommy approached the front, he heard the young female attendant speaking to several of the taxi drivers in *Isaan*.

From Tommy's numerous excursions throughout Thailand he knew *Isaan*, more closely related to the Laos vernacular, to be the dialect of the Northeast region of the country. The *Isaan* language was spoken across the breadth and depth of Thailand as many people from that region were not able to support themselves on the pittance earned from farming sticky rice, the main crop of the region.

While he knew sticky rice to be popular throughout Southeast Asia, it had a low international export demand as a commodity compared to that of Jasmine rice from central Thailand. As a result, many of the *Isaan* people flocked to the cities to find work to support their family farms. And many, it would seem, made their way to Bangkok to work in the taxi trade.

Stepping up to the taxi stand, Tommy spoke quietly in *Isaan* to the attendant, requesting a cab to Soi Twenty, a short ten-minute walk from his prearranged lodging on Soi Twenty-Two.

Surprised, the attendant looked at Tommy and asked, "You are *farang*. Where did you learn Isaan?"

"Had a girlfriend from Isaan."

Tommy was used to being called a *farang*, the term originating from the word *franeze*, which referred to the French colonists in Southeast Asia's history. Today in Thailand, the word *farang* describes any fair-skinned foreigner and has become a common word in their vocabulary. To the Thais Tommy was a *farang*.

Rather than staying at John Smith's selection of the Imperial Queen's Park Hotel, Tommy decided to take a room in a smaller hotel he had used in the past, located in an alley just off of the city's main thoroughfare of Sukhumvit. The only thing Tommy knew about clandestine work he had read in fictional suspense novels, not the best information but his only source of "how to" concerning operating in the situation he currently found himself.

Logic told him that if no one could find him in the interim, the time between arriving in Thailand until the delivery, the better chance for success in a situation that posed significant unknowns and possible danger.

The young taxi attendant handed Tommy a form on which she had scribbled his requested destination then directed him to a taxi. Tommy handed the taxi driver a stub of paper from the form and stepped into a yellow and green taxi. From the airport the cab drove northwest, passing palm trees and banana groves, with Bangkok's distant lights reflecting off low clouds like an outlying beacon.

Heavy rain pelted the cab as it departed the airport complex and occasional bolts of lightning provided brief glimpses of the farms surrounding the highway. More and more structures began crowding sides of the freeway the closer the cab came to the city. The punishing rainfall slowly ebbed as they approached the tall high rises of Bangkok.

# CHAPTER 11

*Bangkok, Thailand, 15 July 2015:*

Twenty minutes from the airport, the taxi climbed an aged and elevated expressway with the downtown Bangkok skyscrapers looming above on either side. The cab wended through expressway connectors and off shoots, twisting through a jungle of forty and fifty-story buildings. Smaller weathered buildings lying beneath the expressway on both sides, built before the city's boom, spotted the capital and appeared as nothing more than stepping stones to their newer and taller companions. The cab exited onto Sukhumvit Avenue, one of the main thoroughfares running through the center of the city that was in a perpetual traffic jam for sixteen hours a day.

Bangkok is a vibrant city, with unique sights, sounds, and smells. Prostitutes, businessmen, tourists, and hawkers walk the streets of the city late into the night, looking to exchange their money, ideas, and wares, all brightened by colorful neon lights and only interrupted the occasional tropical downpour. A surprising amount of trees and flora was mixed in with the urban landscape, along sidewalks and medians. The cab passed by several parks full of more tropical foliage and trees as they inched their way down Sukhumvit.

The Sky Train, one of Bangkok's mass transit systems mounted on high concrete columns, hovered above Sukhumvit. The illuminated shops, restaurants, and bars became nothing more than a backdrop to a sea of people talking, eating, drinking, and shopping along the avenue.

After a tediously slow ride down the avenue, the cab made a right turn, forcing its way across the opposing lanes of on-coming traffic, onto Soi Twenty, one of the many smaller streets bisecting Sukhumvit's broad promenade. Tommy instructed the cabbie to pull up next to the entrance of an alley a short thirty yards from the turn. The alley was L-shaped, intersecting both Soi Twenty and the perpendicularly situated Sukhumvit. The portion connecting to Soi Twenty was narrow and dark, looking like an alleyway in any city around the world. The segment intersecting Sukhumvit was slightly wider and lined with small shops, restaurants, and hotels, whose lights and signs brightened the corridor.

Tommy paid the cabbie and stepped into the alley. He could make out a short row of parked cars to one side, followed by a spirit house topped with a bowl of rice and freshly cut flowers in the shadows. The alleyway smelled a mix of gasoline, spice, and grime. With the lights of a hotel at the bend slightly illuminating the narrow passage, he began to make his way through the gloom.

A shadow silently shot across the alley just in front of him, followed by a hiss and screech—a feline fight brewing in what was presumably a long-fought battle over turf. The wheels of his suitcase rolling along in unison with the soles of his shoes slapping the rough pavement, Tommy smiled at the familiar sight. A small red and green neon sign over the glass double door entrance to the hotel advertised The Drop Inn, his destination.

The Drop Inn Hotel, located on the outside elbow of the alley, provided most rooms a good view of both the dark narrow and bright wide sections of the alley. Small and centrally located, the hotel was hidden from normal tourist traffic. With white stucco walls contrasting against dark wood accents, the five-story structure looked as if it had been transplanted from Portugal or Spain.

Dark wood railings on either side of two front patios bracketed the entrance. Lights glowed from behind thick white drapes hung on the windows above, showing that each room had a balcony with a matching dark wood rail, although, too narrow a space to put a chair.

The employees of The Drop Inn knew Tommy well and as he approached the small staff came out from the lobby, standing on the terracotta-tiled steps leading to the entrance, with wide greeting smiles. The lobby matched the motif of the outside façade with more terracotta tiled floors and matching wood accents.

A small wooden desk with a computer screen mounted on top acted as the reception counter and after a payment of roughly forty-five dollars, Tommy was handed a key to a room on the second floor. Electing to take the narrow concrete staircase over a small-gated elevator that he knew to be slow and cramped, Tommy made his way to the room.

The room, with more white stucco walls, terracotta tiled flooring, and dark wood furniture, was small but clean. Next to a tall floor lamp stood a narrow wooden cabinet with a twenty-eight inch television on top. A matching desk accompanied the cabinet. A small and slightly rusted refrigerator sat under the cabinet and after inspecting its contents, Tommy pulled a single bottle of Heineken beer from the interior. Dropping his luggage on the room's white quilt topped queen size bed he popped the top of the beer and quickly emptied its contents.

Four red silk pillows rested against the wooden headboard and a wide golden strip of fabric was laid across the foot of the bed, giving the setting a unique Thai flair. Taking another beer from the rusted refrigerator, he examined the bathroom with its unusually tiny shower stall.

After finishing his second beer, Tommy took a quick shower in the cramped stall, the curtain clinging to his back as water spilled over its small raised threshold before running into a drain at the center of the room. It was just past midnight when he changed into faded blue jeans and a green short-sleeved shirt. He then pulled from his bag the cell and cell battery John Smith had provided, and a Thai cell phone he had not used in over six months.

Thai cells were all prepaid and recharged with more minutes at any local convenience store. In Tommy's opinion a far better and cheaper system than used in the United States, not to mention more discreet. Most cell phones in Thailand had no name associated with the device.

Slipping the two cell phones and the battery into the pockets of his jeans, Tommy then checked to ensure the flash-drive was still in place around his neck before leaving the room for the short trek to the Imperial Queen's Park Hotel. Stepping from the hotel and wandering down the wider portion of the alley toward Sukhumvit, he walked past the mirrored windows of 'Top Secret Lounge,' and then a beauty shop filled with woman chatting while having their hair cut, combed, and dried. Next he walked past a vegetarian Indian Restaurant with Christmas tree lights wrapped around its large front window. The Queen Lotus Guesthouse with tables and chairs out front was directly across the alley and had large red print across one of its front windows, advertising an attached restaurant. A Chinese noodle shop was next, open, long, and narrow, reaching into the depths of the building it was situated. Each of the businesses lining the alleyway illuminated his path, making what might be considered a treacherous journey, seem bright and safe. At the end of the alley Tommy slipped into the crowd of people moving along Sukhumvit's dirty grey sidewalks.

Dressed in a mix of European and Southeast Asian fashions, bustling Thais and *farangs* crowded the sidewalks, most destined for one of the many small restaurants or bars off the main avenue. Maneuvering through the crowd Tommy caught a glimpse of the towering Imperial Queen's Park Hotel, situated on the next street intersecting Sukhumvit. Cars, trucks, and buses slowly made their way along the busy avenue as he walked. The smell of exhaust fumes from the passing traffic mixing with the humid air created a slightly suffocating effect.

Passing by several street food vendors, the smell of exhaust combined with Thai spices giving it an Asian urban twist. After a five-minute walk along the busy avenue, Tommy turned down Soi Twenty-two.

A hundred yards up the street, the massive Imperial Queen's Park Hotel complex was surrounded by narrow lanes filled with shops, bars, and restaurants. Consisting of two high-rises, each with its own swimming pool mounted on terraces midway up the structures, sprouting from a common four-story base, the Imperial Queen's Park was an imposing sight. The backside of the hotel was situated adjacent to Benjasiri Park, a tropical oasis in the midst of the sprawling city, giving the hotel a slight relief from the city's congestion.

The narrow street leading to the Queen's Park was thick with hawkers and their mobile shops, as well as tourists and businessmen wandering between the hotels and bars. Bargirls stood in front of their workplaces dressed in alluring attire, tempting the passing crowds. Weaving through the sea of people, bargirls called out to Tommy in broken English, promising a night of passion.

The smell of Thai food mixed with that of Indian and European, creating a unique international aroma that might be familiar across the globe but never copied.

Tommy entered the hotel through the parking garage on the lower level and found his way to the lobby pub through a side door. Rarely were there many people in the hotel pub, as the street outside provided cheaper liquor and far more entertainment. Taking a seat in the nearly empty pub and ordering a Jameson on the rocks, Tommy plugged the battery back into the phone provided by John Smith and made a call.

Three rings later, "Hello Tommy, we thought you might be lost. You seem to have far more talents than we discovered in our investigation," John Smith answered, sounding concerned.

"I learned from the best in the business."

"And who might that be?"

"The likes of David Baldacci, Alex Berenson, Steve Berry, and Jeffery Deaver, to name a few."

"All literary geniuses."

"They're all *New York Times* Bestselling authors—don't sell them short."

"Have you checked into the hotel yet? My staff noticed that you didn't use your pre-arranged transportation from the airport. You are at the Imperial Queen's Park, are you not?"

If Tommy's suspicions about a GPS tracker were correct, John Smith already knew the answer to his question. "I reckoned I didn't need a driver. I know my way around and I figured your staff could use the ride. It is a difficult city to traverse for the first time. And yes, I am at the Imperial Queen's Park, but not for long."

"Are you modifying our plan? If so, what can I expect?" John Smith's voice took on a serious tone.

"I am. I'll call you on the morning of the twentieth—let's say ten o'clock Bangkok time. That, of course, will be eleven o'clock the evening prior for you. At that time I will need the details for the delivery. Until then, I plan on keeping a low profile—if that's all right with you, of course.

"Would it matter if it was not?"

"No, I'm just trying to be courteous." Tommy chuckled. "Be assured I'll complete the delivery. Think of it this way, my method will benefit us both."

"Sounds like a familiar excuse."

"It worked for you."

"I look forward to hearing from you, Tommy," John Smith said in a resigned tone.

Tommy disconnected the call and removed the battery from the cell phone. He then made a call on his Thai cell to a number he had not used since his last visit to Thailand.

A soft sweet voice answered. "Hallo?" With a slight variation on pronunciation, the English word of hello had worked its way into the daily language of Thailand.

"*Sawadee Kharp*, hello, my love," Tommy said softly into the cell.

"Tommy? I have missed you. *Rac khun tao faw*, my love for you is as big as the sky."

The sweet voice cracked with emotion.

"I have missed you, as well. I'm in Bangkok and would love to see you. Where are you?"

"*Kalasin*. Can I come to see you?"

"I am at our usual hotel. Please come."

"I will be there tomorrow evening." And then she sighed. "How long?"

"Not long," Tommy admitted.

"I will be there—I have missed you."

After disconnecting the call, Tommy slipped the cell phones and battery into his jean's pockets, and departed the hotel along the same route he had entered. Walking down the narrow and bustling soi leading from the Queen's Park Hotel toward Sukhumvit, he had to step around hawkers and swarms of people crowding the sidewalk. The pungent smell of roasting chilies and sweet curry filled the air around one hawker's stand, and the aroma of simmering chicken at the next. Stopping at a fresh fruit stand and buying a small bag of watermelon, he then had to step out on the street to maneuver around a knot of people swarming around a pirated DVD stand. Walking along the edge of the road, Tommy glanced at a hot pink taxi as it drove past. Inside was the pretty brunette and beady-eyed man.

The pretty brunette recognized Tommy as they drove by. He watched as she turned and frantically began talking with the beady-eyed man inside the cab. Too late, as Tommy quickly turned into a complex of connected bars and pool halls.

Picking a bar at the end of a wide bisecting corridor offering a good view of the street, but well inside the maze of businesses, Tommy found a barstool situated next to a long wooden counter. Although he was told his surveillance team was small, Tommy was sure that John Smith would never rely on merely three employees, two of whose arrival time would undoubtedly be later than his own, to monitor a deliveryman carrying an important package. Tommy wanted to see the rest of the team.

The barstool was topped with worn black vinyl and Tommy could feel its cracks as he twisted around to order a Singha beer, the Budweiser of Thailand. The counter had a matching black vinyl cushion, also cracked with age and showing its fibrous weave underneath, running the length of its edge. The bartender, a slender young woman dressed in a short red skirt and dark green silk blouse, quickly provided an ice-cold beer. From his distant perch, eating the watermelon and drinking the beer, Tommy watched the crowds moving back and forth along the busy Soi Twenty Two.

The pretty brunette and beady-eyed man showed up several minutes later, momentarily stopping at the entrance to the complex. After a brief discussion they entered the complex along a matching corridor paralleling the one he was seated.

As Tommy prepared to leave the bar he noticed two men wearing blazers, one hunter green and the other Navy blue, appear at the entrance to the complex. The two men caught Tommy's attention when they began looking into the various bars near the street. One of the men was tall and tan with close-cropped blond hair. The other was much shorter, slightly overweight, with a misshapen head of curly brown hair.

Tommy took one last drink from the bottle of Singha before dropping a one hundred *baht* note on the counter. Giving the pretty bartender a smiling departure, he began walking toward the restrooms located in a rear corner of the complex. Looking over his shoulder, Tommy saw the two men hesitate, and then enter the complex along the same corridor that John Smith's other employees had several minutes earlier.

Making his way toward the restrooms, keeping an eye out for the pretty brunette and the beady-eyed man, Tommy maneuvered through one of the many narrow hallways that connected the two large corridors.

At the intersection with the next corridor Tommy looked both directions for his surveillance team. There was no sign of the beady-eyed man and the pretty brunette but he could see the two blazer clad men was slowly walking his direction, looking into each bar. Tommy moved across the corridor, masking his movement behind several other complex patrons, into the alcove where the bathrooms were located. Looking around for a place to hide, he finally decided on a small utility closet adjacent to the restrooms.

Stepping inside, Tommy partially closed the door, leaving a crack just wide enough to see through. The utility closet was small, and he had to shift a mop and bucket to make room for his feet. As an odorous mixture of mildew and disinfectant enveloped him, Tommy wished that he had brought along a beer or two.

He could hear several people turn into the alcove from the sound of hard soles striking the dirty concrete floor. Through the small gap Tommy could see the two men wearing blazers come into alcove. Walking just beyond his view through the partially opened door, they stopped.

With a soft and gentle American-accented voice, one asked, "Where have those two gotten to?"

"They are such amateurs," the other responded, his tone much harsher but also with an American accent.

The gentle voice giggled. "Yes, yes, yes."

"How about the bathroom?"

"We're just supposed to watch and see what happens. Let's move back to one of the bars near the entrance and wait." The gentle voice had an unusually calming tone.

"What if something is happening in the bathroom? What if something happens in one of these bars? Let's make sure the bathroom is clear first and then keep looking," the other man said, sounding slightly frustrated.

"Fine, you go in and check. If the bathroom is empty, we'll separate and keep looking," the soothing voice replied.

Tommy could hear a single set of footsteps depart and then return a few moments later, followed by an indiscernible conversation between the two men. He then heard them walk away, their hard-soled shoes once again slapping across the concrete floor.

Leaning against a wall cluttered with mops and brooms, he closed the door and waited. The overwhelming tang of disinfectant began burning his sinuses and eyes. Ten minutes later, enduring the smell as long as he could, Tommy cracked the door open again and listened. Hearing no one nearby, he stepped out of the closet and took a deep breath to clear his lungs. Once he was sure the surveillance team was not around, he began to slowly move toward the far side of the complex, away from the bathrooms but still deep within the cluster of bars and pool halls.

Rounding a corner along one of the narrow passageways, Tommy came face to face with the curly brown haired man with the misshapen head. With a calming angelic face, the slightly overweight man stood about four inches shorter than Tommy and looked surprised at their encounter. Without hesitation, Tommy punched the man in the face, catching him under his right jaw. The man's heavy jowls rippled from the impact, and he stumbled backward. Tommy swung again, striking the man under the left eye. The curly-haired man fell to the ground in a heap. When his head hit the concrete, a thick fold of hair fell to the side, revealing a bald top.

"A comb-over." Tommy quietly laughed, looking down at the crumpled figure on the floor. "That's why your head looks so strange."

Reaching down, Tommy opened the man's jacket and saw a nine-millimeter Beretta handgun strapped to his side. The fact that the Beretta was the type of handgun issued by the US military and used by many CIA agents didn't escape him. Reaching into the man's inner jacket pocket, Tommy pulled out a cell phone. He then quickly searched the remaining pockets. Finding a thin leather wallet in the man's left hip pocket, he pulled several pieces of identification out. Dropping the leather wallet and its remaining contents on the ground next to the man's limp body, Tommy pocketed the cell phone and identification cards.

He then looked down at the Beretta. Hesitating, he finally decided to leave it behind, feeling it would only complicate his standing with John Smith and his surveillance team. Before turning away, Tommy noticed a bulge on the man's ankle. Reaching down and pulling up the man's pant leg, he discovered a stiletto tucked into a leather sheath. Standing up, while wondering about the knife, Tommy decided to leave it in place, as well.

Realizing the short tussle could have dislodged the package, Tommy checked to ensure the flash-drive was still hanging from his neck. Stepping over the man with the comb-over, he moved down a small hallway between two bars. Making his way through a wooden door that led into a restaurant scullery, Tommy knew the business front to be situated on an adjacent cul-de-sac intersecting Soi Twenty Two.

The kitchen staff ignored him as he worked his way between the stainless steel tables and metal stovetops. Tommy entered the restaurant's dining area through a free-swinging door. Only the manager gave him a suspicious look as he wandered past tables and chairs filled with the restaurant's clientele. Departing the restaurant through its front door, Tommy walked up the cul-de-sac and turned down Soi Twenty-Two toward Sukhumvit.

Invisible in the thick crowds along the soi, he walked down to the Sukhumvit intersection and turned toward his alleyway hotel. A block from the intersection, he sat down at a street vendor's stand on a red plastic chair with an accompanying folding metal table that wobbled. Tinny sounding country western music blared from two tiny speakers mounted on a nearby bar on wheels. Several young western men leaned against the short counter trying to gain the attention of the young female bartender. She had a wide grin on her face as the two young men loudly described their exploits across Thailand. Tommy smiled at the scene, as the young bartender's eyes betrayed her hidden boredom.

Buying a small bowl of Thai style chicken noodle soup, Tommy examined the items he had retrieved from the man with the comb-over. Identification from the wallet indicated that the man Tommy had assaulted was named Gene, a logistics specialist at the United States Embassy in Bangkok. Assuming that both men must work for the embassy as logistic specialists, Tommy thought it an unlikely cover for tech firm employees. He also wondered what a logistics specialist would be carrying a nine-millimeter Beretta. Then Tommy opened the cell phone and scanned a registry filled with numerous contacts, some with the North American country codes. The phone gave Tommy no further evidence as to Gene's activities. Tommy then removed the battery from the phone, and crammed the cell and battery back in his pocket with the other phones. After eating his soup, he dropped the man's identification cards into a nearby trash can and causally walked away.

Contemplating why two American embassy workers would be moonlighting for a tech firm, Tommy began to make his way back toward The Drop Inn. Across from the entrance to the alley on Soi Twenty leading to his hotel, Tommy stepped into The Corner Sports Bar, owned and operated by a good friend of his. An impish man of about sixty and a Californian by birth, Jack had operated the pub for several years, making it a favorite hangout with the expatriate community in Bangkok. Jack only employed women and always had a different beautiful girlfriend at his side each time Tommy visited, indicating to Tommy that Jack's libido was likely very healthy, even at the age of sixty.

Standing on the far side of the room with a group of men, Jack saw Tommy enter and yelled his name over a din of loud music and conversations. Maneuvering around tall round tables, crowded with *farangs* and bargirls, and a large pool table, they met in the center of the bar and embraced.

Stepping back, Jack asked, "Where's Lawan?"

"She's coming down from Kalasin. She'll be here tomorrow night."

Jack slapped Tommy on the shoulder. "It's good to see you, Tommy. How are things stateside?"

"The same. Boring. Predictable."

"Let me introduce you to some new faces."

Jack led Tommy over to a group of three men who were chatting loudly with each other. A short round man maybe ten years older than Tommy with a flushed face and large red nose turned and smiled at their arrival. A thin man with thick black curly hair, about Tommy's size, dressed in designer jeans and a black long sleeve shirt continued his conversation with a pale large boned man with harsh facial features. The harsh faced man was dressed in a t-shirt depicting some long forgotten rock and roll band and jeans, stood a good four inches taller than Tommy. Both men appeared to be about five years younger. Tommy correctly guessed the short round one to be an American. He was drinking bourbon on the rocks and the broken veins on his nose told Tommy that he probably started the day early on vodka.

Jack introduced Tommy to the fat American first. Carl's rotund belly strained the buttons on a Thai style collarless white shirt, the thinness of the fabric revealing a thick hairy chest and back.

Reaching out and shaking Tommy's hand, Carl said, "Nice to meet you, Tommy. Another American. It's always good to have an extra yank around this place."

Obviously well into a bottle of bourbon, Carl's hand felt limp and clammy as Tommy shook it.

"Carl works with the Embassy here in town. A business envoy of sorts," Jack commented.

"What type of business, Carl?" Tommy asked more for Jack's benefit than for conversation with a fat drunken American.

"I ensure that the American and Thai business communities continue to prosper together." Carl laughed.

A telling bit of laughter, indicating to Tommy that there wasn't a lot Carl actually did for the US-Thai relationship—other than scam free drinks from unsuspecting businessmen. Tommy was not sure why but he immediately detested Carl. He surely couldn't despise him for his excessive drinking, but there was something to that told Tommy there was a seedy side to this strange American. Tommy told himself to be wary of Carl.

The other two men were from Germany and Turkey. Both had thick accents. The thin Turk was named Aslan. With acne scars on his cheeks, Aslan had a long pointed jaw and smelled as if he hadn't showered in a week. Between his wardrobe choice and an overwhelming musty body odor it was pretty clear to Tommy that Aslan hailed from a region that valued water enough to not waste it on washing. A polyester computer bag draped over his shoulder, Aslan looked somewhat out of place at the bar.

The large pale German, Rudolf, had an oversized brow and cheekbones, and a thick jaw, the appearance enough to give him a distinct advantage in a *Star Trek* Klingon lookalike contest.

To Tommy, Rudolf's black leather athletic shoes and matching black socks marked him as an East German. Laughing and slapping Carl on the shoulder, Rudolf seemed well at home in The Corner Sports Bar.

The five of them moved out to a picnic style table with heavy wooden chairs situated on the street in front of Jack's bar. They drank a few rounds talking about Bangkok and current issues in the business community. Tommy mostly listened to his new friends, answering a few questions about his former business in the Gulf of Thailand. Rudolf seemed very interested in Tommy's presence, quizzing him on his past and current business in Bangkok. Tommy successfully parried the questions with his own.

After thirty minutes of conversation both Aslan and Rudolf excused themselves, claiming that they had early morning meetings the following day, leaving Jack, Carl, and Tommy drinking alone as the two walked away chatting with one and other. Tommy sighed in relief as the air immediately cleared of Aslan's body odor. It was close to two o'clock in the morning when Jack went inside to instruct his staff to start closing the bar.

When they were alone, Tommy asked Carl, "You ever meet a guy named Gene at the embassy?"

Carl looked at Tommy with blurry alcohol saturated eyes. "Yeah, I know Gene. You know him too?"

"I recently met him. Seemed like a nice guy. Said he was working logistics or something?"

"Yeah, he's a logistic guy. Where'd you meet him?" Carl asked, slurring his question.

"In some pub down the road. He was looking for someone at the time. Didn't say who or why, though."

"I talked with him today. He told me that he was working a job tonight. He was supposed to keep an eye on some people or some guy arriving from the States. Maybe it was a girl. I can't remember."

"Who tasked him to keep an eye on some guy or girl? Who's his boss?"

"Gene does a lot of freelance stuff at night. He's been here long enough he has a long list of contacts in the city. I don't know who hired him. Probably not someone from the embassy." Carl slurred his response so badly that Tommy had a hard time understanding. "Gene works a lot of projects. The logistic guys work a lot of projects. I've worked with him but only on an occasion or two."

"What kind of projects do you and Gene work together?" Tommy pressed for information, figuring Carl would not likely remember the conversation the next morning.

"He's a logistic guy. He gets stuff for me. He tells me what people I'm working with are doing. You know—logistic stuff."

"He tells you what people are doing? That's sort of unusual for a logistic guy," Tommy said, continuing to probe.

"He keeps tabs on some of my business contacts for me. It's nice to know if they're trying to trap me or get me in trouble with the government."

"Why in the world would you be in trouble with the government? The Thai or US government?"

"I'm not! Nobody! You know the Thais, always trying to get the upper hand," Carl replied, perking up but continuing to slur his words.

Carl was obviously in no shape to pump for information and the information Tommy was getting from the question and answer period was muddy at best. As Tommy began to move his chair out to leave, a large well-dressed Thai man in a red silk shirt and black tailored pants stepped up to the table. He had a wide flat face and the whites of his eyes had a yellowish hue. A thick gold chain with a large Buddha medallion, not an uncommon sight in Thailand, hung from his neck. The man pulled out a chair next to Carl and sat down. Two young and similarly dressed Thai men, one large and bulky, and the other short and skinny, took up positions behind their boss.

"Carl, I have been looking for you," the well-dressed man said as he reached out and placed his hand on Carl's shoulder. Tommy watched as the man squeezed Carl's shoulder, the Thai's fingers sinking deep into soft fatty flesh.

Quickly sobering up to the man's presence, Carl immediately began looking nervous. Tommy could see Carl's hand shaking as he brought his glass of bourbon up to his lips, a small portion of the drink spilling on his white collarless shirt and staining it light brown. Although, Tommy realized the shaking might have been as a result of Carl's inebriation, some of it was obviously from fear.

"Mr. Jainukul. It is nice to see you," Carl replied with a weak smile as sweat began to build on his brow.

"You have been avoiding me, Carl." Jainukul made it a statement, not a question. Jainukul shifted in his chair so he was facing the fat American and brought his face close to Carl's, as if he was doctor examining a patient's eyes.

"No, not at all, Mr. Jainukul. I have been busy coordinating our deal with outside sources." Carl's face took on every more distinctive red hue, almost matching Jainukul's red shirt, Tommy attributing it to an increase in his already alcohol elevated blood pressure. "I should have our transaction coordinated in a day or so."

"For your sake, I hope so, Carl. I will expect a call from you tomorrow to arrange our meeting. Our final meeting. Correct?"

Jainukul turned to one of the young men behind him and began speaking in *Isaan*, "I wish to meet with this man as soon as he leaves this bar. You will intercept him and bring him to me. You need to make it clear his behavior is unacceptable. You are not to be too kind to this plump pimple of a man."

He then turned back to Carl and began speaking in English again. "We have an understanding." Once again, Jainukul posed it as a statement, not a question.

"Absolutely, sir. Mr. Jainukul, please excuse me, I have been drinking and must use the restroom." Carl's voice quivered.

Having difficult moving the heavy wooden chair, Carl fell back onto the seat. On his second try, he moved the wooden chair, its feet grating across the rough pavement, and stood up. Looking frightened, Carl wobbled inside The Corner Sports Bar.

Void of facial expression, the well-dressed Jainukul then turned and looked at Tommy, asking, "What is your business here?"

Jainukul's yellow eyes glared at Tommy and sweat glistened on his flat face. Tommy assumed the perspiration was not from nerves, but rather from frustration and anger.

Leaning back in his chair, for some unknown reason, Tommy hoped that Jainukul could not see the silver flashdrive dangling from his neck. "To drink and enjoy your wonderful country," he responded, smiling.

"Do you have business with Carl?"

"None at all. As a matter of fact, I just met him tonight," Tommy replied as he once again began to scoot the heavy wooden chair back from the table, the feet of the chair making a similar grating sound as Carl's second attempt.

Still void of facial expression, Jainukul asked, "Are you leaving me, as well?"

"Pardon me, I have just flown in from the United States, and the time difference is fairly significant. I'm tired and wish to go back to my room."

As Tommy stood to leave, Jainukul once again turned and spoke to one of his young companions in *Isaan*, "Follow this man, I want to know where he staying and his business. Take care of him if he becomes a problem. You know what to do."

Stepping inside The Corner Sports Bar, Tommy walked past the girls as they were putting chairs on the tables, completing the final tasks to close. Carl, visibly shaken, was talking with Jack as he tallied up the night's profits at the cash register.

"Wow, Carl, what have you gotten yourself into?" Tommy asked as he approached the two Americans. "Your Thai friend out there is not a happy man."

"It's nothing. I have it under control," Carl said, lowering his gaze to the floor, as if in deep thought, if that were possible in his intoxicated condition.

"Well, expect an early morning meeting with your pal out there. He asked one of his young friends to deliver you to him after you leave, and he's not going to be gentle."

"You speak Thai?" Carl asked, once again slurring his words.

Tommy slowly twirled his half-empty glass of Irish whiskey back and forth, creating a mini-whirlpool effect inside. "He's speaking Isaan."

"Tommy, can we help Carl out here?" Jack asked, in a concerned tone.

Looking at Carl then back at Jack, Tommy shook his head. "Look, Jack, the Thai guy outside, Jainukul or whatever his name, is a gangster if I've ever seen one. He just told his young friends out there to take care of me if I became a problem. I'm not sure what 'you know what to do' means, but I know it's probably not good. I think this is something way over our heads. Carl here is not telling us everything. I've had a busy enough evening without getting involved in Carl's business, as it certainly is not mine. Especially with this Jainukul guy. He's a tough one and undoubtedly, being Thai and wealthy, he has the local police in his pocket."

"I can handle it," Carl repeated, but he didn't look too confident. "I got it all under control."

Ignoring Carl, Tommy continued. "For my part, I'm leaving and will attempt to lose the guy tasked with finding out where I'm staying and what I'm up to." Then looking toward the bar's front doors, he added, "The last thing I need is to get involved with Jainukul and Carl's business. There's enough mystery churning around the reason I'm here. I don't need anymore."

"But—" Jack started to say.

Tommy cut Jack off. "No buts about it, Jack. I'm out of here."

Without a farewell, Tommy departed the bar through the front doors. Noticing Jainukul's two young employees standing across the street in the shadows, Tommy turned and walked toward Sukhumvit. The smaller of the two thugs stepped from the shadows and immediately began to follow. Walking up to cluster of motorcycle taxis parked on the corner next to a Seven-Eleven, Tommy hired one of the orange vested drivers to take him to the Imperial Queen's Park Hotel. When Jainukul's employee realized what was going on, he began jogging toward the Seven-Eleven and yelling at the motorcycle taxi driver to stop. Tommy calmly told the driver that he would pay double if he got them out of there quickly. Hopping on, the driver started the motorcycle, which emitted a sputter and a black cloud of exhaust. Tommy climbed on and the driver throttled the motorcycle, its back wheel spinning and screeching. Speeding away, they raced along the now nearly empty sidewalk, avoiding the slow moving traffic along Sukhumvit Avenue.

A three-minute ride later, the motorcycle taxi pulled up to the entrance of the Queen's Park. Tommy dismounted the idling motorcycle, paid the driver, and went inside the hotel lobby. With the exception of the doorman, a night clerk stationed behind the front desk, and a man and bargirl discussing prices near the elevator bank, the lobby was empty. Tommy walked past the lobby and down a long wide corridor leading to the rear of the hotel and the now empty dining room. Stepping through a large free swinging door into the kitchen, he saw two white-jacketed hotel employees busy chopping vegetables in preparation for the morning breakfast and another employee mopping the floor.

They glanced at Tommy before silently returning to their work. From the kitchen, Tommy took a set of stairs down to the loading dock under the building and then jogged to the vehicle service entrance adjoining Soi Twenty-Two. Not seeing Jainukul's thug, Tommy slipped around the building into a narrow lane that ran along side of the hotel.

The lane took Tommy to Benjasiri Park, locked and empty at that hour in the morning. Bounding over a low black metal gate bracketed by thick hedges, he began walking across the shadowy park. Illuminated from the surrounding city, the shadows from tall trees and wide bushes created a mosaic web of different shades of gray on the short grass and sidewalks. With the refreshing smell of tropical foliage wafting through the air, he made his way to the park's main entrance on Sukhumvit Avenue.

Two small brick buildings, that acted as information booths during the day, flanked a shallow pool with fountain plumbing shimmering just beneath its surface. Tall locked black metal gates, attached to high brick walls, stood to the far side of each of the two buildings.

Tommy jumped up onto a low retaining wall that wrapped around the pool and the sides of two buildings. Balancing on the narrow surface, he walked along the short wall, passing the leftmost building, before jumping down onto the Sukhumvit sidewalk. Flagging down a cab, Tommy rode to the alley entrance that intersected Sukhumvit and led to his hotel. Worried about his friend Jack at The Corner Sports Bar, Tommy then walked the short distance up Sukhumvit to the corner of Soi Twenty.

While it appeared closed, a light was still on in The Corner Sports Bar. Ensuring that Jainukul's two employees were not in the vicinity, Tommy crossed the street and looked through the windows. He could see Jack leaning against the long concrete counter. Trying the front door, he found it open and entered.

Jerking his head around with a look of terror on his face, Jack saw Tommy entering the bar and sighed in relief. Tommy saw that Jack's face and shirt were bloody, and he was holding his left arm with his right.

"Looks like one of Jainukul's boys paid you a visit," Tommy commented, walking over to the counter.

"I let Carl out the back door. They didn't seem to appreciate my patriotism."

Tommy reached across the counter and extracted a cold Singha from a cooler on the far side. "Like I said, it wasn't our problem. Carl's obviously got something going on with the wrong people."

"You know me, always trying to help."

"Let's hope this Jainukul character doesn't want to reinforce the lesson concerning his displeasure with you," Tommy said while popping the cap off the Singha with a church key that had been lying on the counter.

"Shit, I think the guy broke my arm. He was like a Thai kick boxer or something. Legs were flying everywhere."

"I wouldn't worry about that. I'd worry about the Muey Thai's boss pulling in some favors with the local police." Taking a long drink from the beer bottle, Tommy then added, "They could close you down."

"I'm such a fool. I got my ass kicked for a drunken idiot. Hell, I should have kicked Carl's fat ass for bringing that guy and his henchmen into my bar."

"I've had an interesting night," Tommy admitted. "Followed by four Americans, two of which work at the embassy, got into a quick altercation with one, then found myself threatened and followed by this Jainukul fellow's thug—not how I like to begin a vacation in Bangkok."

"Why were the embassy folks following you?"

"They're earning some extra cash from a tech company I'm working a job for, making sure I'm earning my keep—on the straight and narrow, so to speak."

Jack laughed. "I guess they read your dossier."

After some small talk with Jack, Tommy moved to the door and looked for anyone standing in the shadows. Seeing no one, he stepped from the bar and began walking back to his hotel. The color of the sky had begun to change, with red and yellow streaks reaching across the Bangkok skyline as Tommy entered the hotel lobby. Stepping into his room, he closed and bolted the door, and once again checked for the flash-drive around his neck. Lying on the bed fully clothed, he quickly fell into a deep sleep wondering why he had not liberated the Beretta from Gene.

# CHAPTER 12

Bangkok, Thailand, 16 July 2015:

Waking the next day just after one o'clock in the afternoon, Carl rolled over onto his side and the arms of a naked teenage boy lying next to him fell from his chest. Carl wasn't sure how old the boy was, maybe fourteen or fifteen, but he really wasn't young enough. He much preferred boys around ten or eleven years old, their innocence excited him. No matter where the organization sent him, whether Brazil, India, Mexico, The Philippines, or even Thailand, he was always able to find a willing young boy to entertain his wishes for a price.

Lying on the bed listening to the boy's slow slumbering breath, Carl recalled his run in with Jainukul the night before. Carl wished for more courage but Jainukul was a difficult man to work with. In fact, Carl was deathly afraid of the man. Thankfully, Jack had allowed him to use his backdoor to escape Jainukul's henchman and avoid a lone confrontation. With no witnesses, Carl was sure Jainukul could be capable of anything.

Carl looked forward to leaving this country. He would be very happy when his business in Thailand finally came to a conclusion and Jainukul would be out of his life. In Carl's opinion, Thailand was like the Wild West. You had to be a bit crazy to live and work in this country because you never knew when someone would decide it was time for you to die.

Vaguely remembering the other American he had met, Carl recalled the name Tommy. He wasn't sure why but this American had made him feel uneasy. Tommy's eyes seemed to cut through to his very soul and see that he was not a good man. He knew for sure that Tommy didn't trust him, the proof being his unwillingness to help him evade Jainukul. Americans should stick together, Carl thought, just because he wasn't the best ambassador for the nation didn't matter. Carl was an American and this Tommy character should have recognized their common allegiance, aiding him in finding a safe exit.

The apartment was a mess and the sheets Carl climbed off of were yellow with filth and smelled sickeningly sweet. Stepping over sullied clothes strewn across the tan-carpeted floor, Carl stumbled from the bedroom into the kitchen. Dressed in dirty white jockey shorts, whose tight bands made the fat around his waist and thighs resemble farm furrows, his round enormous belly still leached the alcohol out from the previous night. The same odor from the bed sheets emanated from his pinkish body and thick chest hairs, and the few hairs on his head were matted to his skin. He absently wiped his rotund belly then smelled his hand.

The kitchen provided an entirely new disgusting aroma of rotten food and stale cigarettes. The counters were littered with half-eaten takeaway containers of fast food and the cabinets were covered in fingerprints of various unknown substances. An army of cockroaches dashed across the counters and into cracks under the cabinets and appliances as he entered the room. Dirty half-filled glasses and a lone ashtray spilling cigarette butts from its sides stood next to the takeaway trash. Carl pulled open a cabinet and found a half-filled bottle of *Loa Kow*, or Thai whiskey, more akin to grain alcohol than any other substance he could think of.

Plucking a half smoked cigarette from one of the glasses, Carl haphazardly tossed the butt onto the floor. Picking up the bottle *Loa Kow*, his hands shook as he twisted the cap from its top. Filling the dirty glass with whiskey, he downed its con-

tents in three long swallows. With *Lao Kow* now burning his
throat and stomach, Carl felt immediate relief as his forehead
began numb, a familiar and comfortable feeling. Refilling the
dirty glass one more time, he moved into the living room.

More dirty clothes were strewn across the floor and furniture, piles of unread newspapers were spilling from the top of
a side table, and the television was airing an international
news station. Carl remembered leaving the television on several hours earlier as he began to strip the tentative young teenage boy who had been waiting for him to return home.

"Money is a wonderful thing," Carl happily muttered to
himself, smiling at the memory of the interlude with the child.

Pushing the dirty clothes aside, Carl sat his obese body
down in a large brown fabric covered ottoman in front of the
television in time to hear his cell phone ring. Fortunately the
ringing cell was on a coffee table within arm's reach, as he
would have surely ignored the call had it meant having to
move from the comfort of the chair. Reaching over, Carl
grabbed the cell and answered.

"What?" Carl snapped, as the *Lao Kow* he had just ingested
was beginning to revive a fading inebriation.

"Carl, we must talk about the bid," a heavily German accented voice requested.

Slow to comprehend who was on the other end, when Carl
finally recognized the voice, he replied, "Rudolf, the bid is
over. As I told you last night, you didn't win and won't be
getting the merchandise. I am sorry." Carl absently pushed
several magazines off the coffee table and set his glass of *Lao
Kow* in their place.

"I would like to offer more. I want to rebid. I must rebid,"
Rudolf's pleaded, sounding desperate.

As Carl tried to gather his thoughts through the returning
alcohol-induced fog, the young naked boy walked out of the
bedroom and sat on his lap. Stroking the child's back with his
free hand, Carl thought for a moment. After all, this was his
last delivery and maybe another side deal might be warranted.
But he couldn't seem too eager.

"The bid is over. I have taken the down payment from the winner. I can't give the money back," Carl calculatingly replied.

"There must be something we can do?"

Smiling to himself, Carl allowed for a moment of silence, before softly saying, "We might be able to make a deal, but it will cost you."

"Can we meet? I will pay extra. I need the merchandise. It is a matter of life and death," Rudolf pleaded again.

"Where and what time? I'll meet anyplace but The Corner Sports Bar. We can't go back there. We need to meet someplace where the other bidders won't see us together."

It dawned on him the young teenage boy sitting on his lap didn't appreciate his fondling advances. It didn't matter, he would learn. Carl roughly pushed the naked child to the floor and the young boy emitted a short cry before running back into the bedroom.

"Yes, yes. How about tonight at the Suan Lum Night Bazaar? Let's say seven o'clock. I will meet you in the parking lot near the main entrance to the market," Rudolf replied, a familiar confidence returning to his voice. "My employer will pay extra if we can get the merchandise."

Having frequented the Night Bazaar several times in the last few weeks for its vast food and liquor selection, Carl knew it to be a busy location and one that could provide some level discretion by means of its massive international and local crowd. After all, Carl thought to himself, Rudolf deserved the merchandise. He had bought Carl a lot of pleasure during the bidding process, supplying him with an endless number of young boys.

"I'll be there. May be we can come to an agreement."

Disconnecting the call, Carl selected the name "Kimball" from his speed dial list. He had never personally met Mr. Kimball but knew a lot more about his employer than anyone was aware. Carl didn't like being kept in the dark and, over the course of the last four jobs, he had made it his business to find out as much as possible about the organization for which he was working. Absently smelling his armpits, Carl listened to the phone on the other end begin to ring. After three rings the call was picked up.

"Carl, have you arranged everything?" a nasally voice answered.

"Of course, Mr. Kimball, have I ever let you down?"

"Never, now let's hear what you have," Mr. Kimball's voice droned through the cell's small speaker at an irritatingly high decibel.

After Carl had filled in the details for his employer, Mr. Kimball approved the information with a short whinny acknowledgement. Carl sighed in relief as the call was disconnected.

Sitting on the large cushioned ottoman chair, thinking about how much money this one job would make him, Carl thought of all the boys he could have when this was over. *Money does buy happiness.*

# CHAPTER 13

*Fort Meade, Maryland, 16 July 2015*:

Howard Macintyre arrived to the office at his routine time, around eight-thirty in the morning. Judy, his secretary, stood next to the office door with a cup of hot coffee and a wide smile, another daily ritual. As the National Security Agency, or NSA, deputy inspector general, Howard oversaw all internal criminal investigations within the agency. Working to uncover corruption in the nation's top intelligence gathering organization, Howard was a self-proclaimed "spook's spook."

A tall thin man with red curly hair, Howard had a fair complexion and a liberal dousing of freckles. The family name was final proof to his Gaelic heritage. Dressed in a dark green suit and an open collared pink shirt, Howard had a perpetual smile on his face. He was an optimist in everything he did.

"Good morning Mr. Macintyre," Judy said, greeting Howard and handing him the coffee as she opened the office door.

"Good morning, Judy. It's been a whole fourteen hours since I last saw you. What in the world could have transpired in that short amount of time, of which you were presumably at home, I do not know about?"

"Two items, sir. First, the inspector general has asked to meet with you in his office as soon as you arrive. Secondly, a Mr. Rogers, no organization or phone number, called and left a message that you should make contact as soon as possible—for an update. No information beyond that. "

Having worked in her position as the deputy inspector general's secretary for the last two years, Judy knew to never question individuals attempting to contact Howard, nor inquire as to their names or credentials. Above all, she certainly never question Howard Macintyre.

"The inspector general wants an update, undoubtedly," Howard said as he strolled into the office.

Judy picked up a stack of files from her desk before following him into his office. "Undoubtedly," she said as she laid the stack of file folders on top of his desk, all of which would surely need his immediate attention.

Normally, Howard would have instantly headed up to the beaconing inspector general but, on this day, he felt it was prudent to first contact Mr. Rogers.

"That will be all, Judy," Howard stated, his traditional request for privacy.

Judy obediently stepped out of the office and closed the door.

Howard sat down on the NSA-issued black adjustable office chair behind a gray NSA-issued desk. The white walls of the office were adored with framed team spirit posters, another NSA issue item. Using a secure line and a memorized number, Howard called Mr. Rogers. The name alone amused him, for each time he heard it conjured thoughts of the former Public Broadcasting Station children's program *Mr. Roger's Neighborhood* and his *Land of Make Believe*. After all, the Land of Make Believe seemed to be a place Howard spent a large amount of his working hours lately.

After an informative ten-minute conversation with Mr. Rogers, Howard hung up the phone with an even larger smile. Good news was rare in the NSA inspector general's office but occasionally, when an investigation seemed to be on track or providing better than expected results, a smile was warranted. In Howard's case, his perpetual smile widened.

Quickly making his way to the building's elevator bank,

Howard stepped into an open lift, and punched the button for the sixth floor. After a short ride, the elevator doors opened up to the lobby of the executive suites, consisting of little more than a reception area and three hallways leading to the offices of several NSA department managers, one being his boss. Nodding to a young blonde woman dressed in a bright red dress sitting behind the reception desk as he walked past, Howard continued down the hallway to the inspector general's office. The young woman silently returned his gesture with a nod and an alluring smile.

At the end of the short hallway stood a second desk normally occupied by Doris, the inspector general's secretary. Doris wasn't at her desk, so Howard lightly knocked on a thick wooden door. The inspector general title was emblazoned on a brass plate that was affixed on the door and just below that designation was a smaller *Clarence Northman* announcing the name of the person currently holding the position.

"Come on in, Howard," he heard the inspector general call through the door.

Howard wasn't surprised his boss knew who was standing outside the door. The inspector general had a hidden surveillance camera, allowing him to both prepare for visitors and avoid those with whom he did not wish to speak.

Howard beamed as he opened the door and strode into the room. "Good Morning, sir!"

A deep plush navy blue carpet lay across the floor. One side of the office was decorated with a wide oak bookcase filled with pictures of fishing expeditions and books, and on the other was a narrow floor to ceiling window with views of the NSA compound. Two overstuffed leather chairs stood in front of a large wooden desk topped with a wide flat-screen computer monitor to one side, and several personal and department awards adorned the wall behind. Clarence Northman, the inspector general, sat behind the wooden desk, his head and shoulders dwarfed by the size of both the desk and the computer monitor.

The inspector general was a short chubby man with thick curly white hair and bright rosy cheeks and nose. He would have resembled Santa Claus had he worn the requisite white beard. Howard imagined his boss secretly played the character during each holiday season, even lacking the final touch of the beard.

"Good morning, Howard. You are cheery this morning. Let us hope it is a reflection of one of our current investigations."

"I have successfully launched an investigation named 'Black Fly,' and it is coming along quite well," Howard replied, sitting down in one of the overstuffed chairs.

Both chairs facing the desk were canted slightly forward, and Howard knew to firmly press his feet into the thick blue carpet so as not to slide across the slick leather seat cushion and onto the floor. Howard had often wondered if the inspector general had not chosen those chairs with the very purpose of putting his visitors in a physically problematical situation, giving him an immediate upper hand on any conversation.

"Then please tell me about this new investigation and why it has made you are so delighted," the inspector general said with a wide grin.

"I recently discovered a rogue organization has developed within our ranks. This organization has been using NSA computer and decoding assets to hack into corporate databases, stealing secrets, and selling them to the highest bidder. I don't need to tell you the implications of agency employees conducting illegal acts against the private business sector with our assets."

Quickly losing his grin, the inspector general considered Howard's words for a moment before replying. "If word that the government's highest secret caretaker was engaged in corporate espionage were ever to leak to the general public, our near limitless authorization to gather intelligence would likely be stripped by Congress, and our powers to intercept communications across the globe would be severely hampered."

"That is correct, sir."

"This is very disconcerting news," the inspector general

commented, wringing his hands. "How long have you been aware of this situation?"

"It wasn't until several weeks ago that I became aware of the possibility," Howard replied. "As with all investigations into alleged misconduct, I waited to inform you once definitive proof of their history and current activities had been established."

"This seems a bit more important than the usual investigation."

"Yes, but had the information been incorrect, my notification would have created undue concern in the upper ranks of the agency—something you have told me time and time again to avoid."

With a scowl, the inspector general nodded. "Have you identified the members of this organization?"

"Only several low-level associates."

"Then what about the investigation has made you so jovial?"

"I recruited a mole in the organization and the information that individual provided has confirmed the misconduct," Howard said, beaming with pride.

"An infiltrator?"

"Yes, a mole. According to the mole, the organization is very compartmentalized, and command and control appears to be decentralized. The primary source of my pleasure is not the establishment of the mole but, rather the fact that individual has been able to influence the organization's selection of a deliveryman for an upcoming transfer of one of their stolen products."

"Go on." With an expression of concern growing, the inspector general reached into his top drawer and extracted a cigarette.

Howard wished it had been a pipe—it would have been more fitting for Santa Claus.

"The problem confronting me was the mole only had limited information about the other members. Because of the organization's decentralized nature, I knew there would need to be some type of pressure applied to destabilize its structure."

"Get to your point, please."

"In the past, the organization has used deliverymen with questionable reputations and dubious links in the delivery countries. The deliverymen conveniently vanish after each transfer, and because of their lifestyles and associations in those countries, friends and family assume they have disappeared by their own design. Provided the list of possible delivery candidates by the mole, I conducted my own review of their qualifications. I was lucky enough that one of the contenders had all their requisite corrupt habits and connections but also had some qualities desirable to our ends. I passed this nominee's name back to our mole. Our mole was ultimately able to successfully influence his selection."

"And what are the qualities we desire for their bagman?"

"The difference is the deliveryman our mole convinced them to use has a very good reputation for success. He fit all the trademark characteristics of past deliverymen: alcoholic, failed marriages, ties with disreputable contacts in foreign countries, and low on cash. On the surface, our deliveryman was the type of person who, if vanished, would not raise any questions. But, if you dig a little further into this man's past, you realize that, while he has all those less-than-desirable qualities, he also has a reputation for success, imagination, and sheer tenacity."

"And you were hoping that this man could apply the pressure needed to destabilize the organization," the inspector general commented, nodding his head, "even though he is a drunk."

"He is not your normal drunken unemployed loser. I suspect this deliveryman might do something unexpected."

"What's his name?"

"A one Thomas Bacon Luck. His friends call him Tommy. He is a civil engineer and manages high-profile projects. He made a good living as construction site manager. Several years ago, he left it all behind and started up a restaurant or bar on an island in the Gulf of Thailand. He had great success as a small businessman, a publican, but returned to the United States six months ago."

"There must be something more than Mr. Luck's experience as a construction site manager or bar owner that makes you believe his presences will help us. Tell me more about this man's reputation for success, imagination, and tenacity."

"He holds both an undergraduate and graduate degree in civil engineering and quickly proved his adeptness to managing complex construction projects. Working his way up the professional ladder, by the time he was twenty-eight he was managing high-rise projects. He was picked up for assault on a job in Kansas City where the building was later found to have inferior construction materials. The assault charges were dismissed. During an investigation into the building, it was discovered Tommy made a recording of the conversation from which the assault charges stemmed. The recording showed the financier knew of the inferior materials, and Tommy had refused to use the same."

"And Mr. Luck didn't want to be a party to the poor construction and assaulted someone in the process of leaving?"

"The recording also proved his family had been threatened, provoking the assault. He offered to stay on the project for the benefit of a friend, but financier refused. During another job, Tommy Luck saved an employee's life by shimmying out onto a steel girder some thirty floors up. The man was dangling from a lifeline that had been badly frayed. Realizing the man's line could break at any moment, Tommy attached the employee to his lifeline."

"Crawling out on a steel girder thirty floors above the ground sounds rather terrifying."

"There's more to the story. When he cut the man's frayed line, they were both pulled from the girder, dropping several floors before the line abated their fall. Tommy Luck later revealed to a friend that he didn't think his line would hold the both of them."

"But he did it anyway."

"He saw no other way to get them to safety, given the circumstances. There was also an incident at a convenience store. The police report is interesting."

"How so?"

"Tommy was walking past a Seven-Eleven one day when a customer came running out claiming a robbery was going on inside. Rather than seeking to escape the situation, Tommy Luck walked into the store and confronted the two perpetrators."

"And what were the results of that confrontation?"

"Both perps were killed in the incident. The police report is somewhat vague, but a physical confrontation occurred between Tommy Luck and the men. The evidence backed up the claim that Tommy Luck killed them in self-defense."

The inspector general scratched his chin. "Why did he leave a lucrative career in construction management to become a bar owner?"

"I'm not totally certain, but there was a construction accident that killed several men," Howard explained. "Tommy Luck had been drinking the night before and showed up to work late, just after the accident. I believe he felt some guilt over his absence. I think he left the profession because he felt the accident wouldn't have occurred had he been there."

Taking a moment to contemplate Howard's description of Tommy, the inspector general then asked, "Why not use one of our own people as the bagman, a trained specialist who would be able to better negotiate the variables of such an investigation? And how are we to aid Mr. Luck, if needed?"

"We don't know all the players in this organization or where they work within NSA's various departments. An agent from our department or some other within the NSA could have jeopardized our investigation. It would have been a virtual throw of the dice as to whether they would know the delivery person was an IG plant. That's why this investigation has been as secret as our operations come, even among the ranks of our own department. Until now, the mole and I have been the only two people aware that an investigation has begun into this rogue organization. You are now the third to know of its existence," Howard explained. "As far as support, we will keep tabs on Tommy Luck but there is no plan in place to support him. His job is to simply survive the delivery, which will, in turn, cause friction within the organization and create enough havoc to cause the compartmentalized structure of the organization to fail, allowing us to identify the remaining members."

Lighting the cigarette, Howard's boss pursed his lips. "How did they convince this Mr. Luck to sign on to such a shadowy operation?"

While it was against Federal law to smoke in government buildings, being inspector general had certain privileges not extended to every employee. Howard had seen him light up in his office before.

"They discovered him by obtaining a reference from the previous deliveryman, a former good friend, but one that he has not kept up with. That, with the promise of a sizable payoff and a somewhat believable story. Additionally, they used a phony website, all the bells and whistles of a standard covert operation. This organization has become very good at recruiting their deliverymen." Howard added with a chuckle, "What they didn't count on was Tommy Luck's reaction to all the mystery surrounding the delivery."

"Where is the delivery to take place?" the inspector general asked, while looking down and rummaging through his top desk drawer. With the cigarette dangling from his mouth, a thin veil of smoke rose across his face and dissipated above.

"Thailand—probably Bangkok. I was at Dulles to see Tommy Luck off on the adventure. I wanted to make sure he made his flight."

"Go on. What was Mr. Luck's reaction to all the mystery that you seem so pleased with?"

"His actions have even surprised me and been far more beneficial to our investigation than I could have ever hoped. Tommy Luck arrived in Bangkok with the package and disappeared. He did make contact but has now turned the tables on them. He told them how the delivery is going to go down. Apparently, his actions have caused a lot of angst within their organization. Now, it is fair to say this organization does not have the talent for manning a standard operation. After all, NSA employees don't normally find themselves working covert operations of this type. So they have had to rely on relatively new employees and untrained agents, causing some issues, but right now, Tommy Luck is their biggest problem."

The inspector general hesitated. "What can you tell me about the mole?"

"Standard mole recruitment. Our mole had been participating in the organization's activities for some time, believing it was an authorized operation. However, as time went on, this individual began to question the organization's activities and came to me. Learning of the possible criminal activity, I recruited that individual to work with the IG's office to validate the misconduct and gather evidence in order take them down."

Howard knew it was against NSA policy to discuss moles in ongoing investigations, even with the inspector general. A mole could have only one control officer, and that was Howard. Need to know did not exist, so he was intentionally vague.

Looking up from his desk drawer, the inspector general blew a long stream of silver smoke out over Howard's head. "So what's next and why's this good for us?"

"The uncertainty produced by Tommy Luck has forced the organization to open the lines of communication between compartments. We have gleaned a lot of information over the last day in regards to their size and structure as they try to regain control of the delivery."

Howard leaned back to pull the Black Fly file from those laying on his lap and momentarily lost his footing. Slipping several inches out of the slick leather chair, he quickly reapplied pressure to the floor. He then shifted his buttocks back into the chair.

"What are the chances for the bagman, Mr. Luck?" the inspector general asked, putting his cigarette out in an empty Diet Coke can that had obviously doubled as an ashtray for quite some time.

"Two days ago, I would have given him even odds. Today,

I'd give him something slightly higher." Howard lowered his eyes, knowing Tommy Luck was the bagman of their choosing, and he had been deemed expendable from the start of the investigation.

"He knows nothing of the investigation?"

"Absolutely nothing. Chosen by us, but recruited by the organization. We have never made contact him. As I said, he is simply there to cause friction. The good news is, with the information provided thus far, it is shaping up that the organization is relatively small. A half a dozen members at most. As I said earlier, some have been recruited on false pretenses, thinking they're working in an authorized agency operation. That's one reason for the lack of talent within the organization. No seasoned NSA employee would fall for their fantasy operation. However, we are still trying to identify the top players."

Silent for a moment, as if deep in thought, the inspector general then looked up. "Tell me why you named the investigation Black Fly?"

"I can't remember whether I choose it as a play on 'a fly in the ointment' or whether it was a strange reference to that sickeningly sweet Italian liquor, Sambucca with the coffee bean floating on top. They call it a 'Black Fly.' Both seem fitting, to a degree."

# CHAPTER 14

*Bangkok, Thailand, 16 July 2015*:

Tommy woke with a start around two in the afternoon in an unusual state. Having not consumed massive amounts of alcohol the evening prior, he lacked the traditional painful throbs and dry mouth associated with dissipating intoxicants. Not unlike a fish out of water, it was a sensation he had not felt in a long time and made him feel somewhat uncomfortable. Dressing in his jogging gear, he left the room, looking forward to a revitalizing run through the streets of Bangkok.

His daily jog was cut short as the heat, humidity, and traffic became prohibitive to a long workout session along the side streets of Bangkok. After a short shower in the hotel room's cramped shower stall, Tommy wrapped himself in a towel, sat at the end of his bed, and turned on the television. With the cool breeze from the air-conditioning humming overhead and a comical Thai television show providing background noise, Tommy lay back and once again fell into a deep sleep.

A soft knock at his door brought Tommy back to consciousness. With the previous evening's activities fresh in his mind, he immediately became concerned as to who might be at the door. The thought of Jainukul or his young employees as late afternoon guests was an unsettling scenario. He quickly went through a laundry list of people who knew where he was staying: Lawan, but too early as she was traveling from Isaan; a hotel maid, not likely as he had placed the *Do Not Disturb* sign outside the door upon his return from the run; or possibly Jack, who might know where he was staying but had never disturbed Tommy outside of The Corner Sports Bar. Tommy doubted it could be John Smith's people, as he had never used a credit card here, nor had he utilized the room's phone for international calls in the all years as he had been staying at the hotel.

Once again wondering why he had not liberated the Beretta from Gene earlier that morning, Tommy tightened the towel around his waist and positioned himself just inside the bathroom, next to the room's entrance. A door forced inward or, worse yet, his unknown guest beginning an introduction with the use of a weapon was not a position in which Tommy wished to find himself.

"Who is it?" he asked, leaning his head out from the bathroom to simulate the same acoustics as if he were at the door.

"It is me, my love."

Tommy jumped from the bathroom and opened the door for Lawan, a beautiful Thai woman. She dropped a tan cotton bag filled with her clothes onto the hallway floor and fell into his arms. After a long embrace, she looked up and gave Tommy a traditional Thai kiss, a short quick smell on his face or *hom noi*. Tommy laughed, pulling her close and giving her the western counterpart, a long wet kiss on the lips.

Standing just over five feet tall, Lawan had golden skin, shoulder-length pitch-black hair, and dark almond-shaped eyes. Slender and stunningly beautiful, Lawan was dressed in a short jeans skirt, a red T-shirt, and black flats.

"How did you get here so quickly?" he asked while holding her in his arms.

"My friend from the village drove me. She was coming to Bangkok and had room for another passenger. We left very early this morning," Lawan replied while nuzzling into Tommy's chest.

Pulling Lawan's chin up with his hand, Tommy looked into her eyes. "I have missed you so much," he whispered.

Lawan gently tugged the towel from his waist. Tommy began unbuttoning her skirt. It and towel fell to the floor, and the two moved to the bed.

Tommy had met Lawan nearly five years earlier in a Bangkok restaurant while she waited on his table. And while there was a considerable age difference, nearly twenty years, an innocent relationship slowly turned into a love that had made them inseparable. Together the two escaped to an island in the Gulf of Thailand and started a thriving tourist business—a cafe catering to western food tastes during the day and a pub at night that became one of the island's favorites. They thrived, creating a happy life many would envy, until Tommy decided they were too close and returned to his children. To this day, Tommy remained torn between his children and a life he had produced with this beautiful woman so different and so far from his past.

Awaking around six in the evening, both famished, Tommy pulled himself up and leaned back against the headboard. Lawan, lying next to him, wrapped her arms around his waist and placed her head on his chest, the white quilted bedspread covering their naked intertwined bodies.

"Bacon, what are you doing in Bangkok? How long do we have?"

Lawan had always used Tommy's middle name. He asked her why, early in their relationship, and she had explained to Tommy that she wanted to use something to refer to him that no one else did. Bacon had been her pet name for Tommy ever since.

"Couple of days. Maybe longer. I came to do a quick job, but can't seem to stay out of trouble. I've got some Thai guy named Jainukul looking for me for no apparent reason, except I met him in the presence of a man he's very interested in, and the job has shaped up to be anything but straightforward," Tommy said, shaking his head. He explained about the strange delivery job, and how his employer's surveillance team was searching for him. He also explained about the drunken American named Carl and the run-in with Jainukul.

"We must stay away from Soi Twenty and Twenty-Two. They will look for you there. We should go to someplace that is very crowded and difficult to find us," Lawan remarked, having always had a habit stating the obvious at just the right moment.

"John Smith and company expect the unexpected right now. Fortunately, John Smith and company know nothing of Bangkok and don't know what to expect or not expect. As for the Jainukul, he knows nothing about me, but knows Bangkok."

"We cannot guess about this John Smith man, but we do know about this Jainukul man. We should go to where he does not expect. A place with many people. A place with many tourists. He knows you know Bangkok. He knows where local *farangs* who know Bangkok go. The *farangs* who live in and know Bangkok avoid the place of tourists," Lawan responded, her logic process always methodical and normally correct.

"Where's the biggest tourist nightspot in Bangkok?"

"The Suan Lum Night Bazaar, my love. Many *farang* tourists and young Thais go there. We will be impossible to find."

"Lots of people. Lots of food. Lots of drink. Sounds like a great place to hang out with my Thai love."

After a quick shower, Tommy slipped on worn jeans and a faded blue T-shirt advertising some long forgotten bar he had visited. Lawan pulled on cut off jean shorts and a white T-shirt that highlighted her shapely figure and golden skin. After short cab ride from their hotel, Tommy and Lawan arrived at the Night Bazaar.

As Tommy remembered from previous visits, the Night Bazaar was a huge complex made up of three distinct areas, each about half the size of a football field. After being dropped off by the cab, they entered the entertainment section through a street entrance. Having an enormous stage at one end, the entertainment section featured several different live bands each night. Working their way through the crowd,

Tommy looked across the entertainment area and saw large and colorfully lit Ferris wheel slowly rotating its passenger cargo. The area between the stage and Ferris wheel was filled with round metal tables and plastic chairs sectioned off to various beer and food distributors. Waitresses clad in skimpy tight uniforms, similar to those of Hooters in the United States, provided a constant flow of food and drink. To one side and running along the entire length of the entertainment area was a line of kitchens and beer booths supplying the food and drink. Directly opposite was a long boardwalk that bisected the entire complex and separated the entertainment area from a covered market. Tommy and Lawan found an empty table near the center of the chaos and ordered up a pitcher of beer, and plates full of both Thai and western food. A band played rock and roll music which was amplified through four enormous speakers abeam the stage.

Sitting on their plastic chairs Tommy examined the long boardwalk. It was crowded with tourists and youthful locals moving up and down its pathway peering into both the entertainment area and a covered market. The covered market, topped with an enormous white circus type canopy, was filled with hundreds of small shops situated in checkerboard fashion. From his vantage point he could see narrow aisles running its entire length with an equal number positioned perpendicularly, allowing access to the shops. The covered market matched the size of the entertainment area and was teaming with merchants selling anything from clothing to tourist trinkets. Large overhead lights could be seen above the roof of the market illuminating a large parking area Tommy knew was on the far side.

Armed with a disposable plastic cup, Tommy quickly polished off a pitcher of beer, as Lawan sipped a single glass. Not a big drinker, Tommy's Thai counterpart was in many ways his caretaker. Lawan's eyes were on Tommy.

"Time for a trip to the toilet, my dear," Tommy informed Lawan with a smile.

"Please be careful and remember where our table is, my love."

"Of course," Tommy replied as he pushed back the chair. He felt a slight light headiness from the beer working on an empty stomach, a relaxing and familiar feeling.

Tommy weaved his way through the throngs of people seated at the tables enjoying the live music and drink, most of which were young Thais with a few tourists scattered in. The tabletops, littered with half-eaten paper plates of food, were sticky with spilled beer and other drinks. Many of the patrons were far more intoxicated than Tommy, swaying back and forth in concert with the ear splitting music. The Ferris wheel's slow turning colorful lights added a carnival like scene to the Night Bazaar. He finally made his way to the boardwalk.

The walkway was busy and Tommy had to push his way through swarm of people peering out onto the entertainment area and inspecting merchandise in the shops of the covered market. Approaching the restroom entrance he felt a presence on each side. Not other Night Bazaar customers making their way toward a common destination, but two people making an effort to press against him.

Someone reached up and grabbed his elbow, and Tommy glanced over his shoulder to see Jainukul's short thin thug. The young man looked at Tommy with a smile, revealing crooked yellow teeth. Looking over his other shoulder, Tommy saw Jainukul's other, larger employee. He too smiled at Tommy with crooked yellow teeth.

"Good evening, gentlemen," Tommy said over the din of the chatting mob and music, while thinking that Lawan could not have been more mistaken about the Night Bizarre being a good place to hide. "You should consider expanding your wardrobe. Those are the same clothes you had on last night— or earlier this morning, to be more precise."

Saying nothing, the smaller one directed him into one of the corridors bisecting the market. Wondering if they spoke English, Tommy considered speaking Isaan but decided against it, as his ability to understand their language might best be kept a secret talent.

"Ah, a meeting with Mr. Jainukul, no doubt? Could I use the restroom first?"

Ignoring his question, Jainukul's two employees pushed Tommy forward. Walking down the narrow aisle into the market, the three men, abreast to one another, had a difficult time negotiating through the crowds.

The two thugs escorting Tommy broke up knots of people with a push and a growl. Tommy realized that he would have far fewer alternatives once in the approaching parking area.

With just a few more stalls to go before they exited the market into the parking lot, Tommy abruptly drove his body into the smaller of Jainukul's employees, crashing into to a booth selling kitchen wares. Pots, pans, and dishes flew as the two fell over a folding table acting as a counter. The young woman selling the goods screamed and fell backward into the rear wall, ripping through a fabric partition separating it from the next shop. Her fall through the wall was followed by another clatter of falling wares.

To Tommy, it sounded like someone had just pushed over a slack of compact disc boxes, and he wondered if the next shop over might be a pirate video stand.

Tommy jumped up and attempted an escape over another counter on the far side of the shop but a strong hand grabbed his shoulder and began dragging him back. Shoppers witnessing the mêlée began screaming and unsuccessfully attempted to move away from the commotion along the narrow and crowded aisle.

Abruptly twisting a full two hundred and seventy degrees to his left, Tommy led the entire movement with an extended and closed right fist. His fist connected to the larger of two thugs' left ear, and the man went down.

Before he was able to take advantage of the momentary freedom, the smaller of Jainukul's employees threw a matching round house kick, striking the left side of Tommy's jaw.

The blow jerked his head to the right and Tommy felt each of his vertebras pop in sequence as he was lifted off the ground.

Falling over the counter, he inadvertently pulled the table over with the heels of his feet.

Cushioned by fleeing shoppers, Tommy toppled into the passageway between the stalls. Stunned, he looked up to see the smaller, and visibly angry, thug jumping across the overturned counter. Halfway across, a large frying pan met the young man square in the face, knocking him back and on top of his struggling companion. Lawan dropped the pan and began pulling Tommy to his feet. As he spat out a mouth full of blood, Lawan pulled him into crowd of panicked shoppers.

Rubbing his jaw, Tommy said, "Sweetheart, this was a really bad idea."

"It is," Lawan responded, while maneuvering down the aisle filled with tourists milling about the market shops.

"It was," Tommy replied, correcting her English. Tommy could move lose teeth on the left side of his mouth with his tongue, but his neck and spine felt surprisingly good. "That little guy could start a new version of chiropractic service." He chuckled. "Maybe calling it Muey Thai Chiropractics."

"Bacon, please be serious."

"In all seriousness, I need a beer."

As they plunged back into the entertainment area, Tommy glanced to the right in time to see Gene, the embassy logistics specialist, moving along the walkway he had been abducted from several minutes earlier. Realizing that Gene had not seen him yet, Tommy began looking around for his tall blond companion, the pretty brunette, and the beady eyed man.

"It's hard to be serious when our choice to come here could not have been further from a good decision. I just saw one of John Smith's employees."

"*You* are an employee of John Smith," Lawan said matter-of-factly as she dragged him into the crowded venue of the entertainment area.

"That is certainly one to think about."

Tommy and Lawan moved through the tables of drinking youth and tourists. Halfway to the other side, Lawan pulled him down, forcing him to sit at a table with four young Thai men who had obviously been drinking heavily. Asking if it was all right to sit with them, Lawan offered to buy a round of drinks. While she might have thought it was her offer for more alcohol, Tommy realized it really was a matter of her beauty that won the young men over.

The four young men laughed and one pushed a pitcher of beer toward them, its frothy top spilling out onto the metal tabletop. While Lawan was busy waving down a hostess to order more beer, Tommy grabbed a previously used disposable cup with the remnants of a half smoked cigarette floating in an inch of Coke from the tabletop. Unceremoniously dumping its contents on the ground at his feet, Tommy filled the cup to the brim with fresh beer. He then hunched down in his chair in an effort to not be seen by either John Smith or Jainukul's employees.

He could see Gene moving along the walkway, abeam the entertainment area, looking out into the crowd. While he had not seen them yet, Tommy was sure John Smith's other employees were close by. Just as Jainukul's two employees showed up and began a like search along the walkway, Gene gave his up, disappearing into the market area. The crowd at the Night Bazaar seemed to be growing.

Hunkered down in his red plastic chair, Tommy attempted to keep tabs on the men looking for him. The four young men seated with them were deep in conversation about one of the local bands, and Lawan, sitting alongside with a worried look on her face, kept watch on Tommy.

"Looks like Gene moved into the market," Tommy absently pointed out. "But Jainukul's boys are now on the walkway looking for us."

Drinking the last of the beer in his plastic cup, he picked up a new pitcher delivered by a hostess. The base of the pitcher dripped stale beer picked up from the tabletop onto his lap as he poured. Wiping the beer off with his free hand, Tommy took another healthy swallow of beer.

"Where are Jainukul's men?" Lawan asked, looking across to the boardwalk.

"They were about halfway down the walkway last time I saw them."

Having just placed his plastic cup back on the table after a long drink, Tommy was rocked by a blow to the side of his head, the wallop swaying him in his seat. He looked up and saw one of Jainukul's employees had used a serving tray on the side of his head. The other thug jerked Lawan's chair out, knocking her to the ground. The smaller thug had blood stains on the front of his shirt and what looked to be the foundation for two black eyes, presumably a product of the frying pan to the face delivered a few minutes earlier. The four young men seated across from them abruptly stood up, knocking the table over on to its side. Plastic cups, pitchers, and beer became air-borne projectiles, littering the surrounding crowd and adjacent tables. Tommy attempted to standup and grab the larger of Jainukul's two employees but he was met with another blow to the back of his head by the serving tray, knocking him over onto the ground next to Lawan.

The four young men began yelling at the Jainukul's employees and one of the young men pushed the smaller of the thugs. A brawl broke out between the four young men and Jainukul's employees. Their table companions were just drunk enough to pick a fight for no reason other than the protection of their temporary turf, conveniently protecting their unknown guests. Crawling on their hands and knees around the nearby tables, Tommy and Lawan weaved their way through a crowd that had congregated to see what the commotion was about. Tommy could smell the stale beer and spoiled food that had spilled on the ground beneath him as he moved. Their hands and knees quickly become dampened and dirtied by the rubbish.

Several tables away, Tommy hauled Lawan to her feet and began pulling her through the mob of onlookers. No one saw their exit, as all eyes were on the fight in the middle of the Bazaar.

Reaching the edge of the entertainment area, Tommy thought he heard police sirens. Wondering if the police were responding to the struggle in the entertainment area, he looked over his shoulder and saw red and blue flashing lights cutting through the thick humidity above the market's roof.

"That was quick," Tommy commented. "I've never seen the Thai police respond that quickly to anything."

Scampering into a gap between the kitchens servicing the entertainment area, they ran headlong into a tall concrete wall separating the complex from greater Bangkok, prohibiting their escape from the Night Bazaar. They ran along the wall looking for an exit, pausing momentarily for Tommy to take an overdue urination. Lawan frowned and shook her head at the delay. Continuing along the wall, they found a service vehicle entrance opening and ran out onto Wireless Road, the Bangkok avenue on which many foreign embassies were located, including the United States Embassy.

A median, with tall palm trees and decorative light poles illuminating the avenue, separated the traffic flowing in opposite directions. Slowly jogging along the avenue toward Sukhumvit, they crossed the four lanes and median when there was a break in traffic.

"You should go to the American Embassy," Lawan declared as they jogged along Wireless Road.

"And tell them that I've been hired to deliver a high-value computer program but I ditched my employer and he's now looking for me. I've also got a man who wants to find me for no apparent reason, and his thugs attempted to kidnap me and then beat me up. And, oh please excuse me for pouncing on your logistics specialist the other night, stealing his cell phone and identification. I think I need avoid the American Embassy, my employer, and my new friend Jainukul, make the delivery, and get out of town."

Tommy could see the American Embassy coming into view as they jogged down the Wireless Road sidewalk. It was a massive compound with a white concrete wall, tall palm and other tropical trees masking most of the buildings.

"We should catch a cab before they see us. This street will be where they will look," Lawan announced.

"Just like the Night Bazaar is where no one would find me? Maybe walking along an avenue where we expect them to look might be safer? How in the world did they know we were at the Night Bazaar?"

"I don't know, my love."

"I never did get anything to eat and those hostesses we ordered all that food from are probably pissed. We never did have a chance to pay any of our bills."

Flagging down a taxi, Lawan told the driver where to take them as they climbed into the backseat. As if on cue, Tommy looked through the taxi's rear window and saw a black Nissan sedan pull up behind with Jainukul's two employees sitting in the front seats. The yellow eyed Jainukul sat in the back. All three were looking at Tommy, and not one of them was smiling.

"Change of plans," Tommy announced to the driver. "Take us to the Nana Entertainment Plaza."

When Lawan glanced over with a questioning look, Tommy gestured, hitch-hiker style, through the rear window back to the black sedan.

"What are we going to do now?"

"Well, we can't go back to the hotel. Let's try to lose ourselves at Bangkok's sex tourism mother-ship." Tommy then asked the driver, "Can you put some distance between us and the dark sedan behind us? I'll make it worth your while."

The driver didn't say a word, but quickly pulled away from the curb, staying in the far left lane of Wireless Road. The sedan closely followed the maneuver as the cab raced down the avenue.

Rapidly approaching the Sukhumvit intersection, the cab driver stepped on the accelerator and the taxi shot forward. Suddenly, the cabbie made a hard right turn, managing to cross two lanes of busy traffic on Wireless Road and pass through the opposing traffic onto the perpendicularly situated Sukhumvit. Jainukul and his thugs were trapped in the Wireless Road traffic and forced to cross through the intersection. A short distance up Sukhumvit, the cab driver turned right onto Soi Nana and stopped in front of the Nana Entertainment Plaza, fifty yards down the street.

Tommy knew the Nana Entertainment Plaza to be the dirty white sanctuary of pedophiles, transvestites, adulteresses, and lonely men looking for a night in the arms of a young Thai woman or man. Pulling Lawan, Tommy entered the courtyard of the huge three-story U-shaped structure. They made their way through a central court crammed with plastic chairs and tables, trash, and young and old men. Woman served various alcoholic beverages to drunken customers dressed in a global array of fashions. Looking up, Tommy saw outdoor walkways hovering above the courtyard, filled with the entrances to the various bars and nightclubs, and more roaming customers. He moved toward one of the enclosed concrete stairwells, located at each corner of the building. From a previous visit he knew that each of the nightclubs featured young Thai men and woman in various stages of dress who could be purchased for the evening. Scampering up a stairwell to the third floor, they had to maneuver around young and old men from every corner of the globe, all looking for an evening of drinking and short-time love.

In a far corner of the third story, Tommy pulled Lawan into a nightclub called the Purple Haze, featuring *katoys*, or Thai transvestites. It never ceased to amaze Tommy how many of Thailand's sex tourists were attracted to *katoys* and he often wondered why men would come halfway across the world to be with a transvestite.

Tommy and a friend had found the *katoy* nightclub when they had mistakenly entered it on a drunken night in the plaza. Once they realized it was a *katoy* nightclub, they quickly left. The two laughed about the mistake each and every time they talked, always blaming the other for leading them into the Purple Haze.

"I doubt they'll expect us in here," Tommy said as he looked down to see Lawan's reaction to his nightclub choice.

"The only thing I'm worried about is how you knew about this place."

"There are some things a *katoy* can do that you cannot," Tommy teased.

"Now I am worried, Bacon."

The walls of the nightclub were covered in purple satin and multicolored lights, resembling those on a Christmas tree, had been fixed along the edge of a raised platform that ran down the center of the club. Several brass poles interrupted the otherwise unobstructed platform, each with flamboyantly dressed *katoy* grasping them while dancing to music blaring over hidden speakers.

Hiding in the bar for several hours, Tommy and Lawan drank beer and watched the *katoys* dance. Around two in the morning, Lawan grabbed Tommy's hand and led him out of the nightclub. He was intoxicated and stumbled behind her as she led him down the dirty concrete steps, through the still-crowded and trash-filled courtyard, and out onto Soi Nana to catch a cab. Tommy assumed she was watching out for Jainukul and his employees, as he was incapable of the task.

# CHAPTER 15

*Bangkok, Thailand, 17 July 2015:*

It was an impressive hotel room with polished wooden floors spanning across the living room and into the bedroom. A short black lacquer counter was topped with crystal glasses and a decanter was situated next to the room's entrance, a long ivory colored couch stood to one side of the room and faced a large flat-screen television on the other, and a small round table and chairs were nestled next to tall floor-to-ceiling windows with views of the Bangkok skyline. It was a space that should have left any occupant content. Sitting on the couch in the hotel room, aimlessly peering through the floor to ceiling windows, Bob was anything but content. Bob was upset about his current situation.

Flying into Bangkok the day before their quarry, Bob was supposed to have kept track of the drunken deliveryman, Tommy Luck, for the first twelve hours. This plan was in place because Tommy was flying first class, and Becky and Steve, on the same flight, were not. They would undoubtedly leave the airport and arrive at the hotel after Tommy.

Bob had elected to wait for Tommy at the Imperial Queen's Park Hotel, more precisely in the front lobby. After all, Tommy had reservations, and everyone believed that he intended on using them. Not to mention, after a twenty-three hour trip, everyone would need a little sleep. It was supposed to be an easy task, wait in the lobby for Tommy to show up, watch him check into his room, and if he left the hotel, which was unlikely after such a long journey, follow him.

Waiting in the lobby had been a bad decision on Bob's part because Tommy never showed. At least Bob never saw him.

According to his team leader, Tommy had been in the hotel and made a call on the cell phone provided to him for the delivery. A small GPS tracker imbedded in the cell phone verified the fact. Bob would have said the GPS information was wrong but his associates had also seen Tommy near the hotel and followed him into a cluster of bars. They had lost him too, but still blamed Bob.

Sitting on the ivory couch in his impressive room, across the hall from his associate Becky and next door to their team leader Steve, Bob pondered the events of the last six months. Even though Bob had only been with the NSA for two years, he had been reassigned, promoted really, to a unit tasked with preventing the illegal sale of classified information. He had been nothing more than a data analyst, so the transfer had been an opportunity of a lifetime.

The idea was simple—sell foreign agents phony classified information and gather evidence on those agents and the recipients. While this type of operation normally fell under the jurisdiction of the Central Intelligence Agency, or CIA, it seemed a proactive approach, and Bob hadn't questioned why an NSA unit was assigned such a mission.

At first, this had all sounded plausible to Bob.

The first hint of something wrong came with the team's choice of the individuals making the deliveries. Bob had been a part of two other deliveries, thus far—the first in Brasilia, then one in Mexico City, and now this one in Bangkok. In each case, the member making the delivery was not an NSA agent; in each case, the chosen deliveryman led a less than wholesome lifestyle; in each case, the individual making the delivery was not aware of what was really going on; and, in each case, the person making the delivery disappeared after the operation.

For this operation, Bob had made a point to suggest to the team that they should find someone better qualified. "Use an NSA agent," he had offered the team's management. But in the end, they chose a delivery person the same caliber as all those used in the previous deliveries. After his suggestion about going with an NSA agent was rebuked, he had been asked his opinion of Tommy Luck. He assumed they were just trying to keep his morale up and act as if they cared about his opinion, making him feel a part of the team. Bob's reply had simply been, "He looks like the best candidate to me," matching his team's platitude with one of his own.

But Tommy had been different, and Bob was beginning to wonder if they hadn't actually chosen an NSA agent as the deliveryman but used a cover story to hide the fact. You never knew with the NSA. There were shadows within the shadows at the agency. Unlike the other deliverymen, Tommy had immediately been more alert to what was going on around him. Unlike the other deliverymen, who had preferred to hangout in bars getting drunk and hiring prostitutes before the delivery, Tommy kept a very low profile. Tommy Luck had been different. He had been unpredictable and imaginative in his approach to the delivery. Well, they actually didn't really know what Tommy was up to. He had simply disappeared the first night in Bangkok, claiming that he would make the delivery on his own terms.

Bob knew that Steve was taking a lot of heat from headquarters about losing track of Tommy. Steve was generally difficult to be around when not under pressure, intoxicated with the authority he had over his small team, but with management breathing down his neck, he had been trying to find a scapegoat for everything that had gone wrong—and Bob had been his goat.

The cell on a small table next to him began ringing. Hesitantly reaching down, Bob picked it up and saw Steve's number flashing on the caller ID. "Crap," Bob said under his breath, "What will it be this time? Maybe he'll blame me for the poor television reception in his room?"

Steve had recently been complaining about his television reception. Bob answered the phone, trying to conceal the anxiety in his voice.

"Yeah, Bob, we need to split up the search for Mr. Luck," Steve explained. "I've decided to move you to another hotel a little farther down Sukhumvit."

Immediately suspecting that Steve was trying to get rid of him, Bob felt a surprising wave of relief. Bob was ready to get away from his team leader. "Which hotel?" he asked, now attempting to disguise his delight. "I can check out right now if you'd like and head to the new location."

"It's in an alleyway just off Soi Twenty. The hotel is called The Queen Lotus Guest House. It's a long shot, but it will give us more coverage if you hang out along Soi Twenty. Becky can keep an eye here on Soi Twenty-Two, and I'll focus my effort on Soi Thirty-Three and Soi Cowboy." Steve had a way of talking that left the listener with the impression he or she was being talked down to.

"Good idea," Bob replied, noting that Steve had assigned himself Soi Cowboy, a short adult entertainment street, filled with bars and young women selling themselves for the night. "Will you be finding a hotel near Soi Thirty-Three or Cowboy?"

"No, those sois are right across Sukhumvit from the Queen's Park."

His team leader's reply confirmed Bob's suspicions that the move was designed to get rid of him. Soi Twenty was actually closer to the Queen's Park than Soi Thirty-Three, and Soi Cowboy was even farther away. It didn't matter to Bob. He just wanted to get away from Steve.

Quickly gathering his belongings, Bob left his room and stopped by Steve's before going down to the lobby to checkout. He knocked on the door to let his team leader know he was headed to the new location. There was no answer. Bob thought that odd. He then stepped over to Becky's room and knocked on her door with the same result. Standing in the hallway for a moment, contemplating the absence of his team members, Bob finally decided they must be out watching their assigned streets. He knew what was expected of him and headed down to the front desk.

Riding in a taxi along the traffic-packed Sukhumvit Avenue, Bob considered his newly assigned location. Soi Twenty was small by Bangkok standards with three hotels, four or five restaurants, and one or two bars. Not the night spots of Soi Twenty-Two, Thirty-Three, or Cowboy but an area where expatriates tended to congregate, nonetheless. Briefly, Bob thought that moving there might have been a good idea but quickly dismissed the notion. He knew it was too small to focus the entire effort of one agent.

As he stepped out of the cab in front of the Queen Lotus, Bob realized this lodging option was not in the same league as the Imperial Queen's Park Hotel. Not by a long shot. After paying the cabbie and retrieving his bag from the taxi's trunk, Bob stepped into the hotel, and examined his new home. The lobby was a fraction of the size of the Queen's Park, decorated with two large stone guardian lion statues, whose size overwhelmed the small space; Chinese paintings; and paper lanterns. The floor was white marble with thin black highlights and there was a small restaurant attached to the lobby, separated by a waist-high meticulously carved wooden railing, selling Chinese and Thai food. Where the Queen's Park was grand, the Queen Lotus was cliché.

Picking up his room key and taking a short ride to the third floor on a cramped and slow-moving elevator, Bob stepped into a narrow hallway that smelled of mildew. Finding his room directly across the hallway from the elevator, Bob inserted his key and stepped through the door. With floral papered walls, the room was clean but much smaller than the one he had just checked out of at the Queen's Park. These walls were adorned with more Chinese art, and a narrow wooden table stood against one wall topped with a television, a fraction of the size of his previous flat screen. Bob turned on the television and sat on the full-sized bed. Flicking through the channels provided multiple Thai soap operas, several Thai news stations, and one station airing English movies, no Western news. Not the Imperial Queen's Park Hotel, Bob thought again. Showering, he prepared himself for an evening of hunting for the elusive Tommy Luck.

On his way out of the hotel, Bob decided to have a bite to eat before beginning his search. He stepped through the opening in the waist-high carved railing and found a table in the center of the hotel's attached restaurant. The glass-covered tabletop felt cool on his elbows as he sat down, and he glanced out an enormous picture window onto the alley. Large red reverse-oriented lettering announcing the guest house to those on the street partially obscured his view of the people milling around outside. An old man dressed in a neatly pressed black trousers and an oversized white shirt shuffled over to the table, setting a menu in front of him before filling his glass with ice water.

Concentrating on the menu, Bob heard someone pull out a chair from the table behind and sit down. He didn't bother to turn around, assuming it was just another hotel resident looking for a meal before a night on the town.

"Long time no see, pal," a voice rang out behind him.

It took a few seconds for Bob to register that the person was, in fact, talking to him. He began to turn in his seat. "Have we—"

The calm and familiar voice interrupted Bob's movement. "Don't turn around. You're being watched."

"Why would someone be watching me?" Bob asked, feeling a little ridiculous taking instruction from the faceless person behind him. It was a familiar voice but he just could not put a face to it.

"You tell me. It's your team members watching you."

Bob readied himself to turn again. "What do you know about my team?"

"Look, genius, I'm your prey. I'm the guy your team is supposed to be watching. I'm Tommy Luck."

"Mr. Luck? How'd you find me? Why do you think my team is watching me?" Bob now recognized the voice from that day he had parked on the street in Arlington and Tommy pounded on the car window, telling him to go home—or go swimming. He had often wondered how Tommy had known he spent most of his free time swimming.

"What's your name?"

"It's Robert—ah, Bob. My friends call me Bob." Using all his willpower to not turn and confront Tommy Luck, Bob asked, "Why do you think my team is watching me?"

"Bob, this alley has been a circus for the last hour as your team arrived and set up, obviously focusing their effort on this hotel. Then I saw you amble down the alley and check into this place. You don't appear to be connected to their efforts, so you must be the focus. The pretty brunette is across the street in the vegetarian Indian restaurant. She's sitting at the table next to the front window with a good view of the Queen Lotus's lobby door and windows. The beady-eyed man is sitting inside of the Top Secret Lounge, about twenty yards down the alley. It's the bar on the corner with mirrored windows. He has a clear view of the entire alley, both the section that leads to Soi Twenty and the part leading to Sukhumvit. The other two embassy goons are just outside the alley, watching both the exits. I imagine they're waiting for your departure."

"First of all, they are probably watching you. Secondly, I have no idea what embassy workers you're talking about," Bob grunted, while wondering why had his team had not said anything to him about the surveillance operation in this alley. That would explain why Steve and Becky weren't in their rooms, but again, why had they not informed him? Or was Tommy Luck just trying to confuse him?

"They haven't seen me, and their little surveillance operation is not focused on my hotel. I'm not staying at the Queen Lotus, making it pretty obvious they're not looking for me. They were in place watching this hotel before you arrived. Not my destination but yours."

"How'd you see all this if you weren't in the alley? And what embassy 'goons' are you talking about?" Bob mimicked and emphasized the word "goons" to make his point, while trying to think of a reason that his team would be watching him. He could not think of one.

"What are the names of your pals—the other team members?"

"Steve and Becky," Bob replied, immediately realizing he had made a mistake giving up the names of his team, providing Steve with yet another reason to be mad at him. Bob silently cursed himself.

"So Steve is the short guy with the beady eyes and Becky is the pretty brunette?"

"No, the girl's name is Steve. What do you think?" Bob replied sarcastically.

"Glad to see you're keeping a sense of humor, Bob." Tommy chuckled. "Haven't you ever heard the Johnny Cash song, 'A Boy named Sue?'"

"No."

"Yeah, you're probably too young. What about the other two?"

"That's the whole team. We've no one else supporting us. There is just the three of us. There's no embassy support and no reason for my team to be watching me."

"Look, Bob, as I said, I'm not staying here. I came into the Queen Lotus through a side door from a joint connected to this building. Not the main entrance. Your team has spent the better part of an hour moving around this alley, trying to find the best location to set up surveillance on this hotel. They were here when you arrived and they're still here, waiting. So you tell me, why are they watching you and not out looking for me?"

Thinking back to the call directing him to check into this hotel, Bob knew it was an unusual request because Soi Twenty had never been considered a good place to reestablish contact with Tommy Luck. It was too small with far larger and more likely areas to focus on. And why hadn't Steve and Becky answered their doors when he had knocked? It had taken him less than fifteen minutes to pack and leave his room. Had they just finished setting up their surveillance on the Queen Lotus

Guest House when Steve called and made his request? Bob's mind began to whirl. They must be watching him, he just didn't know why.

"I don't know. This operation—this delivery has been a disaster from the start," Bob said in a quivering voice, rubbing his open palms across the cool glass table top.

"Take it easy, Bob. You'll be fine, but you need to think. Why are they watching you and not me? It could be important for both our sakes."

"I told them they should have gone with a trained agent for the delivery." Bob immediately realized he had made another mistake by using the term agent.

"What do you mean a trained agent?"

"Look, Mr. Luck, nothing personal, but you're a drunk and have never done anything like this before."

"What do you mean a trained agent?"

"I just meant that they should have hired a trained professional." Bob knew he could not reveal his NSA identify, for it would surely get him into even more hot water with his team leader, not to mention upper-level management. That revelation could send him back to being an analyst or even cause him to lose his job.

"How many delivery operations have you participated in?"

"This is the third," Bob replied. "The last was in Mexico about two months ago."

"What's so different about this one? What would cause your teammates to decide to start watching you?" Tommy remained calm.

"You—you're different. We've never had a deliveryman disappear before the delivery. Although, all of them have afterward," Bob added. "I was supposed to keep an eye on you the first night in Bangkok, and I never saw you. That's the only reason I can think my team have now started following me. Maybe they think we're working together? I don't know."

"What do you mean all deliverymen disappear after the delivery?"

"All the past deliverymen have disappeared after making

the delivery. I was told that it was individual choice. You know, money in the bank, at home in some foreign country—check off the net for a while. I did try to find out if any of them ever turned up later. None have."

"Jimmy Santos disappeared?"

"Yeah, in Mexico—Mexico City. He hasn't turned up since."

"Why'd you go back and check to see if any of them had turned back up?"

"I'm an analyst by trade. Curiosity runs through my veins. The delivery people all seemed to have less than desirable qualities. Then they all disappeared after each operation. Statistically, maybe one out of two, but both? On the other hand, hire guys that, if they disappear, no one is surprised. It all seems too convenient."

After a moment of silence, Tommy sighed. "Look, Bob, I can help, but it will cost you."

"Why do you think I need help?"

"You got your own people watching you, and you have no idea why. I doubt they'd go to all the trouble to start watching you because you lost me the first night. Something is going down, and you seem to be the focus of effort."

"All right, if you were me, what would you do? And what will it cost me?"

"It'll cost you information. And if I were you, I'd lose these clowns. I'd wander out there, take a walk down the street, and then disappear. Let them call you. They've got your cell number. Let them call you and then tell them when you saw them following you, you went to ground. Ask them why they're following you. Go on the offense."

"All right, how do I lose them?"

"Easy, walk out the front door and take a left. Walk down the alley to Soi Twenty and act like you're looking for me. When you get to the Windsor Suites Hotel, about a block down, go inside and walk through the lobby. At the elevator bank take a right. Keep walking down the corridor. It'll make a sharp turn to the left. At the end of the corridor, go out the doors. You'll be on Soi Eighteen. Walk—no run—down the street toward Sukhumvit. On the corner of Sukhumvit and Soi Eighteen, there's a Seven-Eleven where a couple of motorcycle taxis are always available. Hire one of the drivers to take you to the Chit Lom Sky Train Station.

"Your teammates won't take a motorcycle taxi. Riding on the back of a scooter driven by a guy in an orange vest doesn't fit with their image of a surveillance operation. It doesn't look cool. They'll hire a taxi and the cab will get gummed up in the Sukhumvit traffic. At Chit Lom get on the Sky Train and then get off at the Nana Station. Walk down Soi Eleven. Take the first alley to the left. Take an outside table at Charlie Brown's, it's a Mexican joint. Buy two beers. If no one has followed, you I'll join you there. I prefer Corona. It's a simple plan that will work. In fact, it was the plan I had in the event I ran into your team—that is, before I realized you needed an escape plan more than I."

"How are you getting out of here?"

"The same side door I used to come in through."

"Why can't I use the side door with you?"

"Because you want them to know you recognized and beat their tail. And you want to show them you're in charge of the situation. If you go through the side door with me, they'll think you headed back up to your room and are blowing the surveillance job off. Eventually, they'll realize you skipped out, but it won't have the same effect. You want them to know you're running the show. The head game is a part of the show."

Bob heard a chair move and the shuffling of feet. He then felt a hand on his shoulder. Looking up, Bob saw Tommy give him a reassuring smile. Tommy's expression exuded calm and confidence. Bob watched as Tommy turned and walked through the opening in the carved wooden railing, past the stone lions to the other side of the guest house lobby. Bob watched Tommy disappear through a side door.

Frightened, Bob sat at the table, pondering all that had transpired during the last three hours. He kept asking himself why his teammates were now following him and what had he done to lose their trust and confidence. Deciding he wasn't ready to attempt Tommy's plan, needing time to build his courage, Bob ordered a bowl of green curry from the old waiter.

Between the spiciness of the curry and his nerves, Bob could only finish half his meal. With his stomach upset from the combination, he took a deep breath, stood up, and headed out the front door. It was dark out but the lights from the small hotels and restaurants lining the alley provided good illumination. He glanced into the Indian Restaurant across the alley and saw Becky sitting near the front window. She glanced down at a menu in her hands when she saw Bob looking her way. Walking down the alley, Bob began passing the mirrored windows of The Top Secret Lounge. Before turning the corner toward Soi Twenty, he peeked into the open door of the lounge and saw a cluster of patrons leaning up against a long black lacquer bar. Steve was not among the small group.

Turning the corner—it was darker along this section of the alley—Bob could feel himself become tense. It felt damp and he could smell a mixture of petrol, spice, and grime. With his the soles of his shoes echoing each time they struck the pavement, Bob could see the activity along Soi Twenty thirty yards ahead. Halfway through the narrow part of the alley, Bob heard a shuffling sound, and saw a shadow moving out of the darkness in his peripheral vision.

A hand reached across his face and grabbed his chin, lifting it up. It happened so quickly Bob never had a chance to react. A blade, long based on how it felt when it slid across his throat, cut a deep laceration and severed his jugular vein. Bob instinctively reached up with his hands and felt warm liquid gushing from the wound, soaking his sleeves and the front of his shirt. Immediately, he felt a wave of tiredness sweep over his body. His breathing became labored, his energy began to drain, and his vision blurred. His legs gave out and, as he fell to the pavement, his assailant grabbed him by the armpits.

As Bob's consciousness waned, he felt his heels bumping

and dragging across the dirty pavement. His assailant then tossed him between a parked mini-van and a brick wall. His left cheek hit the pavement hard when he was dropped, but numbness had besieged his body, and he couldn't feel any pain. He felt warm blood pooling around his right ear and head and he could smell its metallic-like aroma. Bob's last conscious memory was wondering how long Tommy Luck would wait for him in the alley off Soi Eleven. Bob died a short fifteen yards from the crowded Soi Twenty.

# CHAPTER 16

*San Diego, California, 12 July 1995*:

Walking along a cracked sidewalk on Ash Street, Tommy felt the sun on his back and could smell the briny waters of the Pacific. Having just finished work at a construction site along Harbor Drive, he was headed back to his efficiency apartment for a shower before heading out for an evening of fun in downtown San Diego.

Suddenly a woman burst from a Seven-Eleven across the street with a panicked expression. She looked left and then right, before running down the street. Tommy stopped, cocked his head to one side, and examined the convenience store. After a moment, he strolled across the street and pushed the door to the Seven-Eleven open, stepping inside.

Inside, he saw a young man dressed in a dirty white T-shirt beating the convenience store clerk. The clerk was laying on the floor next to the counter while the young man, pummeling him with the butt of a .38 special, demanded access to a change machine under the counter. Another man, slightly older, dressed in a black silk jacket and jeans, stood next to the counter watching the younger man beat the clerk. Hearing Tommy walking down the aisle, the older of the two men turned and began raising a handgun. Tommy grabbed a jar of pickles from a shelf he was walking past and threw it at the man.

Unbeknownst to the older of the two hoodlums, Tommy had been the varsity team baseball pitcher at a university he attended and was endowed with a very accurate throw. The pickle jar struck the man in the forehead, knocking him to the floor. The man's weapon bounced and skidded across the floor, coming to rest at Tommy's feet. The younger man, hearing the pickle jar crash to the floor, stopped beating the clerk and stood. The young man looked at Tommy standing in the aisle and then at his companion, lying on the floor. Smirking, the young man began raising the .38 special's muzzle. Scooping up the handgun at his feet, Tommy promptly pulled the trigger three times.

The younger of the two hoodlums could not have known that Tommy's father had been a firearms collector, and Tommy was both familiar and skilled with handguns. The first round struck the young lout in the right eye. The second shot split his jaw and the third took off his left ear. As the young man dropped to the floor, the older of the two men began groggily pulling himself to his feet. Unhesitatingly, Tommy put three rounds into the man's chest. He walked over and placed the handgun on the counter. He then kneeled down and began consoling the beaten clerk, who was moaning on the floor.

Several minutes later a lone stout policeman arrived, bursting through the doors with a raised handgun. The policeman, dressed in a navy blue uniform, had thick dark hair and matching eyebrows. His slightly bulbous nose was bracketed by bright green eyes.

"San Diego Police," the stout policeman called out. "Put your hands where I can see them."

Tommy raised his hands and slowly stood up, turning to face the policeman. "Hey officer, I work down at the construction site on Harbor Drive. I walked in to find these two guys beating the clerk."

Slowly walking down the aisle with his weapon pointed at Tommy, the officer then asked in a low solemn voice, "What's your name?"

"Tommy."

"Tommy, there are two dead men on the floor who have obviously been shot, and I count only two weapons. How is it you managed to subdue two men?"

Tommy gestured to the broken jar of pickles. "I threw the pickle jar at the older guy and knocked him out."

Lowering his weapon, the officer replied, "That doesn't explain the three holes in his chest."

"I used his weapon on the younger guy and then shot him when he tried to get up."

"You shot an unarmed man trying to get up?"

"Well." Tommy scratched his head. "Unarmed would be a subjective description."

# CHAPTER 17

*Bangkok, Thailand, 18 July 2015:*

Tommy was awakened by Lawan, wrapped in a white hotel towel with black bra straps exposed at her shoulders, hovering over him early in the morning. As he sat up in bed his head began to throb and his stomach felt unsettled. He had been dreaming of an incident he had experienced twenty years ago when he walked into a convenience store and found two men beating the store clerk while attempting to rob the business. Tommy had unhesitatingly killed the two hooligans. The problem was that one of the men he killed had been unarmed.

Dealing with the initial policeman at the scene had been fairly straightforward. The officer questioned Tommy in regard to how the death of the two men had occurred with only two handguns, and Tommy had been blatantly honest. The officer, realizing a Good Samaritan would likely be prosecuted for the death of at least one of the preps, quickly readjusted the scene to give the self-defense argument more credibility. With the modified setting, the follow-on officers easily accepted Tommy's claim of self-defense.

Fortunately for Tommy, the clerk had either not witnessed the events of the second shooting or decided to conveniently forget. While Tommy had never felt guilt over the incident, it had been a somewhat shocking experience, revealing a natural ability for him to unleash a large share of violence when need-ed.

"Bacon, you must see what is happening," Lawan said as she gently shook his shoulder.

Hearing a commotion of loud voices on the street below their window, Tommy checked to ensure the flash-drive was still in place around his neck and dragged himself from the bed. Dressed in a set of red and blue plaid boxer shorts, he peered through the window down into the alley. Several police motorcycles were blocking the Sukhumvit entrance to the al-ley, and one police car and an ambulance were blocking the Soi Twenty entrance.

A police officer, in his brown uniform, and an ambulance attendant, in his white, were pulling something from behind a dirty silver mini-van that had been parked in the same spot since Tommy's arrival. It took a moment for him to process the image before he realized that it was a body they were try-ing to remove from behind the van.

Throwing on a pair of shorts, a T-shirt, and running shoes, Tommy told Lawan that he was headed out for a run and he would check out what was going on in the alley on the way out. Lawan kissed Tommy and told him to be careful.

The lobby was empty, as all the on-duty Drop Inn employ-ees were standing in front of the hotel, watching the efforts of the police and ambulance attendants. Stepping out the lobby door, Tommy was met with the hot humid morning air, cool by Bangkok daytime standards, but uncomfortable nonethe-less. Walking closer to the scene he could see one of the at-tendants attempting to keep a blanket over the body as they moved it from behind the van.

As they hoisted the body onto a gurney the blanket fell off, revealing the corpse. Immediately recognizing Bob, Tommy stepped back and scanned the growing crowd. Having recently read in a fiction novel that killers liked to come back to the scene of the crime, Tommy wondered if Bob's assailant could be among the spectators.

The night before, Tommy had waited for three hours at

Cheap Charlie's, an outdoor drinking establishment that provided a good view of Charlie Brown's Mexican Restaurant, their planned rendezvous site. He'd been there long enough to become intoxicated and Lawan had eventually come to gather him up.

The escape plan Tommy had provided Bob had been simple and foolproof, and undoubtedly would have lost any tail, especially one that was not familiar with Bangkok. He now knew why Bob had not made their meeting, having never made it out of the alley. As he began his morning run, Tommy now wished he had allowed Bob to use the side door. It would not have had the same effect as Tommy's plan, but Bob would be alive and Tommy would have had a lot more answered questions.

He ran a one hour loop along city streets, five laps around Benjasiri Park, and then spent another two hours in one of Bangkok's many fitness centers, lifting weights and running on a treadmill.

Entering the lobby of The Drop Inn after his workout, he saw two men sitting in the hotel's closed restaurant. Walking past the restaurant entrance, Tommy recognized one of the men. The older of the men was dressed in a rumpled khaki suit, appearing to be around fifty five years old and standing about five foot eight inches tall. He had a ruddy complexion, premature silver gray hair, and dark bushy eyebrows. The contrast gave him a clown-like appearance. The other man was the blond-closed-cropped-haired man who had been Gene's companion, the embassy logistics specialist. Tommy recognized him from the bar complex on Soi Twenty-Two. There was no indication that the young man recognized Tommy.

"He's either real good," Tommy muttered to himself, "or I've been wrong about this guy and Gene's activities."

"Mr. Luck," the older man called out as he stood from the table. The younger of the two copied the older man's movement, standing as well.

Tommy stopped and turned toward the men, wiping sweat from his brow with the back of his hand.

"What can I do for you, gentlemen?"

"Mr. Thomas Luck?" the older man asked again, walking toward Tommy.

It dawned on Tommy that the man was not sure whether he was Thomas Luck but it was too late to deny his identity.

"Yes, what can I do for you?"

"Mr. Luck, my name is Sid. I am the Central Intelligence Agency station chief here in Bangkok. My companion here is Roy. He's one of my agents." The clown-like man held out CIA identification. The younger man again mimicked the older man's action by holding up his identification. "I was wondering if you had a few minutes to chat?" Sid asked.

"Do I have time for a shower?"

"This won't take long, just a few questions. We can sit down over there and talk," Sid said, gesturing back to the empty restaurant.

With a sigh and nod, Tommy answered, "Sure."

The threesome moved over to a wooden table and sat down in the small restaurant. A maid dressed in baggy black pants and an un-pressed white blouse was mopping the floor near the entrance to the kitchen, and the odor of disinfectant and coffee filled the air, oddly reviving Tommy's hangover.

Sid pulled a business card from his shirt pocket and set it on the table. Tommy picked it up and silently read *Sidney Gilmore, Central Intelligence Agency, Station Chief, Bangkok* with a phone number on the bottom left corner.

"Do you know an American named Carl Anderson?" Sid asked.

"Vaguely. I met him at a bar at the end of the alley a couple of nights ago—The Corner Sports Bar. Why do you ask?"

"What did you talk about?"

"Business in Bangkok and Thailand. We were two in a larger group discussing current events around town."

"But you did talk to him alone," Sid announced, more as a statement than question.

"Not for long. Carl was pretty drunk and not completely coherent," Tommy replied, realizing that Sid had obviously talked with someone else who had been at The Corner Sports Bar that night.

"What did you talk about?"

Tommy thought about that night and wondered if Sid was slowly trying to work the inquiry's questions in the direction of the assault on the embassy logistics specialist, Gene.

"I asked him about his job. As I said, he was really drunk and his answers were mostly incoherent."

"What did you ask him?" Sid persisted.

"I can't remember exactly. Just small talk," Tommy lied.

"Have you seen Carl since that meeting?"

"No," Tommy responded, shaking his head.

"Did he say where he was going after he left the bar?"

"Some Thai gangster showed up before he left. The guy asked one of his employees to bring Carl to him after he left the bar."

"Why do you say gangster? Did you recognize him?"

"No. Just a feeling the guy wasn't just an ordinary businessman."

"This Thai gangster spoke English?"

"English and Isaan," Tommy replied. "He obviously also speaks Thai, but he was speaking Isaan to his employees."

"How'd you know it was Isaan?"

"I speak a little." Tommy leaned back in his chair in an effort to stretch the muscles in his lower back that had begun to tighten up from his run. The wooden joints in the chair creaked at the change in pressure.

"Interesting. Did Carl see the gangster after he left the bar?"

"No idea."

"What did you do after leaving the bar?"

"The man wanted his employees to follow me and find out where I was staying, so I took a motorcycle taxi ride. Once I lost the guy following me, I returned to the hotel."

"What do you know about losing tails? Have you had to do that before?" Sid was obviously trying to pin down Tommy's profession.

"I do a lot of reading—suspense novels. And no, I have never had to lose a tail until that night," Tommy lied again as he thought about the time he lost John Smith's employee Steve, the beady eyed man, on the Washington DC metro.

"Why did the gangster want to know about you?"

"No idea. I assumed it was because I was talking to Carl, whom he was very interested in."

"What was the gangster's name?"

"Jainukul."

"Was that his first or last name?"

"Probably his family name. It's a common Thai family name," Tommy replied, glancing at Roy who was inspecting his fingernails and looking bored.

"Where were you two nights ago?"

"Out drinking on Soi Nana."

"How long were you there? Times? Was anybody with you?"

"I was there from around seven in the evening till around two in the morning. My Thai girlfriend was with me. I got pretty drunk and my girlfriend brought me home," Tommy replied, not lying about who he was with or his intoxicated condition when he left the Nana Entertainment Plaza, but exaggerating how long they had been there.

"Is the woman upstairs your girlfriend? She doesn't speak English."

"That's right. Maybe you should learn Thai. Hey, I'm tired and need a shower. I've answered your questions, and now I'm finished."

"Mr. Luck, Carl was found dead at the Night Bazaar two nights ago. Someone shot him in the head—three times in the parking lot. There was another disturbance at the Night Bazaar on that same night and you fit the description of one of the participants, as well as your friend upstairs. Let me spell it out for you, three nights ago you meet with Carl, Carl doesn't show up to work the next day, and that night Carl is found dead in a location that a gentleman fitting your description was also seen in an altercation."

"Sounds to me like you need to find this Jainukul character," Tommy grunted.

Sid ignored Tommy's comment and continued. "Carl just transferred here from Mexico and there have been some allegations that his activities were of questionable legality. When was the last time you were in Mexico?"

"You know the answer to that. If you don't, then you should check with the Mexican immigration authority. When you do, you will find that the last time I was in Mexico was over twenty years ago—if their records go back that far," Tommy said, scooting the chair out from the table.

Sid ignored Tommy's move to leave. "What do you know about a man named Bob?"

"Never heard the name," Tommy lied for a third time.

"He was found dead just over there this morning," Sid said, while gesturing to the narrow portion of the alley. "Right outside your hotel. He was another American. He was seen sitting in a restaurant last night with someone fitting your description just down the alley."

"I am of average build with common features," Tommy calmly retorted.

"There was also evidence that he was linked with Carl."

"I can't help you."

"Mr. Luck, one call to the Thai Royal Police, and I can make your life a living hell. Have you ever been in a Thai prison? It's not a pleasant experience," Sid coolly threatened.

"I had nothing to do with Carl's death. I imagine you've talked with Jack, the owner of The Corner Sports Bar, and he has confirmed that I did not know Carl prior to our introduction two nights ago. You also probably realize that the Thai man, Jainukul, is a far more convincing suspect than a guy who didn't know Carl. I had nothing to do with this other guy's death, either. If you have tangible evidence linking me with either, then spill it.

"Otherwise, I'm out of here," Tommy said, calling Sid's bluff as he stood. "I am simply a guy who was in the wrong place at the wrong time several nights ago at The Corner

Sports Bar. I don't like being threatened. Have a great day."

"We will be watching you, Mr. Luck," Sid brusquely announced as Tommy turned and began walking away.

Tommy was in deep thought about his discussion with Sid as he entered the hotel room. Lawan was sitting on the bed, watching a Thai soap opera on the television. He walked over and kissed her on the forehead.

She smiled. "There are two men looking for you, Bacon."

"Just met them. Nice move, acting like you don't speak English."

"I did not want to answer any questions. They looked like they could not speak Thai."

Tommy gave her a quick rundown on Carl and Bob's demise and his discussion with the CIA men.

"Do you think Jainukul killed Carl and Bob?" Lawan asked.

"I would bet a lot of money on Jainukul killing Carl. I don't know about Bob. Let's get out of here. I need to try to figure out what is going on."

After a shower in the cramped stall, Tommy and Lawan departed the room and caught a taxi to Soi Eight. Back when Tommy was living in Thailand, he and Lawan would spend afternoons in Bangkok at a small restaurant called Monsoon on Soi Eight. Largely made up of a wooden deck built around several tall tropical trees, it was loaded with squared tables, green-cushioned chairs, and multi-colored umbrellas that, along with the overhead tree limbs, provided shade to its patrons.

As he and Lawan approached the restaurant, Tommy recognized the familiar face of Aslan the Turk sitting at a table with his polyester computer bag at his feet. A mug of beer sat on the table in front of Aslan sweating condensation in the afternoon heat.

"Hello, Aslan," Tommy said, greeting the Turk as they stepped up to his table.

Aslan's over powering body odor hung in the air like a thick fog. "Ah, Tommy, is it not?" Aslan stood, greeting them.

"And who is the beautiful woman?" A wide smile appeared on his narrow pocked face, showing large white teeth.

Tommy made the introductions and Lawan greeted Aslan, putting her hands up steeple fashion in front of her face, Thai style.

"Please join me," Aslan said as he gestured for them to sit at the table he was occupying by himself.

Sitting down at the table, Tommy ordered a bottle of white wine from the waitress. The waitress scurried off with their order, her black skirt vacillating from side to side in rhythm with her long black hair. Soft Thai music could be heard over several speakers attached to the building and the sweet pungent smell of Thai curry wafted through the air, competing with Aslan's harsh body odor.

"Are you staying around here?" Tommy asked while they were waiting for their wine.

"I am staying around the corner on Sukhumvit at the Marriott," Aslan replied with a smile. His face taking on serious look, he raised his dark bushy eyebrows. "Did you hear about Carl?"

"Just heard about an hour ago. Did you know Carl well?"

"Well enough. In his position, as business envoy, I dealt with him on occasion. I would not have expected that he would be murdered," Aslan answered, shaking his head and picking up his mug of beer.

Tommy glanced out onto the Soi and saw Roy, the younger of the two CIA agents standing next to a Family Mart twenty yards from the restaurant.

"Any idea who would want him dead?" Tommy asked, looking back at Aslan.

"No, but he was a secretive man. He was not well thought of by many in the Bangkok business circles, but I think our mutual friend Rudolf was dealing with him concerning some merchandise."

Tommy and Lawan's wine arrived and the waitress poured two glasses before returning the bottle to an ice-filled bucket next to the table.

"What kind of merchandise?" Tommy asked.

"I do not know. I believe it was a prearranged agreement with several people. Carl arrived to conclude the bids. I think Rudolf was one of the bidders," Aslan replied, before looking across the street in the direction of Roy. Tommy thought he saw a fleeting look of recognition on Aslan's face.

"Do you know a Thai gentleman named Jainukul?"

"I know of him but we have never met." Aslan answered, shifting in his chair, as if the question made him uncomfortable. A thin sheen of sweat began to form on the Turk's forehead.

"Where's Jainukul from? He speaks Isaan. He must be from the Northeast."

"He is from Kohn Kaen in the northeast, but I think he owns an industrial complex just outside of Bangkok. He spends most of his time in Kohn Kaen, though. He's in the electronic industry," Aslan said, continuing to nervously shift about in his chair.

"What kind of electronics?"

"All I know of Jainukul I learned from Rudolf. I think automotive components but I don't know for sure. You must ask of Rudolf."

Tommy smiled at Aslan in an attempt to relax him as their conversation was beginning to sound more like an interrogation. Tommy did not want Aslan to feel pressured to answer his questions but he wanted to learn more from the Turk. "You never told me what you do for a living?"

"I'm a purchaser for a large international conglomerate," Aslan replied.

Tommy could sense some hesitation in the Turk's voice and assumed it was due to the inquiring tone of the conversation. Taking another drink of wine, Tommy smiled at Lawan, who was quietly listening to the two of them talk.

After a few minutes of small talk, Tommy asked, "What do you know about the gentleman standing next to the Family Mart?"

Glancing over his shoulder at Roy, Aslan quickly looked

back at Tommy. "Nothing, I have never seen him before."

"He was with another gentleman who questioned me about Carl," Tommy admitted, leaving out the CIA connection, so as to not panic Aslan.

"I would know nothing about that."

"Did someone question you about Carl's death?"

"No one questioned me," Aslan replied, shaking his head and quickly drinking the remaining beer from his mug. He then attempted to call the waitress over but she was talking with another employee and not paying attention. "I must leave now. It has been nice talking with you again, Tommy. It was nice meeting you, Lawan." Standing up, Aslan laid a thousand baht note on the table. "That should take care of my bill." He then picked up his computer bag and briskly walked away, carrying the stench of his body odor with him.

"That was bad," Lawan commented as Aslan stepped off the restaurant decking onto the soi.

"What? His remarks about Rudolf, his reaction to Roy, or his knowledge and then evasiveness about Jainukul?"

"His smell," Lawan said in a perfectly serious voice.

"Sweetheart, Thai people take three showers a day and are likely the most hygienically clean people in the world, but their homes are always in disarray and most are filthy. On the other hand, step into a Persian's home, and it is immaculate and orderly but they smell like goats. I imagine it has to do with the difference in each region's history of water."

"Thai homes are not dirty," Lawan retorted, defending her fellow countrymen.

"I am talking in a relative sense."

After a moment she said, "He got nervous when he saw Roy."

"Maybe his reaction was because Roy looks like a cop. Aslan comes from a place where the police have unquestionable authority and he's probably scared to death of any form of law enforcement—much like Thailand. I've got to figure this out."

"What is it you must figure out, Bacon?" Lawan asked.

"Lawan, I am not a conspiracy theory freak but there is a lot going on with this delivery and some of it seems linked to these other things happening to me. For instance, Bob told me that the last drop was in Mexico and that's where my friend Jimmy did a job for John Smith. The CIA guy, Sid, told me that Carl had been in Mexico before arriving in Bangkok. He also told me that he suspected a connection between Bob and Carl. Coincidence or not?"

"You think that Carl was somehow involved with your delivery? Why would they want you to meet Carl before your delivery?"

"They wouldn't and couldn't have arranged my meeting Carl the way it went down." Tommy paused before continuing. "I had assumed that Gene was working for John Smith. But Roy, Gene's partner, works for the CIA and he didn't seem to recognize me today when I was questioned. So if they're not helping John Smith keep track of me, why do they keep showing up at the most inconvenient times with John Smith's people? If they are not working for John Smith, who are they working for?"

"Maybe they work for the CIA?" Lawan offered.

"But why do they keep showing up with John Smith's people? First on Soi Twenty-Two, then at the Night Bazaar, and finally on the night of Bob's death on Soi Twenty, unless they're watching John Smith's people."

"Bacon, you never saw John Smith's people at the Bazaar. You only saw the embassy man, Gene."

"That doesn't mean they weren't there. The Bazaar was packed." Tommy thought for a moment. "Okay, let's assume that Gene and Roy are working for Sid and the CIA, and they're watching John Smith's people. We know Sid suspects Carl of illegal activities. We know that he thinks Bob and Carl are linked. John Smith's last delivery was in Mexico and, co-incidentally, Carl has just been transferred from Mexico. So let's for the moment say that Carl is working with John Smith—was working with John Smith, rather."

Lawan sat silently, sipping her wine and nodding, confirming Tommy's logic.

"Okay, so Carl is linked to John Smith. Aslan just told us that Carl was brokering a deal with several people for some merchandise, the highest bidder gets the prize," Tommy continued, trying to tie his logic together. "Jainukul was waiting for Carl to coordinate a deal and was upset about his lack of attentiveness. Aslan said that Rudolf was dealing with Carl, as well."

"So, maybe Jainukul and Rudolf were bidding for the same merchandise," Lawan suggested, putting Tommy's logic into a clear statement.

"Yes, and we know that Jainukul's men were at the Night Bazaar the night Carl was killed. Maybe Jainukul lost the bid and killed Carl over the results. He's not a very nice guy."

"But don't forget the embassy man was at the Night Bazaar, too," Lawan stated.

"Yes, but if they were tasked to follow John Smith's people, does that mean John Smith's people were there too?" Tommy posed it as a question. "So maybe John Smith killed Carl?"

"We never saw John Smith's people—not all night." Lawan replied. "Maybe the CIA men connected Carl with John Smith's people and that's why they were there. They followed Carl."

"Okay, Jainukul and Rudolf are the bidders for the same merchandise. Carl is working with John Smith selling the merchandise. Roy and Gene are working for Sid the CIA station chief and watching John Smith's people. They followed Carl to the bazaar. Jainukul kills Carl over the results of the bid." Tommy stated the facts as he saw them and then emptied his wine glass. "So why kill Bob? What had changed that someone needed to kill one of John Smith's people? And who did it. Was it John Smith's people, or the CIA, or even Jainukul?"

"We think Jainukul killed Carl. Maybe he killed Bob?"

Tommy scratched the side of his head. "Or maybe John

Smith is cleaning house? Bob told me that after each operation the delivery boy disappeared. He obviously doesn't have a problem terminating his employees—permanently. So John Smith has bid off a high-value item. His broker was Carl. Jainukul and Rudolf are the bidders. All the while Sid, Roy, and Gene have been working to take the operation down. Carl is eliminated, then Bob follows as John Smith begins to clear house for a reason we don't kno—"

"Maybe John Smith is killing those people because of the CIA?" Lawan interrupted.

"Brilliant," Tommy said then paused for a moment. "That makes sense. Carl and Bob have been on other similar deals with John Smith. Mexico last time. Now Bangkok. So the CIA is onto John Smith and he is methodically taking his own organization down before the CIA works their way to him but he wants to complete this job before closing shop."

Lawan looked confused. "So Jainukul did not kill Carl? It was John Smith?"

"Correct."

"What is the merchandise?" Lawan asked, knowing the answer but stating the question, anyway.

"If the CIA is after John Smith for something that requires him to terminate his bid coordinator and one of his agents, and the flash-drive is the merchandise then that would imply that it contains something illegal or stolen."

"You should go to the CIA. If what you say is true about John Smith killing his people, that means he will kill you after you deliver the flash-drive."

Reaching up to the flash-drive around his neck, Tommy nodded. "You're probably right, my love. But I need to think about this first. Something is still wrong with our logic. I just don't know what."

They ordered another three bottles of wine, most of which Tommy drank, before departing the Monsoon Restaurant. All the while Roy stood patiently next to the Family Mart, watching them.

Walking home they didn't bother to attempt to lose their tail, as Roy knew where they were staying.

# CHAPTER 18

*Washington DC, 18 July 2015:*

M r. Jones sat on a park bench near the reflecting pool with his tweed jacket laying next to him. His sweat-stained light blue shirt was now providing evaporative cooling with the help of a soft breeze blowing across the National Mall. Pulling out his organization cell phone, he scanned the contact list.

The Lincoln Memorial stood proudly at one end of the Reflecting Pool and the World War Two memorial to the other. The traffic along Constitution Avenue on one side and Independence Avenue on the other provided the necessary background noise, and the tourists milling around the memorials provided the visual distraction. The perfect place in Washington DC to make a confidential call, he thought. He did not like conducting organizational business in his office or from home, never knowing where someone might have placed a surveillance devise and who might be listening. The busy and noisy National Mall was his safe haven.

He rotated between five different locations along the Mall each time he made an organization business call but this one, sitting next to the Reflecting Pool, was his favorite. The shade from the surrounding elms and coolness radiating from the pool's brown waters calmed him.

Mr. Jones realized that he would have mixed into the crowd better had he looked more like a tourist, maybe carrying a camera or wearing Bermuda shorts, then he decided he would carry a camera next time. Leaving his office in Bermuda shorts would certainly attract attention.

He had always tried to make as few organization calls as necessary but this delivery was not like any of the others. This was the most important delivery to date and the deliveryman had caused some problems, but there was another. The inspector general office's discovery and investigation into his organization was even more problematic.

Selecting a number from his phone's contact folder, Mr. Jones made a phone call.

"Good morning Mr. Jones," a somber voice answered.

"How are things going with our delivery?"

"Not well. Luck has caused a heap of problems."

The voice carried a serious tone, confirming his concerns about the deliveryman. Mr. Jones was not alarmed by the tone, as his contact was a serious man and his voice always sounded somber.

"He does have chutzpah, doesn't he? Tell me what I need to know."

The somber voiced man filled Mr. Jones in on the details, describing the death of Carl and Bob. He updated him on Tommy's location and activities. He gave him a brief description of the client's activities.

"Should I pass the information on concerning Mr. Luck's whereabouts?" Mr. Jones asked.

"I wouldn't. In my opinion, Luck will be more likely to deliver the merchandise without the added distraction. Our friends have become more of a nuisance at this point than an aid."

"Is there anything more that I can do to help you?"

"No, with the elimination of Bob, the deputy inspector general's investigation should be stalled. I think I've given Luck the appropriate nudge to finish his business and get out of town, and I've calmed the client after the death of Carl."

"How did you manage to prompt Mr. Luck to deliver the merchandise?" Mr. Jones asked, curious.

"I implicated him in both the death of Carl and Bob. He'll want to earn his paycheck as quickly as possible in order to get out of the country. We just need to let this play out."

"My thoughts exactly. Thank you, and, please, call me if anything else arises," Mr. Jones said before disconnecting the call.

Sitting on the park bench, he wondered how this would end. His light blue shirt was nearly dry, its evaporative effect consumed by the heat, leaving a faint salt stain marking the former damp boundaries. Between Tommy Luck doing the unexpected and the inspector general's office investigating the organization's activities, Mr. Jones had concerns. Now with the elimination of Carl the coordinator, things had just become exponentially more complex. He had worked tirelessly to set this delivery up, taking every precaution to ensure success. It now all seemed to be falling apart, due to the actions of an unpredictable deliveryman.

Mr. Jones realized that, in the end, he would need to arrange several terminations in order to ensure that the existence of his organization would never become public knowledge. He smiled and shrugged his shoulders, recognizing that the payoff would be well worth all the work and the deaths of some of the key players. This would be his crown-jewel accomplishment.

Mr. Jones stood, tossing his tweed jacket over his shoulder, and made his way along the aged and cracked sidewalk surrounding the Reflecting Pool. The tourists paid him no attention, as they were busy looking at the Lincoln and World War Two memorials, and the even more distant Washington Monument. Walking up the steps to the encircling road and then past the Lincoln Memorial to his car, Mr. Jones kept glancing over his shoulder. In his business you could never be too careful. Someone could be following.

# CHAPTER 19

*Bangkok, Thailand, 18 July 2015*:

It was an impressive hotel room—a long white couch to one side and a large flat-screen television to the other, with a large floor to ceiling window looking out over the Bangkok skyline. A small black lacquer bar with two chrome barstools stood near the entrance of the room, one of which Steve sat on while sipping a bottle of sparkling water. Thinking about the events from the previous night, he was sure that Bob's death would not adversely affect the delivery, and thankfully, his boss John Smith, agreed with him. In fact, Bob's death might make Steve's job easier as Bob had never contributed much to the delivery operations. Steve had never really trusted him with anything but the simplest of tasks. In some ways, Bob's presence had diminished from the team's capabilities, as each task assigned to him had to have a reliable back up.

Losing Tommy on the first night was just another example of Bob's poor performance. If it had been Steve, he would have waited at the airport and followed Tommy to the hotel—whichever one he chose to stay at.

A light knock at his door broke Steve from his thoughts. He didn't bother looking through the peephole as he assumed it was Becky, his lone remaining agent, or maybe a hotel maid.

Other than Becky and John Smith, no one else knew he was staying at the Imperial Queen's Park Hotel.

Slipping off the barstool, leaving his bottle of sparkling water on the bar, he walked to the door and opened it up. He was surprised when he saw a slightly overweight man with curly brown hair dressed in khaki pants and a light blue polo shirt standing at the entrance. He was equally surprised at the man's height, standing just a few inches taller than himself— and Steve was a short man. As he looked at his unexpected guest, he realized that there was something odd about the man's appearance. At first he thought it was his slightly swollen left cheek, then after a moment or two, he then realized that man's curly brown hair was combed over to conceal a bald top, creating the illusion of a misshapen head.

"Can I help you?" Steve asked his visitor.

"Steve?" the curly haired man asked while looking over Steve's shoulder into the room's interior.

"That's right. Can I help you?"

"My name is Gene. I'm with the United States Embassy here in Bangkok and I was wondering if you had a few minutes to discuss an offer?" His soft voice partnered up with a smile on his plump face, creating an angelic and calming effect.

Even with the soothing aura created by the tone of Gene's voice, Steve immediately became concerned that the man at his door might be an agent with the NSA—or maybe even the CIA. John Smith had told him that the inspector general's office was investigating their activities, and he wondered if this could be someone involved with that inquiry. Steve took a deep breath and tried not to show his panic. "Do you have some identification?"

"Sure." Gene reached into his jacket, pulled out an embassy identification card, and handed it to Steve.

After viewing the identification, Steve handed it back to Gene. "A logistics specialist?"

"That's right," Gene responded with his soft encouraging voice.

"Come in. What can I do for you?" Steve stepped aside, gesturing Gene into his room.

"Nice room," Gene commented, stepping into the hotel room and looking around at the surroundings.

It was a nice and it amazed Steve that such a nice room came at such a cheap rate. He had recently stayed in a standard room at Holiday Inn in Topeka, Kansas, for the same price, and that made this place look palatial. "Yeah, I like it," he replied, wondering if Gene was trying to soften him up for an interrogation about his activities in Bangkok.

"Can we sit?" Gene asked.

Steve nodded to his mystery guest, and they crossed the room in silence, sitting down across from one another at the table next to the window.

"What exactly does a logistics specialist do at the embassy?"

"Shipments, orders in regard to maintenance, some personnel management, but I'm here because I was a friend of Carl's," Gene announced. "We worked together to ensure your upcoming delivery would be successful."

Steve's heart raced, and he tried to hide his astonishment at the man's claim. "You're with the Embassy Logistics Department. Is that another way to say you're with the NSA or CIA?"

"No, I'm not with the NSA." Gene laughed. "I do work with the CIA on occasion, but I'm not an agent. I've been in Thailand for a long time and know a lot of people in Bangkok—throughout the country, really. The CIA department at the embassy asks me to help them out from time to time, using my knowledge and contacts."

"Who is Carl?" Steve knew the name but had never talked with or met the organization's bid-and-delivery coordinator, and, as far as Steve knew, Carl hadn't known him. Steve and his small team's only job during the delivery operations was to watch and ensure the safety and performance of the delivery-man up until the time the merchandise was passed and then conduct any necessary cleanup afterward. John Smith had always handled Carl.

"Look, I know you know the name. He was the guy who conducts the bids and coordinates the deliveries," Gene responded with a kindly smile.

"What deliveries are you talking about?" Steve was required by organizational security protocol to deny anything having to do with their delivery operations to outsiders.

"You can refute everything, and I can walk out of here, but if I do, I'm going straight to the CIA station chief," Gene calmly threatened.

Even with the threat Steve felt Gene's soothing presence. Steve took a moment to ponder his dilemma. If Gene knew his identify, then he likely knew a lot more and, while the thought of killing him crossed Steve's mind, it was almost as quickly rejected for being far too complicated while sitting in a room at a busy hotel. Steve finally decided it would be best to talk to Gene and, if necessary, take care of him later.

"Just listen to what I have to say. Given what I know, you might want to reconsider your claim of ignorance and my offer," Gene continued.

"Okay, for the moment, let's say I know of a man named Carl, and I know something about a delivery."

"Good." Gene took a deep breath. "Carl came to me shortly after he arrived in Bangkok and offered me money to keep an eye on several people he was dealing with. Bangkok can be difficult place to negotiate for the first time. I took him up on his offer and the pay was pretty good. Carl tasked me with watching people who were bidding on some piece of merchandise he was offering. Carl was very happy with my performance and began to include me in more and more of the details of the delivery."

"Do you know what the merchandise is that these people were bidding on?"

"Sure, stolen corporate secrets. This is an especially attractive corporate secret. Carl told me that it was electric car technology from Nissan or one of the other big automakers. The information is worth a lot of money and all contained on a flash-drive to be delivered in two days."

Steve knew Gene was right about the value and time of the delivery, and while he knew it was a corporate secret on the flash-drive, he hadn't known *what* corporate secret. That didn't matter, as this delivery was making John Smith and Steve a bundle of money, more than all the other deliveries combined.

"Why do you think I'm involved?" Steve asked.

"Carl had participated as the broker for your organization for six previous sales and deliveries. He lined up the bidders, conducted the auction, and coordinated the delivery of the merchandise. He was a drunk and a pedophile, but he wasn't a dim guy." Gene leaned back in his chair, looking out the room's window onto the illuminated Bangkok skyline, and continued talking. "And he didn't like working for an organization that he knew nothing about. So over the course of the previous deliveries, he had slowly gathered information on the people he was working for. Using various private detectives and other methods, he was able to identify John Smith in Manila four deliveries ago. Once he had John Smith identified, finding the rest of you was fairly easy. In Brazil, he discovered your name and then in Mexico, during the last delivery, his hired private eye discovered the names of your two teammates. He knew the names of all four of you—well, three now that Bob is dead. He knew there was a larger organization beyond that and had been working to uncover who you three work for."

"Did he ever find out who we work for?" Steve could feel his blood pressure rising, hoping the answer was no.

"I think so, but he never told me the details."

Trying to act as if the information Gene spoke of didn't interest him, Steve asked, "That's all you have?"

"No, that's not all. Carl didn't like all the cloak-and-dagger stuff. He was planning on getting out but wanted a big payoff before he did so. He double crossed one of your losing bidders here in Bangkok. Told the guy that he had won the bid and took a sizable payment."

"He did what?" Steve blurted out, no longer able to control his emotions. "Do you know this for certain?"

"Yeah, he said a couple of things about a week ago that made me believe it was true. Then he confirmed my suspicions on the day of his death. He called and said that he had told another bidder that he was going to sell the merchandise for a price. The impression he left me with was that he had already swindled one of the bidders, and he was working on swindling a second. With his share of what the organization was going to give him for this delivery and what he was able to fleece from the other two guys who had lost the bid, he could disappear and never to have to worry about working again." Gene looked back from the window at Steve with a serene smile on his face.

"Did he ever say who he swindled the money from?" Steve didn't know the winning or losing bidders names, but he wanted to know if Gene did.

"No, he never told me. He did call me on the day he was killed, but didn't tell me any names. I think it was one of the losing bidders who killed him the other night," Gene replied with tranquil sparkling eyes.

Steve was beginning to hate the calmness that radiated from the man sitting across the table from him and fought to not be lured in by his demeanor.

"You talked to him the day he died? What do you know about his death?"

"He called me and asked if I could meet him at the Night Bazaar on the evening he was killed, but, by the time I found him, he was already dead," Gene replied, an innocent sadness crossing his face. "Shot several times in the head—it wasn't a pretty sight."

"Why did he want you to meet him at the Night Bazaar?"

"I think he wanted some back up in the event things went badly. He was meeting someone but was afraid someone else was going to show up."

"You don't know who he was meeting or who he was afraid of showing up?"

"No."

"So what's your offer?" Steve asked.

"Carl had offered me a cut of the payoff. With his death, I've lost that money. I want to try and recoup some of that loss, so I'm offering information. The CIA is looking into Carl and Bob's death. I know all the CIA guys at the embassy pretty well. They're my drinking buddies, and they tell me what's going on all the time. I'll pass you information concerning their investigation and, in return, I want some kickback from this delivery."

"What can you tell me about a guy named Tommy Luck? Have you heard you CIA friends discussing that name?"

"Yeah, he was one of the people identified as to have met with Carl before his death. Carl told me that he was going to meet with several of the clients the night before his death and, according to my friends with the CIA, Tommy Luck was placed in that same crowd."

"*What*?" Steve immediately realized the implications of such an encounter. "Mr. Luck met with the delivery coordinator and several of the bidders?"

"They met at some expatriate watering hole on Sukhumvit a couple of nights ago. Like I said, Carl told me about meeting with the clients, then, after his death, I overheard my CIA friends talking about Tommy Luck being with him on the same night. The impression I got was that he was at the same meeting. They also got an anonymous tip that this Tommy Luck guy was also at the Night Bazaar on the night Carl was killed and he was seen talking to Bob the night he was killed. Who is he?"

Steve ignored Gene's question. "What have they told you recently about Mr. Luck?"

"Not much. I did hear them say that Tommy Luck was drinking at some restaurant on Soi Eight earlier today. Got pretty drunk from what they were saying. He was drinking white wine, and they thought it was funny that he had to be led home by his girlfriend."

"Do you know where he's staying? Mr. Luck, that is."

"No, but I can find out."

"The decision to accept your offer for help is not up to me, but if you find out where Mr. Luck is staying, I think I can convince my boss."

"Who is Tommy Luck?"

"You don't need to know—just get me that information."

# CHAPTER 20

*Fort Meade, Maryland, 18 July 2015:*

John Smith had just gotten off the phone with Steve, and the news from Bangkok was not good. Wearing dark blue pin-striped pants and a light blue shirt, he was sitting in his office, located in one of the many NSA office buildings at Fort Meade, Maryland. His matching jacket and red tie hung on a hanger and then from a hook on the back of his office door. Elbows on the desk top and head in his hands, John Smith was deep in thought, trying to come up with a way to salvage the current delivery.

The office was unspectacular, a black metal desk with a simulated wood veneer top, a black adjustable office swivel chair, and two framed pictures on white walls attesting to attributes of teamwork, all NSA standard issue. It also had a narrow floor to ceiling window with a third floor view of one of Fort Meade's many parking lots.

A cell phone lying on the desk top began vibrating, creating a metallic buzz as it quivered on the simulated wood veneer. Looking at the caller ID, John Smith saw it read *Jones* on the small illuminated screen. Having never personally met the man on the other end of the line, John Smith found that fact did not prevent him from disliking Mr. Jones. He wasn't sure why, he just did not like him. Maybe it was his voice—too fatherly, and John Smith had detested his own father. John

Smith did tolerate his caller for financial reasons. These delivery operations had made him a very wealthy man.

Even if he wanted to, he could never use the man's real name as he did not know it, knowing only his organizational code name of Jones. The organization had strict rules concerning compartmentalization to ensure that damage would be limited in the event of discovery. Of course, all the security protocol protected the upper echelon management—not the operatives. He did know the gentleman on the other end was senior to him within the organization hierarchy, and he was likely John Smith's senior at the NSA, as well. And John Smith could testify as to the value of what Mr. Jones had provided. His information had contributed to the survival of the organization and success of the operations time and time again. In fact, it had been Mr. Jones who had obtained the current merchandize, and it was worth a lot more money than anything they had sold and delivered before.

"John Smith," he answered, leaning back in his black swivel chair. A long and barely discernible squeal announced the change in position.

"Good morning, John, you don't sound too cheery today. I hear there might be some problems with our current delivery operation," the familiar voice droned from the cell's tiny speaker.

"Good morning, Mr. Jones, and, yes, there are some problems."

"Tell me everything I need to hear." A hint of concern could be detected in Mr. Jones's fatherly voice.

John Smith sighed. "Good or bad news first?"

"Is there any good news?"

"There is. Based on the information you provided, we determined the mole's identity and have eliminated him— yesterday evening, I believe."

"I didn't give you that much information."

"It was enough. A new member of the organization who had indirectly influenced the choice of our current delivery person." John Smith swiveled around to look out the window of his office, the chair quietly squealing as it rotated. He began watching a red Ford F-250 pickup that was having difficulty backing out of a space in the parking lot below. "It was a description that fit only one member of the team."

"Who was the mole?" Mr. Jones asked.

"A young man we brought into the organization about a year ago. A former analyst. Not much operational talent. His name was Bob. His absence won't affect the current delivery operation."

"Go on," Mr. Jones requested. "Tell me the bad news."

"Our deliveryman, Tommy Luck, is still eluding my team in Bangkok. We've been unable to find him, but if he holds to his word, he'll contact me in two days for delivery instructions. Secondly, along with Bob, our operations coordinator has also been terminated. We're not sure who's responsible. Could have been the client or even Tommy but, most likely, it was someone other than those two."

"Mr. Luck knew our coordinator? If he is a possible suspect, then you must have knowledge that Mr. Luck knew Carl's identity."

"They met. We're unsure as to how much Tommy knew about Carl," John Smith responded, trying to keep the frustration out of his response. He could not help but notice that Mr. Jones had not been shocked to hear of Carl's demise—a reaction that puzzled John Smith as he had been a key figure in a successful delivery of the flash-drives.

"That's very unusual that our deliveryman met with our coordinator. How did that happen?" Mr. Jones asked calmly.

"From what we can tell, it was chance encounter. We don't know if either of them knew they were participating in the same operation. The only reason I have any suspicion that Tommy committed the act is that there is evidence that he was in the vicinity of Carl when he was terminated. The question is why would Tommy eliminate our coordinator? He had no reason to disrupt the delivery and a live Carl would have benefited him by expediting a successful delivery of the package. Ensure a payday for Tommy, so to speak."

Mr. Jones was silent for a moment as he processed the information, "How do you know he was in the vicinity of Carl's demise?"

John Smith ignored his question because he didn't want to tell Mr. Jones about Carl's relationship with Gene, or Gene's conversation with Steve. "Using the same logic, there is no clear reason for the client to terminate Carl. The client is a rough character, but I can't think of a reason why he would eliminate the coordinator. As with Tommy, it benefits the client to keep the delivery running smoothly. He has paid a large deposit, and terminating Carl threatens a successful delivery. A third possibility is that Tommy is colluding with the client," John Smith divulged.

"How would Mr. Luck and the client collude if they did not know one another?"

"There is a possibility that there was a meeting between them, as well. Like the meeting between Tommy and Carl, it appears that he also met the client." John Smith waited for Mr. Jones's reaction.

"This delivery appears to be falling apart on you, John Smith."

"It is not as smooth running as our past operations. That's a fact," John Smith confessed. "And there is always the possibility that Tommy had prior relationship with the client."

"Did you not conduct a background check on him prior to assigning him as the delivery person?"

"We did, but Tommy does have numerous contacts throughout the country. We checked all the leads we could find but there is always the possibility that we missed one." John Smith paused. "We should also consider that Tommy was the favored candidate in the inspector general's office. They knew he would cause problems. Maybe there is something more than tenacity and the drive to succeed. Maybe the IG's office knew his contacts included the client?"

"I would know if they had chosen him for another reason," Mr. Jones replied in a scolding tone.

"The meetings between Tommy and client aside, chances

are that someone outside of those two, and possibly the operation, eliminated Carl."

"Is there anything in Carl's past that would cause someone outside of the delivery operation to want to terminate him?"

"Carl had been with us since the organization's inception, and he successfully coordinated the delivery of six packages. Prior to working for us, he was a travel agent. Unless one of his past travel agency customers was unhappy with the service he provided." John Smith gave a short dry clucked in a failed attempt to add some levity to a very serious situation.

Mr. Jones ignored John Smith's attempt at a joke. "So why do you believe that it was someone outside of Mr. Luck or the client who terminated him?"

"As I said, both Tommy and the client clearly benefited from a live Carl." John Smith silently shook his head, knowing what he was about to reveal would put him in a problematic situation with Mr. Jones. "There is some evidence that Carl was attempting to double-cross at least one of the losing bidders and that he was receiving help from at least one person at the Embassy in Bangkok. We're not sure if Carl was working with an individual at the embassy to ensure the delivery went well, or for some other nefarious reason."

"What's the evidence?"

"One of my agents stumbled on some evidence that an embassy worker claimed that he had been working with Carl. This individual believes that Carl was in the process of double-crossing one of the bidders. Maybe two. The embassy worker believes that's why he was killed. All secondhand information, so we have no proof of the claim." John Smith went on to describe Gene's story as it was relayed to him by Steve, modifying some of the facts to avoid the question of how a logistics worker had learned the identity of his team.

There was a moment of silence on the line. Mr. Jones then asked, "How did your agent discover this secondhand information?"

John Smith winced. He was hoping that Mr. Jones had missed the flaw in his story.

"The embassy worker just happened to strike up a conversation in some pub with my agent and relayed the story. Carl's death is the talk of the town right now," John Smith lied. "Just happenstance, but a lucky encounter for us."

"That was pretty fortunate, considering the number of bars in Bangkok and our security protocol. Apart from the Carl mystery, what other problems are plaguing our current operation?" His fatherly tone had all but disappeared. John Smith could now clearly hear menace in Mr. Jones's voice.

"That's about it. Tommy continues to elude our people but, as far we know, the delivery will still take place," John Smith said, as he shook his head and wondered how the delivery could have disintegrated to this level. "I believe he will uphold his end of the bargain."

"How will the delivery operation go forward without our delivery coordinator?"

"As you know, none of the members of the organization have ever personally met with Carl, and he was not privy to the NSA connection. I am the only one who had ever communicated with him and that was always via untraceable cell phone. During my last conversation with him, Carl confirmed that he had arranged the delivery and informed the client of the details. As per procedure, he always coordinated the delivery instructions with the client ninety six hours in advance to allow for payment and transportation arrangements. It was all put into place before his termination. We'll pass the information to Tommy on the morning of the delivery. He'll make the delivery as planned. If a problem arises between now and then, I will personally call the client and rearrange delivery instructions. I had planned on calling the client anyway to ensure him that the delivery would still take place, as he undoubtedly has heard of Carl's death."

"That is not protocol. Direct contact between the client and NSA agents associated with the organization is strictly prohibited."

"I can't think of any other way this late in the delivery. The client has not and will not see me, just hear my voice," John

Smith said, trying to soothe his superior's concerns. "He will not be able to identify me."

"There is voice matching technology."

"I will take the needed precautions. I took similar precautions with Carl," John Smith replied while thinking about the fictitious name of Kimball and the voice he had used with Carl.

He had chosen the name simply because his mother had grown up in Kimball, Nebraska, and he had selected a high-pitched voice on the modulator, knowing that the tone would be somewhat irritating. He wanted Carl to prefer limited conversations with Mr. Kimball, rather than ask too many questions.

"What else?" Mr. Jones asked.

John Smith was silent for a moment. "Is there a possibility that Tommy is an NSA agent planted by the inspector general's office?" It was no secret that Mr. Jones had a contact in the inspector general's office, and he was the only one who could answer that question. "Given that the inspector general's office is investigating our organization, it is another possibility that would make some sense of the current issues plaguing the delivery operation."

"No. I would have gotten some indication from my contact that he was a plant. Just get the package delivered," Mr. Jones calmly stated, his fatherly voice returning. "You need to ensure your situation does not become more untenable."

"The delivery is only two days from now. With NSA Inspector General's Office looking into our organization, we might want to delay our next operation until the dust settles," John Smith said as he considered the implications of Mr. Jones's referral to the operation as "your situation." If it failed, it would be John Smith's operation and payment for that failure would likely be swift and vicious.

After a moment of silence, Mr. Jones said, "I agree, it is time to cool our heels for a while. I can handle the NSA inspector general's office for the time being. However, they have apparently identified several low-level operatives within the organization. I'll get the names of the known members from the inspector general's office, and you will need to eliminate them before closing up shop in Bangkok."

"I'll need those names as soon as possible. After the delivery, we will need to move fast," John Smith said, while hoping that his name was not among the known members.

"I'll get them to you as soon as I can," Mr. Jones replied before disconnecting the call.

John Smith sat at his desk, wondering how this would end. During his last conversation with Mr. Jones, he had been told that the NSA inspector general's office had named their investigation of the organization Black Fly, for a fly in the ointment. His deliveryman had turned into the fly in the ointment for John Smith, and he imagined his joy when finally learning of Tommy's demise once the delivery had taken place.

# CHAPTER 21

*Bangkok, Thailand, 19 July 2015*:

The hot morning air felt good to Tommy as he jogged down the sidewalk along Sukhumvit. He turned into Benjasiri Park, through the heavy black metal gates past the shallow pool of water with a high narrow fountain and information booths marking the entrance, to find some shade. A fine mist provided by a slight breeze pushing the frenzied edges of fountain's streaming water out on the sidewalk cooled him as he ran past. The visual coolness from the emerald green trees and plants pooled with actual shade from the towering foliage, granting momentary relief from the rising sun. He ran along a path just inside the fence that marked the edge of the park several times, with neatly laid red bricks passing under him in a smooth cadence. After another hour along the Bangkok sidewalks, listening to the growing traffic sounds and the increasing smell of exhaust fumes, he had sweated out the previous evening libations and returned to the hotel room.

Lawan, dressed in a jeans skirt and white T-shirt, combing her hair in front of the small mirror above the bathroom sink, turned and smiled at Tommy as he entered the room. His hair dripping with perspiration, he pulled the sweat soaked T-shirt over his head and tossed it on the bathroom floor next to Lawan as he stepped past.

"You're up early. What's going on?"

"I want to go see my sister," Lawan replied. "She's off work today and invited us to her home."

"I'll take a pass. I feel like staying in the room. I don't want any unexpected encounters with my fellow employees." Tommy chuckled as he picked up a towel from the bed and began rubbing the sweat from his hair.

Without protest, Lawan departed several minutes later, leaving Tommy to himself.

Around six o'clock that evening, Tommy had become tired of being cooped up in the small hotel room watching movies and the news on television. The maid had not refilled the beer stock in the small rusted refrigerator under the long wooden cabinet, and his hands had begun to shake from a lack of alcohol. Tommy felt the predictable need for a drink and figured the alley would provide a measure of safety, as he doubted that Steve or Becky would venture back after what had happened to their former associate.

Walking through the hotel lobby, Tommy nodded at the desk clerk and then walked across the alley to The Top Secret Lounge. He knew The Top Secret Lounge's large mirrored windows would serve to conceal his presence inside and allow him the opportunity to spot John Smith or Jainukul's employees if they happened to investigate the alley.

Stepping through the entrance, Tommy entered an unspectacular room with alternating black and white walls, and a long shiny black lacquer bar standing along one side. Rows of liquor bottles adorned shelves mounted on a wide mirror behind the bar. Chrome-plated stools with red vinyl cushions stood next to the bar, and five or six chrome-trimmed tables with matching chairs with more red vinyl seat cushions filled the rest of the room. Three ceiling fans turned overhead and soft Thai music filled the empty business. The room oddly smelled like an air freshener dangling from a rearview mirror.

Sitting down on a stool at the far end of the bar, Tommy ordered a Jameson on the rocks from a pretty woman dressed in a tight-fitting black dress. Too much rouge makeup on her cheeks contrasted with her natural light golden skin and her long dark hair disappeared into the blackness of her dress. She smiled at Tommy, revealing crooked but bright white teeth.

After serving him, the pretty bartender retreated to a corner behind the bar and began chatting on her cell phone. Tommy sat at the bar in silence, drinking his whiskey and listening to the young woman's conversation over the soft music. He didn't need conversation as much as alcohol, his shaking hands subsiding after his third whiskey.

Several young Western men came into the bar around eight o'clock and sat several stools down from Tommy. From their accents, Tommy concluded they were from the UK, some-place near London by their brogue. A harsh vocabulary and the loudness of their voices revealed their intoxicated state. The three young men were in the midst of a conversation about the ills of Thai women.

"Aw, I hate them unless their laying on their backs," the one closest to Tommy spouted off.

Standing several inches above six feet with broad shoulders, he was dressed in a blue plaid shirt, jeans and dark athletic shoes.

"Better when they're on their backs with their legs spread," another said and laughed.

This one was Tommy's size with blond hair and soft brown eyes. He wore long canvas shorts and a T-shirt advertising the Manchester United football team.

"They're all monkeys," the third cried out, laughing.

This young man was the fattest of the three. At just about six foot tall, he had wide loose arms and thick shins with bright red pimples that looked to be heat rash. His eyes were engulfed by chubby cheeks, making them look small and too close together. He wore a baggy red T-shirt and wide blue polyester shorts in a failed attempt to hide his obesity. To Tommy, the young man resembled an orangutan.

"They just want our money. They'd screw a dog if it had a wallet," the biggest and closest to Tommy pronounced.

"If you don't like the Thai people, then what are you doing

in their country?" Tommy murmured, more to himself than making a statement to the young men. After all, he had chosen this bar to avoid a confrontation.

"What's that, mate?" The biggest and one closest to Tommy had heard his comment. As the young man twisted his torso to face Tommy and flexed his muscles, a concerned look came over the face of the bartender and she stepped back from the bar.

Looking up from his whiskey, Tommy flatly replied, "I said you three are a bunch of jackasses and should go back to your room and jerk off. I don't know one Thai girl, regardless of their monetary situation, who would let you touch them."

"Who asked you?" the fat one screamed, his chubby cheeks vibrating in rhythm with his moving lips.

"Who the fuck are you?" the closest one yelled at Tommy, pounding his fist on the counter top.

All the beer bottles along the bar and Tommy's glass of whiskey bounced at the impact. The beer bottle in front of the fat man fell over and spilling onto the black lacquer counter top before rolling off the edge onto the floor.

If Tommy had learned anything over the years, it was to never give up the initiative. He picked up his half-filled glass of whiskey and threw it at the largest of the three men, striking him just above his nose on the forehead. The glass shattered and big man fell back into the blond-haired man sitting to his left. In an attempt to keep his friend from falling, the blond-haired man grabbed his blue plaid shirt, ripping it from his body, as the big man dropped to the floor. There was a moment of silence as the unconscious man's two friends gazed in disbelief at their bare-chested friend, lying motionless on the floor.

Breaking the silence, Tommy abruptly stood and threw the stool next to him aside, more to set the mood than for effect. It struck a table just behind Tommy and bounced into the wall, before settling on the floor with a clatter.

The fat one came at Tommy first. Tommy was amazed at the fat man's speed, considering his size, and swung a closed fist that harmlessly ricocheted off the charging orangutan's forehead. Before Tommy could swing a second time, the fat man's plump arms, with surprising strength, wrapped around his body and slammed him into the wall. The entire wall trembled and a black and white picture of Rama Five, the fifth King of Thailand sitting on his throne, fell from its mount. Its glass cover shattered on the floor.

The blond-haired man was right behind his fat friend, striking Tommy in the face with his fist. Tommy brought his knee up between the orangutan's legs, crushing his groin. Reaching for his crouch, the fat man released Tommy and stepped back, becoming entangled in the overturned barstool and tumbling over a table with his oversized red T-shirt fluttering as he fell.

Tommy was struck in the face again by the remaining hooligan. Stunned, he reached out and tried to grab him but the blond-haired man stepped back, kicking at Tommy's wobbling feet. Momentarily clutching the bar to steady himself, Tommy lunged at the man, wrapping his arms around him. As they toppled to the floor, Tommy could see fear in the blond-haired man's soft brown eyes. When they hit the floor, Tommy could hear the wind knocked from the man. Grabbing the beer bottle that rolled off the bar earlier, Tommy pounded it into the side of the man's head.

The blond-haired man went limp.

Climbing off the immobile man, Tommy stood up and looked over at the fat man, who was now on his feet several feet away, rubbing his groin. The biggest thug Tommy had taken down first had regained consciousness and was on his hands and knees, looking up.

"Now, get your dumbasses out of here and don't come back until you learn some manners—and take this clown with you," Tommy growled, while nudging their unconscious blond friend in the side with his foot.

The fat man helped the biggest to his feet, and then they both picked up the comatose one. As the two stumbled out into the alley, dragging their unconscious friend between them, Tommy picked up the blue plaid shirt from the floor and tossed it out the door at the retreating trio, striking the fat one in the back of his enormous red T-shirt.

Turning to the young girl, Tommy said, "I'm very sorry about that."

She responded by placing a fresh Jameson on the bar, saying, "It's on the house," in perfect English. The pretty bartender then began cleaning up the mess made from the tussle while Tommy sat back down at the bar and sipped his free drink.

After finishing his whiskey, Tommy left The Top Secret Lounge and walked back to his hotel, smiling at the same desk clerk he had passed by earlier. Climbing the narrow stairs to the second floor, he entered the room to find Lawan once again standing in front of the bathroom mirror, this time plucking her eyebrows.

"Where did you go, my love?" she asked as he stepped past the bathroom door.

"To the Top Secret Lounge across the alley," Tommy replied while silently looking into a mirror above the long cabinet for any evidence of the fight. He found none.

Stepping from the bathroom, Lawan asked, "You have a nice time?"

"I had a conversation with a couple young guys. It was entertaining. I was getting bored sitting in the room."

"What did you talk about?"

"About how Thai women are the most beautiful and perfect women in the world."

Lawan leaned over and kissed Tommy on the cheek. "You should not start fights over such silly things."

That night, Tommy managed to consume all the beer in the freshly restocked refrigerator, as well as a small bottle of Regency Brandy, before falling asleep.

# CHAPTER 22

*Cleveland, Ohio, 6 June 2011:*

Hovering over the toilet bowl in his apartment, Tommy dry heaved one more time. Glancing at his wrist watch, he saw he was an hour late for work, managing the construction of a new shopping center in Cleveland. Standing up, he shook his head and looked in the mirror. His hair was matted against the side of his head, and he had lipstick smeared across his neck. Stripping off his boxer shorts, he pulled back the shower curtain.

"Fuck," he muttered as he climbed in and turned the water on. "What time did I get home?"

After a quick shower, he hustled over to his closet and pulled a red shirt and jeans from hangers. Glancing over his shoulder at his disheveled bed, he saw a bare leg protruding from under the covers. Hopping on one leg as he slipped pants onto the other, Tommy maneuvered to the side of the bed and sat down. After pulling his pants up, he pulled back the covers, revealing a beautiful blonde woman. The woman's eyes cracked open and she smiled, reaching out to take his hand into hers.

Not remembering her name, Tommy smiled. "Hey, I'm off to work. Can you lock this place up when you leave?"

Rolling over, the woman exposed her naked body. "Can I wait for you? What time will you be home?"

"Sorry, no playing house today," Tommy answered flatly. "I'm not sure when I'll get back. It could be late."

He left the woman and apartment and drove over to the construction site. Pulling past panels of corrugated sheeting that walled the lot off, Tommy noticed activity near a trench they had dug the day before to lay the building's plumbing.

Pulling up to the portable office, he stepped from his Chevy pickup and scrutinized the scene at the trench. The movements of the men around the trench seemed frenzied, so Tommy began walking toward the activity.

As he approached, his assistant stormed up to Tommy, stopping directly in front of him with a scowl.

Tommy head's ached and his mouth felt dry. "What's going on?"

"The trench collapsed."

"Did you get any of the piping laid?" Tommy asked, worried that the collapse might have damaged the material.

"Yes." With a glare of hatred, his assistant continued. "Bill and Connor were inside, trying to shift the pipes into place."

Tommy strode past his assistant toward the men frantically digging out the trench. "Where are they? Where are Bill and Connor?"

"They're inside the trench," his assistant replied. "We're trying to dig them out."

# CHAPTER 23

*Bangkok, Thailand, 20 July 2015*:

Standing in his room's cramped shower stall with hot water dousing his shoulders and back before spilling over the low threshold onto the bathroom floor, Tommy recalled a construction accident that had occurred nearly five years before. Arriving late to work after a night of drinking, he found a trench designed to hold plumbing lines had collapsed. Racing to the scene, he discovered crews frantically digging and learned that two men had been in the trench when the sides came down. Tommy vividly recalled turning to his assistant and asking if the sides had been stabilized with supports before the men climbed in. His assistant's words had been burned into his mind, and even after all the years Tommy could remember the conversation word for word.

"The daily work request simply indicated we were to lay the pipes," his assistant had explained. "Nothing on the request said anything about supporting the sides of the trench."

When Tommy explained it was common sense that the sides should have been supported prior to anyone entering the trench, his assistant had replied, "Common sense to who? You? You come in smelling like a distillery and insinuate I've been incompetent. You're incompetence eclipsed mine when you didn't show up for work this morning because you were drunk last night—again."

The death of the two men occurred not even a year after Tommy had held the hand of Gavin in the collapsed tower crane. Tommy couldn't seem to erase the memory of Gavin's final moments and had turned to alcohol. This incident only increased his anxiety that he had been responsible for the misfortunes.

Pushing the memory aside, Tommy began considering the business at hand. The delivery was scheduled for today, and he was unsure of what to do. As he stood under the shower, he could feel the concern about the delivery mix with an all-too-familiar dull ache in his head from the previous night's libations. He reached up and felt the flash-drive dangling around his neck as he pondered what to do.

Given the history of these deliveries, there was a good chance he wouldn't survive long after turning the flash-drive over to John Smith's client. Based on his conversation with Bob, Tommy knew the moment the delivery was made he would be a marked man. A nagging feeling that he had missed something while attempting to deduct the facts two nights before at the Monsoon Restaurant troubled him, and that realization made the various alternate courses of action equally dangerous. Should he contact Sid, the CIA station chief? Should he rid himself of the flash-drive and run? Or just complete the delivery and hope he could outmaneuver anyone wanting to harm him? None of the options had a clear outcome.

Tommy climbed out of the shower and moved to the bed. Sitting down on its edge, he looked down at Lawan who was still sleeping soundly. Her beautiful round Asian face looked so innocent in the midst of all the violence and mystery surrounding the flash-drive. When he ran his fingers through her thick black hair, she responded by slightly opening her eyes.

"Bacon, I love you," she mumbled before closing her eyes and falling back to sleep.

"I love you too," he whispered.

It was another typical Bangkok morning, but far less suffocating than what the afternoon would offer. Jogging through the back streets of Bangkok for several hours, Tommy then made four laps times around the Benjasiri Park perimeter. The park's shade and green foliage once again fought off the rising sun and heat. When it became too hot and humid to run any farther, Tommy entered a nearby fitness center and spent another hour on a treadmill.

Running provided Tommy with time to think and ponder his options. After his second hour running through the back streets of Bangkok, he had an idea. Several laps into the Benjasiri Park parameter and he had a rough strategy. Thirty minutes into the treadmill, Tommy had a solid plan for how to transfer the flash-drive and, hopefully, survive the delivery.

On the way back to the hotel, jogging down the Sukhumvit sidewalk, Tommy felt that he might survive the day, after all. Given his experience in construction management, he knew that even good plans required modification from time to time. The trick was to create a strategy that was flexible enough to allow for easy and quick changes.

Another shower in the cramped stall and thirty minutes of mindless Thai television helped Tommy whittle the time away. He had told John Smith what time he was going to call and didn't want to show any apprehension or trepidation by calling early.

As Tommy had told Bob, this was as much about head games as anything else. It did cross Tommy's mind that playing head games had cost Bob his life. That was one to consider, Tommy realized.

With Lawan still sleeping, Tommy took the cell phone he had liberated from Gene on the first night and replaced the battery. It took John Smith five rings to pick up his phone. Tommy found that puzzling and wondered what had happened to John Smith's three ring routine.

"Can I help you?" It was John Smith's voice but he clearly had no idea who was calling him. It dawned on Tommy that John Smith not recognizing the caller ID was a good indication that Gene was not one of his employees.

"Good morning, John Smith."

"New cell phone, Tommy?"

"A borrowed cell. I didn't feel like a trip to the Queen's Park for our chat," Tommy taunted.

"Those annoying GPS locators do require a little more effort," John Smith confessed. "I have noted that we must redesign the GPS element to continue functioning even after the cell's battery is removed. Still feeling any affects from all that wine two nights ago?"

"You're good, John Smith, but that is very out of character for you. Snubbing a loyal employee is not your style. Actually, I'm feeling a bit low from all the beer and brandy I consumed last night."

"My apologies. No snubbing intended. I just wanted you to know my surveillance has improved," John Smith replied in a cheerful voice.

Given his conclusions from two nights before, Tommy now wondered if that meant Roy was not working for Sid but rather for John Smith, as Tommy had first believed. As far as he knew, Roy was the only person aware of the cause of his inebriation two nights before. Maybe his first conclusion that Gene and Roy were moonlighting for John Smith was correct.

"I'm not sure two-day-old information concerning the source of my intoxication would qualify as proof that your surveillance has improved," Tommy replied curtly. "You know why I've called."

"Of course, the delivery instructions," John Smith said politely.

"Yes, the delivery instructions."

"The lobby of the Marriott at seven o'clock this evening. There's a raised platform with tables and chairs in the center of the main lobby. The client will be there and can be identified by laptop sitting on the table," John Smith explained in a relaxed tone.

"To ensure you are talking to the correct person, you will ask him for a light. After all, there might be another laptop present on the platform. He will respond by saying that he quit smoking four years ago but still loves the smell of cigarettes. You will then pass him the package and he will verify the program is on the flash-drive with his laptop. At that point, your task will be complete."

"Not very original, 'I quit four years ago but still love the smell.' Sounds like a line out of a B movie."

"I agree, it does sound a little melodramatic. It was not the line I would have chosen but it is the line we are stuck with."

"Sadly, I won't be bringing the flash-drive. I will bring an envelope with a key and the location of a public locker containing the flash-drive. I'll pass the envelope to your client. But before I pass the envelope, you will have one of your minions hand me another envelope with three hundred thousand baht. That's about ten grand and what we agreed to for the job. I'm sure you had planned on having an employee in the lobby overseeing the delivery anyway. I'd rather it be Becky than Steve, his beady eyes are no match for her blue. The client can take the key to the public locker and retrieve his or her flash-drive."

"This is unacceptable, Tommy. The delivery was coordinated with the client three days ago, and he may not agree to the change. And how will my client verify the package?" There was now perceivable frustration in John Smith's voice. "And how in the world did you learn the names of my employees?"

"John Smith, there are two dead people associated with this delivery. The package I am delivering is illegal. And each of your past delivery boys have disappeared after the job was complete. In my view, the change in plans is prudent, considering the facts. Think of it this way, the change in the plan benefits both of us. You get the package delivered, and I get to survive."

"I am becoming a little annoyed with your changes that presumably benefit us both. You should not forget who works for whom."

"If it's not obvious, let me give you a clue. At this point, I'm working for myself."

"Let me give you a clue, Tommy. My surveillance of you has improved. I know everything about you. I know who your friend is and I know where you two are staying," John Smith voice now resonated with a threat.

Tommy noted that John Smith did not disagree with any of his conclusions, meaning that Carl was a part of John Smith's delivery organization and each one of the former delivery boys had disappeared—not to mention, he was carrying a stolen product or information around his neck.

"That's a load of shit. Your employees have been a step behind me the entire week. I am disappointed to find you as naive as your surveillance team. You may claim you know where I'm staying. You may claim you know my partner's name. Sadly, you know nothing," Tommy sternly replied, praying that John Smith's team was not just outside his hotel room door, as he knew he was playing a game of high-stakes poker. He was counting on the fact that John Smith was currently bluffing.

There was a delay as John Smith sorted out his disobedient deliveryman's instructions. "The client will not be happy," he finally said, sounding resigned. "I'll call you if he agrees to the new terms of the delivery."

"Nice try, but you won't be calling me. I'll call you an hour before the scheduled delivery to confirm the changed plan has been agreed to by the client." Tommy then disconnected the call without waiting for John Smith's reply.

Pulling the battery from Gene's phone, Tommy tossed the two components into a small trash can under the room's narrow wooden cabinet.

"Get your stuff together, my love. John Smith might know where we're staying, and we need to leave the hotel as quickly as possible," Tommy announced, looking over at Lawan, who had awakened and been watching him during his conversation with John Smith.

Tommy and Lawan hastily packed their bags and departed The Drop Inn. The alley appeared to be free of any surveillance, but Tommy elected to use the same escape plan as he had explained to Bob three nights earlier. On the Sky-Train, some fifteen minutes later, when Tommy was confident that they had no tail, he and Lawan got off at the Nana station and walked up Soi Eight. They checked into a hotel next to the Monsoon Restaurant, two blocks from the Marriott.

After dropping their bags in their new room, they took a taxi to the bus station on the outskirts of Bangkok, servicing Southern Thailand, and found two empty public lockers side by side. Tommy's original plan called for making copies of the bus terminal locker keys, as Thai lock smiths would copy anything for the right price, but when examining them, he noticed that each had three wide air vents at the top of their doors.

Tommy pulled the flash-drive from around his neck and tested to see if it would fit through. It conveniently fit. He then placed the correct coinage into the mechanisms of two lockers and retrieved the two keys. From there they took a taxi to the bus station servicing Northern Thailand, near Don Mueang, Bangkok's old international airport, and purchased two first class tickets to Kohn Kaen, Thailand's second largest city, on a bus departing that night. They then returned to the hotel to take a break before the evening's event.

"Okay, Lawan, do you understand the plan?" Tommy asked as they were sitting on the bed in their new hotel room.

"Yes, I will go to the Southern bus station and wait for your call. After you call, I will slip the flash-drive through the vent of the locker you tell me and then take a taxi to the Northern bus station and wait for you," Lawan answered in an anxious tone and matching expression. "I am worried, Bacon. What if they do not let you out of the Marriott? Why can we not just call them and tell them where the locker is located?"

"I won't call you until I am out of the Marriott and sure that no one has followed me."

"But why do you have to deliver the key?" she asked. "Let's just send it to them."

"Think of it as a professional courtesy. They know they can't hurt me until their client has received the flash-drive and, by then, we will be well on our way to Kohn Kaen. And don't forget, I need to show up at the Marriot to be paid."

"But there is only one client and you have two lockers. Why do you have two lockers?"

"I'm just trying to create a little flexibility. I'll likely just have to use one envelope, with its associated key and locker, but if I need two, I'll have them."

"What about going to Kohn Kaen? Why are we going to Jainukul's city? Should we not go someplace not so close to Jainukul? He might still be after you. You have enough problems."

"*Farangs* have a saying, 'Keep your friends close, but keep your enemies closer.' Now that saying really isn't meant in the context of physically close but, based on his conversation with Carl on the first night, I think there's a good chance that Jainukul is the client. We need to posture ourselves if things go wrong."

Just before six o'clock, Tommy walked down to the intersection of Soi Nana and Sukhumvit, a block away, and placed the battery back into the cell phone he was provided in Washington DC by John Smith.

Tommy made the call right at six o'clock, and John Smith answered the phone on the fifth ring.

"Hello, Tommy. You are a prompt employee," John Smith stated in a tone that almost sounded jovial.

"You must be using a different security system on your phone, John Smith. What happened to the three ring routine?"

John Smith laughed his dry cluck. "You miss nothing, Tommy."

"I will assume, by your demeanor, that the client has agreed."

"Once again, you miss nothing. A surprising characteristic for a drunkard."

"Once again, I thought it was not your style to badmouth your employees."

"Ah, but I was under the impression you were working for yourself. Let's hope whatever relationship we have ends soon."

"I'll meet with your client at seven o'clock at the Marriott," Tommy replied and then disconnected the call, once again not letting John Smith respond, hoping that it disturbed his employer's current happy disposition.

Taking the business card given to him by Sid, the CIA station chief, out of his wallet, Tommy dialed the number printed on the lower left hand corner.

"Sid, Bangkok CIA station chief," a voice grunted.

"Hello, Sid, Tommy Luck here."

Sid sighed, sounding as if the CIA station chief thought this call would be a waste of time. "What can I do for you, Luck?"

"I'll be meeting with a client of Carl's in about an hour. Apparently, the organization that Carl worked for has sold some merchandise to this client, and it is likely stolen or classified, or both. I thought you might want be a part of the festivities."

Sid was silent for a moment before asking, "What is the merchandise? Who is the client, and how do you fit into Carl's business?"

"No idea what the merchandise is, but I can tell you it's on a flash-drive. I was hired back in the States to deliver the flash-drive, under the assumption that it was a legal deal. I now have evidence to the contrary. That's what I will be doing this evening, delivering a key to a public locker in which the flash-drive is located. Unbeknownst to me last time we chatted, it was a deal brokered by Carl, and I believe the client is the Jainukul, the man I told you of several days ago."

"Where?"

"The Marriott at seven o'clock," Tommy replied.

Hearing soft music in the background, Tommy wondered where the CIA Chief might be. Had he disturbed a dinner between Sid and his wife, or was the CIA man simply having an evening drink at a piano bar or lounge?

"You haven't given me much time," Sid replied gruffly.

"That was my intent. I am having trouble distinguishing between friend and foe. I'm hoping you're a friend."

"I'll be there."

"One more thing, Sid, I'm not sure who your pal Roy works for. He might be moonlighting for this organization that's selling the flash-drive."

"He's loyal to me," Sid said flatly. "You're mistaken."

"Just a warning, my employer was privy to some information that links Roy to this sordid affair. Specifically what I was drinking two nights ago," Tommy replied before disconnecting the call. He began walking back to his Soi Eight hotel and dropped the cell phone into the first trashcan he came upon.

At six-thirty, Lawan prepared to leave for the Southern bus station with their luggage. Standing in front of their hotel, Tommy placed the flash-drive around her neck and then he made sure that she understood the plan. She gave Tommy a passionate kiss goodbye and told him to be careful.

At six-fifty, Tommy left their room, not bothering to check out.

Making his way to the Marriott, he found an open rear door, leading into hotel kitchen. Entering the kitchen, he was immediately engulfed by the clattering pots and pans and the fragrance of an international buffet. While a few kitchen employees gave Tommy suspicious looks, no one said anything to him as he worked his way around the stainless steel counters and gas burners holding pots of simmering food. Tommy found his way to the liquor stock room, directly behind the bar, and peered out into the expansive lobby.

Having been in the Marriott before, Tommy knew the lobby to be nearly three stories high with two enormous crystal chandeliers hanging from the ceiling. He looked up at the second-floor balcony, with a solid concrete banister and a carved teak handrail that encircled the enormous room below, and the two massive chandeliers. As described by John Smith, in the middle of the lobby was the raised platform covered in a plush hunter green carpet. The platform stood a mere two feet off a marble floor with twenty wooden tables, each with four matching chairs. Aligned to the center of each of the four sides of the platform were wide sets of stairs, allowing access.

There were nine customers sitting at the tables on the raised platform, each having an assortment of drinks and appetizers set before them. Some were locked in conversation while others sat alone quietly reading a book, fiddling with cell phones, or watching the crowd. He then spotted Sid sitting on a bench next to the lobby doors, reading a newspaper. Looking up at the second-floor balcony, Tommy saw another ten or fifteen people milling around. Roy was peering over the edge of the balcony down into the main lobby at Tommy. Tommy watched as Roy spoke into the cuff of his jacket, and he glanced to see if Sid would respond. He did not.

Tommy was somewhat surprised to see Aslan standing next to the front desk across the lobby from the bar. Wearing a bright red windbreaker, Aslan was looking out into the lobby with his computer bag slung over his shoulder. Remembering that Aslan had told him that he was staying at the Marriott when they talked at the Monsoon Restaurant, Tommy immediately became concerned that the Turk's presences might hamper the delivery. If Aslan chose to approach and greet him before the transfer was complete, or worse yet, while Tommy was handing over the envelope to the client, things could very well become convoluted.

Focusing on the platform, Tommy could see Jainukul sitting at a table on the raised platform with his back to the bar. A laptop, along with an ice-filled glass full of what appeared to be bourbon or dark rum was also sitting on the table. Tommy wasn't surprised. Based on the conversation he had heard between Jainukul and Carl concerning the coordination of some unknown merchandise, he had suspected that the Thai gangster would be the client. Tommy took a moment to ponder whether Jainukul had murdered Carl. Why kill the coordinator of the delivery when that would just complicate the entire operation? It had to have been John Smith.

Tommy felt the two envelopes he had placed in the each of the back pockets of his faded jeans. Each envelope contained one of the keys and a description of the corresponding locker's location. Looking around for one of John Smith's employees,

Tommy saw none. Taking a deep breath, he walked out from the liquor supply room into the lobby.

Striding through the back of the lobby toward a hallway containing the elevator bank, looking for one of John Smith's employees and his payoff, Tommy heard soft classical music playing over hidden speakers. He noticed Sid saw his advance across the back of the room. While Sid remained sitting, Roy moved to a position along the balcony to get a better view of Tommy's movement. Tommy's stomach twisted into a knot. Something was wrong but he couldn't put his finger on why he was suddenly nervous. He had certainly been in tight situations before and never had he felt the level of anxiety that had currently overcome him. Something was not right, and he was suddenly concerned for no apparent reason. As he walked around the corner of the elevator bank hallway, he was confronted by John Smith.

"Right on time," John Smith said with a smile.

"You know us drunkards. We never want to fit into the stereotypical profile. Now I get the five rings—some overseas technical glitch with your security software?" Tommy replied, returning John Smith's smile while trying to not show surprise at his unexpected appearance.

"Ah, yes. I was wondering when you would figure that one out."

"Why don't I just give you the envelope and you hand it off to the client?"

"Can't do that. I can't allow the client to identify me. It might become problematic at a later date," John Smith responded, shaking his head.

"That doesn't speak well for my future. You have my money?"

Picking up a leather shoulder bag from the floor next to him, John Smith asked, "You care to count it?"

"I would say I trust you, but I don't. However, given the current circumstances, if it's short, I wouldn't want to wait around for you to take a trip to the ATM."

"It's all there," John Smith confidently reassured Tommy.

Tommy looked into John Smith's eyes, searching for the hint of dubious intentions before reaching out and taking the leather satchel, slinging it over his shoulder.

"Let's get this over with," Tommy announced, turning toward the raised platform.

Departing the elevator bank hallway, Tommy walked toward the platform. The soft classical music continued to be piped out through the hidden speakers as he walked up the platform's stepped access at the rear of the lobby. His anxiety seemed to grow with each step. As he approached the client, he could see Jainukul immediately recognize him and then look up to the balcony area. Tommy did not turn to see who Jainukul had glanced up at on the overhead terrace but hoped it had not been Roy.

Sitting down across from Jainukul, Tommy said, "Good evening Mr. Jainukul. It has been awhile—do you have a light?"

"Let's do away with the silly words," Jainukul growled. "Give me the flash-drive."

Tommy thought it was interesting that Jainukul expected the flash-drive and not an envelope containing a key. Standing up from his bench, Sid moved onto the platform. As the CIA station chief sat down in a chair three tables away, Tommy realized why he had become suddenly nervous. The classical music being piped out over the hidden speakers was the same that had been in the background during his earlier call to Sid. Sid had been in the Marriot when Tommy made his call.

Walking up onto the platform, Aslan was now moving toward Tommy and Jainukul with pinched eyebrows and pursed lips. His mind racing, Tommy wondered where Sid fit into all this and how could he delay Aslan's arrival?

"Were you not told of the change of plans?"

"What are you talking about?"

"I don't have the flash-drive, but I do have a key to a locker containing the merchandise," Tommy explained to Jainukul. Aslan was getting closer, and Tommy had hoped to pass the envelope and intercept him before the Turk made his way to the table. His eyes darting from Jainukul, to Aslan, Sid, and then back again, Tommy realized his good plan was coming to a not so graceful conclusion.

"Explain yourself," Jainukul spat.

"The details of the delivery changed this evening—" Abruptly, Tommy stopped mid-sentence, realizing that Jainukul, without the updated delivery plan, might not be the client just as Aslan arrived at their table, sitting down without invitation.

"Hello, Tommy," Aslan said with his thick Turkish accent. Then looking over at Jainukul, he added, "Good evening, Mr. Jainukul. You seem to be attempting to take what is mine." Looking back at Tommy, Aslan held out his left hand, as if waiting for something to be placed in it. His unpleasant body odor drifted over the table and made it difficult for Tommy to take a full breath.

Looking Aslan in the eye, Tommy asked, "So your story that Rudolf was one of the bidders working with Carl?"

"A bit of information to distract you, Tommy. Actually, it is true that he was one of the bidders, but a losing one. It was information to help create a little 'fog of war.' I think it was first coined by a man named Clausewitz, a German military theorist."

"I know the term and yes it was Clausewitz—Carl Von Clausewitz."

"I had a feeling you were somehow involved in this delivery when you began asking questions at the Monsoon Restaurant," Aslan continued, "Now the envelope please." A dark smile appeared on Aslan's face.

"I guess I should ask you if you have a light," Tommy asked, realizing that his simple plan had imploded.

Twitching and fidgeting across from them, Jainukul's rising anger could be sensed by both Tommy and Aslan. Aslan swiftly pulled a small-caliber handgun with a narrow five inch barrel from the pocket of his red windbreaker, pointing the weapons at Jainukul's flat face. The Thai's yellow-tinted eyes glared back at Aslan.

Tommy recognized the small handgun, with its rakish angled grip, as a .22 Colt Woodsman. "I haven't seen one of those in years," he said quietly.

"A small caliber but with a high muzzle velocity, they are very effective when used in close quarters." Aslan's eyes did not leave Jainukul's as he said, "I quit smoking four years ago but still love the smell."

Two young women, dressed in business suits and seated next to their table, saw the weapon and began loudly chattering before scurrying from the platform. A piercing sound of a weapon being fired echoed in the lobby, and Sid turned, pulling a Beretta from under his jacket. Glancing up, Tommy saw Roy's weapon fall from his hand into the lobby with a clatter as it struck the marble floor. Following his weapon, like a choreographed scene from a western film, Roy toppled over the edge of the balcony, landing on the marble floor next to the front desk with a loud slap. More people screamed, knocking over tables and chairs as if they sensed an escalating gun battle. The Marriott employees at the front desk smartly dropped behind the counter.

Aslan continued to point the Woodsman at Jainukul with his free hand still extended to receive the envelope. The lobby of the Marriott became oddly silent, with the exception of the soft classical music and a few remaining patrons pushing their way through the front doors.

Tommy extracted one of the envelopes and placed it in Aslan's hand.

"How did you manage to get Carl to give you the delivery instructions?" Aslan asked Jainukul.

"It became apparent that Carl was attempting to cheat me. He told me that I had won the bid, and I paid a sizable down payment. He admitted to the scheme before I put three bullets in his head. It did not take much to extract the delivery information from the little man before I ended his pitiful life," Jainukul grunted.

"He was a little man," Aslan agreed. "I suspected he was exploiting you in some way or another."

Nervously glancing at to the overhead balcony, Sid moved

over to the table with the muzzle of his weapon raised upward. "Aslan, we need to go now."

"Who are you, Sid?" Tommy asked, sarcastically. "Just another disgruntled government worker? Obviously you're not who you claimed to be the other day at my hotel."

Sid lowered the muzzle of the weapon, his calm demeanor suddenly morphing into a mixture anger and confusion. Watching Sid's expression transform, Tommy sensed a quickly developing danger and grabbed the table edge, forcefully shoving it upward. The table impacted with Aslan's shoulder, knocking him backward. In an effort to balance himself against the rising table, Aslan's held onto the envelope but dropped the Colt Woodsman onto the floor. As Tommy continued to push the table edge higher, Jainukul's glass of bourbon or dark rum flew into his chest and the laptop dropped onto the plush hunter-green carpet.

Sid fired the weapon, its report reverberating across the walls of enormous room, and its round impacting the edge of the table, sending a squadron of wood splinters into the air. Leveraging upward, Tommy forced the table even higher, knocking Aslan out of his chair and onto the floor. Scurrying to one side to avoid the table, Jainukul reached out and grabbed the envelope from Aslan's hand before retreating to the edge of the platform. Sid backed up and fired another round. Tommy could feel the wake of the bullet pass across his left temple and heard it hit a metal object someplace in the lobby behind him. Letting go of the table shield, he rolled to the right and scooped up the abandoned Colt Woodsman.

Stepping back again, Sid stumbled on a chair. Swiftly raising the Woodsman barrel, Tommy pulled the trigger. With a short loud pop the small gun shuddered in his hand, spewing hot chamber gases into his face and stinging his eyes. Grabbing his throat, Sid fell backward over a table. More shots echoed from the walls in the massive lobby and Tommy rolled behind the overturned table.

Glancing around the corner, he could see Steve and Becky firing and running from the elevator bank hallway. It wasn't clear who they were shooting at, but Tommy assumed he was their target. When Jainukul's two thugs appeared on the balcony above and began firing at Steve and Becky, they dove for the edge of the raised platform.

Tommy jumped from the platform and sprinted for the hotel's entrance. Racing across the lobby, he saw Becky peek above the platform. She fired her weapon in his direction. Aiming at a full sprint, Tommy shot back at Becky and the bullet struck a chair next to her head. The chair rocked backward, and Becky, once again, ducked back behind the raised platform. One of Jainukul's men shot at Tommy. The round was so close that it buffeted his shirt as it passed by. Glancing back, Tommy saw Jainukul hunkered down next to a large planter, filled with flowering flora bursting from its top. Continuing his run to the front exit, Tommy could see that Aslan had crawled across the platform toward Sid's motionless body. The soft classical piano music amidst the gunplay provided an amusing audio equilibrium as Tommy raced to escape the pandemonium.

Reaching for the large glass lobby doors, he was tackled by John Smith, the leather satchel wrapping around them both as they fell to the marble floor. Tommy swung the butt of Colt Woodsman handgun down onto John Smith's head. John Smith went limp and withered to the floor. As he was untangling the leather bag, the second envelope slipped out of Tommy's pocket, drifting down and landing atop John Smith's now motionless body. More shots rang out and the marble floor splintered as the bullets ricocheted around him. Leaving the second envelope behind, Tommy began pushing his way through the glass entrance doors. More shots and the glass doors shattered, leaving Tommy holding its unhindered oversized brass handle as he ran from the Marriott's lobby. Dropping the heavy piece of brass, Tommy sprinted down the steps toward Sukhumvit.

He glanced back to see Aslan running over the broken glass of the lobby door behind him, carrying one of the envelopes. His computer bag bouncing against his side, Aslan turned the opposite direction. Another look back revealed Steve exiting the door, turning toward Sukhumvit. Tommy tried to pick up his pace, but he was a long distance runner, never training for speed. Not to mention his flip-flops were difficult to sprint in. Steve began gaining on him.

"Fast for a little man," Tommy quietly panted to himself as he ran toward Sukhumvit.

Rounding the corner, he began sprinting up Sukhumvit, weaving through a maze of pedestrians, and realized that it might not be prudent in Bangkok to be running away from the scene of a crime with a weapon in his hand. Without stopping, he slipped the Colt Woodsman into the leather satchel hanging from his shoulder.

"Mr. Luck! Stop!" a man's voice screamed above the city noises.

Sprinting up the street, Tommy cursed himself for running that morning and not wearing running shoes instead of flip flops to the delivery. His legs began to burn and his pace was rapidly deteriorating.

The man's voice again echoed from behind. "Mr. Luck, I'm a friend!"

Turning his head, Tommy glanced back again and could clearly see Steve catching up. Steve did not have a weapon in his hand, and Tommy realized that there was no way he was going to outrun him. Rounding the corner onto Soi Eight, Tommy stopped and reached into the leather bag, gripping the Colt Woodsman. Steve nearly ran into him as he turned onto the Soi.

"Mr. Luck." He abruptly stopped in front of Tommy, wheezing. "I'm a friend."

"You just shot at me," Tommy panted back, somewhat shocked at how small in stature Steve was in person. He knew Steve was short but he had always seen him either sitting down or next to Becky, who wasn't a tall woman. With sweat bristling from his thick dark hair and his small beady eyes looking up, Tommy grasped the fact that Steve could not have been any taller than five foot.

"I had several clear shots but never fired at you," Steve said, quickly regaining his breath. "Let's keep walking. They'll soon be following."

"So tell me about this friend claim," Tommy asked as he and Steve strode up the Soi, passing several small bars and restaurants.

"I work for the NSA. I've infiltrated the organization you're working for, and I'm trying to gather information on the top players."

Pulling Steve into a small pub with bargirls clad in skimpy bikinis dancing next to brass poles on small round raised platforms, Tommy studied him. "You work for the NSA? Infiltrated an organization?"

Some eighties hip hop song was blaring from cheap speakers into the nearly empty bar that smelled of mildew and stale beer.

"Yes, the National Security Agency," Steve answered as Tommy pushed him toward the bar's well-worn counter.

Over the din of tinny music, Tommy ordered two Singha beers while holding two fingers up to the bartender to ensure there was no mistake as to the number. "How do you know I'm not a member of this organization?"

"I helped them select you," Steve confessed. "I know you knew nothing of the legality of the delivery."

"You helped them select me? Thanks a fucking lot. I should use the handgun in this bag to shoot your ass as a sign of my appreciation," Tommy growled, while patting the leather satchel hanging across his shoulder.

Steve held out his hand. "Speaking of the bag, can I see it?"

Slipping it from his shoulder, Tommy handed the leather satchel over. The bartender delivered two ice-cold beers, and Tommy took a long drink. Steve reached inside and pulled a small electronic device out from under the wide leather flap.

"Another GPS locator? What is it with you guys and GPS locators?"

"We find them useful."

Taking the leather satchel and GPS locator back from Steve, Tommy walked over to a young man standing near the entrance of the bar. He quietly spoke to the young man and then handed him the GPS device with a thousand baht bill. The young man disappeared out the door.

Tommy walked back over to Steve. "Maybe that should have been the first thing we did?"

"Based on the condition of John Smith and the rest of the conspirators last time I saw them, the short delay shouldn't be a problem. Where did he go with the GPS device?"

"I told him to drop the device into the lobby of the hotel next the Monsoon Restaurant. I'm just trying to keep your boss on his toes. The fact that I'm still registered there will add some amusing confusion—at least from my perspective."

"John Smith is pretty upset with you, and he is a very dangerous man."

Ignoring his comment, Tommy asked, "All right, what do you want from me? You know I'm not a part of this conspiracy and, in good faith, I tried to accomplish my end of this delivery deal—sort of, anyway—which is what John Smith wanted me to do. In the process, I nearly got killed. Now, I'd like to take my pay check and disappear for a while."

"Where's the flash-drive now?"

"About to be placed in a locker someplace in Bangkok."

Taking a short sip of beer, Steve stared up at Tommy with his beady eyes. "There were two envelopes."

"Yes, there were two. I hadn't decided who I was going to give the flash-drive to."

"You need to get the flash-drive to the Turk."

"Show me some identification. Although, based on my experience with another member of the party we just left, that's not necessarily a guarantee of your allegiance. I still want to see some ID."

"You know I don't have any NSA identification on me. I'm undercover."

"Not good enough. I want NSA identification. And then I want a ride out of this country on one of your agency's private jets. Right now that flash-drive is the only thing that is keeping me alive, and I don't plan on giving that away until I'm sure you are who you claim." After another long swig of beer Tommy said, "Give me your cell phone number."

Writing out his number on a paper napkin, Steve held it out while Tommy pulled his phone from his pocket and called Lawan.

"Bacon, are you all right?"

"I'm fine. All finished at the Marriott but there's been a change of plans," Tommy announced. "Keep the flash-drive, and I'll meet you at our pre-arranged location."

Disconnecting the call, Tommy took the napkin from Steve.

"You're not going to leave the flash-drive in the locker for the Turk?"

"I couldn't even if I wanted to, I don't know which envelope he got."

"You need to deliver the flash-drive to the Turk," Steve repeated.

"I'll give you a call in two days. I won't be a part of another one of these deliveries, and I won't meet with Aslan, but I will give the flash-drive to you with proof that you are who you say," Tommy announced before setting his half-empty beer bottle on the counter and walking out the front door, leaving Steve standing alone.

# CHAPTER 24

*Fort Meade, Maryland, 20 July 2015:*

Howard Macintyre was sitting at his desk without the customary smile on his face, even though he had just received an update from Mr. Rogers, and it would seem that the Black Fly investigation was proceeding along very nicely. There had been a few bumps in the road, several people murdered within the organization, and a shootout at a high-end hotel in Bangkok, but the overall news had been good. He knew the NSA frowned on unplanned causalities on either side and rated the success of operations in terms of a balance between stealth and results, not pure product, but Howard believed that fatalities were inevitable when dealing with such a seemingly ruthless organization. He was not concerned with the causalities. They were more than offset by the fact his investigation was getting very close to identifying the command structure of the organization. It was the command structure that worried Howard and why he had lost his habitual smile.

His worries about the organization's command structure centered on the death of Bob. He was alarmed because of who had terminated him, the reason he was terminated, and the timing of the termination. The answer to any one of those questions would have been meaningless when considered in singular form, but the three measured together had enormous implications. Bob had been eliminated by the very organization he had worked for, he was terminated because he was suspected of being a mole, and he was killed two short days after Howard had informed the inspector general that he had successfully planted an agent within the criminal organization.

Only three individuals working in the inspector general's office knew of the mole: Howard, Mr. Rogers, and the inspector general. Howard had not told anyone else of the mole, and he was sure Mr. Rogers, the mole, had not revealed the fact. That left his boss, the inspector general.

Howard's Thai intelligence counterparts had informed him of the CIAs involvement in a delivery attempt at the Bangkok Marriot. Mr. Rogers just told Howard that two other men had been working with the Turk during the delivery attempt and one had tried to kill Tommy during the melee. It didn't take Howard too many phone calls combined with a short search on one of the NSA databases to determine the man was Sid, the Bangkok CIA station chief. This presented reasonable suspicions that Sid was mixed up with organization. Mr. Rogers also revealed that the Sid had been one of the casualties during the shootout but was unaware of his condition, whether dead or alive, as he and the records of his treatment had disappeared from a local hospital.

The phone rang on Howard's desk and he dutifully answered, "Howard Macintyre, deputy inspector general."

"Mr. Macintyre, the inspector general would like to see you," Doris the secretary to the inspector general, said through the phone's speaker.

"Good morning, Doris. When would he like to see me?"

"As soon as possible, and he would like you to give him an update on something called Black Fly," she said in a tone that indicated she had no idea how significant this investigation was to the inspector general—for one of two reasons, depending on his allegiance.

Running his long freckled fingers through his red curly hair, Howard sighed. "All right, Doris, I'll be there in a few minutes."

Howard chuckled at the timing of the request for his presence and the topic to be discussed. His dark jovial mood faded as quickly as it had materialized when he considered the implications of briefing a suspected member about his headway in exposing that very same organization.

The inspector general's office oversaw multiple investigations at any given time, but his boss seemed to have an unusual interest in Black Fly. Howard had to remind himself that, under normal circumstances, it would not be surprising that the inspector general would be interested this investigation. If news of an organization working within the United States' top intelligence agency to steal corporate secrets and sell them to the highest bidder were to leak out to the general public, the implications would be profound. The inevitable outcome would be a complete restructuring of the agency in terms of authority. On the other hand, if the inspector general was somehow linked to this rogue organization, he would have an entirely different reason to have unusually high interest.

Howard took a few moments to contemplate the meeting he was about to attend. Considering his suspicions, he needed to decide how much to tell the inspector general. What truths might harm the investigation and, in the event the man was involved with the criminal organization, what mistruths would be helpful? Certainly the wrong answer to one of the inspector general's questions could put Howard in a preverbal corner for future questions.

Howard had become good at lying over the years. It was a required professional trait working at the NSA, and he had nurtured the talent. It was time to put that skill to the test against a man who had spent many more years than Howard working at the NSA, honing that very same talent.

As he pondered his dilemma, Howard realized that he could not give a suspected member of the organization his best lead, John Smith. He needed to keep the organization's delivery manager and his best link to the upper level members a secret. Howard also reckoned his suspicions concerning Sid, the Bangkok CIA station chief, might best be kept a secret until he could figure out the inspector general's allegiance. In fact, if the inspector general was involved, he might know whether Sid was dead or alive, and Howard contemplated for a moment how he might prod Sid's condition from his boss.

Taking the elevator to the sixth floor, Howard considered what he should do to ensure that the information he passed at the meeting would both keep his investigation safe and also create an opportunity to bring it to a successful end, if, in fact, the inspector general was complicit. Stepping out into the executive suites lobby and turning down the hallway leading to his boss' office, he passed the receptionist without a gesture or word. The young woman looked as if she had been snubbed by his disregard.

Doris met him at the door with a smile. "The inspector general is waiting. Thank you for coming so quickly."

Howard nodded to Doris as he entered the office, the door closing behind him with a faint click.

"Good morning, sir." Howard wondered, as he greeted his boss, how the inspector general would take the news of all the chaos in Bangkok.

The inspector general sat silently, watching him, weaving an un-lit cigarette through the fingers of his right hand, his head and shoulders once again dwarfed by both the size of the desk and computer monitor mounted on top. Howard felt as if he was an elf, readying himself for a reprimand by Santa Claus.

"Tell me what I need to know," the inspector general asked in what appeared to be unusually somber mood, making his Santa-like ruddy face and white hair seem that much more imposing, considering Howard's suspicions. "I want to know about the Black Fly investigation. I hear there have been some problems."

"Overall the news is very good, but it has not been without difficulties, causing some problems in our relationship with our clandestine counterparts in Thailand," Howard confessed as he sat down in one of the leather chairs positioned in front of the inspector general's desk. Firmly placing his feet on the plush carpet, Howard attempted to counter the slick leather seat cushion.

"Tell me what I need to know," his boss repeated.

"Three deaths have occurred: a low level operative of the organization, a civilian apparently used for coordinating the bidding process and deliveries, and a member of the CIA stationed in Bangkok. Tommy Luck, the organization's less-than-reputable deliveryman, has continued to create complexities in the delivery by continuing to elude his employer. During a delivery attempt, there was a shootout at a high-end hotel in downtown Bangkok. The hotel was where one of the deaths occurred—the CIA agent," Howard replied, nervously shifting in the chair.

"How do you know he was a CIA agent?"

"Our Thai intelligence agency counterparts discovered his identity when processing the body. I've asked them to keep that bit of information under-wraps until we can sort this out."

"What have we learned about the organization?" the inspector general asked, rocking back in his chair.

"We have identified four organization operatives working this delivery, several who are now dead. We know there are at least two additional people within the organization, maybe three or four at the outside. Those two to four people are our focus of effort. They are the ones using the NSA assets to steal the information and the organization's leaders. The personnel we have identified are the operatives that oversee the delivery of the goods."

"Who were the causalities?" the inspector general asked emotionlessly.

Howard opened a small notebook containing his notes from his recent conversation with Mr. Rogers. "One was a young man who was an operative for the organization, a former analyst."

"He was your mole," the inspector general declared.

Howard's eyes shot up to inspector general's. Mr. Rogers had told Howard that Bob had been terminated because it was thought he was the mole. The inspector general coming to that conclusion without any substantiating information supported Howard's suspicions of his complicity.

"He was," Howard lied, forcing a smile.

"What will you do now without a mole?" the inspector general asked, turning in his chair and looking out his office's narrow floor-to-ceiling window at the NSA grounds below.

It was a windy afternoon and, from his vantage point, Howard could only see the tops of distant oaks swaying back and forth through the window. "We are working with our Thai counterparts, and I have been considering bringing in the Bangkok CIA station chief," Howard said, watching for his boss's reaction.

The inspector general raised his white eyebrows at the news. "If things are getting this out of control in Bangkok, and the CIA is showing up at the delivery sites, then we *need* to bring them in. Under normal circumstances, we wouldn't want the other agencies to find out about our little problem and investigation, but it will reflect like a cover up, at this point, if we do not." He was silent for a moment and then continued, "If the CIA was involved with the shootout during the delivery then they are probably investigating something closely related. Bring in only the station chief. Try to impress on him the need to keep this internal to between the two of you. Tell him everything you know."

"Yes, sir," Howard responded, noting that either the inspector general did not know of Sid's injury or death—or that the Inspector General knew that Sid was still alive and in good health.

"Who are the other people that have been killed?" the inspector general asked.

"A gentleman named Carl, a former travel agent, who has been working with the organization for some time. He was the bid coordinator and was apparently offering the merchandise to two or three different clients. We believe that one of the clients caught on to his plan and disposed of him. And the CIA man killed at the hotel shootout, a low-level agent recently assigned to the Bangkok office."

"The question is, what does the CIA know and where did they get their information concerning the delivery? We need to bring them in so we can combine our investigations and information. But only the station chief. No one else is to know. Now talk to me about the hotel shootout."

"It occurred at the Marriott a couple of hours ago between several players, to include Tommy Luck and two organization members. There was also a Turk and three Thais, as well as a CIA agent. Tommy Luck was to pass the location of the flash-drive to the client, but apparently there was a disagreement over who the merchandise was to be delivered to. As I said, it is believed that Carl had attempted to make a little extra cash, but with the wrong gentleman. This guy didn't appreciate being duped. In the end, both the organization's client and one of the individuals who had been shaken down by Carl arrived at the hotel, which was what spurred a reenactment of a Tombstone street battle. The CIA agent was shot through the abdomen and fell from a second floor balcony. Tommy Luck escaped the bedlam without injury and, once again, disappeared." Howard left out the John Smith's cracked skull and the CIA station chief's participation and suspected part in the commotion, as well as his being shot, followed by his strange disappearance.

"Without your mole, where are you getting this information?"

"The last conversation with my mole before his untimely death, witness statements given to the Royal Thai Police after the shootout, Thai intelligence. I pieced it all together through multiple sources of information," Howard lied.

The inspector general sat silently for a moment then turned to look at Howard. "Who are the identified organizational members?"

Howard hesitated as he suddenly realized that he had unintentionally told the inspector general that there were four organization members he had identified but if he were to leave John Smith's name off the list, he had only three. He was now in the proverbial corner he had hoped to avoid.

"Bob, a low level member but who is now dead; a woman named Becky, who works in the human intelligence verification department; A man named Steve, who seems to be the operational leader, another HumInt Verification member; and finally Carl, the former travel agent, but killed by what we believe was an unhappy client."

The inspector general frowned at Howard. "You are including your mole as a member of the organization?"

"Sorry, sir, my mistake. We only have three organization member names."

"Three names, one of which is dead, is not great progress from my perspective," the inspector general stated as he began tapping the filter of the cigarette on the top of the desk. "I thought you said things were going well?"

Howard was surprised that the inspector general let his mistake of including Bob as an organization member go without an additional challenge.

"I believe we're on the verge of getting a break. All the causalities must have taken a toll on the organization, and they are surely feeling the pressure. Not to mention the strain that Tommy Luck has created with his unpredictable behavior. The possibility of them making a mistake and imploding is a reality," Howard responded, fidgeting in his chair.

All he wanted to do was to get out of the inspector general's office and consider the implications of his boss being a part of the organization Howard was attempting to expose. He needed time to think about all he had learned in his conversation with Mr. Rogers and during this meeting.

The inspector general waved his hand toward the door, dismissing Howard. While a dismissal of this type was very unusual, Howard was happy to escape. He stood up without saying a word and left the office, closing the door behind him. As he walked from the office, Howard considered the inspector general's summation that Bob had had been terminated for being a mole. Howard had only learned of the reason behind the termination thirty minutes before, during his conversation with Mr. Rogers. Was this leap in logic a result of his long-developed experience as the inspector general or because of prior knowledge? While not definite proof, it did support Howard's theory that the inspector general was involved.

Riding the elevator, Howard considered his boss's guidance concerning the CIA station chief. His advice would have been the answer Howard would have expected if the inspector general was involved with the organization and knew of the station chief's connection to the client and organization. What better way to stay one step ahead of an investigation than to have a direct line to the investigator. On the other hand, he had acted as if he knew nothing of the station chief being a casualty at the hotel shootout. If the inspector general and the station chief were both members of the organization, then Sid's injury or death would have been known and the inspector general's answers likely tainted by that information—or the station chief was still alive and wasn't hurt badly enough to preclude his continued participation in the delivery.

Finally, while walking from the elevators to his office, Howard considered why the inspector general had given him an obvious pass concerning his count and names of the organization members. His boss knew Howard to be a very detail-oriented manager who would never make such a simple mistake by including the mole in the list of organization names, but the inspector general had not challenged him. Howard wondered if the inspector general suspected him of withholding or distorting the information and knew of Howard's suspicions.

It would be a long afternoon as Howard tried to sort out the facts and make a plan to prove or disprove the inspector general's complicity.

# CHAPTER 25

*Baltimore, Maryland, 3 June 2012:*

It was a hot afternoon as Tommy stepped from the portable office onto the dusty grounds of the construction site. He could smell the musty aroma of Chesapeake Bay mix with that of traffic racing along the elevated I-95. The sound of men yelling, spinning tires, and sea gulls combined into the rhythmic tune of a waterside city construction site. Making his way to the skeletal structure of the thirty-story building, his assistant Mick took up pace next to Tommy.

"You think you can give me a ride down to Glen Burnie this evening? My kid's going to some birthday party there and the wife wants me to attend."

"Where's your car?"

"Back in the shop. That transmission has been a problem for months, and I'm finally having it replaced."

Stepping up to the elevator cage, Tommy nodded. "Sure. What time do we need to leave?"

"If we get out of here by seven, I make the cake and candles."

"Seven, it is."

The day seemed to move by quickly and, at four o'clock, Tommy pulled a bottle of Jamison Whiskey from the side drawer of his desk for his traditional first drink. By six o'clock, Tommy was incapable of making any sound decisions, but his workers knew that and avoided asking anything difficult.

Just after six o'clock, Tommy stumbled into his truck and drove off, leaving the construction site for the evening.

The next morning at four o'clock, as Tommy was showering, he remembered that he was supposed to give Nick a ride to Glen Burnie the night before, but had forgotten. Taking his cell phone from a small table beside his bed, Tommy tried calling Nick. Nick's phone was off, which was unusual. Tommy had called him earlier in the morning many times, and Nick had answered each and every time.

Driving to the construction site, Tommy parked his pickup in front of the portable office. Several of the crew had arrived and were huddled near a mobile food truck selling coffee. Tommy stepped up the wood plank stairs that led to his office and began unlocking the door. One of the men began jogging toward Tommy, waving to him.

Turning, Tommy called out, "What is it?"

The man came to a panting stop at the bottom of the stairs and wiped his brow with the back of his hand. "Did you hear about Nick?"

"No, what's up with Nick?"

"He, his wife, and child were killed in a car accident last night."

Tommy blinked several times, trying to absorb the news. "Where?"

"His car's in the shop so his wife came up to pick him up. I guess they were all going to some party but were late. Just as they pulled onto I-95, a sixteen wheeler hit their car. The entire car was tossed off the elevated highway not two blocks from here. Apparently it was quite a mess."

"And they're all dead?"

"Nick died at the hospital. The wife and kid were killed instantly."

# CHAPTER 26

*Bangkok, Thailand, 20 July 2015:*

Tommy and Lawan boarded the first-class bus bound for Kohn Kaen at nine o'clock that evening. A first-class bus trip in Thailand reminded Tommy of a flight with a budget air carrier. The bus had a stewardess, providing snacks and drinks, as well as pillows and blankets. And, as on an airliner, the passengers rode in plush oversized seats that reclined.

The bus traveled from Bangkok up to the Khorat Plateau, on which greater Isaan was located. Peering through a white-lace-curtained window that dripped condensation, Tommy watched the scenery turn from lowland farms to mountain jungles as they climbed the ridgeline to the plateau, all shrouded by a moonless night. An occasional car converging from the opposite direction illuminated the surrounding landscape. Once on the top of the plateau, the palm-tree laden jungles gave way to rice paddies surrounded by tall willowing plants with yellow flowers and silver barked trees with wide green leaves.

The bus's air-conditioning forced Lawan to curl up under a thin blue blanket to escape the cool breeze. They passed through the city of Nakhon Ratchasima around midnight. Its city lights and crowded roads provided a colorful break to the dark ride. An occasional downpour beat the roof of the bus as it lumbered along the highway, lulling Lawan into a deep slumber. Tommy remained awake, plagued by a memory of the night he forgot about his deal with Nick.

Tommy had been drunk when he left the construction site the evening and did not remember he was supposed to deliver Nick to the birthday party. As the news spread across the site that day, Tommy would learn that without the agreed upon ride to Glen Burnie, Nick had called his wife and asked her to pick him up. It was a seemingly innocent mistake, but the guilt burned like a hot coal in his belly. Had he taken Nick to the party, the family of three would not have perished. If Tommy had not been drinking, Nick, his wife, and daughter would have enjoyed the birthday party. Nick would have been at work the next morning.

That evening, Tommy pulled the bottle of Jamison from his desk and filled a large glass. Taking huge swallows of the whiskey, he wrote out his resignation. Tommy Luck flew to Thailand the following week to try and come to terms with the guilt brought about by the number of deaths of those in his charge that had been growing for years. Unfortunately, the only thing Tommy found halfway across the globe was the bottom of a lot more bottles of whiskey.

# CHAPTER 27

*Kohn Kaen, Thailand, 21 July 2015*:

Eight hours into their journey, Tommy and Lawan's bus arrived on the outskirts of *Kohn Kaen*. With the sun beginning to peek over the horizon, Tommy could make out hazy and twinkling lights above the tops of tight copses of foliage. An open area, between the thick groves of trees, provided a glimpse to the breadth of the city.

As the first buildings began appearing on the sides of the road, Tommy considered his decision to come to this city. Few tourists ventured to *Kohn Kaen*. On the other hand, a fairly robust expatriate population, whose loyalty was simply a question of one's skin color and native language, inhabited the city. From Tommy's perspective *Kohn Kaen* held the perfect size population of fair-skinned foreigners. As a *farang*, you could chose to stand out as one of the few or mingle in as one of many.

The home grounds of an opponent might seem a strange choice to most, but it made sense to Tommy. While not the winning bidder, Jainukul hadn't let the flash-drive go without a fight. The fight now over, in Tommy's opinion, Jainukul would have two choices after the incident at the Marriot and the disappearance of the flash-drive and deliveryman—remain in Bangkok or come back to *Kohn Kaen*. Given those options, Tommy was betting on Jainukul coming home.

Several skyscrapers, most of which were hotels, dotted the city's five and six-story water-stained building skyline. The streets were busy with colorfully painted Tuk-Tuks—Thailand's cheap three-wheeled taxis that derived their name from the sound their original two-stroke engines made—carrying passengers to and fro in the coolness of the morning. Prompted by the impending stifling heat of the day, the city's business owners preferred those early morning hours to complete tasks that would otherwise have to be conducted during the blistering hot afternoon.

From the bus station, Tommy and Lawan took a Tuk-Tuk to the Kosa Hotel, tucked away between the larger Pullman and *Charoen Thani* in the downtown section of *Kohn Kaen*. The Kosa, twelve stories high, was dwarfed by the Pullman Hotel, two blocks away, and the *Charoen Thani*, across the street. While Lawan checked-in, Tommy headed for a nearby Seven-Eleven to get something to eat. After munching down a Thai pastry filled with sweet and spicy pork, he headed back to the room in an unusual sober state.

As he stepped through the room's door, he was met with a slight mildew smell that was common in the tropical climate and one that would dissipate as the air-conditioning cooled and removed the humidity. The room resembled that of a typical twenty-year-old hotel in the States, with the furniture still being serviceable but the décor lacking a modern touch. With Lawan asleep on the king size bed, Tommy looked into the room's small refrigerator to inspect the beer stock, finally deciding he was too tired to drink.

Several hours of lying on the bed in a failed attempt to sleep, thinking about what they should do next, Tommy began his daily ritual run. Three hours at a slow jog out into the rice paddies just beyond the city limits cleared his head, giving him an opportunity to consider his next move with John Smith. After a cool shower and, with Lawan sitting on the bed watching a Thai television program, Tommy pulled a laptop computer from his bag.

"What are you doing, Bacon?"

"It's about time we looked to see what's on this flash-drive."

"Is that a good idea, my love?" Lawan asked while staring at the laptop screen as the Microsoft logo appeared.

"It probably wasn't a good idea yesterday, but it seems like a great idea today. I want to look and see what has been causing all this drama and violence."

Taking the flash-drive from around his neck, he slipped it into one of the computer's USB ports and double clicked on the computer files icon. Selecting the removable disk icon, the computer showed that there were three files on the flash-drive, two of which were very large. When Tommy selected the smallest file and double clicked, a small window appeared asking for a password. Then he selected one of the larger files and double clicked and another window appeared indicating that the laptop needed a program unavailable on his computer to open it. A quick web search with the help of some Microsoft program for the proper software to open the file proved futile. The second large file provided the same message as the first.

Tommy sighed. "The smallest file is asking for a password. It's likely the execution program for the other two files. I can't get into the other two files. There's something on this flash-drive, but we can't open it."

Lawan sat silent for a moment before softly saying, "I know a man," while looking at the computer screen.

Looking over at her, Tommy shrugged his shoulders.

"I know a man that can maybe help us," Lawan said as she looked from the computer up at Tommy.

"What do you mean?"

"I know a man you would call a...hacker?"

"Where?"

"Kalasin."

Tommy knew Kalasin to be a small city about fifty miles east of Kohn Kaen and the largest population center near the village where Lawan had grown up.

Leaving the room and finding a nearby car rental shop,

Tommy and Lawan leased a small blue pickup. The drive to
Kalasin took them through the heart of the Isaan rice country.
Rising from the river basin on which Kohn Kaen was situated,
the road was a fairly well maintained four-lane highway. As
Tommy drove the pickup along the wide highway, the river
basin terrain gave way to large open pastures with tall scrawny
brown cows and short fat black water buffaloes grazing on
bright green grass.

Tommy could remember making this trip several times
when the grass was brown from lack of water. They passed
several large shallow lakes, dotted with fresh water shrimp
stands made of bamboo advertising their stock to passing cars
and trucks. Beyond the lakes and pastures, and accessed by
hundreds of roads and trails sprouting from the highway,
Tommy could see countless rice farms peeking through breaks
in the thick foliage. Forty five minutes later the roadside rice
farms began to give way to more and more buildings as they
approached the outskirts of Kalasin.

# CHAPTER 28

*Kalasin, Thailand, 21 July 2015:*

Kalasin was a small city of two and three-story buildings located between thousands of small villages that farmed rice. Tommy knew that the area's poor soil was not favored agriculturally, however sticky rice, the staple food of the region which requires poorly drained soil, thrived during the monsoon season when fields could be flooded from nearby streams, rivers and ponds.

Directed by Lawan, Tommy maneuvered the small pickup through the narrow city streets, dodging countless families mounted on scooters and late model faded pickup trucks. It always amazed Tommy how, with their low regard for standard traffic rules, the Thais seemed to negotiate the disorder in an orderly fashion. Lawan directed Tommy to pull up in front of a small store with large windows darkened by age on a side street. As they pushed through a glass front door, with ancient cracked and peeling tinting, a tone sounded from a speaker mounted in the back of the shop, announcing their arrival.

As if stepping into the future from primeval streets and store's dated façade, the walls of the shop were stacked with new and refurbished laptops, computer towers, and every type of electric device that could be found in a New York City Radio Shack. Wi-Fi boxes, bundles of coaxial cable, and amplifiers stood on shelves in surprising order for this chaotic city.

Tommy became mesmerized by the inventory. A clean white tiled floor was topped with glass covered counters holding circuits, computer mother boards, hard drives, and small electronic mechanisms.

An older man with thick black glasses, holding a smoking soldering iron, looked up from one of the counters tucked away in the back of the shop. Dressed in neatly pressed jeans, and a green and red plaid short-sleeve shirt, the man was probably close to Tommy's age, but between the weather and the hard life offered in Kalasin he had prematurely aged, looking more like sixty something.

Lawan approached the man, leaving Tommy gazing that the various electronic supplies stacked on the shelves and locked away under the glass counters. The shopkeeper smiled when he saw her and they immediately began chattering with one and other in their native language. Through their discussion, a background converse to his inspection of the shop's merchandize, Tommy gathered that the two hailed from same village, where many of their relatives still lived and worked.

In the midst of his exploration of the store, Tommy pulled the flash-drive from around his neck and absently placed it on the counter in front of the shopkeeper, letting Lawan do all the talking. After finishing up their conversation about their village's current events, Lawan began to describe the problem concerning the files contained on the flash-drive.

Largely ignoring the dialogue, Tommy found a counter that contained security cameras and motion detectors under its glass top. Next to the security cameras were old style cassette recording devices and hearing aids. Tommy quietly laughed at the shopkeeper's odd sense of organization. Continuing his examination, he saw that the next glass-enclosed counter contained electronic kits to build radios.

The shopkeeper pulled a laptop from behind the counter and plugged the flash-drive into its USB port. After confirming Lawan's description of the files and the computer's response when attempting to open them, he told her that he would need a day or two to examine the flash-drive. Lawan gave the man her cell phone number and dragged Tommy from a counter containing two way radios and small pen-shaped Dictaphone devices. As they turned to leave, Lawan told the shopkeeper that he should not discuss the flash-drive with anyone else. The shopkeeper smiled and said he understood.

# CHAPTER 29

*Kohn Kaen, Thailand, 21 July 2015*:

Returning to Kohn Kaen, Tommy felt the need for a drink. Between his dry spell the evening before and the hot trip to Kalasin, he was ready for a drink. Lawan and Tommy made their way half a block from the Kosa Hotel to the short street of Prachasumran, filled with restaurants and several expatriate watering holes. On their way, they stopped to grab a bite to eat from an old woman sitting on her haunches on the curve making *Som Tam*, or green papaya salad. With leathery hands matching her dark tan face, the woman crushed and mixed the ingredients inside a large clay pot with a wooden mallet. She then poured the salad into a small clear plastic bag before handing over to Lawan.

Eating contents with their hands, Tommy and Lawan walked down the street, looking for a place to buy a long-overdue drink. Tommy's lips and mouth burned from the spicy mixture. Lawan seemed unaffected.

They selected a small pub called Leo's directly across the street from the Pullman Hotel, the highest structure in the city. With an enormous covered and elevated passenger drop off zone and large glass door promenade, the shiny black Pullman seemed out of place in the faded concrete city. Ordering a Jameson whiskey for himself and a beer for Lawan, they took a table looking out on to the street.

Within an hour, Tommy could feel a comfortable numbness beginning to develop on his forehead. Lawan sat patiently, watching Tommy, as he drank glass after glass of whiskey.

With the sun well past its noon apex, the heat was stifling, but Tommy felt relaxed for the first time in days. On his sixth drink, he looked over at Lawan to see her staring across the street at the Pullman Hotel.

"What're you looking at, beautiful?"

"Bacon, look," she replied, pointing over at the Pullman's large covered passenger drop off area.

Two farangs, one dark and the other short and ruddy, were stepping from a black sedan that had pulled up the lobby. Between the distance and his alcohol hindered sight, Tommy could not make out much detail.

"Who is it?"

"Aslan," Lawan said softly.

"No way!" Tommy exclaimed, nearly choking on a swallow of whiskey. "He couldn't possibly know we're here."

Lawan silently watched Aslan and the other man as they stood next to the sedan waiting for their luggage. Neither of the men looked across the street and seemed unaware that Tommy and Lawan were watching.

"Maybe he did not come because of us. The man with Aslan could be the CIA man," Lawan commented while peering at the Pullman's lobby entrance. Tommy was unsure whether her comment was a question or a statement of fact.

"I killed the CIA guy at the Marriott...Well, I know I shot him in the throat." Then after a moment, he added, "If not for us, why else would they come?"

Taking another long drink of his whiskey, he thought about the chance encounter with Aslan and possibly Sid. "My love, I need to go over to the Pullman to see what they're doing. It looks as if Aslan and whoever he is with are taking bags from the car. They're likely staying there, but they could also be meeting someone. I need to go to the lobby and see what they're doing. We also need to see if Sid has been resurrected from the dead. We can't remain on defense. We need to go on the offense if we're to get out of this mess."

"Bacon, I am Thai. You are *farang*. You standout in this city more than I—and you have had too much to drink. I will go," she stated, not as an option, but as what needed to be done.

Lawan set her beer down on their table, pushed back her chair, and walked across the street to the entrance of the hotel. Tommy could see her disappear through the large glass lobby doors. After fifteen minutes, she reappeared and walked back across the street. Her face was without emotion as she sat back down at their street front vantage point.

"Aslan is there," she stated flatly. "He is with the man who came to our hotel room to question me about Carl the other day in Bangkok—the CIA man. You did hurt his throat. It is bandaged. They are meeting with an older Thai man in the lobby. There are two younger men there, as well."

"So Sid survived the Marriott, after all. I must have just nicked him. Aslan and Sid were obviously in cahoots at the Marriott," Tommy said, thinking out loud. "It would make sense they're here together. What does the Thai man look like?"

"A flat pocked face with yellow eyes."

Tommy nodded. "That would explain why they're here in Jainukul's hometown. Aslan and Sid are here for the same reason as us, Jainukul. Sounds like Jainukul, Aslan, and Sid are teaming up. I doubt they could have found us this quickly. I just didn't think it would be this easy to find Jainukul. But in what way are they teaming up? Did Aslan or Sid see you?"

"No, their backs were to me and *pii* Jainukul has never seen me before," Lawan replied, using the *pii* to signify that the Thai person she was talking about was older.

"We need to confirm that the Thai man is Jainukul and see where he goes after their meeting."

Paying their bill, Tommy and Lawan repositioned their leased pickup on the street in front of the Pullman. Thirty minutes later, another black sedan pulled up to the raised entrance, and the Thai man and his two young employees walked out of the lobby. Tommy immediately recognized Jainukul—his wide flat face, yellow eyes, and gold chain with a Buddha medallion glimmering in the sunlight.

Jainukul and his two young employees climbed into the sedan and drove into the streets of Kohn Kaen. Tommy followed, but kept a good distance back. Slightly intoxicated and weaving through the hectic streets, Tommy silently laughed at the thought that his drunken condition might improve his driving skills in the crowded and nonsensical traffic patterns of Kohn Kaen.

Jainukul's sedan traveled south along the main highway into the outskirts of the city. The sedan then turned left off the highway and headed down a small paved road that passed through the same rice paddies Tommy had run along earlier in the day. With papaya trees lining the sides, the road eventually turned to dirt. After several miles Tommy could see a large red roof above the tree tops surrounded by an eight foot tall concrete wall, the large house's architecture seeming to be out of place in Isaan. Tommy laughed at the thought of Frank Lloyd Wright being kidnapped and forced to combine traditional Thai architecture with his own unique style—steep sloped roof lines mixed with a minimalist profile.

When Jainukul's sedan pulled up to the entrance, a guard dressed in a brown uniform opened a heavy black metal gate and the sedan pulled into the compound. As Tommy drove the pickup past the front gate he caught a glimpse of Jainukul and his two employees stepping out of the sedan near a three-step promenade that led up to a large set of carved wooden doors leading into the house.

"I was right about one thing," Tommy commented as they continued to drive down the road.

"What is it?"

"The brown uniform at the front gate—it's not a security guard, it's a policeman. He's definitely in bed with the police."

Driving past Jainukul's compound, Tommy pulled the

pickup off the road into a small recess in a jackfruit orchard. With the shade from the trees cooling the cab of the pickup, they sat in silence, watching several water buffalos feeding on grass growing around the edges of a rice paddy across the road. A hen with seven chicks trotted past the idling pickup as Tommy considered their situation. Lawan silently watched him.

"We need to find out what they're planning," Tommy announced abruptly.

"How will you do that?"

"Without knowing what they're planning, we're wasting our time. Our presence here means nothing unless we find out what they're up to. We currently have the advantage. They have no idea that we're here but that won't last forever."

"You are right. We will not have that advantage long, my love. *Pii* Jainukul has many eyes in Kohn Kaen. He will find out we are here soon."

"Then we should act quickly."

Putting the pickup in gear, Tommy drove down the road away from Jainukul's compound. Using back roads, they made their way back to the Kosa. By the time they had parked the pickup in the parking lot, the sun was down. Tommy and Lawan walked back toward the lights from the bars on Pracharumran Street and found a small bar on the corner that provided a good view of the street. Tommy began his nightly drinking ritual. Lawan began her nightly ritual of watching Tommy.

# CHAPTER 30

*Bangkok, Thailand, 21 July 2015*:

With a scowl on his face and a thin sheen of perspiration on his heavy brow, Rudolf had just returned from a night of drinking. He was slightly intoxicated stepping through the door of his dark apartment. Standing in a small foyer, Rudolf cocked his head one way and then the other, as an unusual aroma that hinted of cloves tickled his nose. It was a fragrance, really, and one that Rudolf's alcohol-saturated mind had difficulty comprehending. Finally, he decided it must be perfume of one of the evening's various tempting girls that had rubbed off on his clothes. Without turning on the lights, he slowly maneuvered around several pieces of furniture to a long black leather couch situated in front of a large picture window. As he sat down, the leather moaned faintly as it stretched and conformed to the weight of his body. The city's bright and colorful lights provided a mild visual stimulant and faint noises from the streets below—horns and cars swarming around the building—provided the partnering audio to the scene. Rudolf let out a long sigh and his shoulders slumped in defeat.

Bangkok was a good place to drink to celebrate one's victories or knock back enough alcohol to forget one's defeats. With cheap liquor and cheaper women, it was a man's paradise. While some nights were for merriment, tonight's outing had been to forget his problems—a goal which Rudolf had failed to achieve.

Four days ago, Rudolf had learned that he had lost the bid for the goods Carl had been auctioning. Considering that he had guaranteed his employer that he would get him the product, it had not been good news. But Rudolf was a salesman by trade and a resourceful person. Using skills Rudolf, had nurtured over a career, he had made an extra effort to keep Carl happy over the course of the auction with the intent of using it as leverage in the unlikely event he was out bid. Rudolf had bought Carl everything he desired and, while disgusting, it didn't surprise him the fat American enjoyed young boys. The thought of Carl fondling a young boy, or worse, disgusted Rudolf. But his job had been simply to bring his employer the merchandise and, in that endeavor, Rudolf had bought Carl an endless supply of innocent teenagers. When Rudolf had lost the bid, it became time for Carl to reciprocate for Rudolf's extra effort.

Rudolf had met with Carl three nights before at the Night Bazaar to convince him to consider a new and higher offer than that of the current winner. Ultimately Carl had agreed and gave Rudolf wire transfer instructions. While he wasn't sure how Carl was going to inform the former winner of the change in plans, a difficult job considering who that person had been, Rudolf had made it worth his while. After wiring the payment for the merchandise, Rudolf felt an immediate wave of relief and ever that more confident in his abilities. Even at the higher price, considering the flash-drive's contents, he knew his employer would be happy.

That was three days ago, and now Carl was now dead. Where was the flash-drive now? Who had eliminated Carl? Was Carl killed when he had told the first winner of the change in plans? Rudolf didn't care who had killed Carl, the problem was that he didn't know who to go to make things right. He didn't know how to retrieve the flash-drive. His employer would certainly not be happy with the turn of events and the loss of the payment.

It was late and a maze of shadows consumed the room. Except for the city lights shimmering through the window, a small red light on the automatic coffee machine in the kitchen, and the glow from an illuminated clock on the living room wall, his apartment was dark. Sitting on the long black leather couch, Rudolf was tired. An occasional bolt of lightning from a thunderstorm moving over the city added a new element to the colorful lightshow of the Bangkok skyline. Realizing there was nothing he could do about the situation, Rudolf decided to go to bed. Placing the palms of his hands on the cool leather of the couch's cushion, he prepared to stand up. He knew it would take the last of his strength to move to the bedroom.

Hearing something shift behind him, Rudolf turned to investigate, the couch's leather whispering another moan as he twisted. Shadows cloaked the source of the sound, and the strange clove smell intensified as he scanned the room. He saw nothing. With the cheap light show becoming monotonous, he once again began to push himself off the couch.

The first blow hit the back of his head, slamming his thick chin against his chest. Something cracked in his neck, and Rudolf fell back onto the couch in the sitting position. His entire body tingled as if struck by high-voltage electricity. His arms and legs did not respond when he tried to stand again. When the second blow came to the side of his head, there was disturbing grating sound in his neck and the tingling sensation disappeared. While the second blow should have knocked him over, he was still sitting upright with his head wobbling on his shoulders. He wasn't sure how he knew, but it was an American style aluminum baseball bat doing the damage. Maybe he had seen the baseball bat out of the corner of his eye, or he had felt the cool aluminum as it struck his head, or maybe he recognized the unique ping sound an aluminum bat makes with it strikes an object.

Two men appeared before him, followed by an even more powerful smell of cloves. Even with shadows cast across their faces, he could make out their unique oriental features. Not the characteristic round facial features of a Thai, but maybe that of

Vietnamese or Chinese. Rudolf realized the unusual smell came from his attackers. One of his assailants was obviously a clove cigarette consumer.

The next blow came in the form of an upper cut and he felt his oversized jaw shatter under the weight of the bat. His teeth came together so hard they too were crushed and broken bits flew from his gums.

He was now looking up at the ceiling, his head laying on the backrest of the couch. He began choking from pieces of teeth that had become lodged in his throat and, with his jaw a fleshy mess, he could not spit them out. It dawned on him that he could die from this surprise encounter, and he oddly became concerned with not being able to follow Carl's wire transfer instructions for the final payment. But then he remembered that he had already made the payment, and Carl was dead.

Rudolf slumped over onto the couch. His head bobbed limply as it struck the cushion. His body continued its downward voyage, and he rolled to the floor. He could not move anything but his eyes. He couldn't feel anything but his cheek on the carpeted floor that smelled as if it needed to be vacuumed. Rudolf could hear two voices and they weren't speaking Thai but rather Chinese—or maybe it was Vietnamese? He didn't understand why these two men had assaulted him but he wanted to.

"You die now," one of the men said in broken English. "You should not to interrupt our desires."

Rudolf did not understand. It must have been an interpretation problem. The Chinese or Vietnamese man's English was obviously not good, and Rudolf wanted to ask him to repeat what he had said. Rudolf wanted to know why he was going to die but his jaw and tongue would not work. His efforts to communicate produced nothing but guttural noises, followed by an uncontrollable gagging as the bits of teeth caused him to choke, spoiling every try.

Rudolf continued to choke as his internal gag reflex interrupted his breathing. Each of his attempts to take a deep lung full of air was cut short by another choking fit. He could feel himself begin to suffocate.

The men moved away, and he heard the front door open and then close, with a click as the lock engaged. The smell of cloves was slowly replaced with that of urine and feces as his bowels emptied onto the floor.

He wanted to reach for his cell phone and call for help, but he couldn't. His hands and arms wouldn't respond. He wanted to stand and go for help, but he couldn't. His feet and legs wouldn't answer calls to move.

Before he lost consciousness, it dawned on Rudolf that his cleaning lady only came once a week and she was not due for another four days. Rudolf wouldn't have to wait that long as it only took him four long minutes to choke to death.

# CHAPTER 31

*Dallas, Texas, 5 May 2005*:

It was a clear afternoon on a construction site in Dallas, Texas, with a bright blue sky hosting several fluffy clouds. Tommy was outlining the afternoon's projects with the foreman at the base of a forty-story building whose beams and joists stood as bare bones against the sky. The tower crane pulleys and lines whined and creaked as it began moving a large beam into place on the thirtieth floor.

Suddenly, a flurry of distant yells raised the alarm that something was amiss. Tommy's radio beeped twice before someone's voice hissed from the speaker, "Man down! Man down on the thirtieth!"

Tommy dropped the papers from his hands and sprinted toward the caged elevator attached to the side of the building. He pressed up the button and then grabbed a leather safety harness from a hook on the wall. His supervisor was at his side as the cage door dropped and the elevator slowly rose upward.

At the thirtieth floor, the elevator came to a halt and the cage door clattered up. Hooking a lead from his safety harness on to a line spanning across open skeletal structure of the building, Tommy walked along a beam toward a group of men at the edge of the building, peering outward.

"What's going on?" Tommy asked, stepping alongside the men.

Gesturing outward, one of the men replied, "Tim Greyson fell from the beam attached to the tower crane."

Looking out, Tommy saw a man dangling by his safety line with his foot wedged between the chain securing the beam to the crane's hook.

"I need a longer safety line," Tommy announced. "Get me a longer safety line."

One of the men rushed away and returned several minutes later with a long length of rope. Metal loops were attached at each end, and Tommy clipped the line to his safety harness. He then attached the rope to the line spanning the building, before releasing the shorter version.

"Tommy, what on earth are you going to do?" the foreman asked. "Let's just lower the entire beam down."

"Look at his line." Tommy pointed out to the dangling man's safety line. "It's trapped in the pulley and is frayed. Any movement of that pulley will cut the line."

Taking several steps back, Tommy sprinted to the edge of the building and bounded out onto the beam attached to the crane. The beam swayed back and forth as Tommy settled on top. Balancing against the beam's undulations, Tommy walked out until the line attaching him to the building became taut.

He stood directly over the where the man was hanging. Getting down on his hands and knees, Tommy lowered the shorter lead from his harness to the trapped man.

"Hook this into your harness," Tommy calmly told the man, who was peering up with a terrified expression.

"That line won't hold us both," the man replied, pointing to Tommy's longer safety lead. "Give me the longer line."

"It won't reach you. It's not long enough. Hook the shorter line into your harness. We'll both be attached to the longer line."

"It won't hold," the man whimpered. "It can't hold both our weight."

"We don't have a lot of options." Tommy shrugged. "Look, I'm going to cut your lead. I will attempt to stay on the beam but if we fall, we'll drop and likely swing into the floor three stories down."

"That lead won't hold."

Tommy chuckled. "Think positive."

With his eyes welling with tears, the man reluctantly clipped the smaller lead onto his harness. "Now that I'm clipped in, can't we get the crane to lower us?"

"The minute that pulley moves, you're line will be cut. Right now we're set up to swing into the floor three stories down. With the beam moving down, I'm less apt to be able to stay atop, and we have no idea where the swinging motion will take us. Just trust me."

Tommy moved to the man's frayed line and pulled a tang knife from his boot. Looking down and smiling at the dangling man, Tommy slipped the knife under the trapped lead and cut it with one swift stroke. The man fell ten feet before the line attaching him to Tommy became taut. The sudden pressure on Tommy's harness pulled them both from the beam.

The two men fell another thirty feet before the longer lead stopped their decent. As predicted, Tommy and the man swung between the exposed beams three floors down. As they arced between the floors, the longer lead broke, flinging them into the open skeletal frame of the building. Tumbling through the air, Tommy grabbed a wide joist between his arms. The edges of the joist cut into his flesh, but he hung on, abating their fall down between the beams and joists. With the joist firmly between his arms, Tommy looked down twenty-seven floors.

The man swinging below him looked up. "That was really stupid."

"That was really lucky," Tommy corrected, laughing.

# CHAPTER 32

*Kohn Kaen, Thailand, 22 July 2015*:

Waking the next morning, Tommy's tongue felt as if was covered with a thick layer of dust as he climbed from bed to find a bottle of water from the room's small refrigerator. He could hear Lawan showering in the bathroom as he fumbled with the plastic cap on the water. Once it was open, Tommy guzzled the bottle. Pulling on his running gear, he silently departed the room, knowing Lawan would realize where he had gone.

Another slow jog through the city streets and out into rice paddies surrounding Kohn Kaen began relieving Tommy of his hangover. As he jogged along the road, he recalled cutting the man from the beam thirty stories above the city. It had been a spur of the moment decision and one that had worked in the end, but as the man had said, looking up from below as Tommy clung to the beam, it had been really stupid. Later that evening over drinks at a local pub, Tommy had admitted to friends that he knew the line would break. Knowing the line was incapable of holding both their weight in a fall, Tommy had simply counted on luck.

Leaving the concrete roads, he found himself jogging through a maze of dirt roads south of the city. Bright green rice stalks shimmered and swayed over still brown water as a soft breeze blew across the paddies. Tommy ran past a slender man dressed in blue jeans and a torn yellow T-shirt leading a black water buffalo with a round silver ring piercing its nose. The man, with a dark leathery smile, nodded to Tommy as he ran by.

Coming to a long white brick wall, Tommy glanced over the top. Above a thicket of trees filled with gleaming foliage, he could see the high red roof of a Buddhist temple. Passing the entrance, Tommy caught a glimpse of a row of small cardboard boxes crowding the parameter of the temple grounds. Filled with candles, string, sand, and food, Tommy knew boxes were the remains of ceremonies bolstering luck and warding off evil. Chickens, cats, and dogs wandered through the grounds, all seeming peaceful and content with each other's presence.

Eventually, Tommy looped around and found himself back in the city, trudging down the hard-topped streets, dodging cars, bicycles, and other pedestrians. His daily jog had proven a good place to ponder his next move, and he knew exactly how to find out what Jainukul, Aslan, and Sid were up to.

Entering the room, Tommy found Lawan was sitting on the bed, talking on her cell phone. She smiled and her eyes sparkled as he stripped off his T-shirt and stepped into the bathroom. After a long hot shower that further eased the effects of his hangover, Tommy and Lawan left the hotel and travelled back to Kalasin in their leased pickup.

# CHAPTER 33

*Kalasin, Thailand, 22 July 2015:*

Arriving in Kalasin, Tommy maneuvered the pickup through the nonsensical traffic back to the electronics shop they had visited the day before. The shopkeeper, again busy with his soldering iron behind the same glass topped counter at the rear of the store, looked up when the tone announced their arrival. He smiled when he saw Lawan step through the door.

"I have not finished with the flash-drive yet," he called out as they approached.

"We're not here for the flash-drive," Tommy responded in Isaan. "We need to purchase some items. We need microphones and maybe a camera—small ones, the type that are difficult to find. With all this electronic gear, you must have something that we can use."

When the man looked startled, Tommy realized that he had let Lawan do all the talking during their first visit, and the shopkeeper was surprised to find that he could speak Isaan.

"You speak the language well," the shopkeeper said.

"I have a good teacher." Tommy looked at Lawan, who smiled at the compliment.

After Tommy described his needs, the shopkeeper scurried around the store selecting items and setting several small boxes on the counter. Tommy ended up with three discrete combined-wireless-camera-and-audio devices that could transmit up to seven hundred feet, and a receiver that plugged into the USB port on a computer. They left the store with the new surveillance gear and a promise from the shopkeeper that he would finished with the flash-drive by the next day.

No sooner had they sat down in the pickup when Lawan stated, "You will have to put the cameras someplace they will meet. That will be very dangerous."

"I'm thinking I'm going to have to enter more than just one place. If you haven't noticed, things are pretty dangerous right now, anyway. We need to find what they're up to and what their intentions are. Only then, can we figure a way out of this mess."

"Why not call Steve, the NSA man?"

"Eventually, I will call Steve, but he wants me to deliver the flash-drive and, if I do, we will be left with nothing to keep us safe. They have to keep me alive until the flash-drive is in the hands of John Smith's client. And what if Steve is not who he says he is? What if he and John Smith's intentions are one in the same? He claims to be a mole for the NSA but could offer no proof. Even if the NSA were to take me back to the United States, there is still the problem of John Smith. He doesn't strike me as the sort to let bygones go and certainly not a bygone that can identify him."

Lawan sat silent for a moment before asking, "Where will you put the cameras?"

"For starters in Sid's hotel room."

"How will you know where to place it? You have never been inside his room."

"I'll have to figure that out when I get inside. Look, this may be as simple as delivering the flash-drive to Jainukul or Aslan, but we'll not know until we hear what they're planning."

Lawan became silent. She knew from experience that once Tommy made up his mind, there was no changing it.

# CHAPTER 34

*Kohn Kaen, Thailand, 22 July 2015:*

Returning to Kohn Kaen, Tommy went inside the Pullman Hotel and paid the receptionist five hundred baht, or roughly fifteen dollars, for Sid's room number. Tommy knew that greasing hands with a little cash was tradition in Thailand and no one thought twice about the morality of such a transaction. From Tommy's perspective, the tradition was all right, as long as you understood the rules upfront. When Tommy saw Sid's key in the slot behind the receptionist he knew the CIA station chief was out.

After riding the elevator to sixth floor, Tommy paid a nearby maid another five hundred baht to borrow her pass key for several minutes while he entered Sid's room. While this was not tradition in Thailand, entering someone's private domicile without permission crossed the Thai morality line, Tommy knew that cash was a formidable temptation to any low-paid employee across the globe.

Once inside, finding a place for the camera and audio device was easy. There was a small kitchenette in one corner of the Sid's hotel room that offered numerous options. Tommy ended up placing the camera-and-audio device on top of the overhead kitchen cabinet with a small scrap of paper under the rear of the mechanism to cant the lens downward. He called Lawan on his cell phone. She was sitting in the back of Leo's bar with Tommy's laptop and the USB receiver. She guided him in the placement, so the camera showed the bulk of the room. He quickly departed, giving the maid her key back, and rejoined Lawan at the table in Leo's. Tommy smiled when he saw that she had ordered a fresh Jameson on the rocks.

Several drinks later, they watched Aslan and Sid walk by the bar and cross the street to the Pullman Hotel. Sid, with a bright white bandage on the left side of his neck, was carrying a brown plastic Seven-Eleven bag and Aslan had his computer bag strapped over his shoulder. Looking at Lawan, Tommy opened the laptop, and, after he clicked the camera-and-audio device icon, a window appeared, showing the interior of Sid's room. Tommy then plugged a set of ear phones into the side of the laptop and handed one of the ear buds to Lawan. Five minutes later, the sound coming from the ear phones indicated someone was entering Sid's room.

"How did you know that they would go into the CIA man's room?" Lawan asked, having wagered the two would venture into Aslan's room first.

"You weren't at the Marriott when all the shooting started. Sid is in control."

"You did not tell me that!" Lawan giggled, pushing at Tommy's shoulder. "That is not fair!"

"Shh—they're coming into the room."

They could hear the soft squeal of the door opening and the shuffling of feet, before the monitor showed a grainy black and white picture of Sid and then Aslan entering the room. The receiver couldn't keep up with the video feed and missed some of the men's movements, creating a choppy visual appearance on the computer screen.

On the other hand, the audio feed picked up even the faintest of sounds and came through the ear phones with crystal clear clarity.

Aslan sat down on a chair next to a small round table on one side of the room, setting his laptop bag on the floor next to his feet. Sid, with his contrasting dark eyebrows and silver hair clearly seen on the screen, entered the kitchenette with his brown Seven-Eleven bag, disappearing beneath the camera's view.

"What time do we meet with Jainukul?" Aslan asked in his heavy Turkish accent.

"Tomorrow at noon," Sid replied dryly.

"What are we going to do with Tommy? He knows that flash-drive is the only thing keeping him alive—he might not give it up that easy, and I must present it to my people in five days," Aslan declared.

"Your people are the least of our worries. It's Jainukul that I worry about. He's a ruthless man. If he gets a hold of Luck, he'll get the flash-drive, and there's a better-than-even chance we'll get nothing. On the other hand, if I were Luck, I'd give it up pronto, knowing what Jainukul will do to him if he doesn't."

Tommy could tell by the volume of Sid's voice on the laptop that the CIA station chief was very close to the hidden microphone.

"You don't know my people. They are as wicked as Jainukul, and maybe more so."

"Your people are not my problem," Sid replied, coming back into view of the camera carrying a can and sitting down across from Aslan. The camera feed was too grainy to make out the label on can in Sid's hand.

"You will be concerned with my people if we do not obtain the flash-drive."

"Let's deal with the closest danger first, that would be Jainukul. Tomorrow, we must be careful. Right now, we have two things going for us. The first is the threat that your people will retaliate if we disappear. The other is that the new coordinator claims to be able to set up another delivery," Sid countered. "We really have no idea how Jainukul will handle our truce. We'll go to Jainukul's estate and see what he says, but we can't trust him. He did kill Carl, which made no sense, making the delivery that much more complex."

Sid pulled a tab on the top of the can in his hand and the microphone picked up the faint hiss of pressure being released. Tommy surmised that Sid was holding a cold can of beer.

Aslan shrugged. "Complex for us, not him. It was to his advantage that Carl was out of the equation. He is very smart and has no conscience."

"That may be true, but we can't just rely on the threat of your people. We must be prepared for anything. We must impress on him that he needs us as badly as we need him. Have you contacted your people concerning the deal offered by Jainukul?"

"Yes, I should hear back from them this evening and find out if it is acceptable." Aslan sat quietly for a moment before continuing. "We should not go to his estate. It is his ground and it will be behind closed doors. Let us meet him in a public area."

"No, we've already agreed to his estate. Changing the location now will make Jainukul suspect we are not planning on honoring the truce. We must go to his estate as we have agreed. We do have something to offer to the partnership. Jainukul may not find Tommy and he knows it, and we still have an opportunity to set up a new delivery."

"I don't like it." Picking up his laptop, Aslan stood up and walked to the door. "He is a criminal and immoral."

"We are all criminals and criminals are inherently immoral," Sid grunted. "At the meeting we need to make it clear that the ball is in our court. We are arranging another delivery."

Looking back, Aslan nodded. "You are maybe right, but if we don't obtain the flash-drive, we will be dead, regardless of who pulls the trigger." He closed the door behind him as he left the room.

"No, only you, my friend," Sid grumbled after the door snapped shut.

Moving over to the bed carrying the can, Sid turned the television on, the camera's position only allowing Tommy and Lawan to see his dangling feet.

Pulling the bud from his ear, Tommy closed the laptop and looked over at Lawan. She was gazing back at him, with the other ear bud in her hand, looking as if she was trying to make sense of what they had said.

Tommy took a long drink from his glass of Jameson. "What do you think?"

"I don't think I understand. They are working with Jainukul, but Jainukul has all the information. Why would Jainukul not just pursue us himself and take the flash-drive?"

"Two things, one Aslan and Sid are still expecting another delivery, and whoever Aslan works for is a formidable force. There's no guarantee that Jainukul can find us, and Aslan's employer must be a big threat to Jainukul or paying him a lot of money—or both." Tommy paused to think. "Maybe that's what Sid meant by the 'deal.' Aslan is to hear back from his employer this evening. We need to find out who Aslan works for. That maybe is the key to dislodging ourselves from this tangle of vying forces."

"How do we find out who he works for?" Lawan asked.

"That's easy, we borrow his laptop."

"But he always has his laptop with him. When would we have an opportunity to take it?"

"While it's on him, of course."

"You make no sense."

As they were making their way back to the Kosa Hotel along the busy street, Lawan's phone rang. She answered and, after a moment of listening to whoever was talking on the other end, she stopped walking and looked at Tommy. "My friend in Kalasin has opened the program. It is…how do you say?…a sickness. A bad sickness. He wants to talk with us."

# CHAPTER 35

*Kalasin, Thailand, 22 July 2015:*

It took forty-five minutes for Tommy and Lawan to make it back to Kalasin for the second time that day. Sitting at a desk at the rear of the shop typing into the keyboard attached to a computer tower, the shopkeeper turned his head when the tone sounded above him, alerting him of visitors. With a thin line of smoke rising from a smoldering cigarette in an ashtray next to the keyboard, he didn't smile at Lawan as they walked toward his counter.

"It is a virus," he stated when they stepped up to the counter. "One file is an execution file written a standard computer language, another is instructions for a language I am unfamiliar with, and the last is the virus written in the unknown language. The execution program instructs two largest files to download separately onto that host computer, passing the security filters as two harmless unexecuted files. The execution file then passes through the security filters as nothing but a sequence of numbers, activating the program. The data file then interacts with the language file and builds the virus in the computer's random access memory. In layman's terms, the two large files interact and the virus is built internally on the computer. That is why I did not recognize it as a virus before downloading the files. It is written in a language that I have never seen—a language that very few people know."

"What kind of virus?" Tommy asked.

"A very strong and very unusual one," the shopkeeper replied, continuing to type on to the keyboard without looking up. "It began by disabling all anti-virus software. It then sent a message over the internet to an unknown site. It also disabled the manual internet controls, followed by downloading all my files to the same site as it sent the message. With the manual internet controls neutralized, I was unable to break the link until I pulled the internet cable from the computer to stop the download. When I did so, the virus recognized the internet link had been broken, and it stripped the computer of all the files and information—destroying them and itself. All files and information on my computer were eliminated. Any evidence of a virus was destroyed, as well."

"What do you mean it sent a message on the computer?"

"It sent a message concerning my location," the shopkeeper answered, glancing back at his computer. "My suspicions were verified when an Englishman called on the phone asking about the download. My English is not very good but I think he was asking to speak to Thom Luc." The shopkeeper reached back and picked up a piece of paper and the flash-drive from the top of his desk.

"Thomas Luck," Tommy whispered.

"Yes, that was the name," the shopkeeper confirmed.

"What did he say?"

"As I said, my English is not good. I did not understand, but he gave me a name and phone number." The shopkeeper handed Tommy a piece of paper from the top of his desk.

"Clarence Northman," Tommy read the name out loud. "How did you know to write this name if your English is no good?"

"He spelled," the shopkeeper responded. "I do not know the language but I do know the English alphabet and can count to one hundred in English. Every Thai is taught the English alphabet and numbers in grammar school."

Pausing for a moment, looking down at the flash-drive in his hand, Tommy frowned. "A virus? Then why does Steve, presumably an NSA mole, want the flash-drive delivered? Why does John Smith, the owner of a high-tech firm, want the flash-drive delivered?"

Shaking her head, Lawan peered at Tommy quizzically as he lopped the flash-drive's cord over his head.

Tommy turned back to the shopkeeper. "Maybe a wrong password prompted the flash-drive to start the virus?"

"No, not the way I found the password. I removed the execution program from the flash-drive to my computer. I then was able to break apart the code of the execution program and extract the password module. With that module, I began a sequential search, digit by digit, for the password on my main frame. That is why it took me so long to find out what was on the flash-drive. I had to break the password. Even after I found the correct sequence of numbers and letters for the password, I continued to try other sequences to ensure it was not a trigger of some kind, but the actual password. Once I was sure I had the correct password, I placed the flash-drive into my computer's USB port and typed in the sequence. That's when the execution program downloaded the virus and its language instructions. The execution program then downloaded the password and activated the two files. The flash-drive is nothing but a virus," the shopkeeper repeated, nodding his head. "I have been doing this for many years."

"We need two things before I call Steve."

"What is that, Bacon?"

"We need to find out what is said in the meeting tomorrow at Jainukul's house, and we need to find out who Aslan works for."

Lawan stared at the front of the shop, as if expecting Jainukul and his two young henchmen to come bursting through the door. "Nothing is easy in this. It is all too confusing—"

"One more thing," the shopkeeper interrupted. "Before I tried to break the password, I made two copies of the contents. I was able to copy the code without opening the program—as a precaution in case something happened to the code on the flash-drive." He reached onto the table behind the counter, grabbed another flash-drive and handed it to Tommy. "This is the second copy. Instead of using the original, I downloaded the first copy onto my computer, and it was destroyed."

Tommy took the flash-drive and inspected it. "So the virus even destroys the code on the flash-drive?"

"Yes," the shopkeeper replied, "even the code on the flash-drive. Everything having to do with the virus and all the data on the computer is ruined."

"The original is intact and this copy contains everything that is the original?" Tommy asked, pointing to the flash-drive dangling by a cord around his neck and holding out the second one.

"Yes, and that is an exact duplicate," the shopkeeper announced with pride. "Computer data is nothing but zeros and ones—it was easy."

Tommy placed the copied flash-drive into his leather satchel and then handed the shopkeeper enough money to cover the price of replacing the lost files and for his time.

# CHAPTER 36

*Kohn Kaen, Thailand, 22 July 2015*:

T he sun was setting by the time they arrived back in Kohn Kaen. Tommy parked some distance from the hotel because he was concerned that Jainukul might have learned that they were in the city. Although Lawan had registered for the room and neither Jainukul nor Aslan knew her family name, Tommy was nervous that they might have stumbled onto his and Lawan's presence at the hotel simply with their physical descriptions. Lawan stayed in the pickup while Tommy entered the hotel through a back door and took the service elevator to their floor. He quickly packed their belongings and returned to the pickup. By the time they drove the back route to Jainukul's compound and parked on the far side of the jackfruit orchard, it was dark.

Lawan broke the silence. "How will we get the computer from Aslan?"

"Let me think about that one," Tommy replied, shifting in his seat to look at her. "I'll figure something out."

"I hope you do—soon please."

Reaching into the leather satchel, he pulled out the Woodsman he had taken from Aslan in the Marriott. "It's really made for target practice, the caliber is much too small to be much a threat, but beggars can't be choosers," he commented while ejecting and checking the magazine to see how many rounds were left. Counting five, Tommy replaced the magazine. He then placed the handgun back into the leather bag.

"There is much that can go wrong," Lawan said while shaking her head. "What about Jainukul's house, what if it has a security system?"

"We're in the heart of Isaan. What's the chance there is a high-tech security system here?"

"Did you not notice all the electronic security equipment my friend's shop has for sale?"

"Good point." Tommy chuckled. "Okay, so I'm no expert, but Jainukul just doesn't strike me like one to worry about his personal security. I think he relies on the fact that everyone is scared to death of him. You just turn that computer on when I call so we can adjust the view of the camera lens."

Around three in the morning, Tommy shook off his sleepiness and nudged Lawan. He then reached into the leather bag and pulled his cell phone out, turning the ringer off before placing it back into the bag. Along with the Woodsman, he slipped the two remaining wireless video-and-audio devices inside. Swinging the satchel over his shoulder, he kissed Lawan on the lips and then opened the door of the pickup.

"Bacon, please be careful," Lawan whispered as she reached out and touched his arm.

It was dark under the jackfruit trees, and the air smelled of freshly turned earth and decayed vegetation, as Tommy silently moved through the orchard. He stumbled on a fallen branch and then tripped on a small vine laying across the ground. Thousands of chirping crickets vied with hundreds of bellowing frogs, masking what little sound he made. Weaving his way through the final row of jackfruit trees, he stepped up to the concrete wall surrounding Jainukul's compound, feeling the coolness radiating from its surface. Reaching up with the end of his fingers, Tommy felt for anything on top of the wall.

"Thai-style security," he muttered, feeling broken bits of glass protruding from the top edge of the wall.

The broken glass had been embedded in the top, when the concrete had still been wet, to ward off intruders trying to scale the wall. Placing his fingers in the gaps between the glass shards, Tommy hoisted his body up far enough to see over the top of the wall. The other side was dimly illuminated by a light near the front gate reflecting off the white walls of the house. It looked as if the ground on the other side was grass. Tommy hoped it was soft grass. He pulled himself up a little farther and slipped his left then right elbow onto the top of the wall. His left elbow stung as it was sliced by a piece of glass.

He then swung his left leg up, wedging the rubber soles of his shoe into the glass. With all his strength, he straightened his arms, push up style, until they were upright and his upper torso was above the wall. The muscles in his arms burned as he pivoted over the wall sideways. His left knee ripped across more broken glass as he rotated over the wall. Dropping to the ground on the far side, he landed on his hip and shoulder with a loud thud. The leather satchel containing the small caliber weapon, and the video-and-audio devices landed on his head, momentarily stunning him.

Lying still in the grass to see if anyone had heard or seen his awkward entrance into the compound, Tommy listened for any sounds. While not as noisy as outside the wall, the crickets and frogs continued their competition for the most deafening inside, as well. The aroma of fresh-cut grass and flowers hung in the air.

Once he was sure that he had not been heard or seen, he stood up and moved around to the rear of the house. Knowing that most of the people in Isaan grew up without air-conditioning and preferred a fresh breeze over mechanical coolness, he moved silently along the wall, checking each window. He wasn't disappointed to find an open window leading into a small room.

He peeked inside to ensure no one was asleep in the space. The room appeared to be a small office. Once he was sure the room was empty, he slipped through the window. Moving across the space, he stood against the door leading farther into the interior of the house for a full five minutes, listening for movement. Other than a few groans coming from the house's structure contracting in the cool night air, there was none. Tommy assumed that everyone was asleep on the upper floor to take advantage of the breeze above the tree tops.

Slowly opening the door, Tommy peered into a massive living area that had two long leather couches sitting perpendicular to one another. A large square coffee table stood between them. One couch was situated with a clear view of a large shuttered opening that Tommy figured was opened during the day and likely provided views of the garden in front of the house. The other couch was positioned to provide views of a flat screen television mounted on the wall next to the office door. A large wooden carved Buddha face was mounted above a shoulder high open cabinet, containing several books and other odds and ends, on the back wall. The darkness of the room obscured the colors of the couches and cabinet. On the far wall was a wide set of wooden double doors that Tommy assumed led to the home's promenade he had seen Jainukul and his two body guards use two days before. Glancing around the corner of the doorframe, he saw a set of stairs leading to the house's second floor and a large arched opening leading to what appeared to be the dining area and kitchen. Stepping from the office, Tommy quietly explored the downstairs. It became apparent as he moved through the lower level of the house that the large living area was the most likely place for a meeting. The second most likely place would be the dining room adjacent to the living area.

Tommy wedged one of the video devices between two books on a mid-level shelf of the open cabinet and then moved the arched opening into the dining area. There was a long low table in the center of the room with pillows scattered around its parameter in lieu of chairs. Placed against the wall was a large standup grandfather clock. Opening a small wooden door, with several openings carved into its design, revealed the clock's the pendulums. He placed the second video and audio device in a position to see through one of the openings and closed the door.

Reaching into the leather bag, Tommy removed his cell phone and dialed Lawan, quietly asking her to see what the camera was showing. After she described the view, he slowly opened the small clock door, readjusted the camera, and closed the door. Lawan described what she was looking at on the screen of the laptop, again. Happy with her description, Tommy then moved from the dining room back to the living area and, with Lawan's help, adjusted the camera on the shelf. Once he was finished, he slipped back out the office window he had entered earlier and walked along the concrete wall back to where he had fallen into the compound.

Looking up at the wall he had bounded over fifteen minutes earlier, Tommy could feel the bruises on his hip and shoulder and his cut knee from the awkward vault, not to mention, the lump on the side of his head from where the leather satchel had landed. After a moment considering his options, he walked down the wall and looked around the corner at the vehicle entrance. He didn't see a guard and slowly moved up to the gate. A small guard house at the corner of the gate revealed a sleeping policeman slumped down in a wooden chair with his arms dangling at his sides. A soft snoring sound emanated from the shack in rhythm with the guard's rising and falling chest. Tommy slipped past the sleeping policeman and between the rails of the heavy metal gate, trotting down the dark road to the pickup.

Startled when he opened the truck door, Lawan hoarsely whispered, "Bacon!"

"I was right. Jainukul is not very security conscious. I could have gone through the front door. Unfortunately, I didn't figure that out until I took an eight foot fall onto my side, trying to get into the place over the wall."

Tommy started the pickup and moved down the road, looking for a place to pullover. Seeing a Buddhist temple in a nearby village, he pulled onto its grounds.

"No one will bother us here," he commented, looking up at the high red roof and gilded façade of the temple behind a small stand of trees.

"What will we be doing tomorrow?" Lawan asked with a tired expression.

"Easy day. We'll attend the meeting between Jainukul, Aslan, and Sid, and take Aslan's laptop."

She laid her head against Tommy's shoulder. "How will we take the laptop?"

"You'll find out tomorrow. You won't be disappointed. I promise," Tommy replied, running his fingers through her long black hair. He then whispered in her ear, "I love you, Lawan."

She was already asleep.

# CHAPTER 37

*Kohn Kaen, Thailand, 23 July 2015*:

After a restless and uncomfortable night's sleep in the front of the pickup, Tommy and Lawan drove into Kohn Kaen early that next morning and ate spicy pork green curry with rice at a sidewalk vendor's stand. They then found a Big C, Thailand's version of a Walmart Discount Store, and perused the aisles looking at the various merchandise while not looking for anything at all. After several hours, they retraced their drive along the back roads to the jackfruit orchard next to Jainukul's estate, arriving at eleven thirty in the morning.

Getting out of the pickup, Tommy found a position in the orchard where he could see the compound. Squeezing himself up next to a jackfruit tree, he patiently watched the entrance. At ten minutes past noon, the brown uniformed policeman began pulling the heavy metal gates open for a sedan approaching the compound. Immediately recognizing the sedan as the car that had delivered Aslan and Sid to the Pullman Hotel two days earlier, Tommy sprinted back to the pickup and joined Lawan, who was sitting on the truck's open tail gate peeling a jackfruit.

Turning on the laptop, he plugged in the USB receiver and, after the desktop screen appeared, clicked on the device icon, bringing up a window showing a grainy view of Jainukul's living room. Tommy could make out the front doors on the left side of the screen, the stairs to the right, and the couches between.

A stroke on the keyboard and the picture changed to that of the dining room, showing the entrance to the kitchen on the far end of the room.

A shadowy figure was moving around in the kitchen and soft music could be heard in the background. Another stroke and the living area came back up on the screen.

Tommy could feel his heartbeat accelerate in anticipation as they sat on the open tailgate watching for movement on the screen. Several minutes later, the front doors opened and Aslan, with his polyester laptop bag slung over his shoulder, and Sid, with his bandaged neck, were escorted into the house by the smaller of Jainukul's two employees. While the picture was again grainy, Tommy could clearly see that Jainukul's young employee had two blackened eyes from their encounter at the Night Bazaar. Tommy realized it had probably been Jainukul's shadow in the kitchen when the Thai gangster appeared on the right side of the screen, coming from the direction of the dining area.

Jainukul greeted the two men, his voice clearly heard through the earphones above the soft music. "Good afternoon, gentlemen,"

"Mr. Jainukul," Sid replied as he held out his hand, greeting the Thai gangster. Aslan said nothing but held his hand out, as well.

Sid, then Aslan, shook hands with their host before Jainukul waved them to the leather couches in the center of the camera's view.

Sitting down on a couch next to each other, Sid and Aslan's position allowed an oblique view of their faces on the laptop's screen. Sid's heavy black eyebrows and silver hair, and Aslan's frowning mouth were easily seen on the computer screen, even with the grainy video feed. While Aslan's fidgeting body language betrayed his solemn facial expression, Sid sat stoically serious.

"What have you found, Mr. Jainukul?" Sid's voice came through the earphones. "Have you found our wayward delivery boy and the merchandise?"

"Yes and no," Jainukul calmly responded as he began moving around the couches. "Mr. Luck and his girl are in Kohn Kaen."

"In Kohn Kaen!" Aslan erupted, his nervousness apparent.

"Yes, they have been at the Kosa Hotel, not far from where you're staying. We waited for them last night, but they did not return through the lobby. They must have used a rear entrance as all their belongings were gone from their room this morning. They have yet to checkout of the hotel, so on the off chance they might return, I have a man there right now."

Jainukul sat down across from Aslan and Sid in a high-backed carved wooden chair that resembled a throne with large drooping cushions. Tommy imagined the cushions to be red satin, adding to the royal setting, even though the video feed showed no color. The chair had not been there the previous evening and had obviously been placed there specifically for this meeting.

"I doubt they will be back. My man is simply insurance. I plan on pulling him off the stakeout tonight. But, mark my word, I will find Mr. Luck," Jainukul said, while lighting a cigarette. He then took a long drag, followed by blowing the smoke out over the coffee table.

"We have heard from our new contact," Aslan said in a much calmer voice. "He is planning on arranging for a second delivery. He says he will be in contact with Tommy sometime today—tomorrow at the latest. He claims that the flash-drive is still with Tommy."

"It would be better if we could find Mr. Luck ourselves and take the flash-drive from him," Jainukul stated, sounding calm in the earphones. "The last delivery was far from successful. What is your new contact's name?"

"Had you not been there, it would have been successful," Sid said bluntly. "We don't know his name, but he was the one who has taken over arranging the delivery after Carl's unfortunate and untimely death." There was thick sarcasm in Sid's voice.

"Had you not turned the Marriott into a shooting range we might not have scared Mr. Luck off," Jainukul said just as bluntly. They were silent for a moment and then Jainukul said, "I will find Mr. Luck. We will take the flash-drive and rid ourselves of him and his girl. It is just a matter of time."

Tommy shook his head and whispered to Lawan, "The contact they're talking about has got to be John Smith. Sounds like Steve, our reputed NSA undercover agent, is not what he claims to be. The fact that John Smith knows I'm to contact Steve clinches it."

"He didn't say Steve's name. You do not know that."

"The fact that they're talking about my redelivering the flash-drive indirectly links Steve with John Smith," Tommy retorted quietly.

"And if our contact can arrange for a new delivery?" Sid asked.

"Then we should agree that there will be no gunplay until after the flash-drive is delivered," Jainukul said, taking another long drag off his cigarette. "What have you heard from your employer, Aslan?"

"They would like to have the flash-drive by next Tuesday. That gives us four days to find Tommy and the flash-drive," Aslan replied, the nervousness returning.

"Have you explained my proposed deal to them?" Jainukul asked.

"Yes, they are willing to pay you a five percent royalty on all sales. However, they asked me to impress upon you that if you distribute your copy or use it for personal gain in any fashion, that they will ensure your profits are short lived," Aslan replied, the camera showing him shifting on the couch as he answered Jainukul.

Jainukul laughed. "A threat?"

"My people do not threaten. They simply act on their promises. You know they have a long arm and keep their pledges."

Jainukul pulled another drag from his cigarette. "As long as I get my five percent I will be happy. But if I find they are shorting me of the profits, I will do whatever I need to do to recoup the losses." Smoke came out of Jainukul's mouth and nose as he spoke.

"What's next?" Sid asked, bringing the conversation back to the task at hand.

Jainukul looked at Aslan and then Sid. "Mr. Luck and his girl are still in Kohn Kaen or maybe in one of the many small outlying villages. We now know the girl's family name from the hotel registry and are attempting to find out if she grew up near Kohn Kaen. They could be hiding with her relatives. Unfortunately, her family name is quite common in these parts, and while it will not be easy to find her. We will eventually. Once we have found Mr. Luck, we will gather him up and bring him back here for a conversation that will convince him to handover the flash-drive. Once we have the flash-drive, Mr. Luck and his girl will disappear—"

"Luck has proven to be very resourceful," Sid interrupted. "You should keep that in mind when you gather him up."

Jainukul ignored Sid's comment. "We will make a copy of the flash-drive. You can deliver the original to your organization, and I will keep the copy to ensure I receive my royalty payments."

"And if our contact can make arrangements for a second delivery?" Aslan asked.

"Then we will both attend the delivery," Jainukul replied. "And we will execute everything the same, starting with Mr. Luck and his girl disappearing."

"Very well, I will continue to communicate with our contact," Aslan stated. "In the event you cannot find Tommy, we will accept a second delivery."

"Agreed," Jainukul said as he began to stand up. "Do we have any other business?"

Tommy could see Aslan and Sid shaking their heads in response to Jainukul's question. Removing his earphone and handing the laptop to Lawan, he then hopped into the driver's seat. Lawan mimicked his movement and jumped into the passenger seat carrying the laptop and earphones. Starting the pickup, he pulled out on the road, stopping fifty yards down the road from the entrance to Jainkul's compound.

He climbed out of the idling truck. "Sweetheart, two minutes after you see me enter the compound, I want you to drive up next to the wall, but not where someone inside can see you or the pickup—and keep tabs on the laptop in the event they discuss something else that is of value before Sid and Aslan depart."

"What are you doing?" Lawan asked, shifting over to the driver's seat.

"I'm going to borrow Aslan's computer," Tommy replied with a smile on his face as he pulled the Woodsman from the leather bag.

As he sprinted down the road toward the entrance, small plumes of red dust erupted under each of his steps. Running up to the compound, he could see its white walls were stained reddish brown along its base from pervious heavy rains and passing cars and trucks splashing mud from the road.

Jogging along the wall he slowed and then came to a stop next to the entrance. Peeking around the corner, Tommy could see the policeman standing just inside, next to the guard shack. Beyond the guard shack, he could see the driver leaning against the sedan at the base of the promenade. Both men were looking toward the front doors. Making Tommy's task that much easier, the policeman had not closed the gates to the compound.

Reaching around the corner, Tommy grabbed the policeman by the mouth and roughly jerked him backward through the gate. Before releasing his hold, Tommy brought the butt of the Colt Woodsman down on the top of the guard's head. A faint crack echoed as the Colt Woodsman impacted the policeman and his limp body fell into Tommy's arms. He then laid the policeman's sagging body along the side of the mud-stained wall. Slipping the Colt Woodsman into his belt, Tommy pulled the policeman's .38 Smith and Wesson revolver from his hoister, placing it on the other side of his belt. He peeked around the corner of the entrance again to make sure no one had seen him extract the policemen.

The driver was still leaning up against the hood of the car, looking up at the front doors at the top of the stairs, patiently waiting. Slipping inside the compound, Tommy maneuvered behind the sedan and driver. A trickle of sweat ran down Tommy's brow into his left eye, and he blinked. He kept his eyes on the front doors, knowing that if Aslan and Sid were to come out before he was ready, he would find himself in a compromising situation and one that would likely lead to his demise.

Silently leaning across the hood of the sedan, Tommy grabbed the driver by the neck. He easily pulled the small man across the hood, clamping the bony portion of his forearm across the driver's neck, squeezing the jugular veins against the windpipe and disrupting the flow of blood to the brain. As he waited for the driver to lose consciousness, Tommy could hear the pickup approach, followed by an idling sound as Lawan waited near the entrance of the compound. The man Tommy held quickly wilted, his arms falling to his sides.

Tommy frisked the driver's pockets for the keys to the sedan but could find none. He then glanced inside the sedan and saw the keys in the ignition. Reaching into the car, he opened the glove compartment and popped the trunk open with the push of a button. He then dragged the driver to the rear of the sedan and dropped him inside, closing the trunk lid over him.

Jumping into the driver's seat, Tommy started the sedan and moved it into a position that blocked the entrance of the compound. The open glove compartment door bounced when the car abruptly stopped at the gate. Shutting the engine off, he then jumped out of the vehicle and put the keys in his pocket.

Sprinting over next to the promenade steps, Tommy thought he could hear movement just inside the front doors. Leaning against the wall, he was out of breath but didn't dare to breathe too hard for fear of someone hearing as the front doors opened.

When the front doors finally opened, Sid was the first to walk out of the house with Aslan close behind. The two men stopped at the top of the stairs leading down to the driveway, apparently confused by the sight of the sedan at the entrance and the missing driver. As Sid and Aslan began moving down the stairs to the driveway, the smaller of Jainukul's employees came out the front doors and pushed past them, rapidly walking toward the sedan. As if on cue, a pounding from within the trunk could be heard as the driver regained consciousness and began to call for help.

The gravel driveway crunched under Tommy's feet as he pushed himself off the wall. He sprinted toward Aslan. The smell of body odor was heavy around the Turk when Tommy grabbed the computer bag. Jerking the bag from Aslan's shoulder, Tommy caught the Turk in mid stride, spinning him to the ground. With the computer bag in his hands, Tommy stumbled a few steps before regaining his stride. Unable to react quickly enough to stop his escape, Sid grumbled with surprise as Tommy raced past him. When Jainukul's young employee turned to see what the commotion was about, Tommy drove his shoulder into the smaller man's chest, knocking the thug up and over the rear corner the sedan. With flailing arms, Jainukul's employee fell to the ground, grunting as he impacted the gravel. At a full sprint, Tommy slipped through the open gate. Jainukul's employee scrambled to his feet and began to chase him. Tommy was into the idling pickup before the thug was able to exit the compound.

With Aslan's computer bag on his lap, Tommy wheezed, "Hit it!"

Lawan stepped on the accelerator and the pickup shot forward, fishtailing as it pulled away from the compound. Jainukul's employee, having just emerged from the gates, shielded his face with his arm as dirt and gravel from under the truck's tires sprayed the front entrance.

Shots rang out from behind them and Tommy glanced back at the entrance in time to see Jainukul's employee standing at the entrance, shooting what appeared to be a black nine millimeter handgun. Tommy assumed that Sid and Aslan had not been allowed to bring weapons into Jainukul's compound, and they didn't draw weapons as they joined the thug at the gate.

None of the bullets struck the pickup as it careened down the road.

"We got to lose this pickup," Tommy announced.

After a few moments of silence, Lawan asked, "Why do we need to 'lose this pickup'?"

"The gentlemen shooting at us can describe it and, considering Jainukul's connections with the police, they'll be stopping every pickup in Isaan looking for us. And to make matters worse, I just assaulted a police officer. The police will likely want to extract a little revenge of their own."

"Bacon, you are crazy. You could have been killed back there," Lawan said, shaking her head without taking her eyes off the road. They shot past papaya and mango trees, racing down the narrow dirt road.

"It's a good thing I didn't take the time to calculate the risk of that move." Tommy laughed nervously. "I would have never attempted stealing Aslan's laptop in the center of Jainukul's compound in broad daylight had I given it much thought."

Shifting the computer bag to the floor, next to his feet, Tommy reached into his pocket and extracted the sedan keys. He then rolled the passenger seat window down and tossed the keys out into a passing rice paddy. The keys ricocheted off a mango tree before landing in the rice paddy he had been aiming at.

Lawan drove the pickup south, away from Jainukul's estate, weaving through the rice farms on narrow dirt roads. After thirty minutes, they turned east, passing more rice paddies surrounded by tall silver-barked trees. Continuing east for nearly two more hours, Lawan only slowed down when they passed through the villages along the route. Parking at the side of the road in a village with a bus stop servicing Kalasin, Tommy and Lawan walked away from the pickup.

Sitting on a bench waiting for the Kalasin bus, Tommy attempted to look at what was on Aslan's laptop, but found it password protected. Worried that the information might be erased if he tried too many times with the wrong sequence, he closed up the laptop.

With a dark plume of exhaust in its wake, a dirty blue and white bus arrived twenty minutes later, its wooden seats worn shiny from years of seated passengers bouncing about on a bus outfitted with poor shock absorbers. Tommy and Lawan enhanced their shininess as it trudged down the road. With no air conditioning, all the windows were down to cool the interior with the speed-generated breeze. A rough and hot hour bus ride later, they were back in Kalasin.

# CHAPTER 38

*Kalasin, Thailand, 23 July 2015*:

Lawan checked into a small guesthouse that didn't ask for identification while Tommy dropped the laptop off at the computer shop and described to the shopkeeper his need to find out who the owner worked for.

The police would be asking around about a farang and Thai woman, and Tommy didn't want the guesthouse attendant to make the connection to her new tenants. He discreetly entered their new room, avoiding the front desk.

Their room was small and sparsely furnished with only an overhead fan for cooling and thin leveler windows. The room did have a small television that sat on top of a water damaged dresser. The bathroom was Thai style, only containing a toilet with no tank, a hose attached to the wall in lieu of toilet paper, and a large open square concrete tank holding about thirty gallons of water for flushing the toilet and rinsing oneself off in place of a shower. A large plastic bowl floated in the tank.

Settling back on the bed, Tommy considered all that had transpired and what they had learned during the day. Several observations stood out: while he was expecting to coordinate with Steve to get rid of the flash-drive, John Smith expected to coordinate a new delivery; Jainukul had made a deal with Aslan's employer for money and, whatever the organization was, it was also posed a threat; Tommy had a message to call a Clarence Northman in the United States; the flash-drive contained a virus that had the capability to download files, in addition, it also provided the virus's location; and if Jainukul found Tommy and Lawan, regardless of whether or not the flash-drive was delivered in good faith, they would disappear. Tommy assumed that killing them would be Jainukul's definition of the disappearing act.

"What should we do next?" Lawan broke the silence as she began to slip out of her clothes.

"I don't know."

"Let's call the NSA man, Steve, and give him the flash-drive," Lawan offered, the bed squealing at the added weight as she jumped up and straddled Tommy's prone body, wearing nothing but her panties and bra.

"Based on the conversation at Jainukul's, Steve's claim to be working for the NSA is bull," he replied while caressing Lawan's shoulders. "He is still on the rolls of John Smith's firm."

"But we need to give the flash-drive to someone else. They will kill us otherwise."

"Before making any decision, we should call this Clarence Northman character," Tommy said, yawning

"Yes, maybe we should call that number before we talk to Steve." The bed squeaked again from the shift of weight as Lawan rolled off and lay next to him.

Sitting up, Tommy pulled the piece of paper with the name and phone number from the leather satchel. Dialing the number into his cell, he calculated it would be nearly five in the morning on the east coast of the United States. Lawan stood up and wrapped a towel around her body. The phone rang five times before a man answered.

"Clarence Northman, can I help you?"

"I got this number from a computer shop in Thailand."

"Ahh, Mr. Luck. I am glad you have decided to call. It is nice to finally talk with you. How are you today?"

"Other than finding myself constantly having to play moving target, I'm doing all right. What can I do for you?"

"You have in your possession something that I need delivered," Clarence Northman said cheerfully.

"It's a virus. There is no database protection software on your flash-drive."

Clarence was silent for a moment before saying, "Please keep that information to yourself. You must not tell anyone what is on the flash-drive. You've become involved in something much bigger than you think. It is important you deliver the flash-drive to whomever you are directed."

"Why do you want me to deliver something that clearly—" Tommy stopped talking as he considered the implications of what Clarence Northman had just requested. "If you're a good guy, you would want to deliver something that is presumed to be a corporate secret, but in actuality, will both identify who the bad guy is while downloading all the files from his computer. On the other hand, if you're a bad guy, you are selling something to another bad guy that can be used to download the good guy's files."

Intently watching Tommy talking on his cell, Lawan began stripping off her bra and panties from under a towel she had wrapped around herself.

"Your first assumption is correct," Clarence Northman answered. "I realize that this has become very dangerous for you, but this is a matter of national security. I need you to deliver the flash-drive."

"Whose national security and what organization do you work for?"

"This is a United States Government multi-agency operation," Clarence Northman answered, his voice carrying a fatherly tone of patience.

"What organization do you work for?"

"The National Security Agency."

"The NSA? I've heard that one before."

"I am the inspector general for the National Security Agency," Northman stated, as if attempting to add more credibility to his claim. "Look it up on the internet if you don't believe me."

"What is the inspector general for the NSA doing talking to a delivery boy in Thailand? Your job is internal investigations."

"I realize that this may seem a little confusing to you, but you have inadvertently high-jacked a very important operation."

"A little confusing? And I haven't high-jacked anything. I feel like I've been kidnapped by your operation. I'm just trying to stay alive."

"What you need to understand that is there are a lot of unscrupulous people, or in your terms 'bad guys,' who are claiming to belong to one agency or another. Some are members of our various government agencies, some are not. At this point, you must consider them all bad guys. But you must deliver the flash-drive."

"Why? Why do I need to deliver the flash-drive? I've been lied to, beaten up, and shot at. Why shouldn't I just throw the flash-drive into the first trash bin I see and run back to the United States?"

"For one, they won't stop looking for you. You know too much. Secondly, the flash-drive is the only thing that is currently keeping you alive. And third, if you deliver the flash-drive, I will make it worth your while," the inspector general said calmly.

"What's worth my while and why should I trust you?"

"Anything you want—within reason. As far as trust, you have no choice."

"Oh, I have choices. It's just that none of my choices are any good. Let's say for a minute that you're my best choice. What can you tell me that might help me survive the next several days?"

"Easy, trust no one and do as you are told by your handler."

"And who is my handler?"

"John Smith," the inspector general stated in a matter-of-fact tone.

"How do you know about John Smith?"

Clarence Northman laughed. "I'm the inspector general for the NSA, I know everything."

"There's a character who claims he's an NSA undercover man. Is there an NSA undercover man working to take down John Smith?"

"You should trust no one. This operation is very complex with various levels of cooperation between and within different agencies. There is or was a mole working within John Smith's organization but he is or was working at a different level than I, and he is allegedly dead."

"Bob," Tommy said flatly.

Lawan looked quizzically at Tommy and moved over next to him in an attempt to hear the conversation better.

"That was the alleged mole, yes. Again, this mole, Bob or not, did not work with me and I have little or no information concerning him. The mole worked or is working for another level of the operation. I cannot, for certain, tell you that the individual claiming to be a mole is, in fact, one. I would trust no one," the inspector general repeated.

Tommy rolled his neck as he thought. "It'll cost you fifty thousand dollars. I'll deliver the flash-drive when I see the money in my account. I'll warn you right now, my safety—my girlfriend's safety—takes priority. If during this next delivery, it looks like my survival requires me to hang on to the flash-drive a little longer, I will. However, I will get it to these people, eventually."

"Agreed. I have confidence in you Mr. Luck. Give me your account information, and I'll transfer the money today." The inspector general hesitated. "One more thing, Mr. Luck, if you can acquire John Smith's cell phone when you see him next, I'll double our agreed price."

"His cell phone? You gotta be kidding me. I just about got killed today taking his client's laptop."

"You've taken the client's laptop?" There was an excitement in the inspector general's voice that had not been there before.

"Yes, his laptop."

"I just doubled your fee for the laptop, but please, if you can obtain John Smith's cell phone, I'll add an additional fifty thousand to the one hundred thousand I currently owe you."

"I'll have to think about that one," Tommy replied as he lightly patted Lawan's towel-covered hip.

Giving his bank account information to the inspector general, Tommy closed the cell phone and sighed. Lying back on the bed, when Lawan curled up next to him, he pulled the towel from her body, nearly rolling her onto the floor.

"Let's get naked and see what happens," he teased her.

As Lawan slid up close to him and began to pull his shirt off, her thick black hair coiled across the pillow.

"Do you think we should shower first," she giggled.

Tommy looked down into her dark eyes and felt an intense love swell in his chest. "Afterward."

After making leisurely love, Tommy lay back and looked up at the ceiling. He was not ready to lose this beautiful woman again. As Lawan's breathing began to take on sleeping rhythm, he lay there, wondering how he was going to survive the next few days. And, while the extraction of John Smith's cell phone was a low priority, it would be a nice addition to the already-hefty fee he was charging the NSA's inspector general.

As he pondered how to deliver the flash-drive, Tommy could feel the warmth of Lawan's naked body fast asleep next to him. The last thing that went through his mind before he too fell asleep was that he needed to go for a run.

# CHAPTER 39

*Fort Meade, Maryland, 23 July 2015*:

Based on the facts surrounding the death of Bob, Howard had become increasingly convinced that the inspector general was involved with the criminal organization he was currently investigating. After several conversations with Mr. Rogers, his mole, and days contemplating the necessary steps, Howard had cobbled a plan together to either prove or disprove his suspicions.

Howard knew from his mole that John Smith was waiting for a phone call from Tommy in order to coordinate another delivery of the flash-drive to the client. Knowing that a new delivery was about to be scheduled, Howard had to work quickly. He also had learned from Mr. Rogers that John Smith received all his guidance from a gentleman referred to as Mr. Jones and all their communications occurred over an untraceable cell phone. Howard believed there was a better-than-even chance that Mr. Jones and the inspector general could be one and the same. This belief was more of a gut feeling than from the gathering of tangible evidence.

The plan consisted of two simple steps. First, Howard would attempt to link Mr. Jones's cell phone to the inspector general. Secondly, he would pass fictitious information to the inspector general to see if it made its way to John Smith and then back to him via the mole. Connecting the cell phone would have been enough but, in the event that he could not, Howard needed an alternate method of proving the inspector general's complicity. On the off chance that Howard was able to connect both the cell phone and the fictitious information, he would have irrefutable proof of the inspector general's involvement with the organization he was attempting to take down.

Having asked Mr. Rogers to temporarily obtain John Smith's cell phone and download the registry or contact list, it was Howard's hope that the cell contained a number that could be connected to the mysterious Mr. Jones. That number could then be used to connect the inspector general. The plan called for registry to be electronically passed to Howard and the cell returned, counting on John Smith never knowing that his phone had been taken. If John Smith were to find out his cell had been tampered with he would undoubtedly inform Mr. Jones, who would undoubtedly rid himself of his cell and link to the organization. With a plan for connecting the inspector general to the cell phone, the creation of a false piece of information that would lure him to pass it along to the organization needed to be orchestrated.

Howard realized that the fictitious information would need to be of such quality that it would be considered worthy of Mr. Jones passing it along to the organization's field operatives. Contacting one of his Thai counterparts, Howard asked him to discreetly search for Tommy. He had received a call late last night informing him that Tommy had been located in the city of Kohn Kaen—more specifically, at a hotel called the Kosa. The room was registered in a girl's name, but a man fitting Tommy's description had been seen staying in the same room. The Thai intelligence agent also indicated that the police were searching for Tommy, and it would only be a matter of time before they found him. Tommy would not likely survive an interrogation with the local police, as he had allegedly beaten up an officer from their ranks, not a smart thing to do in Thailand.

After receiving Tommy's location, Howard asked his Thai

counterpart for a site near the Kosa Hotel that would satisfy
the requirements of a discreet meeting. His Thai counterpart
had told him of a restaurant located in downtown Kohn Kaen,
called MK's, a popular chain restaurant in Thailand. The description of the restaurant sounded much like a Denny's Restaurant in the United States.

"Perfect," he told his Thai counterpart, "discreet is not necessarily the synonym of dark and secretive. Sometimes a
crowded bustling place can provide the ideal venue for a private meeting."

Having always been taught to understand and plan for
one's weaknesses, Howard knew his particular disadvantage
in this situation was that the circumstances in Thailand were
fluid, making it difficult to obtain up-to-date information.
Howard also understood that the key players, Mr. Jones and
John Smith, likely had the same weakness, lacking accurate
information. With this in mind, Howard would keep his false
information simple and based on Tommy's location. In other
words, the wayward deliveryman's general location would add
credibility to the fictitious information because John Smith
and Mr. Jones probably knew the area where he was hiding, as
well.

Howard decided to tell the inspector general that he had located Tommy through Thai intelligence, the truth, and that he
had arranged for him to meet with his Thai counterpart in order to transfer the flash-drive, a lie. If John Smith thought that
Tommy was planning on giving away the flash-drive, he
would want to be there to disrupt the transfer in order to ensure that the delivery to his client would not be compromised.
Mr. Jones and John Smith could not risk Tommy ridding himself of the flash-drive.

Mr. Rogers had delivered the cell registry early that morning via email and the name Jones had been in the contact folder with an associated phone number. On his way to work that
morning, Howard had stopped at a phone shop and purchased
a prepaid cell with cash.

Leaning back in his black adjustable office chair, Howard

went over the plan. The white walls of his office calmed his nerves, and silently reading the team spirit posters that hung above his desk fortified his composure. If he could both connect the inspector general with the cell phone and have his information of a false meeting make the way to John Smith, Howard would know for sure that the NSA Inspector General Clarence Northman was involved with the criminal organization Howard was trying to expose. He felt a wave of confidence sweep through him as he gently rocked back and forth on the chair. While Mr. Rogers, his mole, would confirm if the false information made its way to John Smith, it was up to him to connect the inspector general to the cell phone.

Ready to put his plan in action, Howard picked up the phone on his desk and called Judy, his secretary, asking her to contact the inspector general's secretary in order to arrange a meeting. Howard told Judy to be sure to mention that he wished to discuss Back Fly. He knew that, with the inspector general's interest in Black Fly, the meeting would likely occur within the hour. While he patiently waited for the secretaries to do their part, he loaded Jones's number into his newly purchased prepaid cell phone. He was not disappointed with the secretaries' results.

Calling back a few minutes later, Judy informed him the inspector general would be free in thirty minutes and see him then. Howard smiled.

Stepping from the elevator on the sixth floor twenty minutes later, Howard was greeted by the lobby receptionist. He nodded at the young woman and she returned his silent greeting with a smile of her own, clearly happy he had taken notice. As he approached the inspector general's door, walking along the blue carpeted hallway, Howard silently went through his fabricated story of a meeting between Tommy and Thai intelligence. Doris, the inspector general's secretary, was standing next to the open door and nodded as he stepped passed her and into the office. He heard the door shut with a click behind him.

The inspector general was in his usual jovial mood when

Howard entered the room and sat down in one of the slick leather chairs, firmly pushing his feet into the thick blue carpet.

Howard watched the inspector general closely as he laid out the untrue story about Tommy's meeting with Thai intelligence. He thought he could detect a concerned look cross the inspector general's face as he told the lie.

When the inspector general asked when the meeting was to take place, Howard indicated that the Thai agent and Tommy were to meet that night, only several hours away, considering the time difference. When asked, Howard provided the inspector general with the time and location of the fantasy meeting.

As the inspector general leaned back in his large office chair, looking as if he was pondering the information, Howard discreetly reached in his pocket and punched the speed dial for Mr. Jones's number that he had preloaded into the cell thirty minutes earlier. Several seconds later, Howard could hear a vibration coming from the top drawer of the inspector general's desk.

Pulling the drawer open, the inspector general withdrew a cell phone.

"You'll have to excuse me, Howard, I need to take this call in private," the inspector general said, looking at the cell.

As discreetly as he had made the call, Howard then disconnected the cell in his pocket. Standing up, he said his farewells and left the inspector general's office.

As Howard walked down blue carpet leading to the elevator bank, his prepaid phone began to vibrate in his pocket, indicating an incoming call. Looking down at the small cell, its green luminous screen identified the incoming call came from Jones and he answered.

"Yeah?" Howard answered with brusque tone, attempting to disguise his voice in a lower pitch.

"You just called this number," the inspector general replied.

"Sorry, I must have misdialed."

After a short pause, the call was disconnected.

Howard did not have his usual positive thoughts when he stepped onto the elevator. Instead, his mind was filled with concern.

# CHAPTER 40

*Kalasin, Thailand, 23 July 2015:*

Glancing through the room's thin leveler windows, Tommy could see the reflection of a bright yellow streetlight illuminating the alley next to the guesthouse. He could hear Lawan bathing in the small bathroom, but it wasn't the normal sound of spray coming from a showerhead. It was the unmistakable sound of water striking the walls and floor as she used the large bowl to toss it from the open tank over her body. With Isaan's inconsistent water supply, Tommy had found himself, on more than one occasion, standing next to an open tank of water outside some country house, in clear view of neighbors and passing villagers, washing himself under the thin cloth of a sarong.

Undressing, Tommy joined her in the bathroom and poured a cool bowl of water over his naked body. The cold water felt painfully refreshing, standing the small hairs up on his arms and legs. Lawan scrubbed his back and then pushed him away when he turned and tried to kiss her.

"We need to eat," she said, smiling.

"What if I told you I wasn't hungry?" Tommy tried to look as pathetic as possible to engender some sympathy but a thin smile exposed the tease.

"I need to eat," she said, returning an equally pitiable look.

Then turning and walking out of the bathroom while wrapping up in a bath towel, Lawan left Tommy standing next to the open tank of water. He soaped himself up and poured more water over his body. The cool water felt agonizing and invigorating all at once, each ladle coercing him to take a deep breath and raising goose bumps on his skin. After tormenting himself for ten more minutes, he shook the dampness from his hair and walked out into the bedroom to find Lawan sitting on the bed dressed in a short jeans skirt and white shirt, watching the television.

Without a word, Tommy dressed in faded blue jeans and a bright red, green, and yellow Hawaiian skirt depicting some tropical flower. Concealing his movements from Lawan, he slipped the .38 Smith and Wesson revolver taken from the policeman into his belt next to the small of his back. Hidden under the Hawaiian shirt, the revolver felt both cold and comforting.

Strolling out of the guesthouse onto the dark streets of Kalasin, they found a small karaoke bar. The typical tinny sounding speakers of a Thai Karaoke bar combined with the whiny melody of an Isaan song and an amateur singer promised nothing less than a nerve-racking experience, but Tommy knew the karaoke market in Thailand, like many other Asian cultures, was very popular.

Lawan loved to sing, having no trouble standing in front of an unknown audience and blurting out some sad tune about a difficult life or lost love. Tommy figured that this lack of self-consciousness was likely a trait stemming from her Buddhist roots, never becoming concerned that they would be judged.

While it was the last thing he would ever want to participate in, Lawan kept loading coin after coin into the karaoke machine, trading off songs with the other bar customers. As a mixture of cigarette smoke from the neighboring table and the aroma of roasted chilies from the kitchen drifted over him, Tommy drank beer after beer and slowly nibbled at a spicy Thai pork salad that burned his lips with each bite, while watching his beautiful Thai partner sing. It was the first time he had felt relaxed in days.

"Bacon, let's go to another bar I know of. We can dance," Lawan said as she sat down from her most recent song.

With a peaceful smile on her face, she gobbled up the remaining salad and drained a half-filled bottle of beer. Having not seen her this stress-free in days, Tommy wondered if somehow his tranquil mood was rubbing off on her. Or maybe it was the other way around. He was feeding off her untroubled disposition.

"They might be looking for us," he replied, trying to gauge her frame of mind and ensure she wasn't simply trying to please him by providing an escape from the Karaoke bar.

"I need to have some fun. These last few days have been hard. I need to forget our problems," Lawan said as she bent over the table, giving him a Thai style kiss on his face, before grabbing his hand and pulling him to his feet.

They exited the karaoke bar and flagged down a passing Tuk-Tuk that bounced them down the dark streets of Kalasin, loudly sputtering an even darker cloud of exhaust in their wake. With their hair tousled about from the warm evening breeze blowing through the Tuk-Tuk's open sides and their shoulders bumping together at each of its driver's attempts to avoid the all too frequent potholes, they giggled and laughed at the rough ride. The Tuk-Tuk pulled up to a large dancehall on the outskirts of the city.

The building itself was an unspectacular concrete design, colored a weather stained tan with an entrance that was bracketed by tall trees whose thick trunks and long branches had been wrapped in bright colorful lights. More colorful lights outlined a set of double wooden doors and a large illuminated sign identifying the bar as Pete's Saloon stood above the entrance. Tommy quickly concluded that Pete's Saloon was owned by an expatriate who was either American or someone with an affinity for American western-style bars.

Stepping through the entrance, Tommy saw that the area inside the saloon was enormous, featuring a large parquet dance floor with twenty heavy wooden tables and matching chairs arranged along its edges. Packed with a sea of colorfully dressed people, the room had a long American style bar, with mirrors and shelves of liquor on display at one end of the dance floor, a four foot high stage that matched the length of the bar stood on the opposite. On each side of the room were two wide tiers filled with more tables and chairs presiding over the dance floor. Wooden banisters, darkened and smoothed by a decade of hands rubbing across their surface, ran along each of the levels, presumably to prevent people from stumbling over the edge and falling down to the next tier.

With three large speakers on each side of the stage, the music was deafening, and a thick fog of smoke hung in the air fed by a hundred burning cigarettes. The bar was full of young and middle age couples drinking, talking, listening, and dancing to live music.

Standing next to the bar, Tommy began drinking Regency Brandy mixed with soda water. The smell of cigarette smoke and a collection of cologne and perfume filled the air around him. It didn't take long before Tommy could hear himself slurring his words while attempting to talk over the loud music to a young couple standing next to him. He was comfortably dizzy as he searched the bobbing heads and shoulders of people on the dance floor for Lawan. He caught a glimpse of her long dark hair and white blouse near the stage through a gap in the dancing throng. While his vision was blurred from a combination of age and alcohol, his momentary peek showed her smiling and looking up at the band as she danced next to the platform.

The band was playing a rendition of an old Isaan song and the black haired crowd, standing shoulder to shoulder, was swaying back and forth to the music on the scarred parquet dance floor. Multi-colored overhead lights created a surreal view of the bobbing heads and raised arms freckled with colorful spots reflected from a large mirrored ball hanging from the ceiling at the center of the dance floor.

Tommy was on his fifth Regency and soda when he saw Jainukul's two employees working their way across the dance floor. He closed his eyes and shook his head, in hopes that it had been a liquor-generated illusion. Unfortunately, the two thugs were indeed maneuvering their way through the crowd toward the stage. Jainukul's two employees must have spotted Lawan dancing near the stage as they were headed in her direction.

Feeling the effects of the alcohol he had consumed, Tommy pushed off the bar and stepped into the gyrating masses to intercept them. Lightheaded, he stumbled on the raised threshold of the dance floor. Tommy caught another glimpse of Lawan and could see that she was oblivious to the approaching threat while dancing at the stage's edge. Still looking up with raised arms, Lawan was singing along with the song.

Loud conversations and the shuffling feet of dancers mixing with the music amplified through the large speakers drowned out any sound from the two men and Tommy moving their way. While the two thugs carefully moved through the crowd, slowly working their way toward Lawan, Tommy pushed his way forward. At first the dancing patrons easily moved out of the way as Tommy strode forth but as his pace quickened they became stationary obstacles. One man inadvertently spilled a whiskey and soda on Tommy's shirt as he forced his way past, then a woman dressed in a scarlet red dress tried to grab him for a dance. Another man pushed back as Tommy forced his way between him and his dance partner. Still, it took Tommy just a mere thirty seconds to move up behind Jainukul's two employees as they continued to stealthily maneuver toward Lawan.

Drunk enough to feel invincible, Tommy grabbed the smaller of the two thugs just below the shoulders and tossed him up onto a nearby table at the edge of the dance floor. The small man rolled over the top of the table and fell onto several people sitting on the far side. The table tipped onto its side, raining down half-filled beer bottles and plastic cups of whiskey. The larger of Jainukul's employees spun around, his big shoulders bumping into dancers, to see what the clamor was about, just as Tommy was finishing up with a massive roundhouse. Tommy's fist struck the man just above his left eye.

The big man stumbled backward and then fell onto the packed dance floor. The mixture of alcohol and adrenalin flowing through Tommy's veins numbed the pain his knuckles should have felt. Pushing the dancers aside, Tommy twice attempted to give the big thug a hard kick in the face. The crowd prohibited a long swing of his leg and he was only able to stun the man.

The smaller hoodlum leapt to his feet and rammed Tommy from behind. Tommy stumbled forward into a screaming woman. Hers and Tommy's arms intertwined as they fell to the floor. Once again, in his alcohol-induced haze, Tommy didn't feel a thing.

When Lawan looked over and realized what was happening, she began pushing her way through the bewildered crowd toward the commotion. Lying on the floor, Tommy turned, readying himself for another blow. The larger of the two thugs had risen from the floor and was now looking down at Tommy, while feeling his face for damage from the kicks. The crowd began to scatter as they tried to distance themselves from the disturbance.

Tommy could see the smaller of Jainukul's employees had maneuvered around behind him and pulled a nine-millimeter automatic handgun from his jacket. Seeing the weapon, the crowd began a loud mass exodus, while the saloon patrons sitting in the upper tiers stood, attempting to see what was going on below. Someone pulled the fire alarm and bright strobe lights above the exits began to flash, mixing with the once surreal colorful lights and mirrored ball above the dance floor and giving the violence unfolding an eerie frame-by-frame effect. Instrument by instrument, the band stopped playing.

As the smaller of Jainukul's two employees raised his weapon, Lawan, at a full sprint, hit him from the side. The blow spun the small man and knocked his weapon from his hand. The handgun skidded along the wooden dance floor following the fleeing dancers. Lawan maintained her balance and ran to the far side of the room. The entire band had now quit playing music and began chattering amongst themselves, discussing what they should do as they looked down on the scene from their four-foot perch. Standing up, Tommy sprinted forward, tackling the smaller man at the shoulders. They crashed into more tables and chairs. Out of the corner of his eye, Tommy saw the larger of Jainukul's employees coming at him swinging his foot toward his face, obviously wanting to return the earlier favor. As Tommy rolled through a mess of cups, bottles, and chairs to avoid the blow, he could feel his shirt soaking up the spilled alcohol and soda.

The smaller thug scrambled to his feet, and Tommy pulled the .38 revolver from the small of his back, frantically shooting at the mirror behind the bar while lying on the floor. The report from the weapon in the acoustically designed room created a deafeningly loud pop, followed by shards of mirror and broken bottles showering down onto the bartenders and patrons along the bar. There was momentarily silence before the room broke out into sheer pandemonium, in the midst of which Jainukul's larger employee dove behind a nearby table and the smaller scrambled toward his weapon lying at the end of the dance floor. Jumping to his feet, Tommy shot an adjacent portion of the mirror behind the bar creating the same shattering effect, intensifying the room's chaos. Many of the escaping patrons wrapped their hands and arms over the tops of their heads, regardless of how close they were to the flying shards of mirror and glass.

Tommy raced toward Lawan, who was seemingly mesmerized by the destruction that had taken place above the bar. The band quickly retreated backstage, leaving their instruments on the floor where they had dropped them.

Grabbing Lawan, Tommy pulled her toward a side exit, pushing his way through a small crowd attempting to use the same egress. Running through the door, Tommy and Lawan heard two loud pops. Debris from a shattered door frame rained down on their heads and shoulders as they exited the building. The crowd attempting to use the same exit screamed and dropped to their hands and knees, trying to duck below the gunfire.

Tommy and Lawan ran down a dark alley next to the building. The outside humid air and a musty scent from the alley felt heavy in Tommy's chest as he fought to catch his breath. As they turned the corner into another alley, they heard more gunshots, one bullet striking the corner of the intersection and spraying them with bits of concrete.

Gripping Lawan by her shoulder, Tommy shouted, "Go! I'm going to slow them down." His heaving chest ruined any attempt at providing calm guidance to his beautiful partner.

Lawan glanced at Tommy with a terrified expression then turned and sprinted down the alley. As she disappeared around a corner at the end of the alley, Tommy pushed himself up against the wall. With his back against the cool concrete twenty feet from the corner, he aimed the revolver at the intersection they had just come around. Sweat, dripping down his forehead and cheeks, cut through the alley's thick rank smell that had seemingly stuck to his face.

With his vision blurred and the revolver wavering from the effects his over indulgence of alcohol, he tried to calm himself. Standing next to the cool concrete wall, Tommy quietly told himself that it was times like these that he needed to control his fear, not let it control him. His life and that of his beautiful girlfriend relied on a clear head.

The bigger of Jainukul's employees was the first to round the corner. The big thug, in a dark suit, appeared as a shadow sprinting into Tommy's view. Jainukul's employee quickly detected Tommy's colorful shirt and their eyes met. The man's facial expression clearly changed from determination to one of surprise when he realized a weapon was pointed directly at him.

Looking into the big man's eyes, Tommy hesitated. It was one thing to shoot at people trying to kill him at the Marriot, but here, with Jainukul's employee caught by surprise, Tommy didn't pull the trigger. Confusion at Tommy's inaction produced a matching hesitation from Jainukul's employee. The big man stood looking at Tommy with his weapon at his side. After a moment, a thin smile appeared on the thug's face and he began to slowly raise his weapon. Tommy pulled the trigger.

The shot echoed in the narrow alley and the round struck Jainukul's employee in the chest. The impact of the round spun the big man, and Tommy pulled the trigger again. This round caught the man in the side. Dropping his weapon, Jainukul's employee stumbled back against the far wall of the alley. Slumping, he reached up with one hand, seemingly trying to find purchase on the flat surface. Tommy pulled the trigger for a third time and the back of thug's jacket rippled when the bullet impacted. He slowly slid down the wall, onto his knees, finally rolling onto his side in the filthy alley. A moment later, the smaller of Jainukul's employees rounded the corner wildly shooting without aiming, and Tommy instinctively dove to the ground as one of the rounds struck the wall next to his head. With the young thug shooting at any shadow in the dark alleyway, Tommy scampered across to the other side on his hands and knees.

Once on the other side, Tommy rose up into a crouch and shot at the smaller thug's shadowy figure, scaring him back around the corner of the intersection. Leaping to his feet, Tommy fired again at the intersection to deter the young man from rounding the corner, but the hammer came down on a spent cartridge with a dry click. Realizing that the weapon was out of ammunition, Tommy turned and ran down the alleyway, following Lawan.

Lawan was sitting in an idling Tuk-Tuk at the end of the alley trying to calm the driver, who had obviously heard the gunplay and didn't want to wait. No sooner had Tommy hopped in did the driver gun the Tuk-Tuk's throttle, and it sprang forward, leaving the alley entrance in a hail of gravel and dust.

Checking his neck to ensure the flash-drive was still in place, Tommy then looked over at Lawan. Passing streetlights flicked across her face, showing red puffy eyes and tear dampened cheeks.

Silently, Tommy smiled and winked in an attempt to provide a confident and calming gesture. He surmised it to be a failed attempt when a scowl crossed Lawan's face.

Directing the driver to drop them off at the city's open market, Tommy and Lawan rode in silence. Five minutes later, the Tuk-Tuk pulled up to the market. While bustling with vendors and shoppers during the day, it was empty and quiet at night. Still intoxicated, Tommy tripped as he exited the Tuk-Tuk, nearly falling onto the pavement. Lawan grabbed an arm to steady him, before paying the driver nearly three times the required fare. With a frown on his face, the driver snatched the money from Lawan's hand and only the red glow of the Tuk-Tuk's tail lights showed as he turned down a side road.

They walked through the empty market, over the remnants of that day's sales, and past crudely constructed low wooden tables that would be filled with fresh batches of fruits, vegetables, and other food stock in several hours. On the other side of the market, they caught another Tuk-Tuk which dropped them off three blocks from the computer shop. As they walked toward the shop along a dark sidewalk Tommy pulled the empty Smith and Wesson from the small of his back and dropped it into a nearby storm drain.

Lightly knocking on the computer shop door, a small light came on in the back, and they could see a shadow moving inside. The door cracked, a chain holding it from fully opening, and the weathered face of the shopkeeper peered out into the night. Without saying a word, he closed the door, removed the chain, and re-opened the entrance, gesturing them inside. Dressed in a white T-shirt and faded tan cotton shorts, he re-chained and locked the door after they had entered the shop. They quietly followed the shopkeeper through the dark maze of counters and equipment toward the small light at the back of the shop.

"I was expecting you two. This is a small town and word of the violence at Pete's traveled quickly. When they said an American farang and pretty Thai woman, I knew it was you," the old shopkeeper said as he stepped behind a glass counter and turned a light on above his desk.

"What have you found on the computer?" Tommy asked while steadying himself on the glass counter. Still slightly drunk, he had begun to feel nauseous from the dissipating alcohol and adrenaline. The smell from the spilled drinks on the dance floor and the grime from the alley, that had both soaked into his clothes, wafted in the air.

"Chinese," the shopkeeper stated, "he works for a Chinese electric power company. That firm is a front for something much larger. The company has no power assets but is linked to several other automotive technology companies and the Chinese government."

"How'd you find all that out?" Tommy asked, hoping he had not slurred his words too badly.

"Saved documents on his computer's hard drive led me to his employer, the power company. I then hacked the company website and found linkages to other websites. All seem to be on the same server and share the same security structure or firewalls, making it that much easier to navigate. The power company is listed as a subsidiary of these other automotive technology firms. Very confusing but very obviously connected," the shopkeeper replied, pushing his glasses up on his nose. "The government is in control of these companies, as well. It is as if these companies are nothing more than a front to a government organization. I have written down the names of all the companies that are connected. I had to end my investigation, as someone overseeing the website security became aware of my search. This is all I felt comfortable doing."

"If you don't speak or write English, how did you manage to find all this out?" Tommy asked out of simple curiosity.

"I can read and write Cantonese. Learning a Chinese language seemed to be a beneficial skill in Southeast Asia," the old shopkeeper replied with a slight sarcastic tone in his voice.

"Was there anything else on the laptop?" Lawan asked.

"While the owner did password protect his laptop, he allowed the laptop to save his email username and password. I was surprised to find that he had not changed that password since losing his laptop, so I took the time to print out his correspondence and attachments that have been received or sent over the last month. With the laptop password, you can see the documents saved on the hard drive for yourself. Most are in English." The shopkeeper then turned, picked up a stack of papers from his desk, and laid them in front of Tommy on the glass counter top. Looking at Lawan and Tommy for a moment, the shopkeeper then said, "You must leave me out of this. It is obvious that the Chinese organization is very powerful. I do not want to be a part of your problems any longer."

"We understand," Tommy replied. "Do you know where we might discreetly acquire a vehicle at this time of night?"

The shopkeeper sighed. "You can take mine. I will need it back in several days, but if it will help you, you can take it. Send me the keys and the location, I will come and pick it up. I do not want to see you again until this is over."

Reaching into his desk, the shopkeeper grabbed a set of keys and then held them out to Lawan. Tommy wondered if his intoxication was so obvious that the shopkeeper didn't trust him with the car. The smell of the alcohol and dirt soaked into his shirt and pants had to be overwhelming.

"Are you sure?" Lawan asked, looking at the shopkeeper with concern.

"We are Thai. We share the same village and friends. We must protect one and other," the shopkeeper replied, nodding.

Lawan took the keys and they bid the shopkeeper goodbye in Thai fashion, with a wai. The shopkeeper returned their gesture and directed them to the rear door.

"We'll get the car back to you in two or three days," Tommy confidently proclaimed as they walked out the back door.

Standing in the rear doorway, the shopkeeper pointed out the car and then quickly closed the door. The sound of the deadbolt engaging on the shop's door echoed in the alleyway as they walked toward the car.

"What now, Bacon?" Lawan asked as they stood next to a rusted and faded late model red Toyota sedan.

"Let's pack our things and drive back to Kohn Kaen. We're still checked in at the Kosa. You heard Jainukul, they won't expect us to return there. It's as good a place as any," Tommy said as he climbed into the front passenger seat and placed the stack of papers given to him by the shopkeeper on his lap.

During the drive back to Kohn Kaen, Tommy turned the car's dome light on and began sifting through Aslan's email correspondence in the dim glow.

"Holy cow!" he erupted while reading one of the emails, "Apparently, this Chinese Power company has two men traveling here from Bangkok and, once the flash-drive is delivered, they're going to eliminate Jainukul."

"Eliminate?"

"Kill."

"Kill Pii Jainukul instead of honoring their agreement. Pii Jainukul would be interested to hear that."

"Here's another news flash! According to this email, these two men have already eliminated a man named Rudolf in Bangkok."

"The Rudolf you talked about?" Lawan asked without taking her eyes off the road.

"It could only be him. Apparently, he attempted to bribe Carl to stop the delivery of the flash-drive to the Chinese company and have it delivered to the people he worked for. The electric company wanted to send a message to Rudolf's employers. Poor Rudolf. This flash-drive is proving to be a death sentence to anyone trying to obtain it."

"Bacon, we must get rid of this flash-drive," Lawan whispered.

A few minutes later, reading another piece of correspondence, Tommy announced, "Here they're talking about making plans for a second delivery with a new man. They don't know the name of the new coordinator. This new guy called them after Carl's death. He knows of me, and is trying to organize another delivery. That's sure to be John Smith. They are counting on him setting up a new delivery. They want to leave Jainukul out, if possible."

"Anything else?" Lawan asked.

"Not much, here's another one about the two men the Chinese are sending to take care of Jainukul. Looks like the two men will be in Kohn Kaen by tomorrow and wait for Aslan to get the flash-drive." Then, chuckling, Tommy added, "I wonder if they'll be staying at the Kosa?"

After scanning the last of the emails, he laid his head back on the headrest and watched the passing headlights of the opposing traffic in silence. He needed to come up with a plan to deliver the flash-drive.

# CHAPTER 41

*Kohn Kaen, 24 July 2015*:

The front desk clerk at the Kosa Hotel made no comment on their two day absence and happily handed Lawan the key to their room. Entering the room, Tommy collapsed on the bed fully clothed, and Lawan stripped, stepping into the bathroom.

"Bacon, you need to shower. You smell like whiskey and dirt," Lawan called from the shower.

"I feel like dirt and I need more whiskey," Tommy mumbled as he crawled from the bed and followed her into the bathroom.

With the shower running and steam flowing over the top of the curtain, he could see the outline of Lawan's naked body through the semi-transparent plastic.

"You drank too much again," she stated flatly through the shower curtain.

He stripped off his clothes, dropping them on the bathroom floor, and climbed into the shower next to her. She began soaping his body.

"You're beautiful," he whispered into her ear as he took her in his arms.

The warmth of the shower and her skin aroused him. He felt the alcohol-induced fatigue flowing out of his body as she kissed him on the lips.

"What happened in the alley?" she asked, pushing back and resuming the scrubbing.

"I killed one of Jainukul's men."

"That's not good, Bacon. Jainukul will be upset with that."

"I was mad and just kept pulling the trigger."

"Mad at what?"

"I was mad that we've been pulled into this sorted affair between John Smith, Clarence Northman, Aslan, and whoever else is involved. Not to mention, I was way too drunk to find myself in a gunfight."

They rinsed the soap from their bodies and dried one another off in front of the sink. She took his hand and led him to the bed. He fell asleep before they could make love.

Early the next afternoon, Tommy woke up before Lawan and went for a run. Still slightly drunk, he dreaded the predictable afternoon hangover, especially in the Isaan heat. It crossed his mind that he could always cut his habitual run short and start drinking before the onset, avoiding the pain.

Jogging down the Kohn Kaen sidewalks, Tommy considered the events from the day before. Jainukul's meeting with Sid and Aslan had been informative but the shoot out in the alley had likely complicated his standing with the Thai gangster. The shopkeeper's information had added as much to the mystery as it did to clear it up.

Having sweated most of the remaining alcohol out, Tommy returned after a short two-hour run. Sobering up, he started to feel a powerful hangover as he entered the room to find Lawan was lying on the bed watching television. Tommy picked up his laptop computer and sat down on the bed next to her. Lawan quietly watched him as he checked his bank account over the internet and found it had grown by one hundred thousand dollars.

"At least the alleged NSA inspector general kept his word. Unfortunately that's not much of an indicator as to his righteousness," Tommy commented, smiling at his sudden wealth. "I guess that means I need to keep my end of the bargain."

Tommy then dug his cell phone out of the leather satchel

and dialed the number Steve had given him. Steve answered the call after two rings.

"Good afternoon, Steve. Is John Smith around?"

Steve took a moment before he recognized Tommy's voice. "I'm not sure what you're talking about, Mr. Luck. As you know, I'm in a delicate situation here with John Smith. Working both sides of this delivery is not an easy task."

Tommy listened for any indication of a lie or a noise in the background hinting deception of some sorts. "So what's the plan?"

"Did you miss your meeting last night?" Steve asked.

Tommy was silent for a moment while trying to discern what meeting Steve was talking about. He wondered if Steve wasn't referring to the violent encounter in Pete's Saloon. He certainly hadn't missed that meeting.

He decided to play along. "No, I made my meeting. It turned out to be a very advantageous one from my perspective."

"Hopefully you still have the flash-drive? You didn't give the flash-drive away, did you?"

"Not much time to give them the flash-drive. I was too busy trying to keep me and my girlfriend alive."

"I'm not sure I understand what you mean," Steve replied, seemingly puzzled at Tommy's comment.

It sounded as if Steve didn't know of his run in with Jainukul's men. It was obvious Steve wasn't asking about what happened at Pete's Saloon, and Tommy wondered what meeting he could be referring too. He changed the subject. "What's the plan for the merchandise?"

"As I said in Bangkok, you need to redeliver the flash-drive."

"What a surprise," Tommy calmly answered as he reached into the small hotel refrigerator for a beer. Opening the bottle, he took a long drink before continuing. "I got word yesterday that you would ask me to redeliver again."

"Who told you that? Did they tell you that at the meeting?"

"Look, I have no idea what meeting you're talking about,

and my source of information is none of your business. We'll do the next delivery at the Kohn Kaen Big C."

"Mr. Luck, I need to know everything that's going on. It's important for me to know the source of your information. It could mean the difference between our survival or not. I'll be up front with you. I heard you were to have a meet with a Thai intelligence agent last night. You never showed up for the meeting. I know that because I was at the meeting site waiting for you."

"Oh, yeah, you're the one putting your ass on the line. And any meeting I might have had is none of your business."

"Mr. Luck, I understand your situation, but if we're to both survive this operation, we need to work as a team."

"Look, pal, this is not my operation, it's yours. Kohn Kaen Big C tomorrow at noon. Tell them to be sitting in the food court. I'll come to them." Hesitating a moment, Tommy then added, "And no Jainukul."

"Mr. Jainukul will not be invited, you have my word."

Tommy disconnected the call without responding.

Lawan looked at Tommy quizzically. "What was that all about? A meeting? What did he mean?"

Guzzling the last of the beer, Tommy shrugged. "Let's get something to eat. We'll talk about it at dinner." Opening another beer, he quickly drained it empty, as well.

Before leaving the room, Tommy slipped the Colt Woodsman into his waist. He then picked up his laptop.

"Why are you taking your laptop?"

"I'm assuming that Sid and Aslan are still at the Pullman. I'm also assuming that the camera is still in Sid's room. I thought we might take a look at what they're up to."

"Maybe we should just order room service?"

"Naw, these guys are searching Kalasin for us. Kohn Kaen is the last place they'd think to look."

They found a small restaurant on Prachasumran Street, across from the Pullman Hotel, taking a seat in the rear. Lawan ordered a round of beers and several plates of food while Tommy opened and turned on the laptop. The camera view was slightly cocked, likely from a maid dusting the top of the cabinet, but it was still in place. The room was empty.

When the food arrived, Tommy devoured a bowl of green curry, dousing the spiciness with long drinks of cold beer. The beer did little to end the burning sensation on his lips and tongue, merely moving it around in his mouth. All the while he kept an eye on the laptop screen.

Lawan slowly nibbled away at a som tam salad. "What did Steve say?"

"He asked about a meeting we had with a Thai intelligence agent."

"We had no meeting with a Thai."

"Yeah, I'm not sure what he was talking about." Tommy thought for a moment. "We need to come up with a plan for our next delivery. We need to get rid of this flash-drive."

He wasn't disappointed. After his fifth beer, the laptop screen showed Sid and Aslan's grainy figures entering the hotel room. Tapping Lawan on her shoulder, Tommy placed one of the ear phones into his ear, handing the other to Lawan. Sid and Aslan were in the midst of a conversation.

"...you heard me tell him to be careful when he went after Luck." Sid's voice echoed from the earphones. "He's unpredictable and clever."

"I had no idea that they were his sons," Aslan replied.

"That doesn't fare well for Luck."

"No it doesn't," Aslan said as he sat down at the small table without his customary laptop. "I'm still not sure how it all happened. How could have Tommy gotten such an advantage on them?"

"He's a slippery one, Luck is," Sid said as he lay down on the bed. Like the previous session, the camera only showed his feet dangling over the end. "According to Jainukul, his sons were told of a couple fitting the description of Luck and his girl at some bar or dance hall in Kalasin. They raced over there and saw the girl, not Luck. Luck snuck up and attacked them from behind as they approached the girl."

"But Jainukul's son was killed in the alley out back."

With raised eyebrows, Tommy looked at Lawan as she looked at him. The big thug had been one of Jainukul's sons.

"A shootout when they chased them from the bar," Sid replied. "I warned Jainukul about Luck. He's either very lucky or very good. Just think about the audacity it took for him to enter Jainukul's compound the other day. No one expected that, which is why it worked."

"Lucky, I think. Taking my laptop was crazy and my employer is not happy. Coincidentally they had someone hack into their website the same day."

"It was a brilliant move on Luck's part. He's trying to understand his predator. I have no doubt that he was somehow involved with the hack job on your employer, as well. Too much of a coincidence. He steals your laptop and finds out who you work for, then hacks into their site to find out more. The guy is good. He stays ahead of us because he's being proactive and we've been reacting to his every move."

"What about this new delivery? What should we do?"

"Follow Luck's instructions and meet with him. Once we have the flash-drive, we don't need to worry about him any longer. Jainukul will take care of Luck when he eventually catches up with him."

"We aren't going to tell Jainukul about the meeting, and my organization is sending men take care of him," Aslan replied. "What if my people take care of Jainukul before he takes care of Tommy?"

"Luck doesn't matter and, quite frankly, he deserves to survive this ordeal. He's been playing a good game, staying one step ahead of everyone looking for him. He's running the show," Sid said with a hint of admiration in his voice.

"But won't Tommy want to extract some revenge when it is all over? He is a loose end—is he not?"

"He just wants this to end," Sid grunted.

"What if, after he has had time to think about it, Tommy decides to go to the authorities?"

"He won't. I know his kind. He just wants to get out," Sid's replied, his face coming into view on the laptop screen as he sat up. "He won't want to become entangled in a lengthy investigation and possible court appearances."

Aslan scooted the chair from the table and began standing up. "Meet for breakfast?"

"Sure, how about eight o'clock in the hotel restaurant?"

After Aslan had left, Sid turned the television on and lay back down on the bed. Tommy closed the laptop and looked at Lawan.

"You killed Pii Jainukul's son," Lawan said, speaking first.

"I did. Sadly, I hope Aslan's employer gets to Jainukul before he finds me," Tommy remarked "At least, I have one person in my corner."

"What do you mean?"

"Sid. He wants to forget about me—about us—when it's all over. He just wants to let us go."

Drinking several more beers, Tommy began to feel drunk again. It felt good to him, relieving him of his impending hangover, the stress of the last few days, and his growing concern about Jainukul. After many more beers, Lawan pulled him from his chair and gripped his arm, steadying him on the walk back to the hotel.

# CHAPTER 42

*Kohn Kaen, Thailand, 25 July 2015*:

Reaching up to check for the flash-drive hanging from his neck, Tommy sat at the window, looking out onto the early morning Kohn Kaen skyline. Lawan was lying under the covers in her nightgown, sleeping soundly. Having sat at the window for over an hour, Tommy had been thinking about the evening he had left Nick at the construction site in Baltimore. Nick had requested that Tommy give him a ride to Glen Burnie, a suburb south of Baltimore, so he could attend a birthday party with his wife and child. Tommy had agreed to the simple request, as Glen Burnie was not too far from his apartment. But, as was his tradition, Tommy began drinking at four o'clock and forgot the commitment. And, subsequently, Nick and his family had been killed in a car accident.

Looking out the window onto Kohn Kaen, Tommy wondered how his life had spiraled down to the point he was no longer a reliable friend. How had a once-honorable person, become so incapable of committing to anything—friends, loved ones, or family. Obviously, his drinking was at the heart of the problem, but it alone was not to blame. Watching the early morning traffic below, Tommy pondered his need for alcohol. Had it been holding Gavin's hand and feeling his life wane in Denver? Was it a result of unremorsefully killing the two thugs in San Diego? Did it spawn from being late for work in Cleveland and finding two of his employees had been killed during his absence? Or was it just due to the unintended consequences of life? Sitting next to the window listening to Lawan's rhythmic breathing, Tommy decided it had been a progression of experiences that created the man he had become. It had been all of those events.

Pushing the memories from his mind, he stood up and moved to the bathroom. Splashing his face with water, he donned his running gear and left the room. He was thankful he wasn't still drunk as he hated mid-day hangovers, which, in his opinion, were far more painful than those in morning. Standing in the descending elevator, Tommy's thoughts turned to the conversation between Sid and Aslan, and learning of his misfortune.

The wrath of a man like Jainukul worried him. Not only did he have to survive the delivery of the flash-drive but now he also had to also survive the rage of a forlorn father. And not just any father, for Jainukul was a dangerous man.

The sun was just peeking over the horizon, as he stepped out of the Kosa Hotel into downtown Kohn Kaen. The morning air was cool but the humidity weighed heavy on his lungs as he began to jog. He found a suitable pace, given his throbbing head and dry mouth, and began mapping out a plan for the delivery. With the flash-drive around his neck swinging in cadence with his feet striking the sidewalk, he ran out of the city into the outlying rice paddies and farms. Transient relief from the rising sun was provided by shade from trees lining the road. As his route returned him to the city, he could feel the ambient heat rise significantly from the surrounding unsympathetic glass, concrete, and pavement. Stepping into the hotel room three hours from the moment he had left, he felt the air conditioning cascade over him like a cool stream. He found Lawan was still sleeping under the covers.

Showering and putting on fresh boxer shorts, Tommy climbed into bed with her. Feeling his presence, she snuggled up next to him, her soft breasts pressing against his shoulder.

When Tommy wrapped his arms around her and softly kissed the top of her head, she slipped her hand into his shorts. Within three minutes, Tommy was naked and Lawan's nightgown was pulled up, exposing her bare waist and legs. They made love.

At eleven-thirty, Tommy and Lawan left their hotel room and drove the old Toyota sedan to the Kohn Kaen Big C located on the main boulevard running through the city. A four-foot-high cinderblock wall surrounded three sides of the building's complex. Driving past the entrance, they could see a lone security officer giving out tickets for the parking area. They drove the faded red Toyota sedan down a side road, parking on a narrow street adjacent to the rear of the building.

"You know what you're supposed to do, right?" Tommy asked as he reached over and put his hand on Lawan's shoulder.

Looking concerned, she nodded. "Yes, in twenty minutes I will drive to the front of the building and wait for you."

"Make sure you keep the car running. This operation might require a speedy getaway." The hinges squealed loudly as he opened the car door and stepped out. Slamming the door, he looked through the open passenger window and smiled. "Everything will be okay."

Tommy hopped the cinder block wall separating the back street from the Big C complex and moved to the corner of the building. Looking around the edge of the building, he saw that the four foot wall created a narrow passage leading to the front of the shopping center and parking lot. Other than a Big C employee sweeping up trash next to a large roll-up door, the passageway was empty. Slowly walking along the side of the building, greeting the Big C employee with a smile as he passed by, Tommy paused for several seconds when he came to a window.

Momentarily pondering the penalty of being seen verse getting on his hands and knees, and moving under the window, Tommy shrugged his shoulders and continue walking. The reflection of the sun prohibited him from seeing who or what was behind the window but he assumed it was nothing more than the building's administrative offices. Stopping at the front corner of the building, he could see a flow of customers moving through the parking lot, and in and out of the large main doors. Tommy slipped into the crowd and moved inside.

Glancing at his watch, he saw it had been eight minutes since he left Lawan. She would be there in twelve more minutes, and he wanted to ensure that the time between the delivery and her arrival was as short as possible. He moved into the building to a hall featuring small shops selling cell phones, computers, designer clothing, and other unique merchandise. At the end of the hallway he could see the food court twenty yards away. Milling around the small shops, Tommy kept track of the time on his wrist watch. At four minutes to noon, he began walking toward the food court.

The food court was decorated with a short blue and orange carpet with matching painted walls that reminded Tommy of the Denver Broncos football team colors. Stepping out into the court, he counted five counters selling various styles of Thai food along the back wall and a dessert stand in the center of the expansive room, each having attendants outfitted in white uniforms with big floppy chef style hats. There were a dozen people at various stages of eating scattered amongst the tables, none of which looked like they might work for Jainukul. Tommy saw John Smith and Steve sitting at a table near the rear of the room, watching him as he began moving across the large open area. They did not respond to Tommy's greeting, a smile and nod, as he walked by their table.

Scanning the room, he saw Aslan and Sid sitting at a corner booth near the front of the building next to a large picture window offering views of the parking lot. Moving toward them, he maneuvered through tables and chairs, and around the dessert stand at the center of the food court. The attendant, a beautiful young woman, offered him a free sample of coconut ice cream as he passed by. Without breaking stride, he refused her offer with a smile.

Aslan whispered to Sid when he saw Tommy approaching. Turning toward him, Sid revealed a scowl. It was not a look of concern, rather one of frustration, possibly due to Tommy's selection for the delivery location. Sid did not strike Tommy as one who enjoyed spicy Thai food. Through the large window behind their table he saw Lawan pull up in the faded Toyota and park at the front of the building two minutes early. Looking directly at Tommy her facial expression indicated that she could see him through the window. The plan was coming together flawlessly, and Tommy smiled.

Three feet from the table, he grimaced at the smell of Aslan's unwashed body and hoped it would be the last time he would be tortured with the unpleasant scent. Just as Sid began to say something the large window behind their table imploded, raining shards of glass down. There was a moment of silence, while the customers tried to comprehend what was happening. Chaos erupted and the silence was quickly replaced by food court patrons dashing from their tables, knocking over chairs and spilling trays of food. Tommy dove behind a table, over turning it as he hit the floor.

Glimpsing over the table's edge to see what had happened, Tommy saw Aslan and Sid huddled under their table with weapons drawn, absently brushing glass from their clothes. Outside, Jainukul's smaller son was standing beside the Toyota trying to pull the car's door open. Lawan was inside, unsuccessfully trying to put the idling Toyota in gear. From the sound she had not remembered to engage the clutch, the gears grinding at her repeated attempts. At the rear of the car stood Jainukul, holding another nine millimeter handgun taking aim at Aslan and Sid's table. A flash and pop from his handgun, and wood from the table top above Aslan and Sid splintered, rocking it on its base. Aslan and Sid remained huddled with their backs against the wall under the damaged table.

Tommy glanced back at John Smith and Steve's table and saw them with weapons drawn, crouching down. Both had bewildered expressions. Looking back outside, Tommy watched Jainukul's son fire his handgun into the door of the

Toyota and pull it open while Lawan frantically attempted to move across to the passenger side of the car, kicking the small thug. Grabbing her foot, Jainukul's son jerked her back into the driver's seat and then out of the door.

Becky, John Smith's other agent, appeared near the entrance. Leaping to his feet, Tommy pulled the Colt Woodsman from his waist and sprinted toward the main doors. He felt the wake of several bullets as he ran. Glancing over his shoulder out the window, Tommy could see a look of pure hatred on Jainukul's face as he fired his weapon again. Bullets smashed into tables and the walls as Tommy raced toward the entrance and through the debris of Jainukul's misses. He tried to keep his speed up but was slowed as he had to dodge several customers escaping into the store's interior, away from the commotion. One of the customers caught a bullet meant for Tommy as he sprinted past, the man spinning and falling on the blue and orange carpeted floor. Becky watched Tommy with a confused look on her face as he raced toward her. She made no attempt to stop him and their shoulders brushed as he ran past.

Running through the front doors, Tommy sprinted toward the Toyota. He saw that Jainukul's son had Lawan by her shoulders and was dragging her, as she attempted to squirm from his grip, across the parking lot to a waiting sedan. The driver of the sedan, dressed in a dark suit and tie, nervously stood next to an open trunk. Jainukul trotted after his son, changing the magazine in his handgun. Tommy took aim at Jainukul with the Colt Woodsman but didn't shoot for fear of hitting Lawan. Jainukul turned and began shooting at him again.

As Tommy dove behind the idling Toyota, he could hear Jainukul's bullets impacting the car, one shattering a side window, another punching a hole in the door. Hearing several shots behind him, Tommy looked back and saw Becky shooting at Jainukul. He yelled at her to stop but she couldn't hear him over the turmoil and noise from all the gunplay. Tommy glanced over the hood in time to see Jainukul's son and the driver unceremoniously throwing Lawan into the trunk of the black sedan.

The driver slammed the trunk lid down over Lawan and raced to the driver's door, jumping in, while Jainukul and his son hopped into the backseat. The sedan's tires squealed as the car began speeding away.

Tommy sprang up and leaped over the hood of the idling Toyota, jumping into the driver's seat. Before he could put the Toyota in gear and chase the sedan, Becky hopped into the passenger seat next to him. Slapping the stick into gear, Tommy slammed his foot down on the accelerator and the old Toyota shot forward. The Toyota, with its lighter weight making up for its smaller engine, kept up with the heavier sedan as they weaved in and out of parked cars. The damaged driver's door on the Toyota swung open and closed in tempo with the turns, as Tommy chased after the sedan.

"What are you doing here?" Tommy yelled at Becky.

"I'm trying to help," she shouted back, hanging on to the dashboard. "I'm an undercover NSA agent."

"I've heard that one before," Tommy replied as he jerked the Toyota's steering wheel to the right to avoid colliding with an approaching car. "Your pal Steve claimed to be the same."

The mouths of the other car's occupants hung open in panic as the two cars chafed sides. A piercing grind, in tune with flying sparks, marked their passage. Both cars' side mirrors broke off with a loud bang when they collided. The Toyota's mirror impacted the window next to Becky, exploding it inward and raining small blocks of glass throughout the interior.

"John Smith told Steve to tell you that to get you to trust him," Becky yelled, brushing broken glass from her shoulders.

"What about the tracking device he pulled out of the bag? Why would he do that if he weren't a mole?"

"To gain your trust. They knew you'd find the GPS tracker eventually. It was all a set up, in the event the delivery went wrong."

Jainukul's sedan burst through the parking lot's wooden toll gate next to the security guard shack, sending it flying and twisting down the sidewalk. Several pedestrians had to dodge the gate as it clattered to a stop. The lone security guard stood in the guard shack calmly watching the mayhem, looking as if the scene before him was a daily occurrence. Ignoring a red light, the sedan veered out onto the main avenue. The passing vehicles on the boulevard swerved to avoid colliding with the sedan and honked their horns in protest. Following after Jainukul's sedan, Tommy rapidly shifted the gears of the Toyota, keeping its RPM needle bouncing off the red line limits of the gauge. Its broken side mirror hanging from the adjustment cable viciously bounced against the Toyota's side. There was more honking and screeching of tires as the old Toyota bounced out onto the boulevard after Jainukul's sedan. The damaged driver's door on the Toyota swung out and bashed a car as they passed by.

Pressing the accelerator to the floor, the Toyota pulled up behind the sedan as it turned into the oncoming traffic lane. The two cars careened across the wide avenue onto a small narrow road, the tires of both screaming in objection as they made the turn. As they raced down the narrow side road, the Toyota a mere ten feet behind the sedan, onlookers stepped back against the walls of the buildings lining the street. The sedan rapidly slowed to make a turn onto an intersecting street.

The Toyota slammed into the rear corner of the sedan as it was turning. The driver's door flew forward, ripping from the Toyota. It took several bounces down the sidewalk, smashed through a large display window, and knocked over two mannequins dressed in Thai style wedding dresses, before clattering to a rest. The Colt Woodsman flew from the center console, where Tommy had placed it, and disappeared under the dash board. Tommy slammed into the steering wheel and his head bounced off the dashboard, stunning him. Out of the corner of his eye, just before his head crashed into the dashboard, he could see Becky's body propelled forward, striking the window with her right shoulder. The collision cracked the glass in spider-web fashion and almost pushed the entire windshield from its mount. With most of its forward momentum drained from the collision with the sedan, the Toyota rolled to a stop, lightly bumping into the building on the corner of the intersection.

The impact to the rear fender of the sedan spun it perpendicular to the street, where a corner of the rear fender side struck a tall aluminum light pole, knocking it over. The lamppost lazily fell across the street, dragging down a handful of phone and cable wires, bouncing when it hit the top of a parked pickup. Pivoting around the light pole, the momentum of the sedan sliding sideways caused it to roll over on its side, skidding half on the sidewalk and half on the narrow street. Hitting a fire hydrant and breaking it from its mount, the sedan rolled over on its top and continued its slow slide on the roof. The last of its momentum dissipating, the sedan came to a stop. No water spouted from the broken hydrant.

Sitting in the driver's seat, Tommy slowly shook his head. Slivers of glass dropped from his hair. He took in several deep breaths, attempting to regain full alertness, and reached up to ensure the flash-drive was still around his neck. Though thick steam billowing from the left front wheel well of the wrecked Toyota, Tommy could see the sedan's trunk had popped open and Lawan was curled up next to the spare tire which had come loose from its mount. Becky was lying back in her seat with a baffled look on her face, and several small lacerations on her forehead were oozing blood. Small bits of shiny glass were clinging to her hair and clothes. Tommy wasn't sure if they were from the impact of the mirror on the side window or her collision with the windshield.

His legs screamed in agony as he pulled himself from the doorless Toyota. Tommy moved toward the sedan, ducking under the downed light pole. Once he reached the sedan, he jerked the spare tire from next to Lawan, gently lifting her from the wreckage. Becky, wiping the blood from her forehead, joined them. He could hear movement inside the sedan as they turned and jogged from the scene. Lawan, in Tommy's arms, moaned quietly as they turned the corner and trotted down the street. Onlookers slowly approached the smoking and wrecked cars as Tommy, carrying Lawan, and Becky made their escape into the suburbs of Kohn Kaen.

Lawan slowly regained consciousness four blocks from the crash and Tommy set her down on a bench at a bus stop. Becky stepped up next to Lawan and began to caress her hair.

On his knees in front of Lawan, Tommy studied her. "Where do you hurt?"

"I'm all right. I think I was just banged up. What happened?"

"I hit Jainukul's car with the Toyota. I'm sorry. I didn't know what else to do. If they had gotten away, they would have hurt you and probably killed you."

"I am all right. We must go. We must get out of here," she whispered confidently. "Did you deliver the flash-drive?"

"No time. Jainukul began shooting before I could even talk with Aslan and Sid."

Standing from the bench, Lawan's wobbling stance was clear evidence of her condition. Looking over at Becky Lawan asked, "Who is she?"

"A friend," Becky responded.

"I feel bad about the Toyota," Lawan said hoarsely, looking back to Tommy. "What will we tell the man about his car?"

"I'll transfer money into his account when this is all finished. Enough to buy a new car."

They slowly walked along a side road until finding a parked Tuk-Tuk with its driver eating at a small sidewalk stand. After a brief conversation and the passing of a small amount of cash, the Tuk-Tuk driver left his half-eaten meal and took them to the Kosa where Tommy helped Lawan up to their room. Becky stayed in the lobby to keep lookout for Jainukul and his men.

Packing their belongings, Lawan and Tommy returned to the lobby ten minutes later.

"You go," Becky said to Tommy. "I'll stay and join backup with John Smith."

"Stay with us," Tommy requested. "If you are who you say, you'll never explain away what you did. You could have stopped me from leaving the Big C on at least on two occasions."

"But if I leave, we no longer have someone on the inside of this operation," she replied shaking her head, her long dark hair had falling across her damaged forehead.

"You don't have a choice. You need to come with us. We can separate in Bangkok if you like but your actions back there will be questioned and, based on how quickly John Smith decides to eliminate questionable employees, you won't make it out of Kohn Kaen."

Becky finally agreed. The three of them took another Tuk-Tuk to the bus station and boarded a bus bound for Bangkok. Bruises began to show on their heads and bodies from the accident and the bus attendant, with a curious look on her face, provided three bags of ice. Tommy and Lawan lay back in the large seats with their fingers intertwined, holding their ice bags to the spots that hurt the most. Lawan fell asleep as Tommy pondered their next move, and Becky sat across the aisle, watching.

When Tommy's cell phone rang, he pulled it from the leather satchel on his lap. The small glowing screen on the phone identified Steve as the caller. Becky looked over at him with a questioning expression when he turned the cell phone off and put it back into the leather bag.

"Your pal Steve. I'm not ready to talk," Tommy said while looking back at Becky trying to figure out whether to trust her or not. "Steve said he was undercover too. Why should I trust you?"

"John Smith had Bob terminated because they got word of a mole and Bob fit the description. Thankfully, it was a vague description. He thought you might be in contact with the NSA's inspector general's department and know of the mole. He figured it would give Steve's claim instant credibility."

"Why would he do that instead of just killing me when he had a chance? And you shot at me at the Marriott."

"I missed you by a mile." Pushing back a lock of hair that had fallen across her blue eyes, she continued. "Steve claiming to be the mole was the backup plan. They need you to deliver the flash-drive so the client can't identify them. I think they eliminate the deliveryman after each delivery. In other words, once you deliver the merchandise, they kill you and no one can connect them to anything. Simple, really."

"What do you know about the NSA inspector general? Do you work for him?"

"Yes and no. It is likely that the inspector general is mixed up in this, as well," Becky confessed.

Tommy laid his head back on his seat. "Great, I talked to him yesterday. He told me I needed to deliver the flash-drive too."

Her eyes widened in shock. "You what?"

"Yeah, we talked. I guess I know why he wanted me to re-deliver."

Reaching across the aisle, Becky brushed a piece of dried blood from Tommy's arm. "That clinches it, he is involved."

# CHAPTER 43

*Nikon Ratchasima, Thailand, 24 July 2015*:

Just outside of Nikon Ratchasima, at a planned bus stop for passengers to eat at a small restaurant and use the facilities, Tommy shook Lawan awake and told her to gather her belongings. With their bags in hand, the three of them slipped off the bus, stepped behind the detached restroom at the complex, and waited. The other riders and attendant didn't notice their departure.

"Why?" Lawan whispered.

"If Jainukul is still alive, he'll be searching for us. If I were him, I'd search all the transportation options for getting out of Kohn Kaen," Tommy whispered. "We had to provide our identification to buy the tickets, so it won't be too hard to find how we left Kohn Kaen and where we're headed."

"They might be waiting for us in Bangkok," Becky said, nodding her head in agreement.

"Or more likely they'll stop the bus before it gets to Bangkok. Once in Bangkok, we can easily disappear into the crowds."

The bus sat there a few extra minutes while the attendant and driver decided what to do about their missing passengers, finally climbing on board and driving down the interstate to maintain their schedule. After the bus departed, Tommy, Lawan, and Becky approached a man standing next to a dirty blue Ford pickup that was pointed in the direction of Bangkok. Speaking in Isaan, Tommy asked the man where he was going and offered to share the price of gas if the three of them could ride in the back. The driver indicated that he was headed for the outskirts of Bangkok and agreed to Tommy's offer. Noticing Lawan's condition, the driver offered her the seat up front. Lawan accepted and climbed into the cab, while Tommy and Becky jumped into the bed of the pickup and arranged the baggage as pillows.

As the pickup bounced over the curb and sped down the highway toward Bangkok, shade from the cab of the pickup provided a cooling relief from the setting sun as the two tried to get comfortable on the hard metal bed. Becky's soft skin rubbed against Tommy's in sync with the vibrations of the engine and bumps along the road. As sun dipped below the horizon, glowing street lamps flashed overhead, replacing the daylight. In the light of passing lampposts, Tommy could see Becky's blue eyes watching him.

"You have really made a mess of this delivery." Becky finally broke the silence, her soft voice barely audible over the noise of the spinning tires on the pavement and wind blowing into the bed of the pickup.

"I'm just trying to stay alive but yeah, they hired the wrong guy for this job."

After a moment, Becky asked, "Why do you drink so much?"

"My reputation precedes me."

"No, really, why do you drink so much?" she asked again.

"I find it comforting and it helps me sleep. All my regrets and worries vanish after a few drinks," Tommy admitted. "Is that all that bad? I still manage to function. I don't hurt anyone with my drinking, and it helps me get through another day—or another night, to be more precise."

Reaching over, Becky pushed the hair back from his forehead. "You could be so much more without the drinking."

"Becky, you're a beautiful woman, but mind your own business. One of the reasons I love Lawan so much is because she never complains about my drinking." Then chuckling, he added, "Well, almost never."

Thirty kilometers out of Bangkok, the pickup began slowing. Tommy raised his head over the edge of the bed to see what was causing the delay. The pickup slowly drove past a bus on the side of the road. The passengers were all peering out the windows at the driver and stewardess while they talked to two men dressed in dark suits. The driver used his hand and arms to accentuate an explanation to the two men. There was a look of concern on both the driver and stewardess's face.

Recognizing the stewardess as the one who had provided the ice packs to help alleviate the pain from the bruises on her three strange passengers, Tommy decided the two men were obviously more of Jainukul's employees. Jainukul had apparently survived, and the small group was discussing Tommy and Lawan's whereabouts.

Several hours later, the pickup driver dropped them off in a Northern Bangkok suburb. From there, they caught a taxi to Suvarnabhumi International Airport and bought tickets for the last flight of the day to Koh Samui in the Gulf of Thailand. Becky chose to stay with Tommy and Lawan instead of rejoining John Smith and risking possible elimination.

After a forty-minute flight, the aircraft began to descend toward Koh Samui. Looking out his window, Tommy could see the high mountains of Koh PhaNgan, just north of Koh Samui, in the moonlight. While a thin line of lights illuminated the two thirds of the coast of the island, its sparsely populated eastern shores and interior were almost completely black. The plane descended farther and Koh Samui came into view. Unlike Koh PhaNgan, the entire northern third of the island was lit with dense urban sprawl. It was obvious that the island of Koh Samui was far more developed than its sister island of Koh PhaNgan.

# CHAPTER 44

*Koh Samui, Thailand, 25 July 2015*:

They were dirty and tired as they climbed down the silver sided mobile stairs onto the tarmac. High light posts illuminated the airplane and four open-sided and canvas-topped buses waiting to take the passengers to the terminal. The buses resembled a hybrid between a bus and golf cart, each with a unique Koh Samui beach scene painted on its side.

Rain began to beat their bus's canvas top as it delivered them to the main terminal. The Koh Samui airport was new and modern with ornate wooden pillars and beams supporting enormous white tent like roof. Tall palm trees stood between the buildings and walkways. They climbed off the buses under a large covered entryway leading to the baggage claim area and retrieved their luggage before proceeding to an anticlimactic parking lot filled with taxis and minivans.

Tommy hired a yellow and green cab to take them to Bo-Phut Fisherman's Village on the northern coast, a favored expatriate destination on Koh Samui. As the cab drove from the airport, it was immediately swallowed up by urban sprawl. The narrow airport road weaved between small homes and businesses along a tight winding street that fed onto a slightly wider coastal road. The taxi followed the coast road west along the north shore of the island where palm and other tropical foliage mingled between the densely packed buildings. Locals and tourists alike risked their lives darting across the busy roadway.

The cab finally made a sharp right turn under a large wood and metal banner announcing they had arrived at Fisherman's Village. The cab then made a left turn onto the village's main street, running parallel with the beach. With one thin line of buildings standing between the main road and the gulf, the long narrow street provided dark glimpses of water between the structures. Few cars ventured along the street, but the cab was quickly engulfed in and slowed by a sea of tourists wearing bright shirts and skirts or pants. The lights from numerous Western-style restaurants and pubs provided a colorful scenic backdrop to the slow and peaceful chaos of rambling tourists.

The cab stopped in front of the Beach Lodge, situated directly on the beach. The building was a combination of dark wood mounted on a white concrete base with a steep Thai style roof. The lobby was in a narrow breezeway leading to the beach and adorned in matching dark wood. The breezeway did not easily fit all three of them and their luggage as they checked in.

There was only one room available on the ground floor and they took it. All first floor rooms had exterior doors located on the main street. The interior of the room was beautifully decorated in more wood trim and a slow turning ceiling fan. In the center of the room sat a king size bed standing against a white concrete wall. French glass paned doors, partially hidden by thick floral designed drapes, looked out on to a small private patio and the beach.

While they took turns taking a shower, the lapping of the waves against the beach provided a calming background harmony. Lawan dressed in her nightgown, and Becky borrowed panties from Lawan and a T-shirt from Tommy. With the girls tucked under the blankets of the bed for desperately needed sleep, Tommy sat down on chair in the corner. Beer by beer he consumed the contents of their refrigerator. When that was finished, he emptied the bottle Regency brandy that had been sitting next to a display of peanuts and crackers. In a drunken stupor, he finally fell asleep, listening to the waves rolling across the beach, the turning overhead fan, and rhythmic and slow breathing of the two sleeping woman.

# CHAPTER 45

*Koh Samui, Thailand, 26 July 2015:*

Waking in the chair early the next morning with a faint scent of perfume in the air and the gently sound of waves breaking on the beach outside, Tommy sat watching the slow moving ceiling fan. Pondering the night in the alley with Jainukul's son, he wondered how he could have become so callous over the years that he could coldly shoot a man not once, but three times without any hesitation. He wondered how he could have let himself get to a point that he could take another human life without a second thought. Tommy wondered whether it was the regret for the act in itself or his heartlessness during the act that bothered him more. The two seemed too closely tied to separate.

He looked over at Lawan and then Becky, who were both sleeping soundly. Deciding he was too sore from the car accident to go for a morning run, he examined the two women's bodies. Lawan had a large dark bruise over her left eye and contusions all up and down her arms. The contusions made him wondered if the damage on her body, under her nightgown, looked as painful. Becky's forehead looked better with only a few scabbed over scratches surrounded by a raised red bruise but a deep purple discoloration under the right sleeve of the borrowed T-shirt looked painful. He assumed that the bruise on her arm was from her impact with the windshield.

Standing up, he pulled his cell phone out of the leather bag, put the battery in, and turned it on. After a quick scan of the contact list, he called Steve.

"Good morning, Mr. Luck. You left quite a mess in Kohn Kaen," Steve answered.

"I thought Jainukul wasn't invited to the party. You gave me your word."

"Jainukul knows a lot of people, especially in Kohn Kaen, and his presence didn't surprise me. Where are you and where is Becky?"

"None of your business. I assume Jainukul is still kicking?"

"He and his son survived the ride with just a few bruises. His driver is in the hospital in a coma, somehow striking a fire hydrant with his head. I'm not sure how that happened," Steve said without emotion.

"You had to be there."

"There is no word on the driver's chances," Steve continued. "Based on Jainukul's reaction to your departure, I'm guessing you've headed back to Bangkok? Is Becky with you?"

"Like I said, that's none of your business."

"You need to deliver the flash-drive—that was the deal. Don't trust Becky if she is with you. She works for John Smith."

"If you haven't noticed, the flash-drive is the only thing keeping Jainukul from killing me and my lovely girlfriend, and as far as Becky, I trust her like I trust you. Not at all."

"I think that Jainukul is beyond wanting the flash-drive. He just wants you. Flash-drive or not, you killed one of his sons outside that bar in Kalasin. He wants you dead." Steve hesitated and then asked again, "Is Becky with you?"

"I know I killed his son, but I didn't *know* it was his son," Tommy admitted. "Give me two days, and I'll give you a call for a new delivery site for the flash-drive. As for Becky, I don't know where she is. I left her at the wreckage in Kohn Kaen. She was unconscious the last time I saw her."

"Not good enough. We need the flash-drive delivered today, tomorrow at the latest. Our client has a deadline."

He didn't ask about Becky again and Tommy hoped that meant he believed him about his last sighting of her.

Recalling Aslan's claim that his organization had only given him four more days and his deal with the inspector general, Tommy sighed. "Tomorrow evening on the island of Koh PhaNgan. I'll call you by noon tomorrow to tell you when and where."

"Where is Koh PhaNgan?"

"Koh PhaNgan is the island just north of Koh Samui in the Gulf of Thailand. There's no airport on the island. The only access is several ferry options from Koh Samui or a number of ports on the mainland." What Tommy did not tell him was that Koh PhaNgan is also the island he and Lawan had opened their restaurant on the beach and he knew his way around. He also knew a lot of people on the island.

"Agreed," Steve replied.

"Can you try to keep Jainukul out of the loop on this one? This flash-drive would have been delivered long ago had he not become involved."

"I'll try, but it seems obvious that someone is leaking information to him. You need to plan on Jainukul being present and still delivering the flash-drive."

As Tommy disconnected the call, Becky stirred next to Lawan, rubbing her eyes and then sitting up. The borrowed T-shirt had hiked up on her during the night, showing her panties as she climbed out of bed. He looked away and grunted a good morning.

Standing up and walking into the bathroom, Tommy stripped his shorts off and stood in front of the mirror, examining his damaged body. The most obvious was a pronounced raise red mark across this forehead where his head had hit the Toyota's dashboard. He also had matching contusions above each knee and on his chest from the impact with the steering wheel.

Hearing a faint squeal from the door hinges, Tommy turned and saw Becky entering the bathroom.

Grabbing a towel, he quickly wrapped it around his waist. "How about a knock?" he exclaimed, glaring at Becky.

"I grew up with three brothers. There's nothing there I haven't seen before." She yawned. "You're pretty shy for a forty-three-year-old."

"My mother was a Baptist from the deep south."

"No she wasn't. She was a Catholic from Tulsa," Becky countered. "I read your file. So what's the plan?" Stepping up to the sink next to Tommy, Becky pulled the T-shirt over her head, revealing her small round breasts. Her light brown skin glimmered next to the white towels hanging on the wall. She whipped her head to one side and her long dark hair swung from her face. Struggling to get the top off the hotel-provided toothpaste, she looked over at Tommy with playfully pleading blue eyes.

Reaching over and grabbing the tube, Tommy quickly twisted and removed the cap. "We're meeting them on the next island over tomorrow night sometime. I haven't got a plan," Tommy admitted. "Give me some time, I'll figure something out."

Yawning again, Becky brushed past him and stepped over to the shower, her skin feeling warm and soft as it rubbed across his arm. Reaching in and turning on the shower, she stripped the borrowed panties off and turned to Tommy. Her thin naked body immediately aroused him.

"Time for a run," he grunted as he turned to walk out of the bathroom. "You're too young for me, anyway."

"Like Lawan isn't too young for you?" She giggled. "She's only six months older than me. I'm twenty seven."

"Did she tell you her age or birth date?"

"Age. We're the same age. So I asked her what month she was born in. I was born in April and she in October. I'm only six months younger than her."

"Then you're actually six months older than Lawan. Thai's count their age differently than westerners, they're one year old the minute their born. You really need to learn the culture," Tommy said as he glanced back over his shoulder for one last look at her beautiful body. He heard her giggle again and call him a sissy as he walked out the door.

Pulling on his running gear, he headed out of the room for his daily exercise

"Time to come up with a plan," he mumbled to himself as he picked up the pace along the beach, the soreness of his body and limbs dissipating with each stride. He shook the vision of Becky's naked body from his mind and began thinking about the next day's events.

Tommy ran for three hours along the beach before returning to their room. When he stepped through the door, he saw Becky sitting next to Lawan helping her eat a container of noodles that looked as if it had been purchased at the local Seven-Eleven.

Wearing a green bikini top with a red and blue flower print sarong wrapped around her waist, Becky had obviously purchased new clothes during his absence. Her blue eyes shone when Tommy entered the hotel room.

"How are you feeling, my love?" he asked, sitting on the edge of the bed.

Wincing at the shift in the mattress, Lawan replied, "I am very sore, but feeling all right."

"We should take you to the hospital."

"No. Can you call Mew? She used to be a nurse. She can help," Lawan responded weakly.

Tommy and Lawan had several good friends on Koh Samui, one whom was a tall attractive Thai woman married to an English expatriate. Mew had been a nurse at a Bangkok hospital before marrying. The couple now owned and operated a small resort ten minutes from Fisherman's Village.

Tommy turned to Becky. "Have you given her anything for the pain?"

"Vicodin. These Thai pharmacies will sell you anything without a prescription. I just gave it to her five minutes ago. I pretty sure it hasn't taken affect."

Scrolling through the numbers on his phone's contact list, he found Mew's and called.

After a brief explanation of Lawan's condition, Mew agreed to come to the hotel.

Locking the bathroom door to ensure Becky didn't try to seduce him again, Tommy took a long hot shower while waiting for Mew's arrival.

Mew arrived twenty minutes later and immediately began tending to Lawan. The Vicodin had obviously begun to numb the pain as Lawan was feeling better and, after a cursory look with a few questions, Mew told Tommy it was just the bruises that were causing the problems. She said it would take a day or two for the pain to become tolerable, assuring Tommy that there were no internal injuries. She then offered to take Lawan back to her resort to look after her.

After packing Lawan's bag and placing it in the trunk of Mew's car, Tommy put one change of clothes in the leather satchel. He then put his remaining clothes, his and Alsan's laptops, the papers the shopkeeper printed out for him, and the copy of the flash-drive in his suitcase, placing it in the trunk next to Lawan's bag. Carrying Lawan out of the hotel room, he gently set her in the passenger seat.

"Bacon, be careful."

"I will. I think I'll set the next delivery up to occur at Haad Sadet. Only two ways in and out that most people know. And neither is easy. And we know of a third route, don't we?"

"And, Bacon." She pulled him close and whispered, "I don't trust Becky. She made at least one phone call on the patio while you were showering."

"What did she say?"

"I couldn't hear too well but I think she told someone something about where we stayed last night and about Koh PhaNgan."

"I'll be careful. I promise. I'll see you in two days."

As Mew drove down the street, Tommy could see Lawan painfully shift her body around to watch him.

Looking over at Becky standing in the hotel room door, Tommy sighed. "No hanky-panky. We've got things to do."

"You're no fun," Becky replied with a mocking frown.

Gathering up her new belongings, Becky placed them into a plastic shopping bag. From the size of the bag, Tommy estimated she had purchased several changes of clothes. He collected his, swinging the leather satchel over his shoulder before checking out of the small hotel. The hotel clerk called a cab and they made the ten-minute journey to the Big Buddha Pier, hidden in a thick cluster of buildings along the same stretch of road they had traveled from the airport the night before.

The long crooked dock derived its name from an enormous golden Buddha statue built on a flat finger of land that jutted out into a wide bay, some two hundred yards northeast of the pier. Standing at its threshold, under a bright blue sky, Tommy could see the old Haad Rin Queen tied up at the end of the equally old wooden pier, rocking back in forth in cadence with gentle waves. As he walked down the narrow misshapen dock, each plank groaned under his weight while the pier's joints grunted and moaned from the water swirling around its supporting bamboo pylons. Tommy and Becky climbed onto the ferry, joining a crowd of young tourists outfitted in an assortment of colorful sunglasses and revealing clothes, sitting along plank seating that encircled the aft deck of the boat. With a pile of luggage and backpacks stacked at the center of the deck, the surrounding conversations were in a medley of European languages and accents, all seemingly to be focused on discussing and identifying their distant destination across the expanse of water, the village of Haad Rin on the island of Koh PhaNgan.

With a heavy canvass canopy protecting them from the bright sun and the possibility of rain, the diesel engine sputtered to life and a small crew cast off the mooring lines. As the old wooden ferry drifted away from the dock, the captain throttled the boat in reverse, stirring a cloud of silt in the shallow green water under the stern. With the throttles again at idle, the boat gently turned, bringing the distant island in line with its bow before the captain throttled up again, leaving a wake of black diesel exhaust and more stirred silt. The boat pushed its way forward, foamy green waves lapping at the bow, and a fresh sea breeze blew across Tommy's face as he peered at Koh PhaNgan's high emerald green mountains that beautifully contrasted against the surrounding clear blue sky and waters.

Koh PhaNgan was largely undeveloped and some beaches were in remote locations, advertised as being only accessible by boat, but Tommy knew otherwise. Nearly all the beaches had seasonal road access and many had trails leading to them. Tommy also knew the island was home to the infamous Full Moon Party, occurring monthly in the village of Haad Rin with twenty to fifty thousand tourists converging on a two-kilometer length of beach to listen and dance to music under a full moon. The participants also did a lot of drinking and taking of illicit drugs, in many cases becoming so overcome with the affects that they could no longer function. Most found themselves incapable of lasting the entire party. The party would end the late following morning, several hours after the sun had risen. Tommy had seen some astounding sights on the few occasions he had attended the party. Passed out party goers surrounded by oblivious dancing tourists, public vomiting, defecation and urination, public nudity, and couples making love on the beach were not uncommon sights.

Several of Tommy's acquaintances who had lived on the island before the Full Moon Party had gained international prominence told him what Haad Rin had been. Situated on a narrow peninsula on the southeast side of the island, the village had once been a peaceful palm tree grove but grew at astonishing rates to support the rapidly growing popularity of the once-a-month party. The end result was a small seaside village that was a jumble of buildings and roads, all focused on supporting a monthly mob attending its chaotic lunar celebration. Lacking supporting infrastructure from its rushed growth, the town provided an unlikely mix of lavish and austere lodging and eatery options.

Halfway across the expanse of water on the old wooden ferry, the details of Haad Rin began to emerge. With a tall

jungle covered mountain, spotted with large gray rock for-
mations separating the peninsula from the greater island acting
as a backdrop, the village was built at the water's edge and
had an assortment of colorful bungalows speckled along its
southern beaches. Tommy knew that the village spanned the
entire width of the peninsula with its widest and most popular
beach on the north side.

# CHAPTER 46

*Koh PhaNgan, Thailand, 26 July 2015*:

Forty minutes later, the ferry arrived in Haad Rin, with aged rubber tires separating the boat from the pier's thick concrete pylons squealing in displeasure as they pulled alongside. The crew laid out a warped and heavily used walkway for the departing passengers, its metal base scratching against the concrete pier and rocking wooden boat, adding a whole new chorus of inanimate pain to the setting.

Walking across the ramp, Tommy and Becky were met by a small group of dirty and bedraggled tourists with slumped shoulders and red eyes, waiting to depart on the Haad Rin Queen's return trip to Koh Samui. Looking as if they could be extras in a documentary of a tropical version of a Siberian labor camp, several had arms and legs wrapped in white bandages. At the end of the pier Tommy and Becky found themselves surrounded by hundreds of young Western tourists walking, shopping, eating, and drinking along the streets of the small seaside village.

Two tall radio and cell towers could be seen hovering over the roofs of brightly colored shops and restaurants lining a street bisecting the village. With the fragrance of body odor, stale beer, and fresh sea breeze in the air Tommy maneuvered through the mass of tourists and approached a scooter rental shop. Knowing the answer beforehand, he asked the shopkeeper why so many people were in Haad Rin and was told that Full Moon was the next night.

"Great," Tommy mumbled to himself.

"What?" Becky asked.

"Big party tomorrow night," Tommy answered. After a moment to think about the circumstances he shrugged. "You never know, it might work in our favor."

With scooters being the customary way to get the around Koh PhaNgan, they rented the second to last in the shop. Even though scooters were the leading cause of injury on Koh PhaNgan, as most tourists had never ridden one till arriving on the island, where the roads were challenging even for the experienced, Tommy found them to be a convenient and easy method of travel on the island's narrow roads.

Tucking their bags between the handlebars and front seat, Tommy looped his leg over the seat and sat down, gripping the handlebars. Becky climbed on the back, wrapping her arms around his waist. They maneuvered through the narrow streets of Haad Rin, avoiding large groups of wandering tourists, other scooters, and the occasional van or truck forcing its way along the crowded roads.

It was a confusing town to navigate. Mostly made up of bars and hotels, Haad Rin had no clear layout of roads, many winding back and forth, sometimes doubling back to their point of origination. The roads also alternated back and forth between pavement and dirt, catching inexperienced drivers by surprise, to the detriment of their health, and bolstering the island's leading cause of injury. Having spent time in the small town Tommy was accustom to the road network and maneuvered the scooter to a steep road leading up a jungle burdened hillside.

The scooter struggled up the road leading out of Haad Rin, taking them high up on the mountain separating the peninsula from the rest of the island. Views along the road were spectacular, revealing long white sandy beaches trimmed with tall lazy palm trees. The road reached its apex midway up the mountain side, spilling down to the beaches on the southern coast. Cruising west along the coast, Becky twisted back and forth on the scooter's seat, fascinated with the island sights.

The narrow road left the palm tree laden beaches, coiled through dense jungle, then quickly returned to the coast. They caught glimpses of incredible vistas of the surrounding water and neighboring islands between the thick stands of palm trees. Becky peered through the palm groves at the beaches and sparkling blue water with a thin smile on her face.

They once again veered away from the beaches and sped along a long straight road lined with numerous businesses— passing schools, Seven-Elevens, restaurants, bars, and hardware stores. Ten minutes later, they came upon the largest town on the island, Thongsala, with more faded two and three story buildings that resembled those of Kalasin. Both the town's stop lights stood dark, either turned off due to a lack electricity or maintenance.

Tommy easily navigated the organized turmoil of cars, trucks, and scooters working their way through the intersections. Turning north, Tommy and Becky drove into the interior of the island, passing open meadows ringed with more palm trees. They passed a fat black water buffalo grazing on green grass, and then a man with a monkey sitting on the back of a slow moving scooter and a long dirty thin rope leash coiled up in the driver's hand.

"What's that all about?" Becky shouted over the din of the scooter engine.

"The monkey picks the coconuts so the man doesn't have to climb the tree," Tommy shouted back.

The jungle closed in on the road the farther north they drove and another large tropical forest covered ridgeline loomed ahead. The road twisted over bridged washes and through rolling hills and then turned upward, and toward a low narrow pass flanked by two tall mountains.

At the top of the pass, Tommy pulled over to the side of the road and gazed out at the spectacular view of a northern bay, the blueness of the water highlighting the bright green of the surrounding jungle. Over thickets of palm trees several red and blue roofs could be seen on the shores of the distance bay. They sat on the idling scooter next to a large wooden sign engraved with *Welcome to Chaloklaam* on the side of the road. A soft hot breeze blew through the narrow pass and Tommy smiled.

"This was your home?" Becky asked, not seeing his smile. "I read about Chaloklum in your file."

"Yeah."

Throttling the scooter, nearly knocking an unprepared Becky from the rear seat, they sped down the far side of the ridgeline. They passed an ornate Chinese temple, then several elephants grazing in a small meadow, their human handlers squatting and smoking cigarettes. The smell of the sea breeze intensified and buildings became more frequent along the roadside. At a sharp bend in the road, a Seven-Eleven appeared and Tommy pulled up.

Giggling, Becky asked, "We staying at a Seven-Eleven?"

"We need supplies."

She pointed at a sign post with the word *Chaloklum* printed on it. "So why the different spelling from the one at the top of the ridgeline?"

"If you haven't noticed English is a second language around here, and a second alphabet," Tommy explained, pointing at the curly Thai language translation shown below the English print. "You want a laugh, go to Japan. There they may spell the words correctly but their translation is lacking."

Becky sat on the back of the bike, taking in the sights, as Tommy disappeared into the Seven-Eleven. A mix of tourists and Thais wandered in and out of the small store. Across the street, a small outdoor restaurant with a bamboo shroud that provided shade was filled with more tourists. The air had a heavy smell of garlic and roasted chili peppers, creating a sinus burning aroma.

Returning five minutes later, Tommy was carrying a case of Singha beer under his arm and roughly placed it on Becky's lap.

"Needed supplies? I should have guessed," she commented, shaking her head, while trying to shift her new load into comfortable position.

"The frig is bare."

They drove the scooter slowly down a road lined with shops and restaurants, dodging bathing suit clad tourists. A minimalist Chinese flair to the architecture attested to the village's heritage. Becky balanced the case of beer on her lap as they turned down an intersecting road that ran parallel to the beach. She could see the bay between the buildings as they sped down the street. They passed an open area filled with palm trees and high grass, resembling an unmaintained park that revealed a full view of the bay. They passed by racks of drying squid lying in the sunlight, its odorous presence unmistakable. They passed a long concrete pier jutted out into the bay with colorful fishing boats bobbing alongside. As one of the boats pulled away from the pier, a string of firecrackers tied to its bow began popping and snapping.

Peering at the sight of white smoke and falling paper debris, Becky asked, "What's that all about?"

"Ward off evil spirits and promise a bountiful catch."

Passing the pier, more Chinese minimalist buildings with wide wooden accordion style doors closed in, concealing the bay once again. Tommy pulled up to a faded yellow building with tall royal blue accordion doors and took the case of beer from Becky. Several tourists, walking past speaking in Italian, scrutinized Tommy and Becky. Another group standing across the street purchasing cigarettes from a vendor talked in Russian.

Becky grabbed her plastic shopping bag filled with clothes as Tommy directed her down the narrow space between the yellow building and a white one next door. Following her with the case of beer and his leather satchel down the passageway, Tommy had to move sideways to fit the bulky load.

At the end of the passage, they stepped out onto a terrace next to the crystal clear waters of Chaloklum Bay. Water lapped against a wide ribbon of sand that sat below a four-foot-high concrete seawall protecting the buildings along the beach from the seasonally turbulent bay. Tommy climbed a set of steep wooden steps leading to a deck attached to the rear of the yellow building. At the top, he dug into his satchel and pulled out a set of keys, unlocking two large glass doors that led into an upstairs apartment.

He smiled again as they entered a gray-tiled living area with light blue walls. Teak colored water stains on the walls pointed to the floor and a wood planked ceiling with two dusty white ceiling fans stood overhead. A small arched space containing two wooden doors leading into the bedrooms stood at the rear of the room, next to a wide set of steps with a thick concrete banister leading to the buildings first floor. To one side of the living area sat a long wicker couch with soft green cushions and to the other was another wooden door leading to one of the apartment's two bathrooms. Next to the bathroom door was a small refrigerator and washing machine.

"So this was home?"

"It was and hopefully will be again someday," Tommy answered as he twisted a plastic knob just inside the glass doors, cycling the overhead fans that immediately filled the room in a light rain of dust. Opening the door to the refrigerator, Tommy was met with a hot stale smell. He turned the dial to the coldest setting before loading it with beer.

Dropping her bags on the couch, Becky pulled the sarong from around her waist revealing a tiny green bikini bottom.

Looking at Tommy with a smile, she asked, "Swim?"

"Swim."

Knowing that the bay water offered a guaranteed way to cool down, Tommy retreated into the larger of the two bedrooms. After rinsing his face in the en suite bathroom, he then dug into the closet, coming out with a pair of faded blue swim trunks. He quickly stripped and put the trunks on.

Moving back out to the living room, Tommy could see Becky standing ankle deep in the water below the deck. Before stepping out on to the balcony, he dug into Becky's belongings and found her cell phone. Taking it back into the larger bedroom, he placed it in the closet.

He met up with Becky below the yellow building's terrace, and they began wading out into the bay. The water was just cool enough to be refreshing but not cold. They could easily see the sandy bottom, each step creating a small plum of dusty water that would momentarily obscure their feet. Becky's skin radiated under the bright sun and against her green bikini.

Chest deep in the clear bay water, she turned to Tommy and gently took his arm. "I've never done anything like that before."

"What, swim or wade in a bay, or what?" Tommy asked, having no idea what she was talking about.

"This morning. I have no idea what got into me."

Tommy could see what looked like a blush under her light brown skin and realized she was talking about their morning encounter in the hotel bathroom. "Happens to me all the time," he joked.

Reaching up and caressing Tommy's cheek, she giggled. "To see you in action here in Thailand has been thrilling. I feel like a little girl with a crush on a teen rock star."

Tommy took her wrist and moved her hand away from his face.

With a sad expression, Becky asked, "You don't trust me?"

"Not one bit, but knowing that going in makes all the difference. While I was changing I took your cell phone. You won't get it back until the flash-drive has been delivered." Pausing, letting what he had just said sink in, Tommy then said, "If you are what you say, then you'll want to help me deliver the flash-drive and, hopefully, glean some information that you can use against John Smith and his crew. On the other hand, if you work for John Smith, you'll still want to help me to complete the delivery in order to please the clients. I'll just have to watch my back as soon as I hand over the flash-drive. It's a win-win situation for me."

"Actually, I need two things to satisfy my boss. I need a copy of the flash-drive, to show what John Smith and associates acquired illegally and tried to sell, and I need evidence you delivered it to a foreign agent. Pictures would be nice."

"I'm delivering the flash-drive but I happened to have a copy of the contents to show what John Smith allegedly acquired illegally. You can have that copy and I'll set you up to get your pictures."

Becky thought for a moment and then said, "That'll work," before stepping back up to Tommy.

With the sun directly overhead, he could feel it beginning to burn his shoulders and pushed her away, diving under the cool water. Becky swam up when he surfaced and put her arms around his neck. Tommy pushed her away again.

"No messing around. We got a job to do," he said before wadding back to the beach.

She giggled, following him back to shore. "Can't we take a quick nap before getting down to business?"

Climbing the stairs to the deck soaking wet, Tommy entered the apartment and took one of the beers from a small refrigerator. As he was taking a long swallow of the warm beer, Becky stepped up next to him and took a bottle for herself, brushing her hip against his.

"Have you got a one-track mind or what?" he grunted as he stepped back from Becky.

"We've got nothing else to do. Are you worried about Lawan?" Placing a hand on her hip, she frowned. "So what's your problem?"

"Call it personal integrity. While I will admit that my personal integrity concerning women has been lacking over the years, there is always time and room for improvement. I've been faithful to Lawan for a number of years, a record for me. Not to mention she's lying on a bed, in pain, recuperating from injuries inflicted by me. Sleeping with you would inflict mental anguish on top of the physical pain she is currently feeling."

"She doesn't have to find out."

"I would know."

After showering, they sat on the deck and drank several more slightly cooler beers, watching the sun dip below a ridgeline on the western side of the bay. Becky kept her distance from Tommy but was outwardly pleased to be with him.

As darkness fell over the bay, they left the deck, finding a seat at a beach front restaurant two doors down from the yellow building. With bamboo and wicker tables arranged on a flat sandy surface adjacent to the water's edge, they sat down on matching chairs with faded floral designed cushions. Colorful lights hanging above the tables on thick beams gently swayed with the breeze. Tommy slipped off his flip-flops and pushed his toes into the cool sand.

After a spicy dinner of squid and rice, Chai, the restaurant owner and a good friend of Tommy's, joined them. Dressed in blue jeans and green T-shirt, Chai was tall for a Thai with big ears and droopy eyes that hinted at Chinese heritage. Tommy switched from beer to Lao Kow when he sat down to chat. They spoke in Thai, and Becky and didn't seem to mind.

"So what brings you back, Tommy?" Chai asked.

"I've gotten into a bit of trouble and Koh PhaNgan offers a place I can sort it out on my own turf."

"What kind of trouble? Can I help?"

"I was hoping you would ask. I have some very dangerous people to whom I must make a delivery. They will likely try to kill me afterward."

"Why would they do that?"

"So there is no one left who can identify them. They want no trail or evidence connecting them to the delivery."

"Who is the girl?" Chai asked, gesturing toward Becky who was watching one of the fishing boats, lit up with hundreds of lights on long wooden poles hanging over its sides, moving out of the bay.

"She is likely one of them, but I don't know that for certain."

"How can I help?"

Becky ignored the two as Tommy explained how he was going to make the delivery. His friend, the restaurant owner, nodded as Tommy laid the plan out. When he was finished, they toasted with their glasses of Lao Kow and soda, and switched back to English.

Becky quickly joined the conversation.

As the evening wore on Tommy could tell the Lao Kow was taking effect when he began slurring his words. Chai began slurring, as well, and took on a silly expression. She had switched from beer to Lao Kow and also began to act drunk, making childish comments and laughing louder than anyone else. They sat drinking the Thai whiskey with their bare feet in the cool sand, talking about nothing important, all the while watching the reflection of moon and stars off the dark surface of the bay for several more hours. Eventually, Tommy stood up and announced their departure. Becky nearly fell over as she stood next to him. It was clear to Tommy and Chai that Becky was unable to walk.

Tommy picked Becky up and carried her from the restaurant. He had difficulty carrying her through the narrow passageway between the buildings and bounced her head off the concrete walls several times, each infraction producing a yelp, followed by a giggle. Somehow negotiating the steep steps to the apartment, Tommy stumbled into the living area with Becky in his arms. Becky, still conscious, talked gibberish about one aspect or another concerning the NSA.

Dumping her on the bed in the guest bedroom, he fell down next to her. Becky stripped off her bikini top and wiggled out of her bikini bottoms before pulling Tommy's shirt over his head. He lay there semi-conscious, not moving, feeling her soft skin brush against his. Once she had pulled Tommy's shirt off, she swung her naked leg over his waist, straddling him, and began fumbling with his belt. Tommy opened his eyes and saw her smiling down at him, her small naked round breasts arousing him for the second time that day.

"I'm not known for my performance in this condition," he mumbled.

She giggled again. "We could just try."

Tommy pushed her aside, standing up and walking to the door. Becky lay on the bed, watching him with a pouty expression.

"Tomorrow is a big day. I don't want to be thinking about

what a lousy boyfriend I am while trying to outwit Jainukul and John Smith," he announced before leaving the room and closing the door behind him. He entered and locked the door to his bedroom, falling on the bed. Reaching up, he checked the flash-dive around his neck before falling fast asleep.

# CHAPTER 47

*Kohn Kaen, Thailand, 26 July 2015*:

In the living area of his Kohn Kaen residence, Jainukul sat on one of the long leather couches waiting for the phone call. A thin ribbon of smoke rose from a burning cigarette clinging to the side of a wide glass ashtray at the edge of the coffee table. The tint of his normally golden skin nearly matched that of the red silk shirt he wore, a physical effect from an elevated blood pressure bought on by the unfortunate turn of the events. The television was on, but he wasn't watching or listening to the program airing. Jainukul was in a foul mood and filled with hatred.

Tommy Luck, the man who had killed his oldest son, had out witted and eluded him once again. And much to Jainukul's displeasure, Tommy's girlfriend had obviously survived the chase from the Big C and subsequent car crash, as she had been seen with him both at the hotel and the bus station. He also learned that Tommy had teamed up with another woman. It was unclear where this woman had come from, but she was at the crash scene and had boarded the bus with Tommy. According to his contact in the bus company, her name was Becky. He had no idea who this woman was, but he could easily add her to the list of people who would pay for his son's death.

After the chase from the Big C, then the accident and the

escape, Jainukul quickly discovered how Tommy and his en-
tourage departed Kohn Kaen. He had arranged for several of
his employees to stop the bus north of the city, but Tommy
had outsmarted him and gotten off at the rest stop two hours
prior. Tommy had once again disappeared.

Jainukul was enraged. He had been close to exacting his
revenge on the American, having had his girlfriend in his
clutches with the intent of using her as bait. Jainukul knew
that a promise to release her would have pressed Tommy to
turn himself over. But he would have never let her go. Once
his captive, Jainukul had planned on tying Tommy to a chair
and allowing several of his henchmen the pleasure of raping
his girlfriend while he helplessly watched. Jainukul then
planned on killing her with his bare hands. He wanted Tommy
to see the life fade from her eyes.

He wanted to see the same rage and sorrow in Tommy that
he currently felt. Fanaticizing about using a knife to carve his
skin from his body, piece by piece, Jainukul wanted Tommy
to live long enough to think about what he had witnessed before finally killing him. Jainukul wanted Tommy to beg to die.

Everything had gone as planned up until the car crash.
Jainukul had received a phone call telling him where the new
delivery was to take place. He then focused his effort on cap-
turing Tommy's girlfriend. He had laughed out loud when he
saw her waiting for Tommy to complete the delivery, the perfect set up for his plan. Everything had gone right until the
moment the American had done something no one expected.
Who would have thought that Tommy would ram the car that
carried his girlfriend? He could have easily killed the very
woman he was trying to save.

And what about Aslan and Sid? They had doubled crossed
him and not told him of the new delivery. It was only because
of a call from an anonymous person that he knew where and
when it was to take place. He didn't know who the person was
that gave him delivery information and didn't care. At this
point Jainukul could care less about the flash-drive, but he
couldn't allow people to think someone could double cross

him without consequences. Word would spread, and his respect would be diminished. His ability to get things done through coercion would be jeopardized. He would take care of Aslan and Sid as soon as he had captured Tommy.

A cell phone sitting on the coffee table began vibrating and ringing. Methodically, Jainukul picked up the burning cigarette with a long cylindrical ash protruding from its end, marking its former length, and took a deep lung full. The long ash fell from the cigarette onto his belly, shattering into a pile of gray dust. He then placed the cigarette back onto the ashtray and picked up the phone.

Swiping the small pile of ash from his shirt, Jainukul answered with a curt, "What?"

"The new delivery will be tomorrow night," the same voice that alerted him to the last delivery droned through the cell. The caller's American accent grated Jainukul's ear like fingernails on a chalkboard, reminding him of Tommy.

"Where?"

"Koh PhaNgan," the voice replied.

"That's a big island. Where on the island and what time?"

"I don't know yet. As soon as I find out, I'll let you know."

Thinking about the information for a moment, Jainukul then asked, "Why are you helping me?"

"Like you, I want revenge." The caller paused. "Like last time, I need the delivery to take place before you grab him."

"Why does that help you?" Jainukul asked as he picked up the stub of the cigarette and crushed it in the ashtray, the tips of his fingers burning as he smothered the last glowing embers.

"We both want Tommy Luck dead. That should be enough. I'll call when I find out the details of the delivery. But you must give me your word that you will allow the delivery to take place before you grab him."

"I will wait until it is done," Jainukul grunted.

"You must not interfere with the client, either. He must be allowed to leave with the flash-drive."

Through clinched teeth, Jainukul hissed, "Agreed."

"I'll call as soon as I get the information on when and where. You should make arrangements to travel to Koh PhaNgan. It has no airport."

"I know it has no airport, you American monkey," Jainukul snapped before disconnecting the call.

Jainukul looked at the number that the informant had called from. Like previous call, the caller ID read *private number*, indicating that it came through a calling bank—maybe from overseas, but Jainukul couldn't tell for sure. He thought about calling one of his contacts within the Thai telephone service. They could find out who and where the calls were originating, but it really didn't matter. He was just glad this person was helping him track down Tommy Luck.

Sitting on the long leather couch thinking about his last encounter with Tommy, Jainukul decided that he had not had enough man power during the last delivery. With more men, he could have slowed Tommy down and gotten away with his bait. He would not make the same mistake a second time.

Calling his youngest son on the cell phone, Jainukul brusquely said, "Get us plane tickets to Koh Samui on this evening's flight. I want to bring three of our best men. We need to be on Koh PhaNgan tomorrow morning."

Disconnecting the call and leaning back with a smirk on his face, Jainukul quietly said to himself, "I will get him this time. No doubt about it, Tommy Luck will be mine."

# CHAPTER 48

*Koh PhaNgan, Thailand, 27 July 2015*:

Tommy rolled over to find Becky sleeping naked next to him. His mouth was dry and his head hurt. The side effect from a dozen glasses of Lao Kow, no doubt. He remembered locking the door the night before and wondered how she could have possibly entered his room. He knew that nothing could have happened, as he had been incapable in his alcohol-induced state.

He could not help but look over at her exposed bare hip and breasts. She was a stunning woman and every bone in his body wanted her.

Glad to be back on the island of PhaNgan where he had developed different jogging routes over the years, Tommy changed into his running gear and headed out for some morning exercise. He ran a route that he used many times before. Jogging down the beach, along a trail that led up a steep mountainside into the jungle, and then out onto a road leading back into Chaloklum, Tommy could feel the previous night's over indulgence leach from his skin. Pushing himself to keep a rapid cadence, he considered his plan for the delivery and all that he had asked of his neighbor.

If Chai was able to come through with all the required equipment and Aslan choose to use the access road to Haad Sadet, both of which were likely, the delivery should go well.

If either of those necessities did not materialize, he would have to modify the plan and hope for the best.

Reaching the outskirts of Chaloklum, Tommy slowed to a jog. He could smell the racks of drying squid as he passed the Seven-Eleven, long before ever seeing them. Several small roadside coffee shops stood empty, even at that late morning hour, as most of the village residents were still sleeping after a long night of fishing for squid. Tourists were lying on one of the local beaches, soaking up the sun, or sleeping in their bungalows after a long night of partying.

He slowed to a walk as he drew near the yellow building. His friend Chai stepped out of his restaurant and called from two doors down. Standing on the street holding a small sports bag in his hand, Chai looked as if he'd had a good night's sleep that had not involved drinking several bottles of Lao Kow.

"Good morning, my friend," Chai called out as Tommy walked down the street to meet him.

"Good morning. You're looking well. You must have not drunk as much as me."

"I have been drinking Thai whiskey since I was fourteen." Chai chuckled. "You have not. It does not affect me like it does you."

"Sort of like the American Indian's intolerance for firewater." Tommy laughed. "I have an intolerance for Thai whiskey."

A quizzical expression on Chai's face told Tommy that his friend had no idea what his American Indian and firewater comment meant.

"I was able to get everything we need," Chai said, while holding out the sports bag. "You will need to take this along with you. I will bring the other items."

"Thank you, Chai," Tommy said, stepping up to his friend, taking the bag with one hand while placing his free hand on Chai's shoulder. "I owe you much."

"You are my friend. You owe me nothing. I will see you later."

When Tommy re-entered the second floor apartment, Becky was sitting on the green cushioned couch in brown shorts and a white T-shirt, waiting for him.

"Morning jog?"

"Felt good to run all the alcohol out of my system," Tommy admitted.

"I don't remember getting home last night. I hope I behaved myself."

Tommy chuckled. "If you call trying to seduce me good behavior, then you succeeded."

"I awoke on your bed with nothing on. Did anything happen?"

"No, you're safe. I wasn't at my peak performance last night. Incapable might be a better description. I'm just not sure how you got past the locked door."

"They train us to pick locks. It's a professional skill." Then pointing to the bag in Tommy's hand, she asked, "So what's in there?"

"You'll see," he replied, walking past her into the bedroom. Closing the door behind him, he didn't bother to lock it.

After a quick shower, he dressed in khaki cargo shorts and an olive drab T-shirt and then slipped on fresh socks and his running shoes. He picked up the flash-drive from a bedside table and looped it around his neck before sitting down on the bed and calling Steve.

"Haad Sadet, six o'clock this evening," Tommy told Steve when he answered.

"The client is on the island. He'll be there. Don't blow this one, Mr. Luck."

"You're not sounding like the NSA undercover agent and ally you claim to be, my friend. You should be giving me the team spirit speech right about now. What do you gain from a successful delivery?"

"Just deliver the flash-drive. You wouldn't understand why we need it delivered."

"Right, I'm just the delivery boy who has outwitted you at every turn—I couldn't possibly understand."

"Screw you, Mr. Luck. Deliver the flash-drive and then run for your life," Steve replied in a frustrated tone.

Tommy's proclamation had obviously touched a nerve. "Well, that's incentive, isn't it? 'Run for my life.' I truly hope you're a bad guy and I get to see you go to prison. Although, you'd probably enjoy shower time at Leavenworth. That is where they send NSA agents who are convicted of crimes, is it not? That is, if you really are an NSA Agent."

"Screw off, Mr. Luck. You could have played the game but instead you choose to be a loner," Steve retorted, disconnecting the call before Tommy could tease him any further.

"It is such an easy plan," Tommy quietly muttered to himself as he lay back on the bed, "What could possibly go wrong?"

At four in the afternoon, Tommy and Becky hopped on their rented scooter and began retracing the route back to Haad Rin. With the flash-drive looped around his neck, Tommy had placed the contents of the sports bag Chai had given him in the leather satchel and hung it over his shoulder. They raced past the Seven-Eleven and then the elephants with their roadside smoking handlers. As they sped through the low pass, a stunning view of Koh Samui in the distance presented itself. While there wasn't a cloud over the island, Tommy eyed a large dark formation to the west. Seeing the approaching storm, he wondered if he shouldn't have considered weather in his delivery plan.

They passed through the lightless stoplights in Thongsala, avoiding the chaotic converging traffic, and down the long road with an assortment of businesses and schools. In the small fishing village of Baan Tai, halfway along the southern coast to Haad Rin, Tommy turned left onto a paved road leading into the jungle. The road twisted through stands of trees with monkeys and birds hidden in the dense foliage screeching around them as they passed by. They passed an enormous tree with wide yellow ribbons tied around its massive trunk. The road turned upward and began a long trek up the side of a tropical-forest-laden mountainside. Maneuvering around portions of the road that had been washed away from heavy rains, Tommy and Becky caught glimpses of the picturesque beaches below. Becky twisted back and forth on the scooter's rear seat, trying to take in the passing scenery while Tommy focused on the avoiding potholes and cracks in the pavement. They could feel the ambient temperature dropping the higher they climbed. At the crest of the mountain under a thick jungle canopy sat a small bamboo hut with a hand written wooden sign proclaiming *last gas before the jungle* in red paint.

"I thought we were already in the jungle," Becky commented sarcastically.

Tommy laughed. "Wait, it gets better."

Turning to coppery-red dirt, the road narrowed and dust began pluming behind the scooter. As they maneuvered along the top of a thin ridge, the trees surrounding them provided a triple canopy of shade from the sun. Suddenly, the road plunged downward. Deep ruts carved into the road from water runoff threatened to knock them from the scooter. After a twenty-minute treacherous ride down the side of the mountain, the road flattened and the jungle opened into a tropical meadow. They passed a small concrete building along the road, advertising food and gas, and they dipped into several washes, splashing through muddy water. At a road juncture, a sign advertised Thong Nia Pan straight ahead and Haad Sadet to the right, a young teenage boy, dressed in jeans and a red and blue plaid shirt, sat on his scooter at the edge of the road smoking a cigarette. Tommy nodded to the boy while making the right turn to Haad Sadet. The boy smiled and returned his nod.

The road narrowed once again and the surrounding jungle began closing in on them. They passed a memorial carved out in the dense foliage for the much beloved Rama Five, a child of the King made famous in the Hollywood movie, *The King and I.* Tommy knew Haad Sadet had been one of the king's favorite vacation spots, visiting more than a dozen times. Next to a small coconut wood shack with a large overhead sign proclaiming a scenic waterfall nearby, the road once again spilled downward.

This road was in much worse shape than the one they had just used to descend off the mountain. Even switch backs could not lessen the sharpness of its decent and, making it that more challenging to traverse, boulders and large rocks had fallen onto the road from above. Deep ruts again complicated maneuvering the scooter, and Tommy had to slow to a crawl as the weight of Becky's body pressed against his. When they came around the corner of one switch back, the condition of the road was so bad that Becky had to get off the scooter and walk. At the bottom, the road flattened and its condition improved. With Becky back on the rear of the scooter, they wended through the jungle, finally arriving at a small beach between a rocky hillside with colorful bungalows built up its steep face and a smaller boulder strewn hill.

Parking the scooter under a grove of palm trees, Tommy and Becky walked to a small restaurant situated on the south side of the beach. The restaurant looked as if it had been constructed of wood planking scavenged from the sea that had faded to a silvery gray. Coconuts husks were wrapped around the building's supports, hiding its wooden pillars. Bamboo tables and chairs with an assortment of faded cushions sat on the beach in front of the restaurant with tall lazy palm trees hanging overhead, providing late afternoon shade. A hand painted sign above the restaurant declared it *Mai Pen Rai*.

Pointing to the sign, Becky asked, "So what's that mean?"

"It doesn't matter," Tommy responded, shrugging his shoulders.

Hung over and saddle sore, Becky snapped, "I just wanted to know what it meant. You know I don't understand Thai."

"It doesn't matter."

"Fine," she said, shaking her head.

"No, it means it doesn't matter." He laughed. "Like no worries."

Becky shook her head, leaving Tommy wondering if she understood him or still thought he was ignoring her request for a translation.

Becky took a table on the beach and waited as Tommy

walked into the restaurant. He came back several minutes later with a key, gesturing for Becky to follow as he walked past. He trudged along the sandy beach toward wooden steps leading to the cliff face bungalows with Becky silently trailing behind.

With a cool fresh sea breeze blowing across their faces, Tommy and Becky climbed old wooden stairs leading up between the bungalows, the planks swaying and groaning with each step. Halfway up, Tommy stopped and used the key to open a bungalow that had a nice view of the beach below. He stepped inside and pulled a thirty five millimeter digital camera with telescopic lens for his satchel, revealing what Chai had handed to him in the sports bag.

"I'll be meeting the clients at the tables you were just sitting at," Tommy explained as he handed her the camera, walking out onto a cantilevered balcony hanging over the cliff.

Becky followed and saw it provided a perfect view of the tables below.

"You should be able to get your pictures from here. I'll be hiding in the jungle waiting for Aslan and Sid to show up. You need to call me if you see anyone else arriving by long tail. I'll be watching the road and won't have a good view of the beach."

"What's a long tail?"

"You probably saw a couple on the bay yesterday. Long tails are the younger cousin to the outrigger and the most common mode of water transportation around here. With large engines mounted on the stern turning a propeller at the end long shafts, the 'long tail' name either originates from the long shaft or the rooster tail of water the turning propeller creates, I don't know which. The designer was remise in not widening the hull. They're really too narrow for heavy seas. They typically move people and supplies between beaches and resorts, or between islands when the weather is calm. You can thank me for the history and cultural lesson later," Tommy answered, before handing Becky her cell phone. "I put my number into your contacts. Make sure that you remember to call if anyone arrives by Long Tail."

"I thought you didn't trust me with a cell phone."

"The clients will be here in about forty-five minutes. I imagine Jainukul will be here before that."

"I thought Jainukul wasn't coming."

"Based on recent events, I would be surprised if he wasn't here."

After a brief hesitation, she said, "Thank you."

"Wait till this is over before you thank me," Tommy replied as he turned to leave, hoping Becky had not heard the note of deception in his parting words.

Leaving Becky on the balcony, Tommy walked back down to the stairs to the beach, the wooden stairs mimicking their earlier complaints. From the beach, he jogged back up the jungle road they had ridden down, taking him nearly ten minutes to reach the steep section that Becky had had to walk down. Striding up the steep road, Tommy heard a whistle from the thick vegetation on the left side, and Chai stepped out from behind a grove of banana trees, waving.

Tommy hopped across a deep ditch and walked up to his friend. "Are we ready?"

"Of course, my friend. My son is at the intersection above. He will call you when they approach," Chai replied, gesturing in the direction of the intersection with a second digital camera and telescopic lens in his hand.

Knowing that Chai was a simple man who did not indulge in luxuries or frivolities, Tommy asked, "Yeah, I saw him. Where'd you get the cameras?"

"My second cousin owns a photographic studio in Thongsala. Don't let me forget to give you this," Chai said while pulling a Walther P-99 semi-automatic handgun from his waist.

"Thank you again," Tommy replied, clapping Chai on the shoulder and taking the handgun.

"You are my friend and I am Thai. What would you expect?"

Gesturing across the road, Tommy said, "I'm going find a place on the other side. It has easier access to the road."

"What of the girl?"

"She's settled for the moment. She'll be fine."

"How will she get back to Chaloklum?"

"I left the key in the scooter. She's resourceful and will figure out how to get the scooter out."

Jumping back across the ditch and climbing up a steep embankment on the other side of the road, Tommy found a hiding place behind a large tree. He then sat down and waited for the arrival of Aslan and Sid.

Twenty minutes before the scheduled delivery Tommy's cell phone rang. It was Becky telling him that a long tail with five Thais had just arrived at the beach. She identified two of the passengers as Jainukul along with his son. The other three men she didn't recognize.

Five minutes later, he received call from Chai's son telling him that a truck carrying two farangs had just passed the intersection. Tommy waited in anticipation, hoping it was Aslan and Sid.

Ten minutes later, a green Nissan pickup turned the corner of the switch back above them. As it drew closer, Tommy peeked around the corner of the tree and saw John Smith in the front passenger seat with his window down and Steve driving the truck. Tommy pressed his back up against the tree and let the truck inch past.

Becky called a short time later to tell him that John Smith had arrived at the beach with Steve.

Fifteen minutes later, Chai's son called again telling him that another pickup carrying two more farangs with a Thai driver had just started down the road. Tommy again hoped it was Aslan and Sid.

If they were to arrive by boat, he would need to return to the beach and deal with Jainukul, face to face. Not something he wanted to do. Ten minutes later, Tommy saw a white Ford crew cab truck begin descending down the steep switch back, slowing to maneuver around the deep ruts and rocks.

Tommy could see Sid in the front passenger seat holding onto the dashboard, and Aslan, sitting in the rear, hanging on to the driver's seat with white knuckles.

When the pickup came abreast of his position, Tommy slipped out from behind the tree, raced to the embankment, sliding down on his backside. A plume of red dust rose around him as he skidded to a stop on the road. The truck's driver and passengers were intently watching the road in front of them and didn't see Tommy's approach as he sprinted across the road and around the rear of the truck. Next to the truck, Tommy tapped the borrowed Walther P-99 against the passenger window next to Aslan's head. The driver looked back and the truck jerked to a stop. Aslan sat frozen with fear, looking at Tommy through the window.

Tommy calmly tapped on the window again with the handgun. "Roll the window down, Aslan."

Aslan looked flustered but quickly rolled the window down, engulfing Tommy in the stench of his filthy body.

Tommy greeted the Turk, trying to hold his breath to avoid the initial onslaught of foul odor. "Hello, Aslan."

Looking over his shoulder from the front seat, Sid asked, "A surprise delivery or were you planning on assassinating us?"

"A delivery," Tommy replied while pulling the flash-drive from around his neck. Aslan watched in silence as Tommy passed the flash-drive through the window.

"Will you allow me to check the contents?" Aslan asked, regaining his composure.

"As long as you're quick."

Aslan picked up a new laptop from the seat next to him, placed it on his lap before opening and turning it on. Sid waited quietly as Aslan plugged the flash-drive into the computer's USB port and looked at the contents.

"It checks out," Aslan said after a few moments, nodding his head. "As described to me, two large files and an execution file providing security."

"Then our business is concluded."

Aslan looked at Tommy. "I need my other laptop back."

"Consider your old laptop collateral damage."

"You could very well be sorry about that decision," Aslan replied, shaking his head. "I work for some very powerful people."

"Just for your information, Jainukul is waiting at the beach," Tommy responded, ignoring Aslan's threat while looking across the interior of the pickup at Sid. "You might want to avoid the party. Jainukul will be displeased that he missed this little transaction and certainly will expect his copy of the flash-drive. Now please continue down the hill, there is a turnaround about fifty feet beyond the next corner."

"You seem to know a lot about our truce with Jainukul," Sid grunted.

"I was listening in on your meeting in Kohn Kaen."

"How did you know about our meeting?"

"Never underestimate the lubrication power of money." Tommy smiled at Sid. "I wired your hotel room and Jainukul's living room."

Nodding in an approval-like manner, Sid then gestured to the driver to continue down the road. Tommy stood in the middle of the road, holding the borrowed weapon at his side, watching the pickup resume its slow descent. When it rounded the corner, he jumped across the ditch and ran up to Chai's hiding place.

"You get the pictures?"

"Many pictures," Chai replied, with the sound of the pickup turning around on the road below. "It was the perfect set up. I even got one with both your and his hands on the flash-drive."

Pulling a small dark chip from the camera, Chai and Tommy swapped the handgun for the digital memory.

"What of the girl?"

"Like I told you, she'll be fine. The pickup will turn around and never go to the beach. John Smith and Jainukul will eventually realize that something interrupted the delivery and leave. The girl will see everyone leaving and find her way home. All that will allow you and I time to get out of here."

"It has worked well—your plan."

"It has. Were you able to arrange for my ride?"

"Of course, my friend, but why not come with me? I can get you to your destination much quicker than walking."

"These guys are pretty smart. They would be remise if they had not put a lookout on the road leading out of here."

Jumping back across the ditch together, they separated at the road. Chai began walking to meet up with his son at the intersection and Tommy climbed back up the embankment on the other side, disappearing into the jungle.

He found the trail leading from Haad Sadet with a little probing, a path climbing up the ridgeline north of the beach. The jungle was dense but the trail was in fairly good condition, likely due to it being used by the wild boars and deer on the island. Cicadas and monkeys audibly competed, and the occasional bird outperformed them both. As Tommy maneuvered along the trail, the wind began to pick up, thrashing the exposed palm tree tops, and dark clouds quickly formed overhead, unleashing heavy rain for several minutes.

It took him forty minutes to reach the top of the ridgeline where, in a small clearing, Tommy could clearly see a deep blue bay surrounded by the two half-moon-shaped strands of sand. With the sun beginning to recede toward the horizon, the trail became a shadowy wash as it descended toward the bay and two beaches. Runoff had created cavernous cuts, forcing Tommy to jump from one side of the trail to the other in an attempt to negotiate the easiest route. Coming upon a deep ravine, he had to jump down into the crevasse and slosh through its fast-flowing muddy brown waters, before climbing back out on the other side. Eventually rounding a corner, Tommy found himself on a high meadow overlooking a village situated between the two half-moon-shaped beaches of Thong Ni Pan Yi and Noi. More rain and wind swept across the bay.

The trail finally ending in the village, Tommy followed a dirt street east, making his way down to Thong Ni Pan Yi, the larger of the two beaches, where resorts and bungalows crowded the shoreline. Stepping out onto the beach, Tommy immediately found the long tail waiting for him, captained by a short stocky man dressed in faded blue shorts and a torn T-shirt advertising Chang beer. It was a ride Chai had coordinated after their drunken night together. The long tail captain, Tommy's junior, initiated a Thai wai, greeting him according to custom, and he responded in a like manner. They climbed into the long tail and the captain directed the boat out of the bay into the turbulent open waters of the Gulf of Thailand.

It was a rough evening on Gulf of Thailand, water rising ten feet at each swell, and the long tail struggled. The long propeller shaft would rise and fall in the swelling and tumultuous water, varying its torque and swerving the boat back and forth. Even the seasoned captain had difficulty keeping the boat moving in a straight line.

"We must go south," the captain shouted over the din of the engine running at high RPM. He knew the plan was to take Tommy around the northern end of the island to Koh Samui but realized the dangers of the rough water were too great. As Tommy had explained to Becky several hours earlier, long tails were not known for their stability in rough water.

"We might run into the people looking for me," Tommy warned the captain.

"The weather is coming from the west. We cannot go that way, it is too rough. Traveling along the east side the island will protect us from the big waves." Hesitating, the captain added, "I will not be able to get you to Koh Samui in this weather. The waters between the islands will be bad tonight."

Tommy nodded while holding on to the sides of the boat, water continually dousing him from the high winds and turbulent sea.

"Drop me off in Haad Rin," Tommy shouted back to the captain, hoping that the hordes of partiers at the Full Moon Party would provide cover from anyone searching for him. He would figure out how to get to Koh Samui once there.

The captain headed south, nearly capsizing as the boat

turned sideways in the heavy seas. It was a rough ride and Tommy felt nauseous as they cruised south along the eastern shoreline of Koh PhaNgan.

The clouds momentarily cleared and the rough water reflected a frantically dancing full moon and stars in its irregular waters. As they passed the Haad Sadet cove, the lights from the bungalows and restaurant glowed onto the beach. Tommy looked for some sign of Jainukul or John Smith but saw none. While the next two coves were dark and empty, the ensuing beaches became progressively developed, starting with small resorts and graduating to larger the farther south they traveled. Soaked with seawater, Tommy looked up at a second round of approaching thick dark clouds as he was tossed back and forth in the long tail. Holding onto the sides of the narrow craft, Tommy could see the glow of Haad Rin and the Full Moon Party looming in the distance.

The beach-side party was in full swing as the captain drove the boat up to the shore, the hull dragging across a sandy bottom in the shallow waters, slowing it to a halt fifty feet from the beach. Party-going tourists waded out into the water and crowded around the long tail, inspecting its cargo as Tommy hopped out. Waving to the captain, as the loud music would have undoubted drowned out an attempted conversational farewell, Tommy began wading to shore. The captain jumped from the long tail with a gentle splash and pushed the boat off the sandy bottom, before leaping back in and throttling up the engine, pulling away from the beach and the curious and drunken tourists.

As Tommy trudged through the shallow water, he could see young men and women, adorned in revealing swimsuits and florescent paint, dancing on the beach to the loud music with a background of colorful strobe and neon lights, all oblivious to the foul weather. Something under thirty years old was the norm. However, as Tommy moved through the crowd, he caught glimpses of several older tourists trying to relive their youth.

Pushing his way through the throng, he had to step over

four passed-out partiers lying on the beach midst the dancing hordes.

Kicking one young man in the head who was fondling a young girl passed out amidst the chaos, Tommy knocked him over in the sand. When the young man turned and looked up at his assailant, Tommy pointed his finger at him in a way that threatened more violence if he were to catch him doing the same again. Yelling at the young man would have been futile in the earsplitting music. The young man scurried away through the crowd.

Working his way to a street that led away from the beach, Tommy was met with a crushing flow of partiers heading out to the lunar celebration. He laughed when the vision of a salmon swimming upstream came to mind, best representing his situation. Halfway up the street, Tommy stopped next to a concrete wall to examine the best route to move against the steady flow of people when chips of concrete splintered above his head. He looked up at the wall, wondering what had happened. The concrete splintered again. As the chips of concrete rained down for the second time, Tommy realized that someone was shooting at him and the chips were coming from bullets impacting the wall. In their drunken and drugged state, none of the partiers noticed, nor had they heard the shots in the loud music. Tommy ducked and ran to the other side of the street before looking back. An extensive variety of aftershave and perfume scents mixed with body odor swirled around him.

An out-of-place, well-dressed man was standing at the top of a stairwell near the entrance to the beach, talking on a cell and holding the same type of nine-millimeter handgun Jainukul and his son used. Tommy had never seen the man before but assumed his assailant was one of the men Becky had told him arrived with Jainukul at the Haad Sadat. Tommy quickly concluded that Jainukul was someplace close by and his employee had just warned the Thai gangster of his presence. Sprinting up the packed street, Tommy roughly pushed his way through the onslaught of tourists. Jainukul's employee started after him.

At a crowded intersection, Tommy turned the corner and put his back to the wall. As Jainukul's man raced around the corner, Tommy stuck his foot out, tripping his assailant. Falling face first, the man blocked his impact with the ground with his gun-free hand and rolled onto his side. The man's eyes jerked up, just in time to see a knee dropping on his head. Tommy heard something crack as his knee struck the man's jaw bone. Reaching down, Tommy grabbed the handgun from the man's motionless hand. Passing tourists chose to ignore the sight, as if it was not out of the realm of possibilities for the Full Moon Party.

Trotting down the busy street, Tommy tucked the nine millimeter handgun into his waistband. He turned a corner and passed a sandwich shop filled with hungry partiers standing in a long line leading up to a small counter. Beyond the sandwich shop, the area to the right was under construction, separated from the street by a four-foot-high cinderblock wall. Glancing down the street, Tommy saw two more men walking toward him, looking as if they shared the same tailor as his first assailant, their dark pants and patent leather shoes marking them as outsiders. Tommy recognized them as the two men who had stopped the bus traveling to Bangkok three nights before. The two thugs spotted Tommy and began walking toward him while pulling handguns from their waistbands. Tommy hopped over the four-foot-high barrier into the construction site, and the two men quickly appeared at the wall.

Making his way across the dark construction site, Tommy felt the wake of a bullet pass his back, missing by several inches. He turned and fired back while jogging between newly raised concrete pillars. A second round skidded across Tommy's upper back, knocking him off balance and spinning him to the ground.

Lying on the ground, he immediately realized the injury was only a flesh wound. As he hesitated, pondering his situation, a second round grazed the left side of his face. The impact of this bullet, far more damaging than the first, jerked his head to the side and rolled him into a shallow ditch. Lying face down on the ground, he could taste blood and dirt in his open mouth.

Taking a few moments for the fog to clear from his head, he rolled behind one of the newly erected pillars in the construction site, placed his back up against the cool concrete, and breathed deeply, trying to force oxygen into his lungs. Concrete chips spat at him as bullets bounced off the pillar.

More heavy rain began to fall on Haad Rin and large droplets pounded a nearby corrugated roof. The echoing sound blended with the music from the beach, creating a stereo-like reverberation. The rain washed the blood and mud from his face. Tommy leapt up and began sprinting back toward the wall, firing two shots in the direction of his attackers. The men ducked behind the wall at the sight of Tommy running and shooting.

Tommy dove onto the ground and rolled up next to the four-foot-high barrier, raising the nine millimeter weapon and aiming at the top of the wall. When one of his attackers raised his head above the wall, Tommy shot him under the jaw. The impact of the nine millimeter round raised the man off his feet and threw him backward. The other man, seeing his partner lying on his back with the top of his head blown off, ran back down the street, likely looking for reinforcements. Several partiers running up the street in the heavy rain stopped and examined the dead man before continuing their trek toward the party, either not comprehending the sight or not wanting it to interrupt their night of frolicking on the beach. Tommy breathed a sigh of relief for the momentary reprieve and wondered what he was going to do. After a few moments, he pulled himself to his feet and jogged to the far side of the construction site, hopping into the streets of Haad Rin over a matching low wall.

Using back alleys and trails, Tommy made his way to the pier that he and Becky had arrived at the day before. Standing in the shadow of a palm tree on the beach near the pier, he spotted a small speed boat tied up between two tall wood pylons protruding from the dark and turbulent water. The ropes holding the gyrating speedboat in place, as frenzied waves swirled around its keel, strained from side to side. Bracing himself to the violent waves rushing into the small bay, Tommy wadded out into the water next to the pier. Churning around the pier pylons and then his legs, the water threatened to knock him over each time a wave struck the harbor. Salt water stung the wound on his back and face.

Swimming the last twenty feet, Tommy grabbed the rocking speedboat and pulled himself over the edge, falling onto the deck. With the heavy rain making the boat's fiberglass deck slippery, he moved up to the console on his hands and knees before tinkering underneath, finding the ignition wires. With thick clouds overhead now obscuring the moon and stars, the only available illumination came from a single overhead light at the end of the pier. Working by feel under the dark console, he pulled the wires down into view and then separated each from the ignition devise. Not immediately hot wiring it, Tommy moved back to the rear of the boat and found a fuel shut off valve. He opened the valve and then found the soft plastic bulb on the fuel line leading to the engine, pumping up the fuel pressure. Finally, he untied the lines anchoring the small craft. The speedboat drifted to one side and began pounding against one of the wood pylons, each blow nearly knocking Tommy off his hands and knees.

Crawling back over to the ignition wires, Tommy hotwired the speedboat while manipulating the throttle. It started quickly with a smooth hum, and Tommy pulled himself up off the slick deck to wheel and throttle. Looking over the bow of the boat, he pushed the throttle and the boat vaulted forward but was immediately slowed by a crushing wave hitting the harbor. The wave slipped past and the boat leapt forward once again, roaring in testimony to its powerful engine. Tommy did not turn the navigation lights until well away from the pier, for fear of being seen departing the island.

The boat was tossed back and forth, and the engine struggled against the waves. The bilge pumps were unable to keep up with the surging sea. Water began sloshing at Tommy's feet from waves coming over the edge of the boat onto the deck and, looking down, he became concerned that the boat would become swamped long before he could make it to the distant shores of Koh Samui.

Trudging through the weather, the boat teetered over the top of each swell and the engine screamed a high whining pitch as the propeller became exposed to the foul night. Tommy was relentlessly being soaked from the heavy rain and waves crashing across the bow and sides of the boat. Salt water coursed down his forehead into his eyes hindering his ability to see.

The violent waters between the two islands pounded the boat mercilessly as it moved toward Koh Samui. The bilge pumps got farther and farther behind as the water inside the boat rose above Tommy's ankles. The added weight of the water further slowed the boat as the lights of Koh Samui seemed to languish in the distance.

A mile from its shores, just as Tommy began to believe he might make Koh Samui, the propeller hit something heavy in the water, bucking the craft. The engine whined loudly in affidavit to a severed propeller shaft, and Tommy immediately pulled back the throttles. The drifting boat was quickly hit sidelong by a large wave, knocking him to the deck.

Grabbing his leather satchel, Tommy swung it over his shoulder and dove over the edge of the floundering boat. Surfacing, he looked back to see the boat listing heavily to one side in the dark churning water.

Swimming toward a distant beach, he could make out the illuminated shore of Koh Samui at the top of each swell. Between the currents and the drag of his clothes and satchel, it took Tommy nearly two hours to traverse the rough water, finally crawling up a sandy beach on Koh Samui.

# CHAPTER 49

*Koh Samui, Thailand, 27 July 2015*:

Moving to the top of the beach and leaning against a palm tree, Tommy gasped for air. The rain slowly turned to a drizzle and then stopped altogether as he sat under the palm tree, recovering. It took him a full thirty minutes to regain his strength and, after stretching his legs and back, he began trotting away from the beach down a narrow dirt road. After a short distance his clothes began to dry, the salt chaffing his legs and arms as he jogged toward his friend's resort.

It was after midnight by the time Tommy showed up at the resort. With most of the resort's small villas dark, he moved toward a bright light in the main building. Looking through the window, he saw Lawan and Mew sitting around a low table drinking beer. Lawan's bruised face had a look of concern, as Mew tried to console her. When Tommy stepped through the door both jumped to their feet and hurriedly approached him.

"Bacon, what happened? You look awful," Lawan announced.

"Thanks, sweetheart, words of encouragement."

Mew rushed into the kitchen, directing over her shoulder for Lawan to move him to the couch. With Lawan's help, Tommy pulled the leather satchel from his shoulder.

"Your phone is off," Lawan said. "Why did you turn it off?"

"Mother nature turned it off. It's soaked."

"How did you get here? Why are you wet?"

"Too many questions, I promise to tell you everything later."

Mew returned with a medical kit and, after examining and cleaning Tommy's facial wound, she pulled a needle and thread from the medical box, making quick work of a stitch job.

When Tommy told them, "Don't forget to look at my back," the two women looked at each other then turned him on his side. They let out a simultaneous yelp at the sight of the grazing flesh wound across his shoulder blades.

"One more question," Lawan demanded. "Where is the flash-drive?"

"Delivered."

# CHAPTER 50

*Koh Samui, Thailand, 28 July 2015:*

Tommy woke, lying on his stomach, dressed in boxer shorts on top of a king-size bed. With the room's dark furniture contrasting against its white stucco walls, a large hunter green quilt shielded him from a cool breeze humming from an air conditioner mounted on the wall above the bed.

Curled up next to him, Lawan was asleep with her arms entwined around his. Gently lifting her limbs to slip free, Tommy moved to the side of the bed and placed his feet on the floor. The gash on his back began to burn as he stood up. The heavy quilt slipped to the side and the chill from the air conditioner began to revive his senses. His jaw stung as he attempted a yawn and he reached up, touching the wound.

Moving to a mirror above the dresser, Tommy inspected his face. The four inch laceration started near the back of his jaw and extended up to the corner of his mouth. Mew's stitch job from the night before tightly pulled the wound together. While his jaw was sore, the bullet seemed to have driven across the meatiest part of his face, avoiding a direct encounter with a bone and cartilage. He then reached around and pulled off the bandage that Mew had placed on his back, turning around and scrutinizing the damage in the mirror. Like the facial wound, this bullet seemed to have missed all the bony protrusions, skimming across his flesh just below his shoulder blades. A red raised line marked the bullet's path that ended in a three inch lesion where it had cut into the skin under his right shoulder blade. Like the facial laceration, Mew had stitched the small wound snugly together.

Looking over at Lawan under the thick quilt, Tommy could only see her face and left arm. Two days before, when he had said goodbye to her in Fisherman's Village, she had angry purple bruises on her face and arms. She looked much better now, as the once colorful contusions had begun to turn a yellowish brown.

He found the leather satchel and removed the handgun, the saltwater exposure already beginning to erode the dark blue finish on the weapon. Tommy took it apart, wiping down each piece, before using some baby oil he found in the bathroom for lubrication. The remaining rounds in the magazine concerned Tommy as he was sure that water had seeped into the bullet casings and dampened the gunpowder. He then looked around the room and found the shorts he had been wearing. Digging in the front right pocket he extracted the camera memory chip. He wasn't sure what the effect of saltwater would have on the memory chip but realized it wasn't worth worrying about. There was nothing he could do if the chip was damaged.

Placing the handgun and the memory chip on a desk near the door, Tommy then looked around the room for his cell phone. Finding it on the bedside stand, he could see the screen was water damaged and assumed that the rest of the phone was spoiled as well.

He then dug into Lawan's purse and removed her cell phone, replacing her SIM card with his. Turning her phone on, he punched the appropriate keys on the keypad and his contact list appeared on the screen. Tommy found the inspector general's number and then looked at his watch.

"Seven o'clock in the evening Washington DC time," he quietly said to himself before calling the number. "The inspector general is probably still at work."

"Hello, Tommy, I hear you made the delivery," the inspector general's answered, his voice sounding cheery.

"You heard correctly," Tommy replied, smiling to himself, the wound on his face stinging but not dissuading him from silently showing joy that the delivery was complete. "I've got a laptop for you. Where do you want me to drop it off?"

"Did you get John Smith's cell phone?"

"No, I was never presented the opportunity."

"Fair enough. Are you coming back to the United States anytime soon?"

"Not for a while."

"I'll have a gentleman come by and pick up the laptop. Where are you staying?" The inspector general queried, clearly happy, even with the news that Tommy had failed to get John Smith's cell phone.

"No chance, Inspector. I'll drop it off someplace and let you know where to find it. I'm still following your advice, don't trust anyone. That sage advice is still good, as far as I'm concerned."

The inspector general laughed. "If you ever want a job, Mr. Luck, give me a call. I'll await your instructions."

Disconnecting the call, Tommy then scrolled through his contacts to Becky's name and number.

Becky answered the call somewhat flustered. "Where have you been? I've been calling for over twelve hours."

"How was your evening at Haad Sadet?"

"You left me there. Why did you leave me there?"

"I told you, I don't trust you," Tommy announced as he walked across the room into the bathroom and closed the door so as not to disturb Lawan. "What happened at the beach while I was delivering the flash-drive?"

"You promised me pictures," Becky retorted, refusing to answer his question again.

"You'll get your pictures and the flash-drive, as promised. Where are you?"

"The Beach Lodge. In the same room where we stayed the other night. When can you come?"

"I'll drop it off tonight. I'll give you a call ten minutes before I get there. You can meet me at the hotel's bar." Tommy ended the call with an, "I see you tonight."

Placing Lawan's cell next to the bathroom sink, he climbed into the shower, slowly rinsing his body off. He heard the bathroom door open and the familiar sound of Lawan's bare feet patting across the tiled floor. When the shower curtain was pulled aside, she was naked and climbed in, taking the soap and washing him without saying a word. Tommy saw that the yellow bruises extended from her forehead down to her thighs.

"You look much better," he said pulling the hair back from her face.

"I feel much better. Who were you talking to?"

"The inspector general and Becky."

"What do they want?"

"The inspector general wants the laptop. Becky wants the photo chip and the copy of the flash-drive."

"This won't be over until you give them those things," Lawan stated, looking at Tommy with a serious expression. "You must continue to be careful. I do not trust Becky, and I do not know this inspector general man."

After their shower, Lawan and Tommy, with Aslan's black polyester computer bag draped over his shoulder, walked down the narrow dirt road leading away from the beach and their friend's resort. Tall palm trees and wide tropical plants crowded the sides of the street, and there was the scent of fresh flowers in the air. The sun felt hot on Tommy's back but refreshing, nonetheless. They entered a small wooden building on the side of the road with a corrugated metal roof that housed a small restaurant for a leisurely breakfast. An overhead fan mounted under the exposed roof failed to provide cooling relief from the hot day and an occasional car or scooter would drive past, leaving a fine cloud of dust hanging over the road that would drift into the restaurant. After breakfast, they walked farther down the street to the island's main thoroughfare that was crowded with small businesses and traffic.

Cars and scooters loudly sped pass, and tourists and locals jockeyed for room along the thin ribbon of a sidewalk. They walked along the road, dodging others on the sidewalk, until finding a cell store where Tommy bought a new phone. Several hundred feet farther up the busy street they found a sporting goods store where Lawan bought a box of nine millimeter ammunition for the handgun.

They then rented a scooter and drove down the busy street to a storage facility near the airport where Tommy leased a large space for one month, paying cash to the attendant. With a galvanized roll up door, the storage space was large enough to fit an entire car. Tommy placed the laptop in the center of the space with the stack of Aslan's emails and list of linked companies the shopkeeper had made for him in Kalasin on top. Rolling the door down and placing a lock on the hasp at the bottom, they returned to the front counter where Tommy gave the attendant the key.

"Could you please fill out the access form?" the attendant asked, looking at Lawan.

Taking the form from the attendant, Tommy printed 'Clarence Northman, United States NSA Inspector General.'

Walking across the street from the storage facility, they sat down at an outdoor table in front of a small café where Lawan ordered two drinks. With a red coke can and bobbing white straw sticking out of the tops sitting on the table in front of him, Tommy pulled his new cell phone out and called the inspector general.

"Mr. Luck, tell me what I need to know," the inspector general's cheery voice answered the phone.

Tommy gave him the address of the storage facility and number of the space. "Your name is on the access list."

The inspector general laughed, seemingly amused at the information. "I hadn't planned on coming out that way."

"You're the inspector general of the National Security Agency. Please tell me that you can retrieve a laptop from a low security storage space in a country where bribes are a tradition."

"You sure you don't want to work for the NSA?"

"I thought I was working for the NSA. At least that's what my bank account tells me. How long before you think you can pick it up?"

"It'll be a while. I haven't got anyone on the island," the inspector general replied. "A couple of days at the earliest."

Disconnecting the call, Tommy turned to Lawan who was watching him. "Let's hang out here for a while. I want to see if someone comes."

"Did he say he could pick it up that soon?"

"No. He said he had no one on the island. I find it hard to believe, considering his interest in the delivery of the flash-drive, that he doesn't have someone close by. I think he's lying."

"Bacon, why do you care? It is almost over. We need to give Becky the flash-drive and photos, and then it is over."

"Curiosity, I guess. You were right when you told me not to stop being careful this morning. This won't be over until Clarence Northman, the alleged NSA inspector general, decides it's over."

They sat at the table for two hours where Tommy drank two Jameson on the rocks and ordered a small bowl of curry and pork.

The food wasn't very good, but Tommy ate it anyway. After finishing his meal, he leaned back in his chair and stretched. The injury on his back throbbed as his muscles extended. Five minutes later, a black Toyota sedan entered the storage facility.

"Look," Tommy said to Lawan, pointing at the sedan.

"Who is it?"

"I can't see that far. You have better eyes. You tell me."

Lawan squinted across the street. "Bacon!" she cried out, looking at Tommy with a frightened expression. Leaping to her feet, she reached over and tried to pull him from the table.

"*What*? Who is it?"

"We must go," she exclaimed. "We need to get out of here."

Refusing to budge from the table, Tommy again asked, "Who is it?"

"Sid. It is Sid the CIA man," she cried. "It's the man working with Aslan."

"Whoa, are you sure?" Tommy replied, laughing at her answer. "I doubt he's there for something else. You're sure it's him?"

"Yes. I am positive."

"Okay, let's get out of here."

Riding back to the resort in silence along the busy road, Tommy pondered the connection between Sid and the inspector general. Finally, shrugging his shoulders, he decided that it didn't matter. He had delivered the flash-drive and computer, earning a hundred and ten thousand dollars. Not bad for a week-long job.

"What does it mean?" Lawan asked later, as they sat next to the resort pool on wooden deck chairs.

"I'm not sure. Maybe he was retrieving the laptop for Aslan? But why was Aslan not there and how does the inspector general fit into this? As I said, this is over when the inspector general says so."

"What about tonight with Becky? Do you not worry about tonight?"

"Other than the fact that they allegedly work for the same organization, I doubt that Becky and the inspector general are connected. He would have backed her story of being an undercover agent. He didn't even know her name, and Becky said that he was involved but didn't give any details. I think Becky just wants the chip and flash-drive. I believe she is who she says."

Tommy departed the resort at eight o'clock that night, leaving Lawan with her friend Mew. Dressed in faded jeans, a white T-shirt advertising some Washington DC pub, and flip flops, he tucked the semi-automatic weapon and its magazine filled with the new rounds into his belt, under his shirt. He placed the second flash-drive around his neck and camera memory chip in his pocket.

Riding the rented scooter into Fisherman's Village, he parked a block from The Beach Lodge and walked up the street into a pub across from the hotel. Standing next to a concrete bar with a tiled mosaic sea scene along its surface, he ordered a beer and positioned himself to see Becky's room. Colorfully dressed tourists crowded around the bar, smoking and laughing, and more strolled up and down the narrow street as Tommy leaned against the counter watching the hotel room door. While the door was shut, he could clearly see a light through the crack at its base.

After three Singha beers, Tommy causally walked across the street and entered the hotel, making his way through the narrow breezeway lobby with its ornate dark wood onto a short walkway leading to the beachfront bar. Sitting down at a long half-moon-shaped counter facing the water, he ordered another beer, the young bartender quickly delivering a cold Singha. Tommy swiveled his seat away from the water and the distant lights of Koh PhaNgan so he could see Becky's beachfront patio. The lights in the room showed above the thick drapes covering the room's French doors.

Finishing his beer, Tommy then walked up to Becky's patio and unsuccessfully tried to peek between the closed drapes. The room's overhead fan gently dimmed the light reflecting above the drapes with each passing turn, masking any movement from within. Tommy could hear the television on airing some Thai program, hampering him from hearing other noises. He then walked over to the patio next door and sat down on a wicker chair with a tan and brown checkered cushions, its fibrous weave stretching and moaning as he sat down. With the water gently lapping against the beach below the terrace, Tommy leaned back in the chair and called Becky on his new cell phone.

"Tommy, where are you?"

"I'm sitting on the patio outside. What's going on? And why in the world are you watching a Thai television program?"

There was a rustling sound over the phone just before the

French doors leading to her room burst open, several of its small glass panes shattering as doors struck the stops on the outside wall. Jainukul's son and the man who had run away from Tommy the night before in Haad Rin surged out the door with weapons in their hands. It crossed Tommy's mind, as he rolled out of his chair, that the Thai television show was for Becky's other roommates—she didn't understand the language. The two men looked surprised not to find Tommy on Becky's patio, but quickly spotted him leaping from the chair on the next patio over. Tommy dove behind a nearby tropical bush.

Reaching around and grabbing his weapon as the two men began to shoot, Tommy could hear the rounds snapping branches and twigs as they smashed into the bush. At that time of night the beach was nearly empty as most of the tourists were dinning and drinking in the various restaurants and bars along the main street.

The few tourists still wandering the beach stopped and look in the direction of the loud racket before scurrying away.

Not returning fire for fear of hitting Becky, Tommy jumped down to the base of a low seawall, sprinting past the patio toward the beachfront bar. Debris from rounds striking the top of the concrete seawall sprayed Tommy's neck and back as he ran.

He dove behind the beachfront bar and turned to see Jainukul's man chasing after him. Bringing his weapon up, Tommy shot the man in the face as he stepped on top of the seawall.

Tommy could see the round entered just under the man's nose before the back of his head exploded in a red mist. The man crumpled and fell over onto the beach. It then became oddly quiet.

"I will kill her," Jainukul's voice broke the silence.

Tommy remained silent.

"I will kill her," Jainukul repeated his threat.

"You let her go and I'll come out," Tommy replied.

Tommy nearly shot the young bartender as he jumped over

the edge of the beach bar where he had been hiding. The bar-tender raced down the beach.

"You throw your weapon out first," Jainukul yelled back.

Inching his way to the backside of the bar on his hands and knees, Tommy slipped over the low seawall and maneuvered between tropical plants and palm trees.

"Throw it out! Or I will kill her," Jainukul said again.

Peeking through a narrow gap between the bar and hotel, Tommy saw Becky silently crying while standing next to Jainukul. Jainukul's son stepped into view and whispered something to his father, then disappeared into the hotel lobby.

"Let her go, Jainukul," Tommy called out.

Jainukul jerked his head toward where he heard Tommy's voice and stepped behind Becky. Quickly making his way back down to the beach, Tommy's movement was once again masked by the beach bar. Tommy then crawled along the base of the seawall.

"Where are you, Luck?"

Once Tommy was sure that he had crawled past Jainukul and Becky's position, he stood up with his weapon raised. Jainukul was still looking at the gap between the hotel and beach bar where he had heard Tommy's voice. Tommy quietly climbed up on the seawall and stepped closer to Jainukul. As Tommy took aim on Jainukul's back he heard something behind him. At the same moment, Jainukul spun around, dragging Becky back into a blocking position. Ignoring the sound, Tommy took another step forward as Jainukul's began to smile.

"You're dead, Luck," Jainukul laughed. "Drop your weapon or my son will blow a hole in the back of your head right here."

Realizing someone was behind him, Tommy didn't bother to turn, knowing that Jainukul's son would be standing there.

"Maybe I prefer the quick end solution vice the long version that you will undoubtedly perform if I drop my weapon."

"Because I will kill your friend right here and now, if you do not."

Becky whimpered as Jainukul forced the muzzle of his weapon into her throat.

"Tommy, I am so sorry," She softly sobbed. "But you left me at Haad Sadet—he caught me when I tried to leave."

"Guess I should have planned that part of the delivery a little better," Tommy calmly confessed.

Dropping the weapon onto the sand and grass at his feet, Tommy shrugged his shoulders. Jainukul's son stepped up behind him and forced the muzzle of his weapon into Tommy's back, unknowingly pressing the thin barrel against his wound. Tommy winced.

Jainukul's son pushed Tommy forward, directing him through the narrow breeze way. Jainukul pushed Becky in similar fashion behind them. Turning down the main street, Jainukul and his son didn't bother concealing their weapons. Tommy took their impervious attitude as a confirmation of Jainukul's deep connection to the Thai police, as no sirens could be heard. He was convinced that the commotion at the Beach Lodge was expected and ignored by the police dispatchers. Onlookers in the bar across the street gazed in amazement at the foursome exiting from what had sounded like a violent encounter.

In Isaan, Tommy asked, "So Jainukul, who was your spy? How did you know to be at the Big C in Kohn Kaen and then on the beach in Haad Sadet?"

Jainukul laughed. "So you know my language? Your Isaan is good, Luck. Too bad you will not be able to use it much longer. Maybe the first thing I will do is cut the tongue from your mouth so I don't have to listen to you beg for your life in my language." Jainukul then became silent as if deciding whether to answer Tommy's question. After a moment he switched back to English and said, "My source was John Smith, of course. He knew after you killed my son that I had a desire to present you with an especially painful death. He has been very upset at the method in which you conducted yourself during his delivery operation. He prefers to be in control of his deliveries and you caused him many sleepless nights.

He was upset with me in Kohn Kaen when I acted too early but he knew without my aid you would likely get away. He wants you dead, like me, for revenge."

"I should have known," Tommy mumbled.

"I did not know who John Smith was until Haad Sadet, where he introduced himself for the first time," Jainukul said, laughing again. "He is the one who told me to use the woman on the deck above us to find you. I did not even know she was there, but John Smith saw and recognized her. He knew she could contact you and he told me that your loyalty would be the end of you. He was right. He only requested that she disappear along with you."

"John Smith does look after the details, doesn't he?"

As they were walking down the main street, Tommy noticed two men standing next to a building dressed in dark pants and jackets calmly watching the foursome approach. Tommy figured them as more of Jainukul's men. It seemed odd when Jainukul and his son paid no attention to the men, no greeting or order by their employer, as they passed by.

As the foursome walked by, the two men slipped their hands into their jackets and, at that moment, Tommy remembered the team sent by Aslan's organization to dispatch Jainukul. Spinning around, Tommy smashed his fist into Jainukul's face just as the two men pulled handguns from their jackets.

Tommy tried to push Becky between two parked cars but she tripped. Becky and Tommy tumbled to the ground between the cars. As Jainukul's son spun and began to bring his weapon up the two men fired their weapons simultaneously, striking him in the back. The impact of the two bullets forced Jainukul's son forward onto the trunk of one of the parked cars, where he then rolled off sideways, lifelessly landing on top of Tommy.

Jainukul quickly recovered from the strike to the face and responded by firing his handgun at the two men as he dove behind the rear bumper of one of the cars that Tommy and Becky were hiding between. The two men found cover behind a low concrete wall that separated a small outdoor restaurant from the entrance to an alley. The adjacent restaurant was filled with blue plastic tables and chairs but empty of patrons and staff.

Wrenching the weapon from the lifeless body on top of him, Tommy then pushed Jainukul's son into the street. Crawling over Becky, Tommy pulled her until they were on the sidewalk, leaning against the side of one of the cars.

One of the men provided covering fire for his partner by spraying the parked cars with bullets, their windows shattering, raining down small blocks of glass. As the rounds were striking the car, the shooter's partner hopped over the low wall, knocking over several of the plastic tables and chairs as he sprinted across the empty restaurant. Jainukul emptied his handgun, trying to stop the man, but was distracted by the bullets impacting the cars. The sprinting man slipped inside a bar across the street from Jainukul's position, the sight of the armed man quickly persuaded the bar patrons and staff to empty the premises. They ran down the street away from the gunfight.

Tommy pushed Becky to the end of the line of parked cars, opposite from Jainukul, and pulled the flash-drive from around his neck and camera chip from his pocket, pushing them into her hand.

"When I start firing, I want you to sprint around the corner of that building," Tommy explained while pointing with the handgun where he wanted her to go.

She signified her understanding with a nod.

When Tommy rose up over the hood of the car and began shooting in the direction of the low concrete wall, Becky leapt to her feet and sprinted toward the corner of the building. The man in the bar began shooting at Becky, and Tommy shifted his covering fire to the bar. Jainukul also began shooting at the bar, unaware he was providing cover for Becky's escape.

Becky disappeared around the corner, and Tommy continued to shoot until the automatic handgun's bolt locked into the empty position. As if synchronized, the two men exposed themselves from their positions and began shooting at Tommy and Jainukul. Jainukul moved to the sidewalk, looking surprised when he saw Tommy squatted at the other end of the line of parked cars.

Throwing his empty weapon at Jainukul, Tommy jumped to his feet and sprinted across the street amid a hail of bullets. He dove over a low wall into a darkened and undeveloped section of the village filled with palm trees and tall grass. When Jainukul attempted to follow Tommy, he was struck in the shoulder by a bullet, spinning him to the sidewalk. While the man behind the concrete wall peered down the street trying to see where Tommy had gone, his partner rushed from the bar to the sidewalk next to the line of parked cars. Tommy heard a single shot behind him and hoped that it was from a weapon that had just killed Jainukul.

Surrounded by smell of freshly turned soil, Tommy crawled through the palm trees and high grass, knowing that the two men would come looking for him—and he was unarmed.

# CHAPTER 51

*Fort Meade, Maryland, 28 July 2015*:

Howard received a call from Mr. Rogers late that morning while he was sitting in his office reading reports from the various NSA internal investigations. Judy, his secretary, answered the call then transferred it back to his office.

"Good morning, Mr. Rogers," Howard answered. "Or is it good evening for you? I was beginning to worry. I haven't heard from you in three days."

"Code names aren't necessary any more. The delivery is complete and my cover is no longer needed. I have photos showing Tommy delivering the flash-drive and a copy of the information passed to the foreign agent.

Howard smiled at the news. "Excellent."

"Just to let you know, I never liked the cover name Mr. Rogers. It has a sexist twist that I don't like. Not to mention, every time your secretary answers the phone, I feel like an idiot giving her a man's name."

"Sorry about that, Becky. The name came out of an electronic assignment system. There was no sexism meant." Howard quickly changed the topic. "The pictures and copy of the information on the flash-drive with John Smith's phone registry should be enough to take the organization down. Good work."

"I'm just glad it's over," Becky replied in a tired voice.

"Where have you been? Why haven't you checked in? You are all right, aren't you?" Having not heard from her in several days, Howard had been worried that his mole had met with an ill fate.

"Barely." She laughed softly. "Tommy is good at this cloak-and-dagger stuff. You should consider putting him on the payroll. As I told you last time we talked, he set the delivery up on the island of PhaNgan. He arranged to deliver the flash-drive on a remote beach and set me up with a camera and a good view of the delivery site."

"So that's where you got the pictures?"

Becky spent the next ten minutes describing the events on that took place on Koh PhaNgan and Samui. Howard could hear her voice tremble when she talked about being Jainukul's captive. He heard sadness when she described the shootout in Fisherman Village.

When she was finished, Howard asked, "Do you think Tommy Luck survived?"

"The gunfight in Fisherman's Village? I have no idea. Last time I saw him, he was emptying his weapon in order to give me cover to get out of there." Becky sighed. "He was out numbered and out gunned—that doesn't speak well for his prospects."

"He seems to have come through a lot worse. You might be surprised."

"You're right," Becky replied. "He does seem to have an unusual knack for surviving."

"As I said, between the copy of the flash-drive, pictures of the delivery, and the phone registry, you've given me all I need to bring the organization down. Not to mention pictures from my Thai counterparts of John Smith and Steve showing up at a meeting at the MK's in Kohn Kaen—a fictitious meeting between a Thai agent and Tommy Luck that I only told the inspector general about. He won't be able to wiggle out of this one. Thank you."

"When will you go for him?"

"As soon as you get back. You need to get back here and bring the camera chip and flash-drive so we can process the evidence and present it to the director."

"I have a flight out in the morning. I'll see you tomorrow, around five in the afternoon."

Howard hung the phone up and looked out the window, thinking of what needed to be done. Pulling the Black Fly file from his desk, he began reviewing it.

# CHAPTER 52

*Koh PhaNgan, Thailand, 28 July 2015*:

John Smith and Steve had just finished a late dinner and were sitting in the hotel restaurant, waiting to pay their bill. They were planning on leaving the island the next morning. A soft warm breeze blew across the outdoor restaurant and a waning moon stood high in the night sky, creating a fine network of shadows amidst the palms trees surrounding them.

Both men looked tired after their previous evening at Haad Sadet. It took them nearly two hours to realize that the delivery was not going to take place on the beach, and when John Smith spotted Becky on a balcony of one of the cliff side bungalows, he knew that Tommy had once again outwitted him. At that moment, John Smith realized he would be hard pressed to ever find Tommy again. Especially if he had successfully delivered the flash-drive to Aslan.

It was then that John Smith decided to breach the organization's security protocol and approach Jainukul. John Smith had secretly kept Jainukul informed of the deliveries, hoping he would save him the trouble of eliminating Tommy, and he knew that any death at the hands of the Thai gangster would be slow and painful. He liked the idea of a slow and painful death for his deliveryman.

Jainukul still had the best chance of finding and killing

Tommy so John Smith gave the Thai gangster his disobedient agent, Becky. Becky had obviously teamed up with his deliveryman and knowing that Tommy's one weakness was his loyalty, she could be used as bait. Giving Becky to Jainukul would also save him the trouble of eliminating her.

John Smith was now silently pondering how he would eliminate his companion, Steve. Sitting at the table next to his lone remaining agent, John Smith decided that he would enter Steve's room later that night and complete the task. He would then depart the hotel and hire a speedboat to Koh Samui before the sun came up.

He could be on a plane to Bangkok before the hotel staff found the body.

"Did you ever reach Aslan?" Steve asked.

"Aslan called this morning as he was getting ready to climb aboard his employer's private jet. Considering I spent most of last night trying to contact him to find out whether he received the flash-drive, it was nice of him to have the courtesy to call back," John Smith answered with thick sarcasm in his voice.

"What about Mr. Jones?"

"He called last night, wanting an update. All I could do was to tell him I thought the delivery took place but wasn't sure. He seemed oddly relaxed at the news. After I called back this morning to confirm the delivery had taken place, he congratulated me." Then after a brief hesitation, John Smith added, "Something about this whole delivery has been off. Mr. Jones's part was far more prevalent than our previous delivery operations."

"What do you mean?"

"He provided the merchandise. He wanted daily updates. He demanded that we deliver the merchandise even when things were well out of control. In the past, he would only call when he had pertinent information."

John Smith's cell phone began to ring, interrupting their conversation. Looking down at the cell's small screen, he saw Aslan's number on the caller ID. A smile crossed John Smith's face as he thought that at least one person was truly happy with the outcome. "Aslan, what can I do for you? I hope you had a pleasant trip back home."

"You are a dead man," Aslan's thick Turkish accent growled.

"What's the problem?"

"You are a dead man. My organization will find out who you are. They will find out where your family lives. You and your family will be dead within the week."

"Aslan, I have no idea what the problem is," John Smith replied, sincerely confused. "Why are you threatening me?"

"You merchandise was a computer virus. It was not what you advertised. When it was downloaded, it sent all my employer's electronic files to another site and then erased everything. We are dead. I am running from them now, and like you, they will find me."

Aslan disconnected the line before John Smith could reply.

"What was that all about?" Steve asked, seeing the concern on John Smith's face.

"According to Aslan, the flash-drive was nothing more than a virus," John Smith responded as he pushed back his chair. "I'm going to bed. Let's meet in the lobby tomorrow morning at six."

Leaving Steve at the table, John Smith walked back to his room. He was deep in thought about the recent events and all the problems he had had to overcome to ensure a successful delivery. But in the end it appeared he had failed. John Smith was tired and confused.

The hallway was dark as he placed his key into the room's lock, and, as he turned the handle to open the door, he felt a blade slip between the ribs in his back next to his spine. It was a quick upward thrust that buried the blade to the hilt and, before he could react, his attacker shifted the angle of the blade. John Smith's lower torso and legs exploded in a tingling sensation, as if he had been hit with a Taser. The door swung opened, and he stumbled into his room, painful surges blasting down his legs with each step. His attacker entered behind him and closed the door.

John Smith turned, his back screaming in agony, but he couldn't make out his assailant's features in the darkness. He could feel energy draining from his body.

"Sorry, John Smith. Orders are orders," a calming voice said, strangely easing John Smith.

"Whose orders?" John Smith weakly asked, as he crumpled onto the floor next to the bed, the tingling sensation painfully accentuating his impact with the floor.

"Mr. Jones requested that I take care of you," the soft voice replied. "The inspector general's office has identified you as a member of the organization."

"Something's wrong. Someone has played me," John Smith muttered, looking up at the shadowy profile above.

"The only thing wrong is that you are dying. Goodbye, John Smith. The world won't miss you."

John Smith's last thought before losing consciousness was wondering if Jainukul would ever find Tommy. Little did he know that Jainukul and his remaining son had been killed just an hour earlier in Fisherman's Village on the island of Koh Samui.

# CHAPTER 53

*Fort Meade, Maryland, 29 July 2015:*

Howard was busy at his desk, sifting through a pile of file folders lying next to his computer's key board. Looking down at his wrist watch then up at wall, he realized that his black and white government-issued plastic clock was once again running five minutes slow. Howard had been planning on replacing the batteries in his wall clock for nearly two weeks, but seemed to always find himself distracted from the task. As he began rummaging through his desk drawers, looking for a set of AA batteries, his secretary stepped into his office with a puzzled look on her face.

"What is it, Judy?" Howard asked, once again interrupted from the task.

"I just got a call from the director's office," Judy explained while standing in the doorway with her hands on her hips.

"Go on," Howard prompted, wondering why the director's office would be calling him? They normally conducted inquiries through the inspector general.

"You presence is requested immediately. The director wants you to bring the Black Fly file with you."

"My presence and the Black Fly file? Who in the director's office requested me?"

"You don't understand. The director, you know, the big guy, wants to talk to you."

"That is unusual," Howard replied, trying to hide his astonishment.

"You can say that again," Judy said, nodding her head in agreement.

Howard immediately began packing the Black Fly file into a large blue and white banded document size envelope with the word *CLASSIFIED* stamped across the front and a small black and white bar-code in one corner. He had only been to the director's office on one other occasion, during his promotion to deputy inspector general, two years prior.

With the director's office in a different building than that of the inspector general and his offices, Howard rode an elevator to the lobby and began the procedures for exiting the building. He first stepped up to the security desk and used a pen like device to log the bar-coded envelope out. The security guard then nodded as Howard swiped his identification badge across the electronic reader, logging his departure and automatically moving a waist high barrier to the side, allowing him to pass.

He exited the building, the sun warming his shoulders as he walked along a wide sidewalk that connected two white buildings. A bright green lawn, punctuated with several tall oak trees, surrounded the gray path, and the smell of freshly cut grass filled the air. The director's building, standing ten stories high, with wide glass doors at the top of a concrete staircase, loomed at the end of the walkway.

The lobby of the director's building was covered in marble and featured a dark wood security desk. The building had a duplicate security process as the one his office was housed in, but with a much more elaborate facade. Howard signed into the building by swiping his NSA identification badge across the electronic reader, registering his entrance into the building's electronic logs.

The guard nodded at Howard, after viewing his credentials in a private screen at the security desk, and a clear Plexiglas barricade slid aside, allowing him to pass. Howard then logged the envelope in at the security desk by scanning the barcode with an identical pen like device as the one he used to exit his building.

Howard could smell the guard's overpowering aftershave as he stood at the security counter registering the envelope and was happy to get away from the odor when he made his way to a row of five elevators along the back wall. More marble outlined the entrance to each elevator and the doors were covered in the same ornate wood as the security desk. Stepping into the elevator at the end of the row, used strictly for accessing the director's office, he swiped his identification card across another electronic reader and the doors automatically closed.

After a quick ride, he stepped from the elevator into a large lobby adorned with more decorative wood and the same plush blue carpet as that of the inspector general's office. A secretary sitting behind an appropriately sized desk for the massive lobby had obviously just finished viewing his credentials on her computer screen, sent automatically when he swiped his card in the elevator.

"Mr. Macintyre, they're expecting you," she said in a deep southern drawl that seemed somewhat out of place in the elaborate setting. Standing up, she moved to a set of heavy wooden doors, opening one side.

"They?" Howard asked, looking puzzled as he approached the open door.

"Go right in," she answered, ignoring his question as Howard walked past her and into the office. He could hear her close the door behind him.

Dressed in a dark suit, white shirt and red tie, the NSA director greeted Howard as he stepped through the door. Behind the director stood the inspector general and a man Howard recognized as the director of the Central Intelligence Agency. The inspector general was dressed in his usual brown tweed jacket and khaki pants, and the CIA Director looked as if he shared the same tailor as the NSA director. As per protocol, Howard shook the directors' then the inspector general's hands, in descending order by rank.

The office was enormous, with a rich oak chair rail running along each wall and a large mahogany desk with two wide computer screens on top, situated at one end of the room. On the other end of the room stood eight leather chairs, surrounding an eight foot long mahogany table. Three forty-two-inch flat-screen televisions were mounted on the wall behind the table, airing the CNN, Fox News, and Al Jazeera stations. The volume for all three had been muted.

"Please have a seat, gentlemen," the NSA director requested, gesturing toward the leather chairs and mahogany table. Silently, all four men moved to the table, the soles of their shoes whispering scuffs against the thick carpet, and took seats around the table. The soft leather of the chair cushion compressed with a soft hiss as Howard sat down directly across from the inspector general. Howard laid the envelope containing the Black Fly files on the table top between the men.

"Mr. Macintyre, tells us your progress concerning the Black Fly investigation—give us the reader's digest version, please," the NSA director asked with a hint of a humor in the tone of his voice.

"Investigation 'Black Fly,' concerns a rogue internal—" Howard began.

"We know all about the rogue internal organization," the NSA director interrupted. "Tell us the results of your investigation."

Howard turned red with embarrassment from not understanding the director's instructions. Quickly regaining his composure, Howard started again. "Tell me if I've fast forwarded too much, gentlemen. The flash-drive containing corporate secrets was delivered two days ago to foreign agents. We have obtained pictures of the delivery, as well as a copy of the information on the flash-drive—"

"Keep a tight control of that copied flash-drive," the inspector general interrupted. "Do not let anyone download the information. Especially onto an NSA mainframe."

"Yes, sir," Howard replied, finding it ironic that he was

getting ready to tell the NSA and CIA directors of the inspector general's complicity, and yet he was taking orders from him in the meantime. "As I was saying, we have photos of the delivery to a foreign agent, a copy of the information passed, and the call registry of the lead field operative's cell phone. We have identified all the field operatives and one leading member of the organization. My hope is that these individuals will cooperate in identifying the remaining members."

"How did you obtain this evidence," the CIA director calmly asked, his voice a husky low baritone that echoed across the room.

"We were able to place a mole within the organization, and she was able to sway the selection of their delivery person. This delivery person was instrumental in gathering much of the evidence we currently have."

"She?" The inspector general asked, clearly surprised at the sex of the mole. "Then Bob was not your mole?"

"No, sir, we believe he was mistakenly terminated for being the mole. My mole was the female member of the organization's operatives," Howard responded.

"You told me your mole had been assassinated," the inspector general stated flatly, but seemed unusually calm at the news that Howard had lied to him.

"It doesn't matter, I'm sure he had a good reason to mislead you," the NSA director interjected. "Go on Howard."

After a brief pause, Howard continued. "In a nutshell it was the bagman, Tommy Luck, who provided the atmosphere that allowed us to obtain most of the information. He took control of the delivery and caused the organization to begin breeching its security protocols. He also had the flash-drive copied and had an accomplice take pictures of the delivery. My mole provided the information necessary to discover the identity the organization leader, through the lead operatives call registry."

Looking first at CIA director and then at the inspector general, the NSA director leaned back in his chair, its metal swivel giving off a faint squeal. "Where do we begin, gentlemen?"

"Who is the lead member you've identified?" the inspector

general calmly asked, peering at Howard from across the table with his Santa-Claus-like rosy cheeks and nose.

Howard paused again, thinking about how to break the news that it was the inspector general he had identified. "I have proof that the lead member of the organization is a man whose organization code name is Mr. Jones—and Mr. Jones is you," Howard declared, looking directly at the inspector general.

The three men sat in silence, none seeming even slightly surprised at his allegation.

"You did some excellent work, Howard," the inspector general declared, breaking the silence. He turned to the director. "If you don't mind, sir, I'd like to explain."

"Go ahead," the NSA director responded, again leaning back in his chair, its metal swivel whispering another soft squeal.

"Howard, your discovery and investigation Black Fly interrupted a very important interagency operation," the inspector general began. "The rogue internal organization was created by several disenfranchised members of the NSA several years ago. I learned of the organization from our friends at the CIA, after they had stumbled on to its existence in India, over a year ago, as it was making a delivery. The target of our interagency operation was not the rogue organization itself but one of the criminal elements buying the stolen information. We believed the Chinese government was deeply involved, using a front company to steal technology from corporations across the globe. Rather than assigning you to investigate and take them down, we—the directors and I—decided to highjack the organization to uncover evidence against the Chinese."

Dumbfounded, Howard blurted out, "But you were aiding this organization's operatives."

"Yes, I needed to ensure that this particular flash-drive was delivered," the inspector general replied. "Let me back up a little. After discovering the existence of the organization, I was able to link the stolen information to a specific NSA asset's activities. From there, I discovered the information technology specialist stealing the information by simply finding out who was assigned to the asset at the time the theft occurred. Unknowingly, he led me to one of the organization's leaders, and I was able to convince that individual to pass the organizational leadership to me.

"This gentleman has taken a long vacation from his duties here at the NSA. I continued to provide corporate secrets, but those that I could buy legitimately from private corporations, and then direct the specialist hacking into the corporate sites to steal information I had already purchased. We would then sell the information via the organization's field operatives. This delivery was to be our final.

"We advertised a flash-drive containing electric auto technology, something that the Chinese have been aggressively pursuing in recent months. We had done business with this Chinese organization before, and had their trust and confidence as to the quality of our merchandise. We hoped that with our reputation from past sales and with the method we used to design the software on the flash-drive, that the information would not be reviewed in detail before they downloaded it onto their mainframe. Even if it had been reviewed, there was a good chance that they would not recognize it for what it was—a computer virus."

"A virus?"

"Yes, this last delivery was nothing more than a computer virus," the inspector general confessed.

"What about Bob?"

"Unfortunately, I needed to slow you down and told the lead field operative about your mole. I provided him with all the information you gave me about the mole. He obviously identified the wrong person. I would have given them my mother to get this flash-drive delivered," the inspector general answered emotionlessly.

"This was an important operation." The CIA Director's baritone voice boomed across the room, showing support for the inspector general's actions.

"You knew they would kill the mole," Howard replied.

"We needed to get the flash-drive delivered," the inspector general said, closely watching Howard's reaction. "Your ability to get Mr. Luck chosen as the deliveryman had caused enough problems. The organization nearly imploded due to the actions of Mr. Luck."

"I didn't know," Howard admitted, "or I wouldn't have moved forward with the investigation."

"While the inspector general managed to discover the identity of the information technology specialist, one of the organization's leaders, and the lead operative, we had no idea who else within the NSA was involved. This organization had very rigid security protocols. For all we knew, one of your team was a member—or even you. We could not afford letting the organization know what we were doing. Our team needed to remain as small as possible," the NSA director added flatly. "You did your job well. Unfortunately, your efforts were threatening our operation, and you needed to be slowed down."

The inspector general looked at the two directors and smiled. "The good news is that the delivery was successful and the flash-drive has been downloaded onto a mainframe in China. The information we have retrieved is very revealing."

"I don't understand."

"When downloaded, the flash-drive transfers all the data from the host mainframe to ours, here at Fort Meade. Once the download is complete, or if interrupted, it strips all the information residing on the host mainframe, destroying every bit of it," the inspector general said, laughing. "As of eleven o'clock this morning, mission accomplished. We have our evidence and they were left with a database that resembles a reenactment of Pompeii. Mr. Luck also provided me with the laptop of the Turk who was acting as their middleman and that has been as enlightening, as well."

"Tommy Luck was working with you?"

The inspector general laughed again. "Not directly. I contacted him after he discovered what was on the flash-drive and made a financial deal with him to redeliver. He was ready to call the delivery off after the first attempt and needed a little monetary prodding."

"What of John Smith and his accomplices?"

"I arranged for John Smith to take a similar vacation as the one leader I was able to identify," the inspector general said, his smile quickly fading and his facial expression taking on a solemn look. "We could not afford a public trial."

"Sid, the CIA station chief?"

"He was been working for me during the delivery. He was able to befriend the Turk, a known Chinese operative, and help him win the bid. Sid tried to ensure a smooth delivery but, again, your deliveryman, Mr. Luck, made that much harder than anticipated. Sid was my mole in the operation," the inspector general replied.

"But, according to my mole, he tried to kill Tommy Luck at the Marriott during the first delivery attempt," Howard exclaimed, clearly surprised at Sid's part.

"Mr. Luck was about to reveal to the Turk that Sid was with the CIA. He could not allow that to happen. It would have jeopardized the entire operation and, under those circumstances, Mr. Luck was expendable," the CIA director chimed in, his baritone voice once again reverberating off the office walls.

"What of the Turk—Aslan?" Howard asked, leaning back in the leather chair trying to take in and sort out all the new information.

"Found several hours ago, face down in a rice paddy in central China," the NSA director replied. "He had failed his organization, much the same way as John Smith had failed his."

"What of Steve, the remaining operative?"

"He will meet with the same fate as John Smith. We don't want any surviving organizational members, for obvious reasons," the NSA director answered again. "If the media were to get a hold of this, the outcome would be disastrous."

"Does that mean Becky, my mole, is scheduled for a similar fate?"

"She's safe," the inspector general calmly stated.

"What of Tommy Luck?"

"We won't be hearing from him," the inspector general responded.

"What do you mean?"

"He's dead," the CIA director declared.

# CHAPTER 54

*Chaloklum, Koh PhaNgan, 29 July 2015*:

Tommy and Lawan traveled back to Koh PhaNgan the morning after the shootout in Fisherman's Village, thinking it might be a good idea to put some distance between themselves and the unknown assailants that he had escaped from the previous night in the empty lot. After sleeping the day away to recover from their wounds collected during their two-week adventure, they lay on wooden lounge chairs on the yellow building's deck that evening. It was a dark overcast night and the bay appeared as nothing but a black hole. The only indication they were over a bay was the sound of water lapping against the beach and a long thin line of fishing boats luring squid with bright lights on the horizon. With a silky glow below provided by the downstairs terrace lights, Tommy and Lawan appeared to each other as nothing more than dark shadows, even though they were only three feet apart.

Shifting on the lounge chair, Lawan asked, "Is it over?"

"I have no idea. This thing has become so complicated that I don't know which side anyone is on—or was on. I don't even know which side I was on." Tommy chuckled, before taking a long drink from a glass of Jameson on the rocks.

"You are on my side and I am on yours," Lawan softly whispered.

"Jainukul is dead. Aslan got the flash-drive with the virus. John Smith got his delivery. Becky got a copy of the flash-drive and the photos. Sid and the inspector general got Aslan's laptop—maybe they gave it back to Aslan and he got that too."

"Does that mean it's over?"

"Well, I think everyone got what they wanted, except for Jainukul. He probably didn't want his sons or himself to die. I'm still not sure Aslan knew what he was getting."

"We need to go out and eat. We need to celebrate. We should celebrate, even though we don't know if it is over," Lawan said, standing up and looking down at Tommy's shadow.

The terrace lights illuminated the base of the stairs as they climbed down and walked through the narrow passageway between the buildings, making their way to Chai's seaside restaurant.

Sitting at the same bamboo table that he had shared with Becky several nights earlier, Tommy and Lawan slipped off their shoes and toyed with sand beneath their feet with their bare toes. The sand felt cool and comforting. Colorful lights strung above them fluttered in the light breeze and mixed with the heavy humidity creating a rainbow like effect around each bulb. Two bottles, one of Lao kow and one of soda water sat on the table next to a small bucket of ice and Tommy mixed drink after drink into a glass, quickly polishing off three servings of the Thai whiskey. After they finished their food, Chai walked up to the table and joined them with a fresh bottle of Lao kow.

Pulling a bamboo chair from the table, its legs scratching furrows in the sand, Chai sat down. "Is it over?"

"What? Did you and Lawan rehearse your questions?" Tommy laughed. "I think it's over, but I don't know for sure."

Mixing another Lao kow and soda into the glass, Tommy pushed it over to Chai. They talked about the events of the last two weeks, oddly laughing at the fight at the Night Bazaar, the car crash, and Tommy's shootouts in Haad Rin and Fisherman's village. The mood became somber when Bob's death came up.

After drinking for nearly two hours, Tommy pushed back his chair. "I think that'll be enough for tonight."

"Enough what?" Chai asked, raising his eyebrows.

"Enough drinking. I think I want to go home and spend some time with my beautiful Thai girlfriend. Sweetheart, let's go get naked and see what happens."

"Bacon!" Lawan giggled. "You should not say that in front of our friends."

Leaping to her feet, she pulled Tommy from the table, and they walked down the street to the narrow opening between the yellow building and the one next door.

As Tommy stepped out onto the yellow building's back terrace, he felt a thin blade strike his back, colliding with the center of one of his ribs, the tip partially penetrating the bone. His assailant quickly pulled the blade back and began to reinsert it between Tommy's ribs.

The pain was intense as the blade began to work past the nerve sack around his bones, and Tommy swung his elbow backward, impacting his attacker's face. The blow dislodged the knife's hilt from the assailant's hand and, with the thin blade dangling from his back, Tommy spun to face his attacker.

Standing under to soft glow of the terrace lights was Gene, with his angelic eyes looking up at Tommy. Grabbing him by his thick brown fold-over, Tommy threw him against one of the supports to the upper deck. Quickly recovering, Gene stepped back, his fold-over in disarray.

"You picked a very bad time to try and kill me," Tommy said calmly with the water gently lapping against the beach in the background.

"You're a loose end," Gene replied in a soothing voice, the lights illuminating his innocent face.

"Was Jimmy Santos one of your loose ends?" With Lawan nowhere to be seen, Tommy assumed she had run back down the passageway to get help. As Tommy reached around and pulled the blade from his back, Gene retrieved a Beretta hand-gun from his waist.

"Mexico," Gene answered. "He went down quite easily for such a big man."

"You picked a very bad time to try and kill me. You should have waited for me to get drunk."

"When are you not drunk? Timing of that was never an is-sue. While it is tradition for me to use a blade to clean up loose ends, this will work fine," Gene stated as he began to raise the Beretta.

With his right hand, Tommy lightly tossed the knife up, grabbing the blade by the tip as it came back down, and then threw it at Gene. The blade struck off center, to the left side of Gene's neck, tip first, sinking a full six inches into soft flesh. The Beretta dropped with a metal clatter on the concrete ter-race, and Gene sank to his knees, all the while looking up at Tommy with his comforting brown eyes.

"You obviously didn't do your homework on me, jackass. I won a Boy Scout trophy for knife throwing when I was fif-teen—it's a skill that stays with you," Tommy lied. He had never been a Boy Scout.

From the amount of blood running down the front of Gene's shirt, Tommy figured he hadn't hit a jugular vein and his assailant was obviously on his knees more from the shock of having a long thin blade sticking from his neck than the damage inflicted. There was a distinctive sucking sound as Tommy stepped up and pulled the knife from Gene's neck. Gene whimpered as the blade slid out, an oddly soothing sound to Tommy, and more blood began to flow. A small drop of blood appeared at the corner of his mouth.

"Help me," Gene pleaded weakly, his voice a calming melody.

"Yeah, let me help you," Tommy said as he grabbed Gene by his plump shoulders and raised him to his feet.

"Help me," Gene innocently repeated.

"Who sent you to kill me?"

"Mr. Jones."

"Who in the hell is Mr. Jones."

"I don't know. I've never met him. I only talk with him over my cell," Gene replied with blood now running freely from the corner of his mouth.

While holding him up with one hand, Tommy frisked Gene with his other, finding a cell phone in his left hip pocket. He scanned the contact list and found a listing for Jones.

Pushing the small glowing cell screen in front of Gene's face, Tommy asked, "Is that his number?"

"Yes. Yes. Please…"

Turning Gene so he was facing the beach, Tommy drove the knife into the small of his back. He could feel it grinding into Gene's spine as he pushed the blade in, twisting it between the vertebras. Gene legs gave out as his spinal cord was severed and he let out another soft whimper. Urine flowed from his bladder and soaked his pants. Tommy pushed the blade into Gene's back up to its hilt. Holding Gene's body up, Tommy leaned forward and whispered in his ear, "You won't be sneaking up on unsuspecting people anymore. Yours will be a slow death, my friend."

Tommy pushed him over the seawall and Gene's body hit the dark beach with a thud. Stepping up to the edge of the seawall, Tommy looked down. The yellow building's terrace lights faintly illuminated the beach below, and he could see Gene lying on his belly, his fingers groping at the sand.

Tommy then called the number for Mr. Jones on Gene's cell phone.

"Is it finished?" a man asked on the other end of the line.

Recognizing the voice, Tommy disconnected the call. Lawan appeared from the passageway between the buildings with Chai and another man.

Looking around, Lawan asked, "Where is he?"

"Gene decided to take a midnight stroll through the village," Tommy replied, smiling at Lawan. "I don't think he'll be back."

Looking at Tommy quizzically, Chai asked, "Are you all right?"

"Just a scratch on my back. No first aid necessary." Placing his hand on Chai's shoulder, Tommy asked with a wink, "Can you take care of some trash on the beach for me? But wait for a while. It's not quite ready to be moved."

"Trash?"

"Yes, some trash. I think it will be ready in about an hour or so."

"I am not sure I understand."

Leaning over and placing his mouth next to Chai's ear, Tommy whispered, "He needs to die first."

A smile appeared on Chai's face. "I do not think you are *farang*. I think you are really a Thai."

"I would never qualify. I can't handle Lao kow like a Thai."

Nodding, Chai turned and walked back down the passageway with his friend. Climbing the stairs to their apartment, Tommy led Lawan to the bedroom and began unbuttoning her blouse. Lawan pulled Tommy's shirt over his head as he reached around and unclasped her bra.

"It's almost over," Tommy whispered into her ear.

Giggling, while wiggling out of her pants, Lawan asked, "You promise?"

"I promise."

# CHAPTER 55

*Washington DC, 15 August 2015*:

C larence Northman, was sitting on park bench next to the Reflecting Pool on the National Mall, the coolness radiating from its soft brown waters calming him. Lincoln sitting on his marble throne, under its heavy roof supported by thick marble columns, could be clearly seen from the bench to one end and the tall white spirals of the World War Two monument to the other. The elm trees provided shade and masked his presence from traffic both on Constitution and Independence Avenues. It was still too early for many tourists, as few wandered the grounds.

This was his favorite place to conduct business that he did not want known back at Fort Meade. He checked to ensure the syringe was there and ready for use, laying at the bottom of the outside pocket of his tweed jacket, in anticipation of a quick jab into a nearby thigh. Normally he would have instructed someone else to take care of loose ends like Tommy Luck, but he had already tried that, sending what he considered a very capable person to dispatch the deliveryman. Somehow their rolls had been reversed. Gene, his long-time private employee, had disappeared, not Tommy Luck.

The inspector general did not like loose ends, especially ones that could jeopardize the NSA. He was proud of his institution and would do anything to protect it. And while neither the NSA nor CIA director would ever condone what he was about to do, the inspector general knew it had to be done. The amusing paradox was that he actually liked Tommy. Unfortunately, Tommy knew too much and was unpredictable—not to mention, he was a drunk, an unfortunate mix of knowledge, personal traits, and habits.

The inspector general knew before the delivery that he would need to kill Tommy, as he had tasked Gene to do with all the other deliverymen. After Gene had failed to dispatch Tommy, the inspector general had lured him back to the United States with a promise of an additional monetary reward in return for a private debriefing. Tommy had rejected a proposed meeting at less open venue but the inspector general had been in this position before. With the use of a primitive and untraceable tool, his syringe, he would end Tommy's life. The yellowish liquid contained in the syringe, a powerful muscle relaxant, would paralyze Tommy within seconds and the inspector general would simply walk away. Several minutes later, Tommy's heart would stop, and he would be found some time after, his death attributed to his heavy drinking, no doubt.

It really didn't matter what they blamed Tommy's demise on or whether they could link the inspector general to his death. He would ultimately be protected by his standing at the NSA. Investigations would cease and documents disappear.

He saw Tommy approaching from the Lincoln Memorial, walking along the edge of the Reflecting Pool. The inspector general had obtained Tommy's picture from a file created by his deputy, and while he looked a bit skinnier than shown in his picture, the approaching man was undoubtedly Thomas Bacon Luck.

The inspector general chuckled at Tommy's attire, a colorful Hawaiian shirt depicting orchids or some other tropical flower, faded blue jeans, and flip flops. Tommy had obviously looked him up on the NSA website as well, as he was walking directly toward the inspector general with the clear look of recognition.

"Good morning, Inspector General," Tommy said as he sat

down next to him. "Has anyone ever told you that you resemble Santa Claus? Lacking the beard, of course."

The wood slats of park bench groaned under the added weight. The inspector general smiled. Tommy sat in the perfect position for the surprise attack with the syringe.

"The mark on your face, is that from the delivery?" the inspector general asked while looking at the grazing wound that rose from the corner of Tommy's jaw to the edge of his lips.

"Yeah, it has a twin brother on my back."

"You are either a very lucky man or very talented. You managed to thwart several attempts on your life over the course of the delivery."

Tommy laughed. "I do seem to have a bit of luck."

"How many people did you managed to eliminate in the end?" the inspector general asked, curious to hear Tommy's admission to see if he might have missed one or two in his own count. He fingered the syringe, wondering when he should sink it into Tommy's thigh, not wanting to draw their encounter out too long.

"They're a drop in a bucket of regrets. I once had someone ask about my regrets. I told him that every regret we create in life is like putting a pebble in your pocket. The pebble never goes away. You can always feel the added weight next to your thigh, it chafes you when you walk, and you can feel it every time you put your hand in your pocket. I have a pocket full of them. The few I added in Thailand really don't make a difference."

"Other than luck, what do you attribute your knack for survival on?" The inspector general was beginning to enjoy their conversation. Maybe he'd wait a few more minutes before killing Tommy.

Pausing for a moment to think about the inspector general's question, Tommy finally replied, "When I was a young man, working on a construction job, I had a friend come to me. He was a close friend, one who I both worked and drank with.

"What did he want of you?" the inspector general asked. A

breeze across the National Mall caught his thin white hair, standing it straight up on his head.

"His car was in the shop and he asked me for a ride home one evening so he could attend a birthday party with his child." The bench groaned again as Tommy shifted. "And I agreed to take him to his house in Glen Burrie, Maryland."

"So what happened?" the inspector general asked, genuinely interested in Tommy's story.

"As was my habit, I began drinking in the afternoon and I forgot about our deal. His wife and child drove up to the construction site that night to pick him up."

"And what happened?"

"They all died in a car accident on the way to the birthday party."

"And you could have stopped it?"

"For years, I believed that it wouldn't have happened had I given him a ride home. The guilt over that one day caused my life to spin out of control. But it was more than just the guilt. The whole experience brought into question the plausibility of destiny. I became reckless with my wives, my children, and my own safety," Tommy confessed, as he ran the fingers of his right hand through his wavy brown hair, realizing it was a subconscious act prompted by the inspector general's white hair standing on end in the breeze. "My lifestyle provided me with the perfect venue to entertain my recklessness—or so I thought."

"Guilt is a human frailty, is it not?" the inspector general commented. "The construction trade was not the perfect venue?"

"The venue is immaterial. It's bigger than the venue. While I was trying to disprove the possibility that our lives are scripted, I came to realize that our path makes the venue, not the venue making the path."

"You obviously believe in destiny, then?"

"I do now. Maybe by genetics or maybe by some higher power or maybe by both, there is a destined path we all fulfill. He and his family's path was already predetermined."

"You're not saying that our every move is predetermined, are you?"

"No, what I mean is that our path is predetermined. The bible, or more specifically Ecclesiastes, says that 'to everything there is a season and a time to every purpose.' It goes on to say 'there is a time to be born and a time to die; a time to plant and a time to pluck up that which has been planted.' Now the bible has been translated and rewritten more times than we can count, and, in some cases, written describing events that occurred long before ever being scribed to paper. One can find as many interpretations as pages but, based on my experiences, I can see only one interpretation for these Ecclesiastes verses. We all have a charge in life, and both it and our end are unavoidable."

"Your path was to be an unemployed drunk and mine to be the inspector general of the NSA?"

"That's simplifying it too much. You're missing the point, Inspector General," Tommy replied, shaking his head. "We all have a charge in life that contributes to moving this world forward. It might be something big like becoming the President of the United States and making a decision that changes the world for better or worse. It might be as small as helping an old lady across a busy street that is witnessed by someone who uses that experience to do something even more magnanimous. I believe destiny creates those events, and those events shape us for our task. My destiny has been anything but a straight road. I did everything I could to avoid my destiny after leaving the construction business, but it found me again in Thailand during this delivery. My past has shaped me into the person I am and will or has contributed to my contribution to this world. Your destiny has been to live in a world of lies, deceit, and secrecy. It shaped you into the person you are and will or has contributed to your charge. More to the point, our destiny prepares us for our final day. We all have a time at which we are scheduled to die. 'A time to be borne and a time to die.' It could be today, tomorrow, or next week. It could be when we're ninety years old."

"So you believe that destiny determines who we will become, aids us in some predetermined task, and then shapes us for our last day? What has been your contribution to the world?"

"No idea and I will likely never know. But I do think Nick's death was his contribution, shaping me for mine."

"And that our last day on earth is a foregone conclusion?"

"Yes, our destiny drives us toward and contributes to our death. You might be destined to die on a high rise in Kansas City, or in a Bangkok hotel, or in the comfort of your home, or on interstate 95 outside of Baltimore. No matter what you do to avoid your final moment, it will happen and your past experiences will play a part in your demise. The minute you believe that, you lose all your pebbles." Tommy softy chuckled. "That is, if you want."

"What do you mean?"

"If you have no control over your death, then neither does anyone else. If you are destined to die at this moment, and if I elected to not pull the trigger of a revolver I have pointed at your head, you would still die. If that's true, why would I be responsible if I did pull the trigger?"

"So we should forgive people for the act of murder? That seems a little outrageous."

"No, we still must be held accountable for our actions. That's all a part of destiny. But you can't lose sight of the fact that most murders, and criminals in general, are typically victims of their situation. Murders grow up in an environment that breeds a lack of respect for human life, or they have something in them that creates that same shortcoming. We are groomed for our purpose."

"What do you mean you lose the pebbles only if you want?" the inspector general asked.

"You never really want to lose your pebbles. Those pebbles are a part of what defines you. We use our pebbles to better ourselves. Losing your pebbles would be equivalent to losing your moral compass."

An uneasy feeling overcame the inspector general as he sat

next to Tommy. For some reason he began to feel vulnerable. "And what of this gun to my head? Do you have a weapon with you?" he asked while wrapping his hand around the syringe, preparing to plunge it into Tommy's thigh.

"No, of course not." Tommy laughed and then paused a moment before continuing. "But I did come here to kill you. Destiny brought me here. Which of us will die is a foregone conclusion. Relax, we are mere puppets in the outcome."

"If you have no weapon, how do you plan on killing me?" the inspector general asked, his voice betraying his unusual calmness.

"I'm pretty sure you'll provide the instrument. After all, you intended on eliminating me at this meeting, as well. You must have something up your sleeve."

The inspector general panicked and began pulling the syringe from his jacket pocket, but the tip of the needle hung up on the fabric. Before he could untangle the instrument, Tommy's hand was in his pocket and wrapped around the inspector general's, grasping the syringe. Tommy turned the inspector general's hand and forced the tip of the needle into his hip, pushing it through the fabric of his jacket and the top of his pants, into soft flesh.

The tip of the needle broke off as it struck the edge of the older man's hip bone but Tommy kept pushing it until the broken end was buried deep in the inspector general. Tommy then squeezed his hand, forcing the man to depress the syringe's plunger.

The yellowish liquid flushed into the inspector general's body, the tussle between the two men lasting only a matter of seconds. None of the tourists wandering past them seemed to take notice.

The inspector general looked at Tommy, wide-eyed. "How did you know?"

"Never underestimate a man just because he's a drunk. Pretty easy. Your boy Gene told me that a Mr. Jones had requested my elimination. I used Gene's cell to call Mr. Jones and you answered the phone," Tommy explained, watching the drug slowly take effect on the inspector general's body, the man's eyes beginning to glaze over.

"I remember the call," the inspector general muttered.

"Your desire for a personal debrief at a secluded location was, in my opinion, a transparent attempt to lure me in for the kill."

Tommy steadied the inspector general's body as he began to sag to one side on the park bench. The man tried to say something, but no words came out.

Looking into the inspector general's eyes, Tommy said, "Maybe I do know my contribution, after all—ridding the world of the likes of you." Standing up, Tommy instinctively stretched his back before looking back down at the inspector general. "Not my day to die, Clarence, but it looks as if it is yours."

Clarence looked up at Tommy with frightened eyes.

Turning away, Tommy began walking down the path next to the Reflecting Pool, the brown waters rippling and the tops of the elms fluttering as a strong breeze blew across them. Walking toward the white marble Lincoln Memorial standing at the end of the pool, he glanced back over his shoulder at the park bench. The breeze had nudged the inspector general over onto his side, making him look like a napping vagrant.

As Tommy approached the steps leading up to the road encircling Lincoln, proudly sitting on his marble chair, Lawan stepped out from behind a small building selling military trinkets at the entrance to the Vietnam War Memorial.

Taking Tommy's hand, she asked, "Is it over?"

"It's over."

# About the Author

Growing up in the Rocky Mountains and graduating from the University of Colorado, Patrick Ashtre chose a career in the military opposed to one slugging it out in the office cubicles of corporate America. After serving twenty-six years in the Marine Corps as both an infantryman and aviator he took a fancy to a horizon of water over that of mountains. Spending his final tour in Japan, Ashtre retired from the marines and moved to the small tropical island of Phangan, located in the Gulf of Thailand, where he owned and operated a popular beachfront pub. After eight years of living, working, and traveling throughout Southeast Asia, he is now in the process of moving back to the Colorado Rockies. With a misspent youth and experiences from around the globe as a canvas, Ashtre will likely fill the pages of many more books before he closes his laptop for the last time.